# Quarter Past Two on a Wednesday Afternoon

# Linda Newbery

**Doubleday**

LONDON · TORONTO · SYDNEY · AUCKLAND · J

TRANSWORLD PUBLISHERS
61–63 Uxbridge Road, London W5 5SA
A Random House Group Company
www.transworldbooks.co.uk

First published in Great Britain
in 2014 by Doubleday
an imprint of Transworld Publishers

A CIP catalogue record for this book
is available from the British Library.

ISBNs 9780857522498

Addresses for Random House Group Ltd companies outside the UK
can be found at: www.randomhouse.co.uk
The Random House Group Ltd Reg. No. 954009

The Random House Group Limited supports the Forest Stewardship
Council® (FSC®), the leading international forest-certification organisation.
Our books carrying the FSC label are printed on FSC®-certified paper. FSC
is the only forest-certification scheme supported by the leading environmental
organisations, including Greenpeace. Our paper procurement policy can be
found at www.randomhouse.co.uk/environment

Typeset in New Baskerville 12/15pt
Printed and bound in Great Britain by
Clays Ltd, Bungay, Suffolk

2 4 6 8 10 9 7 5 3 1

*For Linda Sargent – writer, guide, friend, polisher of sea-glass.*
*Thank you.*

❖ ❖ ❖

## August 1990

It was the day when everything stopped, and something started that was quite different, that couldn't be controlled or shaped or ended. From then on, a ringing telephone could terrify; a knock on the front door could numb the house into petrification.

Prompted at first by her parents, then by the police, and ever after by her own search for overlooked significance, Anna went over and over the events of the morning, the lunch time, and her parting from Rose. She replayed and replayed until she couldn't tell if she was really remembering what happened. Maybe she was only recalling memories.

For Anna it had started as an uneventful weekday in the summer holidays, a Wednesday. Mum and Dad were at work, and the girls spent most of the morning in Rose's room, Rose sketching with the radio on, Anna sprawled on the bed, reading. Early haze cleared to unbroken sunshine; after a sandwich lunch, Rose fetched the garden lounger from the garage and put it under the pear tree, then sat sideways to paint her toenails before settling with a book.

Bored with being at home, Anna decided to go the shops.

'See you later,' she called from the back door, and Rose, already engrossed, replied without looking up. What were her exact words? Anna couldn't remember, though in the days to come she strained to hear, squeezing her eyes tight shut to open her ears to the echo of what she'd missed. Rose had said nothing, she was sure, about going out, or meeting anyone. She looked as if she intended to stay all afternoon in the quiet of the garden, reading and sleeping in the tree's dappled shade.

Asked what time this was, Anna thought it must have been about a quarter past two, because the radio was still on in Rose's bedroom and she'd heard the two-o'clock pips as she went upstairs. Some two hours later she returned, letting herself in with her own key. She had felt no more than mild surprise to find the house empty, the garden deserted. Sometimes, still, she dreamed of returning to that day and making it so ordinary that it would merge into dozens of similar featureless days. Rose would be in the garden, or if not she would soon come home, preoccupied, a little impatient at being questioned. But *there*.

No sign of a break-in; the police asked her closely about that. No sign of anyone having visited. Nothing any different from how it usually was. The blue garden lounger was there under the tree, with an empty glass tipped over on the grass. Anna poured a cold drink, took Rose's purple varnish and painted her own toenails, although it was forbidden by Mum, who said that Anna was too young, so she'd have to keep her feet hidden in socks and shoes. Soon after five, Mum returned from work and asked where Rose was; six o'clock came, and seven, and now Dad was home as

2

well. At eight-thirty, Mum phoned Rose's friend Christina. No, Chrissie hadn't seen Rose that day, and had no idea where she might have gone. They'd spoken on the phone last night, when Chrissie got home from her holiday, and were to meet tomorrow, A-Level results day. They planned to be at school to open their envelopes together, compare results and go into town to celebrate or commiserate.

Anna didn't see why Mum was getting so worked up; it wasn't particularly late. Dad reassured them both that everything was fine, that Rose would be back any moment now. She'd met someone she knew, or she and Jamie had got back together and were making up for lost time. Or, likeliest of all, Dad said, she was anxious about her A-Level results. 'Remember the state she got into about her O-Levels?'

'GCSEs, Dad,' Anna corrected.

'You know she's set her heart on getting three As,' said her father. 'Let's hope to God she gets them. It's the waiting, it's got to her. She's met someone from school, gone home with them.'

'She'd have phoned,' Mum said flatly; it was her reply to all his suggestions. 'She wouldn't stay out without telling us.'

'She's eighteen now, love, old enough to take care of herself. We're not going through this every time she goes out for the evening. She'll turn up, right as rain.' Dad kept saying that, as if saying it over and over could make it so.

Sent up to bed, Anna stood for a while with her elbows on the windowsill, looking out at the garden. Dusk was falling now; the shrubs were heavy with leaf, and it had begun to rain – light, refreshing rain that Anna could hear through the open window as a faint hissing, and smell as wetness on dry earth. It was almost the middle of the school holidays. At first, the six weeks had stretched out with no end in sight, but already the nights were creeping in earlier. It didn't seem fair that midsummer, the longest day, was back in June, before the holidays had even started. After what Dad called 'the year's turning', the days immediately began to shorten towards autumn and September, and the return to school.

In bed Anna propped herself up, reading *Forever*, her library book, anticipating drama, and the earful Rose would get when she turned up. Eventually she turned off her light. It was a way of hastening Rose's return; when she woke up it would be morning, Rose would be asleep in her room, and no one would remember why they'd been so worried.

But she woke instead to Mum's voice from the downstairs hall. 'It's Sandra Taverner, Rose's mother. I'm sorry to bother you so late, but we're a bit worried about where Rose is. She's not with Jamie? No, no. Yes, I know, but I thought perhaps . . .'

And it was still dark; not morning, but a few minutes before midnight. Anna sidled to the top of the stairs. Her mother stood for a moment still holding the phone, then replaced it and went back into the sitting room. Surely Rose would come in at the stroke of midnight, or risk being turned into someone else or frozen into a statue. Anna waited, her eyes on the front door, confident. The hands of her watch aligned themselves at twelve, and the minute hand moved barely perceptibly into the frightening orbit of next day. It was tomorrow now, and Rose hadn't been here since yesterday, and that made it immensely more serious.

She crept halfway down the stairs.

'I'm going to phone the police,' her mother was saying.

'Don't you think we should—'

'No! No! I can't wait any longer!' And now Mum's voice rose in a wail; she ran to the telephone table in the hall, both hands clamped to her mouth. Seeing Anna, she stopped dead. Dad followed, put an arm round her shoulders and led her back into the sitting room. He hadn't seen Anna huddled on the stair, shivering in her pyjamas.

She heard him say soothing words, and Mum's quiet sobs. When he came back to the phone there was a long moment of breathing as he reached for the receiver, hesitated, then picked it up. He was going to dial 999, Anna supposed, and although this was exciting she wanted to yell at him *No, don't*, because to make that phone call was to stop pretending everything was normal, and to move into a new phase.

'I want to report a missing teenager,' Dad said. 'Yes, yes. My daughter.'

❖ ❖ ❖

# 1

She is thinking of her garden.

Soon it will be snowdrop time. Maybe already they're stirring underground, getting ready to push through frozen earth. Each year there are more, their circle widening like ripples. She has planted them in the green to encourage them to spread, after they flowered, when the stems wilted softly and the small bulbils could be trowelled up and separated. Last year she did that, and the year before, and the year before. Two or three weeks from now, she'll have her reward: the lawn under the pear tree will be pooled white, as if the tree has sprung into blossom early and dropped its flowers wet and shining into the grass. Soon after that will come the hellebores, and the first daffodils, and then the great rush of spring that comes upon her every year with no time to register each change.

Now, in the hollow after Christmas, everything seems frozen into suspension, waiting for the date that will soon be marked on the calendar. The end. The beginning. On that day, yet to be decided, she and Don will walk out of the house and hand over the keys and never come back. She would never have believed she could do it, but it's easy after all. She can register quite dispassionately that the Christmas just gone is the last one here. There will never be another summer. Almost certainly she'll see the hellebores and the *tête-à-tête* narcissi, but by the time her roses flower (*Cécile Brunner*, *Veilchenblau*, *The Pilgrim*; she loves the names as much as the roses themselves) the house will belong to the Baverstocks. 'It's what the house needs,' Don said, after phoning the estate agent to accept the offer. 'After so long.'

Yes. The house has been waiting for years, echoing to the memory of children's voices. For too long the rooms have been full of absence, full of reproach. Now it will be a family home again.

'You'll love working on a new garden. You can take some of your favourites with you,' Anna has suggested; 'divide them, or dig them up altogether?'

But that would have meant starting two or three months ago, in the autumn, assembling a nursery of cuttings and divisions. Now isn't the time, with the ground hard-frozen. Something obstinate in her refuses to salvage. Instead, she'll walk away, leaving her treasures behind. It will be a final parting. Isn't that the point?

The estate agent brought the Baverstocks on their first and second viewings, but on their third visit, with the offer accepted and solicitors engaged, they came unaccompanied, to take measurements for curtains and furniture. Don did most of the talking, while she smiled and made tea and listened, retreating into silence.

'We've looked at so many, but this is the house for us. And it's the garden that sold it to us.' Mrs Baverstock was a young woman of, surely, Rose's age, sleekly casual. 'It'll be wonderful for the boys.' Too sure of herself, assuming the right to have anything she wants. The husband had a notebook and an air of wanting to get on with things, looking around the room as if for flaws.

Three boys, they told Don in answer to his questions; eight, ten and five. They asked about schools. They expressed polite interest in the house in Cranbrook, in the reasons for the move; Don said that it was time for a change, for downsizing.

They can't wait for us to move out, she thought, so that they can take over, bringing their boys and their noise. They'll dig up my plants and install decking and a swing, a barbecue.

'It'll be a wrench, I'm sure.' Mrs Baverstock has asked them to call her Joanne, and her husband Tim; but, having taken against them for planning to live here, she doesn't intend to call them anything. 'Your children grew up here, did they? That's a lot of memories to leave behind.'

Children. They'd seen Rose's room, of course. They'd tramped in, talking loudly about bunk beds for the two older boys.

She knows Don can't lie. He nodded, looking at her uneasily, but this time she did speak. 'A daughter, Anna. She lives in London.'

What business of theirs, anyway?

'Boys!' she said to Don, when they'd gone. 'I can't see this as a boys' house. Boys in my garden! They'll kick footballs. Scuff the lawn. Break stems off plants.'

'Come on, love. It can't be helped. And you'll have your new garden.'

Always, to hold herself steady, the garden is where she retreats. Mentally she places herself in dappled light under

9

the pear tree, looking across at the wide border and the massed flowers of the *Veilchenblau* rose – mauve, almost blue, against the fence.

And whenever she wants to, if she listens, she hears the girls' voices, one calling to the other from the swing, or Rose giving Anna instructions. Eventually they will come in, hungry, in search of biscuits, or choc-ices from the freezer: Anna with dirty fingernails and dishevelled hair, Rose as if from a world of her own devising. There they are, playing, secure in the green enclosure of childhood, where it is always summer.

Anna was painting the bedroom walls. Martin was at Ruth's today, and she'd decided to get on with the job alone, to surprise him when he came in. As soon as he left, she caught a bus to B&Q, taking a taxi back with her purchases; then she changed into jeans and an old T-shirt, moved and covered the furniture, and spread newspaper over the carpet. The hours passed in a succession of radio news and CDs, mugs of coffee going cold on the windowsill while she painted and painted.

She and Martin had put off the job of redecorating, getting only as far as choosing a colour. Now, giving the whole day to it, she found an unexpected pleasure in the task: the dip into cool green, the loading of the brush with enough but not too much paint, the nudge against the side of the tin; then the custardy glide, as scuff-marks and small blemishes disappeared beneath a skim of perfection. It was years since she'd painted. The feel of the brush in her hand recalled the art rooms at school and at college, years ago when there had been time to think of nothing but making marks on paper or board. Then, earning a living had seemed irrelevant, a worry she needn't face yet; devoting herself for hours on end to the picturings of her imagination could be seen as a virtue. An artistic future had surely been her due, waiting for her to claim it. She had almost forgotten, but this felt good, the ache in her neck and arm as she edged colour along below the cornice, standing on a stool to reach. Stepping down to the floor, she admired her work, the stretch of wall gleaming and flawless.

Martin had suggested that her picture could hang here, above the bed, but now Anna wasn't sure. Expecting him to dismiss it as immature, she'd felt touched that he liked it and thought it too good to be hidden in a cupboard. She washed her hands and went to fetch it from the spare room, laying it on the old curtains spread over the bed.

For her A-Level exhibition she had given it the title *Shore*. In a tall, narrow frame, it showed a stretch of shoreline, low tide lapping at the left-hand frame. In the foreground, the prints of bare feet were sharply delineated, fading into the tideline as they receded to the small, indistinguishable figure walking alone by the sea's edge. Only her art teacher had understood that she meant the title ironically: *Shore*, when she was sure of nothing but absence and uncertainty. The painting asked a question that had never been answered, even now.

Anna admired the light through sea-mist, the smudged suggestion of low cliffs at the horizon. I painted that, she thought, wondering if she could still do as well. Perhaps she ought to make time, join a class; there were plenty of opportunities. She had forgotten what it meant to her, back in the days when she was never without a sketchbook and pencils. But – she angled her gaze at the picture, and at the point on the wall where she supposed it might hang – did she really want to invite Rose into the bedroom? To install her, even that imagined glimpse, above the bed?

She would stow it back in the cupboard, after all; tell Martin that she didn't like it any more, and they could choose something together, something new. She slid the picture back into its sleeve of corrugated cardboard, thinking that next time she went home she'd take it with her, replace it in the portfolio with the rest of her work.

*Home* – she was doing it again. Home was not here but her parents' house, the home that would soon belong to someone else. It was the only real home she knew; everything since had been temporary, and after more than a year she still thought of this flat as Martin's. Home was Sevenoaks, the quiet cul-de-sac, the shady garden, her old bedroom. Once her parents moved out, it would be gone from her life, an idea she was finding impossible to grasp. She had been astonished – dismayed too – by her mother's decision to leave, but, knowing that her father thought it a good thing, had helped all she could, searching RightMove, making contacts, even accompanying them on some of their viewings. Soon everything would be packed up and moved; she'd have to go through the belongings stored in her bedroom and in the loft, and either bring them here or dispose of them. More significantly, Rose's things would have to be confronted, and decisions made. Who would do that?

In her parents' spare bedroom – Rose's room – Anna's student portfolio was kept in the cupboard. She hadn't looked at it since the time when Martin had shown an interest, but the other Rose picture, the watercolour she'd kept back from the exhibition because it was too private, was among the paintings and sketches stored there. It showed the garden, and the pear tree where the swing had been hung when she and Rose were children. Anna had painted Rose under the tree, reading: bare legs stretched out, feet with toenails newly painted a dark and somehow provocative purple. The bottle of nail polish was on the grass beside the lounger. Sunlight dappled Rose's face and glossed her hair; her head and shoulders turned towards the onlooker with an expression that was partly smug self-containment, part annoyance at being interrupted.

Anna had never shown that painting to anyone but her art teacher. Now, with it clear in her mind, she couldn't tell whether it was painting or memory she was seeing. She had expected to feel relieved – a sense of closure, as people said – that once the house was sold she would never see the garden again, never stand in the silence of Rose's room. Instead she felt only loss; the loss of her childhood, of herself as Rose's sister.

Briskly she carried the *Shore* painting back to the spare room and put it away. She wished she hadn't been tempted to look; she should have known better than to poke a stick into that particular pond. Again she looked at the bedroom walls, now drying nicely; she was glad to have finished before Martin got back, to tidy away the sheets of newspaper, the brushes and tins. Martin hated clutter.

At the sink, washing out her brushes, she realized how late it was: nearly eight o'clock. Looking out at the street below, the canopy above the jeweller's and the lit windows of the Cantonese restaurant opposite, she heard someone calling, and a siren from the direction of Clerkenwell Road.

Voices carried in the chilly air; people hurried along the pavements, faces half hidden in scarves and upturned collars. It had been a day of piercing cold, the kind of January day that felt marooned in midwinter, the hours of daylight a brief reprieve before darkness fell again.

She was hungry now, her thoughts turning to food. It was Monday tomorrow and Martin was due to make an early start, driving to an appointment in Aylesbury. She took a ready meal out of the freezer – beef stroganoff, his favourite – and put it in the oven, then changed her clothes, brushed her hair and checked her mobile. He hadn't left a voicemail or text message. When she called there was no answer, which presumably meant he was on his way, driving.

Anna thought of calling Ruth, but instead phoned her parents. It was her mother who answered, sounding cheerful and a little distant.

'Yes, everything's fine. Our buyers came round yesterday, Mr and Mrs Baverstock. Fortyish, I should think, or late thirties. Nice enough. They've got a young family. Boys.'

'Oh.' Anna couldn't adjust to the speed of this; her mother's decision to move, and now, barely two weeks after her parents had put in their own offer, a buyer for the Sevenoaks house. *And how did you feel about meeting them?* she wanted to ask. *The thought of them taking over our house?* But something in her mother's tone discouraged her, a note of bright determination that might be too easy to flatten.

'What are you doing?'

'I've been painting the bedroom,' Anna said. 'Now I'm waiting for Martin.'

'Why, where is he?'

14

'He's been over at Ruth's.'

Usually her mother showed faint distaste when Ruth was mentioned; much as she approved of Martin, and his stabilizing influence on Anna, she preferred not to acknowledge his previous life, his marriage and his two sons. Anna expected her to change the subject, but instead there was a pause, then: 'Ruth's? Do I know who Ruth is?'

Anna felt cold. This wasn't the first lapse.

'Mum, of course you do. *Ruth*. Martin's ex-wife. He had to help her sort out some financial stuff – her mother's accounts and suchlike.'

'Ah, that one,' her mother said, as if Martin had had several wives. 'Her mother died.'

'Yes, that's right.' Anna was thankful not to have to explain again.

'Of course I remember. It's just that there's such a lot to think about, with the move.'

'I know, Mum. It's a huge upheaval. I'll come over and help you sort through stuff whenever you like.'

'Oh . . . not yet,' said her mother, vague again. 'There's plenty of time to think about that sort of thing.'


When another hour had passed and Martin still hadn't returned, Anna gave in and phoned Ruth. Was it breaking a taboo? But if a rule did exist, it wasn't of her own making.

Ruth answered at once. Yes, she told Anna, Martin had just left. He hadn't expected to stay so late, but there'd been a lot to sort out.

'I could come too, another time,' Anna offered, wanting the conversation to be more than transactional. 'You know, if there's anything . . .'

'Thanks, Anna. Actually, that might be good, in a week or two.'

'Whenever you want. Are you OK?'

Silly question.

'Yes,' said Ruth, though she sounded doubtful. Even, perhaps, a bit sniffly.

'I'll call next week, shall I?' Anna told her, already planning to do it when Martin wasn't around.

The drive from Woodford would take about half an hour, depending on traffic. Anna set the table and put out salad, then made up the bed in the spare room.

When he came in, Martin gave no sign of noticing the cooking smells or the laid table. Anna went to him for a kiss, and he gave her a peck on the cheek, perfunctory, almost irritable.

'What's wrong?' she asked, more sharply than she meant.

'Nothing. I'm tired, that's all.'

'Come and see what I've been doing!' Taking him by the arm, she pulled him towards the bedroom door. 'What do you think?' She stood triumphant, looking at the immaculate walls, and the bed still covered with old curtains; childlike, she waited to be praised and petted.

He glanced around. 'You didn't say you were doing this today. I thought we'd agreed on the blue?'

'This is the one,' Anna told him. 'You called it blue, but it's the one we chose. Bluey-green. Greeny-blue.' Last weekend she had bought sample tubes and had patched each colour on the wall near the window, writing the names in faint pencil.

'No, that one was blue. This is green. Definitely green.'

'I *know* it's green! Jackman's Green. It was you who said— Oh, never mind.'

'It's fine,' Martin conceded. 'I'm not saying I don't like it. And you've done a good job. We can't sleep in here tonight, though. It'll take a day or two for the paint smell to go away.'

'I know. The bed's ready in the spare room, and I've moved our things. Let's go and eat.'

Martin moved away. 'Actually I don't need anything. Ruth made us a meal.'

'Oh, great.' She followed him back to the kitchen, all expectation of pleasure draining out of the evening. 'Why didn't you let me know? And why are you so cross? Didn't you have a good time with Liam?'

'I'm not,' Martin said, looking directly at her for the first time. 'Liam was fine. It's all a bit wearing, that's all.'

'What is?'

He puffed out his breath. 'So much to sort out. I thought Ruth would have done more by now.'

'But you're helping her, aren't you?'

'Yes, with the financial stuff. But she hasn't even started on the house, and it's becoming a bit of an albatross. It's about time she . . . you know, moved on. Started to get over it.'

'Well, it's tough, losing a parent,' Anna said, leaning against the sink. '*Both* parents, now. You wouldn't know, would you?' It sounded like an accusation. She didn't know, either, but she did know absence: the bewilderment of it, the gulf it left.

Martin didn't respond. He went to the fridge for a beer, an eloquent silence in the turn of his shoulders.

'But . . . you think she's taking advantage?' Anna said. 'Using this to keep hold of you?'

17

'No.' Martin gave a quick, impatient shake of his head. 'That's not what I mean.'

But maybe I'm right, Anna thought, knowing that Ruth's devotion to Martin had somehow survived the break-up of their marriage. Her friend Bethan said that Ruth would soon meet someone new, and then Anna could stop worrying. But Anna wasn't worried, only curious, seeing Ruth's continuing love as a measure of Martin's worth.

She rather liked the way Martin helped Ruth, not making a big deal about it – with her tax self-assessment forms, and part-exchanging her car. An only child, Ruth was now parentless, her father having died some years ago. Her mother, chronically ill, had been in and out of hospital for several months until being admitted to a hospice. Then, early in December, Ruth phoned with the news that her mother had died.

Anna couldn't have faulted Martin's conduct. He cancelled his meetings for the next two days, and went straight over. He knew how to register the death, and who else had to be informed; over the next fortnight he helped Ruth with the funeral arrangements, went through her mother's savings and accounts, dealt with the solicitor. If Anna had any possible cause for complaint, it would have been on her own behalf. She felt excluded. Martin refused all her offers to go with him or to take Liam out for the day. He didn't want Anna involved, not even to go to the funeral. 'What's the point? You didn't know Bridget. Ruth wouldn't want you there.' He always sounded certain of what Ruth would and wouldn't want. To Anna's frequent questions he gave only the blandest of answers: 'She's OK . . . She's coping . . . She's taking it one day at a time,' – as if life could proceed in any other fashion. A kind of morbid curiosity pulled Anna towards Ruth, like a driver reducing speed to stare at a crash on the opposite carriageway. Ruth had become glamorized by her closeness to a death.

But Martin's sympathy, it seemed, was time-limited, now approaching its expiry date.

'She's upsetting Liam,' he said now. 'It's not as if Bridget's death wasn't expected – it's been on the cards for nearly a year.'

'Still! It's a shock. Expecting it can't take that away. When it comes to it, we don't know what death means.'

Martin rubbed his eyes with the back of one hand. 'All I'm saying is she needs to pull herself together, for Liam's sake.'

'That's not something she can *decide*,' Anna said. 'It's not surprising Liam's upset, either. He's lost his gran. And Ruth's on her own now, isn't she? You could be more sympathetic.'

'Well, thanks for that, Anna.'

What a range of nuances he could place on the mere pronouncing of her name! It could sound aloof and disapproving, as now; at other times, when his breath was warm on her neck, his hands roving, it was a caress, a declaration of love, or at least of lust. When he looked like this, wearing the shut-off expression Anna was beginning to know, it was hard to believe they could ever be intimate.

'I'm only trying to have a conversation.'

'Trying to put me in the wrong, more like. Let's face it – whether I go to Ruth's, or don't go, you'll take offence.' He moved to the sink to rinse the tumbler under the tap; in his way, she made no effort to move aside. 'At first you

19

complained about me spending too much time with her. Now I'm being callous. Why not accept that it's nothing to do with you, and let me get on with it?'

'Of course it's to do with me! And I *didn't* complain, not once—'

'Not in so many words. You didn't need to,' Martin said, in an *I know I'm right* tone that made her want to hit him. 'Weren't you going to eat? I've got papers to sort out for tomorrow.'

'Fine! Don't let me hold you up,' Anna flung at him as he left the room. She stood undecided for a few moments before taking the over-browned stroganoff out of the oven. She no longer felt hungry, but obstinacy made her serve a portion for herself and sit at the table to eat. A hard lump in her throat made swallowing difficult. She could have wept if she'd wanted to: whether from sympathy for Ruth, self-pitying frustration with Martin or sheer petulance, she couldn't tell.

# 2

Anna walked along High Holborn, wrapped up against the cold in winter coat, scarf and beret, the heels of her boots tapping authoritatively with each stride. Catching a glimpse of her reflection in a full-length window, she took a moment to recognize herself – a tall woman dressed in black, with a frowning expression. She looked in dismay at this forbidding double – was that who she was? This other person had taken her over. She couldn't see her own self looking out from inside.

She was meeting Bethan for lunch. Until Christmas, the Italian restaurant had set out tables and chairs under its awning on milder days, and patio heaters wastefully radiating warmth, but today there could be no question of anyone sitting outside. Bethan waved from their favourite table, in an alcove near the bar. She was dressed more casually than Anna, in a printed tunic over a long-sleeved T-shirt. Anna brightened, seeing her.

'It's all right, you're not late. I got here early to read something through.' Bethan had a pile of papers on the table in front of her; she gathered them into a folder, which she stashed in her saggy fabric bag.

'I thought you did everything electronically these days?'
Anna said.

'We do, but this author doesn't. He isn't even on line, can
you imagine? We have to *phone* him, or send a letter. But he
writes like a dream.'

'Anyway, how are you?' Anna settled herself next to
Bethan on the cushioned bench. 'You look great. Positively
blooming.'

Bethan always did have a look of robust health: slightly
plump, rosy-cheeked in what she disparagingly called her
milkmaid look. 'Oh, I'm fine,' she said, smug and self-
conscious. 'I've got over the sickness now, and I can't tell you
how good that feels.'

'So you're doing all the right things? Laying off alcohol
and coffee, going to pregnancy yoga?'

'Course!'

Briskly the waiter took their order, geared to quick
service for people on lunch breaks.

'It's a girl,' Bethan said, spreading the fingers of one
hand over her stomach. 'I just know it's a girl. Not that I
mind, either way. But Cliff wants a girl. Actually, Anna,
I want to ask you something. A huge favour.'

'Oh, what?'

'I – that is, we – we'd really like you to be godparent.
Would you?'

'Godparent? Me?' Anna absorbed this. 'Well, thanks,
Beth. I'd love that. Only – what do you mean by the God
bit? I don't think I could make promises in a church without
feeling like a hypocrite. Will it be a church christening?'

'I did look at some websites, and you can have a naming
ceremony, anywhere you like, and do it your own way. I

know, I know. It's all a bit early to start planning, and Cliff says I shouldn't tempt fate, in case something goes wrong.' Bethan held up both hands to show crossed fingers. 'Anyway. By godparent, I mean as in supporter. Special auntie. Pagan parent, if you'd rather.'

'In that case . . . but do you really think I'm, you know, reliable enough?'

'You are now.' Bethan gave her a teasing look. 'I might not have thought so once.'

'Then – thank you. I'd love to. I was hoping to be honorary auntie, anyway.'

'Brilliant! Thanks so much!' Bethan gave her a hug, then took out her mobile to text Cliff the news. The waiter brought their pasta dishes and salad; putting her phone away, Bethan asked, 'How about you? How's work? How's Martin?' She began to eat hungrily.

Anna shrugged. 'Everything's fine, thanks.'

'What about you two? Do you think you'll, you know, have children?'

'You sound like my mum,' said Anna, unfairly, as her mother had never given such a hint.

'Still! You're thirty-three. Biological clock ticking.'

It always jolted Anna to remember that she had reached such an age; surely she ought to feel adult by now, responsible, in control of her life.

'Martin's already got the boys,' she said.

'Yes, but you?'

'Haven't really thought.'

Bethan made a *puh* face. 'You expect me to believe that? You've never so much as thought about having a baby?'

'I don't want to be pushed into anything, that's all.'

'Who's pushing?'

'No one. Just – you know – people's expectations.' Anna filled Bethan's glass with mineral water. 'Yours, now,' she added lightly. 'Like it's the obvious next thing to do.'

Bethan shrugged. 'Only asking. What about the job? How's that working out?'

'Fine, thanks. Keeps me off the streets.'

'You don't sound keen. You're not chucking it in, are you?'

'It's only a trial period. I'm not sure I want to stay there for ever. I quite like the work. I like houses, property. I like matching people to homes, or dreaming about what I'd do if I had the money. It's just – just I don't like feeling tied down.'

'But why think of it like that?' said Bethan. 'You've got a lovely man, a nice flat, and now you can have a good job as well. All this flitting from one thing to another – wouldn't it be more rewarding to stick at something?'

'Beth! You're definitely turning into my mum.'

Bethan sagged into her seat in an attitude of surrender. 'It's only common sense. What's the problem? No one's asking you to sign up for life, are they? You haven't found a vocation, that's your problem.'

'But how many people do?' Anna said. 'What's yours – massaging the egos of pushy authors?'

Bethan giggled. 'I won't mind taking a break, that's for sure. Anyway. How was your weekend?'

Anna told her about the decorating, Martin's visit to Ruth, his late return.

'Hmm.' Bethan lowered her eyebrows. 'You're not thinking they're—?'

'No! Definitely not.'

'It's just that you mentioned it. I asked about your weekend and that's what you chose to tell me.'

'It's not what you're imagining,' said Anna. 'I *like* Ruth. She and I could easily be friends.'

Bethan gave her a comically sceptical look.

'Why not?' Anna countered. 'If it wasn't for Martin in the way.'

'Yeah, right. You'd be soulmates.'

The waiter came for their plates; Bethan turned down coffee, but Anna looked at her watch, and ordered an Americano.

'Martin's the one I feel sorry for,' Bethan said. 'He's afraid you'll start comparing notes.'

'Typical man, that'd be. Assuming we'd have nothing else to talk about.'

'She did seem nice,' said Bethan; she had met Ruth recently at Martin's fortieth birthday party.

'Sister substitute, obviously. Is that what you're thinking?'

'Yes. I wasn't going to say.'

No. No one ever did say. There seemed to be an unspoken agreement that Rose's name must never be mentioned. Anna had come closer than usual to breaking the rule.

Bethan looked at her sidelong, tilting her head. 'You seem a bit . . .'

'What?'

'I don't know. Unsettled.'

Anna made herself smile, trying to regain the celebratory tone they'd started with. 'Sorry. I don't know why. Except it's not because I want a baby, and *definitely* not because I think

Martin's sleeping with Ruth. Let's not get sidetracked. Honestly, Beth, I'm thrilled you asked me to be godparent. Will you give me a crash course?'

'We'll talk more, sometime soon.' Bethan glanced up at the clock. 'I'd better get back. Publicity meeting at two-thirty.'

Anna downed her coffee and summoned a waiter to settle the bill. Outside on the pavement she and Bethan stood for a moment, buttoning their coats, pulling on gloves.

'I'll text you. Take care,' said Bethan, as they hugged.

'And you! Great to see you. Look after yourself.'

Bethan walked away quickly in the direction of Bloomsbury, a jaunty figure in her purple tights, boots and butcher-boy cap. Anna watched her go, wishing she had Bethan's gift for happiness. It looked so easy, for those who had the knack.

❖ ❖ ❖

Years ago, when they were children, Rose showed Anna the Seven Sisters.

Standing by the back door, Anna was shivering so much that her teeth hurt; she could have made herself stop, but it added to the excitement of being out in the dark. Night-time transformed the garden into a strange, unknown place, even though indoors was only a few steps away, with Mum and Dad watching TV. As long as she could reach back and touch the house wall, she'd be safe.

They had come out to look for a hedgehog that sometimes scuttled across the lawn, nosing its way to the dish of cat-food Rose put out for it. Anna hugged herself, peering into the stalky, spidery place beside the shed. Her eyes sought the thicker patch of darkness that might, if she willed it hard enough, clump itself into a hedgehog and trundle over the grass as if on wheels. It gave her a shivery thrill to think of other lives so close to her own, of creatures huddled in darkness, waiting for nightfall, their time for creeping out. Then Rose, distracted from hedgehogs, called, 'Look, look at the stars! There's the Plough, and the Pole Star. And the Seven Sisters – how many can you see?'

'Where?' Anna's head jerked up, her eyes adjusting to a different scale. The stars giddied her; how could she not have noticed them?

Rose pointed. 'See? It's like a blurry bit. Look at the very top of the tree, then go up a bit, like two o'clock. Have you got them?'

Anna gazed, anxious not to make Rose impatient. There were bears and lions and hunters if you knew how to see them; Anna imagined them chasing each other across the night sky, trailing stardust like glitter. She knew there was meant to be a swan and a lion and a pair of twins, and now sisters too. Her eyes searched for faces, flowing robes and hair, like those pictures made of joined-up dots. Star-sisters. But all she could see, following Rose's pointing finger, was haze, a smudged thumbprint of light. She was disappointed.

'Did you make that up?' she asked Rose. 'About sisters?'

'No! It's true. They've got names – Dad showed me. We looked them up in a book.'

He didn't show *me*, Anna thought. Resentment prickled her. She thought of Rose and Dad in the garden looking at stars, finding the pictures, joining the dots; herself left out, sent up to bed on her own. The Seven Sisters belonged to

Rose and Dad. She was only being let in on something that was already theirs.

'I can't see them,' she said, huffily.

'You're not looking properly,' Rose told her. 'That blurry place is made of stars. How many can you see?'

Anna stared. She narrowed her eyes, trying to make out the individual points of light. 'Seven,' she said, sure of a right answer.

Rose shook her head. 'There's supposed to be much more than seven. If you had really good eyesight, you'd see more. But you won't if you look straight at them. Look to one side, then try.'

Anna tried. She fixed her gaze to the left of the smudge, pretending not to look, as if she could play a trick on a star cluster thousands of light years away. There was an impression of clarity, of the separate stars just out of her eyes' reach. But when she stared straight at them, trying to catch them unawares, the vision blurred. The stars wouldn't be caught that way.

It's funny, she thought: the more you look, the more you can't see.

❖ ❖ ❖

# 3

On Friday evening Anna phoned Ruth.

'Thought I might come and help tomorrow, while Martin's out with Liam?'

Now that she was offering, it seemed a stupid idea. She waited for a polite brush-off, but instead Ruth said, 'Would you? If you really mean it, I could do with some help over at the house. My mum's place, I mean. I've got to make a start on sorting out her things.'

'Yes, of course I'll help.'

Ruth sounded relieved. 'I'm not looking forward to it. It'll be easier with company, but not much fun for you.'

'I'll come down on the tube,' Anna told her. 'Martin's bringing Liam back later, isn't he, so I can go back with him.'

'Good – I'll meet you at Woodford station. I'll be putting Liam on the train at ten-thirty – does that sound OK?'

When Anna told Martin of this arrangement, he gave a shrug, as if recognizing he'd been outmanoeuvred.

'It's nice of you to do that. It'll be a bit dismal, though.' He'd just come in, and was looking through the post.

'Not really. It's not as if I knew Ruth's mum.'

'I'd have thought you had enough house-clearing on your plate, with your parents' move coming up.'

'Mm. This is a practice run, perhaps.'

'Must be worth a bit, that place. She'll be glad of your advice. Either she could do it up and sell it, or let it and get the income. That's what I'd do – wait till prices go up, then sell. It'll only increase in value if she hangs on to it.'

'I don't suppose money's the main thing on her mind,' Anna reproached. 'It'll be a big wrench. Did she live there as a child?'

'No – her parents moved there the year we got married.'

It still jarred Anna to hear Martin say 'we' like this as if it was still current; to come up against this other, earlier *we* that was Martin-and-Ruth. Martin didn't mention Ruth much, beyond the transactional details of his days with Liam, and had never told Anna why the marriage had ended, apart from an all-encompassing 'Things didn't work out.'

She and Ruth saw each other only occasionally, when Liam – usually Liam on his own, now that Patrick's visits were less frequent – was being collected or returned, but Martin's presence always emphasized the triangular nature of their relationship. Ruth, a little younger than Martin, was diffidently attractive, with quick movements and an air of anxiety. When she came to Martin's birthday party in November – alone, there never being any suggestion of a new partner – she had been quite uncharacteristically dressed up, trying to use clothes and make-up as a shield, giving herself extra height with heeled shoes that made her self-conscious. Till then, Anna had felt ambivalent about her, but now she was oddly touched by this brave effort.

Not knowing many of the other guests, Ruth had stood awkwardly with her wineglass, affecting close interest in the bookshelves until Anna went to her rescue. She knew from Martin that Ruth had given up her job in a hospital pharmacy to work as a gardener, a backward career move in his view. Asking about this, Anna drew out details of the course Ruth had taken in horticulture and garden design, and of various projects she spoke about with enthusiasm. Gratitude and warmth shone from Ruth's eyes, not the wariness Anna might have expected.

When Anna compared herself to Ruth, she couldn't see what Martin had gained from the substitution. Though tempted to probe further into his dismissive 'Things didn't work out', she never did, fearful of the not-workings-out that were emerging in their own relationship.

Saturday was bright and frosty, more cheering than the bleak greyness of the previous week. As Anna came out of the Underground station at Woodford, Ruth pulled up in her black Fiesta, nosing into an empty parking space. Liam got out of the passenger seat, wearing his Chelsea scarf. Anna felt disconcerted, as she always did at first sight, by his resemblance to Martin, the sleek dark hair and dark eyes. Martin was taking him to a home match today, and being allowed to go to London alone on the Underground was a new concession.

''Lo.' Liam gave her a perfunctory wave.

'Hi, Liam. Hi, Ruth.'

Ruth startled Anna with a kiss and a warm hug, which she hastily returned. 'It's really great of you to do this,' Ruth told her. 'You must have loads of better things to do on a Saturday.'

'You don't have to come *with* me,' Liam mumbled, but Ruth insisted on going as far as the barrier, and seeing him through. Martin, who would meet him at Holborn, considered Ruth over-protective; but now Anna sensed Ruth's anxiety as they waited for the small and suddenly vulnerable-looking figure to cross the bridge to the opposite platform, where a train was already pulling in.

They went back to the car. Ruth's mother's house was in a village near Epping, and their route took them between leaf-strewn banks and stands of trees. Even in midwinter, the copper of the beech leaves was dazzling; the forest floor was thickly strewn, and the few still clinging to branches were burnished into fiery bronze by shafting sunlight. Anna saw, in a hollow, flecked ice on a pond, with hollies huddling close, a trodden path leading through the stand of trees, and grasses bleached strawy pale.

'I know,' said Ruth. 'It's beautiful, isn't it? I try not to take it for granted, seeing it most days. We used to go for long walks with the boys.'

That *we* again; Anna wasn't used to hearing it from Ruth, and it hung awkwardly in the air for a few moments.

A stretch of common marked the edge of the forest; then Ruth took to narrow lanes, crossing the M25 and reaching, after another few miles, a settlement hardly large enough to be called a village: a few houses, a post box at the junction of two lanes. A pair of cottages stood together beyond a farm entrance. Ruth and Anna got out of the car. Motorway traffic hummed faintly in the distance; nearby, rooks cawed in the treetops, and wings beat against cypress branches as a woodpigeon took clumsily to the air.

While Ruth stood for a moment holding her bunch of

32

keys, as if reluctant to go in, Anna couldn't help looking at the house with the speculative estate agent's eye she was fast acquiring. Probably built as a farm cottage, with its conjoined twin, it was quite substantial, with a generous front garden and driveway separating it from the lane. An entrance porch was twined all over with brown stems and feathery seed-heads, like old man's beard.

'*Clematis tangutica*,' Ruth said, as Anna reached out to touch. 'Lovely in September. The garden's gone wild. I used to help Mum with it, but then things got out of hand. I should have got someone round to keep things tidy, but, well . . . I didn't.'

'There must be such a lot to think about,' Anna said, dismayed by the prospect of dismantling a home, a life. The house must be stripped of personality. The similar task soon to confront her parents would be as daunting; to leave their home would mean leaving Rose, acknowledging at last that she would never come back.

This was easier, by comparison; the house and its contents meant nothing to her, other than that Martin had been here with Ruth immediately after Bridget's death. He'd known his way around, of course; Bridget had been his mother-in-law. She pictured him, capable and re-assuring, collecting what he needed, making notes, ticking things off a list. He must have comforted Ruth too – allowed her to cry, in those first days. Anna imagined Ruth sobbing against Martin's shoulder, her fine hair tickling his face, his arms holding her.

'Martin's been brilliant,' Ruth said, as if reading her thoughts. 'I wouldn't have known where to start, but he's thought of everything.' She unlocked the door, looking in dismay at a heap of post on the mat. 'Oh, look. I expect it's mostly junk, but I must get it redirected. Something else I should have done.' She tugged at a fat envelope wedged in the letter box.

Never having met Ruth's mother, Anna felt like an intruder as she stepped inside. The chill struck at her. She would have thought it impossible for a house to feel so cold; the air and space inside might have been rendered deep-frozen by the death of its occupant.

Gathering up the letters and catalogues, Ruth carried them through to the kitchen; Anna stooped for a dropped envelope, and followed. They both stood in silence for a few moments. The kitchen was large, furnished with units in the dark, rustic-looking wood that had been popular some thirty years ago. A frilled blind was half lowered in the window. On the sill, and on every other surface, were bits and pieces of china, jars, ancient cookery books, dried teasels. Clutter, Anna thought; so much clutter. What will we do with it all? For a moment, thinking Ruth was about to give way to tears, she searched for something to say; but Ruth briskly took control of herself.

'I thought we'd start upstairs.' She dumped the post on a worktop, with a slither of paper and cellophane. 'But first I'll check the oil and turn on the heating, or we'll get hypothermia.'

There were only two bedrooms, the back one over-looking a large, bedraggled garden with a bird table and empty seed feeders. Beyond, hedgerows stretched away in hazy sunshine; a green slope of meadow, still frosted at its shadowed edges, was dotted with well-spaced parkland trees. Bridget's room at the front, large and square with a washbasin in one corner, was less feminine than Anna had expected, the clothes in the wardrobe tending towards tweed and corduroy, quilted gilets and sensible skirts.

'We need a system,' said Ruth. 'Most of this can go to the charity shop – the shoes as well, unless they're too battered. Anything past it we'll bag separately for the recycling centre – there's a bin there for fabrics. I'm going to choose some scarves and jewellery to give to her friends.'

They got to work. Ruth turned on the bedside radio and tuned it to Radio 3. They didn't talk much, beyond 'What do you think?' or 'Oh look, this can't have been worn,' and 'Where on earth did she get this?' as Ruth pulled out a flimsy purple top with feather-trimmed neckline.

Anna carried the bulging bin-bags down to Ruth's car, and stowed them on the back seat for Ruth to take to the hospice shop later. The hanging space and shelves were soon emptied, quickly stripped of character and the accumulation of years: hints of bargain purchases, special outings, threadbare favourites. Now it was as bland as a fixture in a hotel bedroom. Only the shoes remained.

Ruth made a start, but said, 'I can't do this. Could you?'

She didn't say why, but Anna understood. Shoes took on the shape of feet; kept the imprint of toes, their uneven heels recording how their owner walked and stood.

'OK. Let me.'

'I'll do the airing cupboard, instead – the sheets and towels.'

Anna knelt, and began taking out the shoes, pair by pair. Sturdy lace-ups and flats, comfort sandals, ballet pumps, size five, were neatly arranged on racks, several with shapers inside to keep them stretched. Most were well-worn, though

35

one brand-new pair had labels still stuck on the instep. It was easy to sort them. Most, still wearable, went into the charity-shop bag; Anna rejected only frayed slippers and a pair of pumps whose toes had almost worn through.

She found herself thinking of Rose's new sandals.

Rose's bedroom, the two of them on a summer Saturday; the window open, and Mum and Dad outside, gardening and reading respectively. Rose had been out shopping with Chrissie, her best friend, and had come home with new sandals in a box. The smell of fabric and newness, when Rose took off the lid, made Anna long for new shoes of her own.

'They're like the ones I saw in *Honey*,' Rose told her, 'the ones I showed you. Only cheaper.'

She held the box possessively, as if Anna's gaze might be too covetous. Then she lifted one out. It had a high wedge heel made of cork; the upper – just a broad strap over the instep – was crocheted in cream cord, and there was a triangular piece to fit over the heel; long ties ended in wooden beads.

Anna touched it; felt the pitted smoothness of cork, and the round shininess of the beads. It was infinitely desirable, because chosen by Rose.

'Put them on!' she urged.

Rose made a ceremony of it, placing the shoes side by side on the mat, sitting on the bed to unlace the old canvas plimsolls she had on. She pushed her feet into the new sandals, then criss-crossed the laces around her ankles and tied them at the front. She stood tall in the wedge heels, and practised a few steps in front of the mirror. The pale cream deepened the tan of her legs and feet. She turned this way and that, lifting her skirt to admire the effect; she stood pigeon-toed, like the models in *Honey* often did. Not satisfied, she frowned at herself. 'They'd look better with shorts. You can have the box if you like, Annie.'

She dropped her skirt so that it fell like a puddle on the floor, stepped out of it and posed again, giggling. 'Perhaps I should wear them like this.'

How slim and coltish her legs were, how slender her waist above the surprising fullness of her bottom in brief blue spotted knickers; how aware she was of herself, the way she turned, tilting her hip, pushing out her chest, flicking her hair. Rose had turned into something Anna could never imagine herself becoming. There was a gloss and preen about her, a sense that admiration was her due. Rose was like the girls Anna saw in magazines, sleek and groomed, leggy as racehorses, their beauty allowing them to attract and dismiss boys according to their whims. Anna imagined Jamie Spellman staring at Rose's legs; she knew how his face would look, and how Rose would tease him, knowing he wanted her. She uses him, Anna thought; she'll soon drop him for someone else.

Rose pulled on her denim cut-off shorts, and went downstairs, wobbling slightly, supporting herself with a hand on the banister rail.

'Good God! You'll break your ankles in those heels,' Dad said; and Mum, from her lounger, shading her eyes, 'Very nice, dear, but wouldn't they look better with a pretty skirt? Those shorts are so scruffy.'

Soon after Rose left, Anna took the crocheted sandals, scuffed and a little grubby now, to her own room. She was only borrowing them, she told herself; Rose would want them, of course, when she came back. They fitted Anna now. She tried them on, criss-crossing the ties. She paraded in front of the mirror in bra and knickers, remembering how Rose had looked. If she narrowed her eyes, she could just about see herself as one of the magazine girls, but open them wide and she looked ludicrous, a girl teetering in heels too high for her, a girl in shoes borrowed from her big sister. Instead of Rose's lovely slender curves, her own body was almost straight up and down, and podgy around the stomach; her legs were long and quite slim, but somehow didn't belong with the rest of her.

She unlaced the sandals and held one in both hands. The insoles were made of coiled fabric like thin rope, slightly rough to the touch. The pressure of Rose's heels had worn it flat, with a faint dark rim of sweat and dirt. An indentation showed where the ball of her foot had pressed, and her big toe. Anna traced these shapes with her forefinger, as if Rose could be summoned like the genie of Aladdin's lamp. She held the shoe to her nose and smelled sweat, the particular cheesy sweat of feet: the smell of hot summer days, of throwing off sandals to feel the coolness of grass.

Anna sat quite still and listened. If she listened always and always, maybe she'd hear a whisper. Maybe Rose wasn't really gone; just playing a joke.

❖ ❖ ❖

'Lunch!' Ruth called from downstairs; Anna hadn't realized she'd gone down. One end of the kitchen was a dining area, with a pine table and two chairs; Ruth had spread a cloth, and set out French bread, olives, cheeses and salad, and a carton of apple juice.

'Oh, I forgot plates.' Ruth went to a cupboard. 'It feels so weird, everything in its place where it's always been. And knowing that soon it'll all be gone. I won't start on the kitchen today. It sounds daft, but I keep thinking Mum'll turn up and say, *What are you doing with my things? Why are you giving all my clothes away?*'

Anna was silent, thinking of Rose's drawings, Rose's clothes, Rose's books; the remnants she had clung to as if they had talismanic qualities. It was pointless, keeping them; the breath of life that had once clung to them had evaporated. They were only objects now.

'Oh . . .' Ruth looked at her in consternation. 'I'm so sorry. Your sister – Martin told me. You must have been through all this, only much worse, because it has to be worse when a young person dies.'

'Dies? Martin said that?' Anna's voice came out gruffly. 'He told you Rose was dead?'

'Not exactly – I think he assumed, or maybe I assumed—'

'People do assume,' said Anna. 'But we don't *know*. She was eighteen when she disappeared, and that was nearly twenty years ago. Twenty years ago this year.'

'And you've got no idea what—'

Anna shook her head. 'We don't know any more now than we did then. She went out one day and didn't come back.'

'Anna, that's *awful*.' Ruth's blue eyes welled with tears. 'Your poor parents. Poor you. If it were Liam or Patrick . . . I can't bear to think about it. What a terrible thing to live with.'

39

'They don't talk about her,' Anna said; Ruth's compassion made her feel inadequate. 'Don't even mention her name. It's like we've agreed not to. Martin and I never talk about her either – I'm surprised he told you.'

'Well, I asked if you had any brothers or sisters. What was her name?'

'See, you're talking about her in the past tense. Rose, her name's Rose. *Is*, not *was*. We were Rose and Anna – Rosanna, we called ourselves, like we were one person . . .'

Herself and Rose together, facing the mirror. 'Look! We're Rosanna now. Two people in one. One person made of two.' Rose stood behind, chin resting on top of Anna's head, draping her long hair on either side of Anna's face so that it looked as if it belonged to both of them. Mum had once told them to stop it, as if it was naughty, but when they were alone they couldn't resist. Rosanna seemed to have a presence of her own, half Rose, half Anna, but somehow more than that.

Anna pushed the thought away. 'Now there's just me. She'd be thirty-eight now—'

'Same as me,' said Ruth.

'So, if she's alive, more than half her life has been spent somewhere else.'

'But – do you really think she could have made another life and not have been in touch?'

'Yes. No. I don't know what I think. I've thought every-thing there is to think, and all of it leads to the same dead end.'

Ruth put a hand on Anna's arm. 'I'm so sorry. I don't know what to say.'

Anna shifted away, clasping her hands together under

the table. 'Thanks. But that's why I don't talk about it, I suppose. Either people tiptoe around the subject, or we go over and over the same questions. There's nothing new, nothing we haven't thought of a hundred times over. I had a sister and now I haven't. I'm used to it.' Her eyes drifted hungrily towards the food. 'Let's eat now. I'm starving.' She tore a piece off the French loaf and cut a generous piece of Camembert.

Dusk came early, the moon rising in a clear indigo sky. There were no streetlights here. Frost sparkled on the road, and an owl hooted, quite close, as Anna and Ruth went outside. It felt like the middle of the night, although it wasn't yet six. Anna imagined how long and cold the hours of darkness would be, out here; you'd want to close the curtains and huddle indoors. She wrapped her scarf more closely into her neck, and pulled down the cuffs of her sweater. But it was wonderful to be out in the dark; elemental. In London, everything was muffled by traffic noise, obscured by tall buildings and twenty-four-hour lighting. Here you'd be acutely aware of every variation in light, weather and season.

If it hadn't been for the need to get back to Woodford before Martin arrived with Liam, she might have said, 'Let's go for a walk – look at the stars!' And she had the feeling that Ruth might agree, with enthusiasm.

Ruth was locking up. The house, with everything turned off, looked bleak and deserted. Hadn't Ruth's mother felt isolated, living here on her own? You'd feel more vulnerable inside than out. Outside, you were like some feral creature, all senses awake and alert. Indoors, you couldn't tell who

41

might be prowling out there, watching. Anna shivered.

'Well!' Ruth said brightly, getting into the driver's seat. 'We've made a good start.'

'But there's loads still to do.' Anna fastened her seat belt. 'I can come again – tomorrow, if you like.'

'Thanks, Anna! That's lovely of you, but I go to Holtby Hall on Sundays. If you really mean it, how about next Saturday?'

'Of course I mean it. Maybe Martin'll come too, but if not I'll come anyway.'

Even as she said this, Anna hoped he wouldn't. Martin would bring briskness and practicality to the task, but it wouldn't be the same. Anna had enjoyed today, although she couldn't have said why.

Holtby Hall was a garden restoration project Ruth had taken on, working there three days a week and now Sundays as well, to supervise weekend volunteers. Anna remembered now that Martin had told her this, speculating that Ruth had met someone there.

'Do you mind if she has?' Anna had asked him, and he'd looked at her as if the idea were preposterous.

'No. Why would I?'

'You might find it interesting,' Ruth was saying, as the main beam threw a swathe of light between the high hedgerows ahead. 'Holtby Hall, I mean. Come over one Sunday, if you like.'

'Thanks. I might do that.' Anna almost added, 'Do you mean Martin as well?' but thought better of it, deciding Ruth didn't. Martin was quickly bored by what he termed stately homes and gardens; and besides, Anna didn't want him to get in the way of an overture of friendship from Ruth.

*　*　*

Martin was late back with Liam, apologizing, blaming the traffic in the East End. By that time Ruth had cooked an omelette for herself and Anna, and they'd shared a bottle of wine. It was Anna's first introduction to Ruth's home, and she was intrigued, a little wary. She couldn't help thinking of it as Ruth and Martin's house, the one they'd lived in since Liam was born; she noticed Martin's ease as he made tea for himself and Liam, knowing where to find an unopened packet of biscuits. He could move back in, Anna thought, pick up his old life, and no one would see the join. He could be a proper dad to his boys. She had seen only the kitchen and hallway and the downstairs loo, but wondered, Is this Ruth's taste? Or Martin's? Or both of them together, Ruth-and-Martin? The kitchen they were sitting in had cream Shaker-style units, with pale green tiles; the Krups coffee machine was the same as the one Martin had recently bought for the flat.

Anna's tentative new rapport with Ruth couldn't flourish in Martin's presence. Thankful for Liam, Anna gave him her full attention, encouraging him to tell her about the match, the two goals, one in extra time, and the substitution of his favourite player. Patrick had gone to Edinburgh with his girlfriend, Ruth said; she'd been expecting him back, but now he was staying on indefinitely. Anna saw Martin's disappointment when Ruth told him this. The relationship between father and son had become difficult lately, though Martin was never forthcoming when Anna tried to draw him out.

It was gone ten by the time they got back to the flat. Anna drew the bedroom curtains, yawning. She thought

43

Martin would want to watch TV – a film or Sky News – but instead he said, 'Let's go to bed.'

'Mmm. I'm so tired.'

But Martin wasn't tired. He was in bed first, his eyes following Anna as she twisted her hair into a grip and stripped off her clothes, throwing her jeans and T-shirt into the washing basket. She lingered in the shower, soothing away dust and aches, thinking about various remarks Ruth had made. Was Ruth really as guileless as she seemed – as open, as willing to be friendly? Had there been a barbed edge to some of the things she said?

Anna's skin was warm and fragrant as she towelled herself dry. She slipped on her bath robe and went back into the bedroom. Her nightdress was under the pillow, but as she reached for it Martin caught her wrist and pulled her to him, wrapping her in his arms.

'You're doing it on purpose,' he murmured. 'Taking ages.'

'I wasn't!'

His mouth was on hers, and her tiredness forgotten as he slid the robe away from her shoulders. Moments ago she had wanted nothing more than to curl herself into warmth and sleep, but now – the deliciousness of his hands roving over her, sweeping, lingering, over and down and between her legs, pushing them apart, and his body so firm and compact as she held him close. He had pulled the duvet over them, but now it was too hot and constricting; he knelt upright and flung it off, exposing them both to each other's gaze. The cool air tingled against her skin. She reached for him, pulled him down to her. His lips and his tongue, so expert, so knowing, roused her to a pitch of greedy desire she could hardly contain. He knew exactly when to shift himself, waiting, waiting for tantalizing moments, then pushing into her with slow, deep thrusts, kissing her neck, her hair, while his breath rose and quickened, hot on her skin.

*Oh Martin, Martin . . .*

She knew he was claiming her back.

# 4

What's the point of this? She dabs powder, applies lipstick, grimaces at herself to check for smears on her teeth. The face in the mirror looks tired; blue-grey eyes, with a little red veining, gaze back at her. But when she looks more closely, the eyes are quite empty. She can look right into them and there's nothing.

Sometimes, catching unexpected sight of herself, she sees her mother's face; even, more alarmingly, her grand-mother's. Where has the smooth-faced young girl disappeared to, in this fast-forward rush through the generations? Can it really be hers, this face? How odd that people think it's her they're seeing. It can nod and smile and do all the things faces are meant to do, and that's enough to fool people. It's become an irrelevance. Other people seem closely associated with their faces, but hers is an encumbrance, something she has no choice but to wear, patching it up and trying to make the best of it whenever she's going to meet people. Like plumping up cushions or dead-heading the roses.

She'd rather stay in. She isn't hungry and she doesn't want to spend the evening in pointless chit-chat, but Don has said they'll go and it's too late to back out. There's no escape from what she can only see as an ordeal. He's like that. If he says he'll do something, he does it.

'Ready, then?' Don is jingling his keys, just short of impatient. She puts on her coat and a silk scarf, picks up her gloves and follows him downstairs.

Malcolm. That's who they're going to visit. A golfing acquaintance of Don's, and his wife, Kathy; she's met them both briefly, but can hardly picture their faces. Why not keep it like that? Why make the effort to *get to know each other better*, as Kathy put it when she invited them? Other people's lives. Other people's children and grandchildren and holiday plans. She wants to float away, look down on it all from an aloof height.

'But we won't be living here much longer,' she objected, when Don told her about the arrangement. 'What's the point of making new friends?'

'For Pete's sake! Cranbrook isn't a million miles away. We won't be cutting ourselves off from everyone we know. That's the point.'

Perhaps they *should* move a million miles away. Perhaps that's what she wants. Cranbrook is no more than a feeble gesture of change, barely forty minutes in the car.

Don has remembered to pick up the wine and chocolates she bought yesterday. All she has to do is belt herself in and be transported.

'You'll like Kathy,' he tells her, wiping the inside of the windscreen.

'Will I?' She always bridles when people tell her that. Are her affections so logical, so easily predicted?

There's a pause, then Don says, as he pulls out of the

47

drive, 'I wish you'd tell me what's wrong. You don't seem very happy. I thought you'd be pleased everything's going so smoothly.'

She takes a deep breath and sighs it out, wondering if she can pick something from the confusion that will make sense. 'It's – oh, something at work. Not important enough to bother you with.'

'No, go on.'

'Well – I wish they wouldn't try to change things. Afternoons. I can't do afternoons. I told them.'

'Have they asked you to?'

'Yes, two a week, but I said I couldn't.'

Don looks at her. 'Is that all? It's sorted, then. Why worry about that? You'll be leaving, anyway, when we move.'

She wonders why she started this; she has no intention of elaborating. And yes, he's right. Just a few weeks more. It's part of her routine now to get well away from the health centre by one-thirty; she can't risk being even five minutes late. Mondays, Wednesdays and Fridays have become dangerous now, evenly spaced, waiting to trap her. The others in reception have no idea, seeing no difference between those days and the others. But she doesn't have to keep putting herself through this – it's the one thought that keeps her going. She could resign now if she liked: say she's got too much to do, getting ready for the move. Don wouldn't mind. It's only a kind of obstinacy that makes her reluctant to give in. With so much about to change, she wants at least to hang onto the shape of her days.

She keeps noticing, lately, how carefully he treats her, with a mixture of concern and exasperation, as if she's a frail-tempered convalescent who must be humoured. It's making her *feel* frail, her nerves about to snap, as if she's entitled to outbursts of temper or irritability. She has to remind herself that there's nothing physically wrong with her, nothing at all. It's only a house move they're facing, not life-threatening illness.

Soon the tyres are crunching on gravel and they're outside an ivy-clad house with a pillared entrance porch. The woman, Kathy, comes to the door, wearing some sort of Eastern-inspired, bead-encrusted garment, her hair held back by jewelled clips. In the gush of *How lovely to see you* and *You found us, then*, she registers her own dullness and drabness, her safe clothes. Fortunately Malcolm is far scruffier than his wife, dressed as if for gardening in saggy trousers and a zipped top.

Everyone seems to kiss nowadays, the double air-kiss that once looked flamboyantly Gallic, even people who are barely acquainted. Reluctantly she submits. Kathy, one hand still on her shoulder, says, 'Come through and sit down, Sandra. Such a cold night! Malcolm's lit the wood-burner.'

'Cassandra. My name's Cassandra.'

Why's she saying that? Sometimes it's as if a different person speaks for her; the words are out so quickly that she hears them before they've formed in her mind.

'Oh! I'm so sorry. I thought Don said Sandra.' Kathy recovers quickly. 'Well, Cassandra is lovely – I don't blame you for preferring it. Do you predict the future?'

'No.' The answer yips out of her. 'I can't even predict the past.'

Kathy laughs, as if this is immensely witty, but there's an awkwardness now, affecting all of them. Malcolm rubs his hands together. 'Drinks! Let me get drinks organized. White wine, er, Cassandra – Soave? Or there's soft drinks if you prefer.'

While Kathy takes the coats and Malcolm officiates in the kitchen, Don gives her a puzzled, warning look, and mouths, 'What's that about?' She doesn't answer. Drinks are brought in; there's bluesy piano music in the background, and warmth from a log-burning stove. Sinking into a too-soft sofa, she stretches out her feet and assumes a vaguely genial expression, saying nothing. Kathy is answering a question from Don: something about her grandson, how naughty he is; how she looks after him every Tuesday and Thursday morning, how he plays her up.

'Have you got grandchildren?' Kathy asks, looking at her.

'No. Not yet.' Her voice sounds much louder than she meant. 'Not until Rosanna . . .' The pause stretches into silence; they're all looking at her.

'Rosanna?' Kathy prompts. 'Don mentioned your daughter – an estate agent, isn't she? That must have been useful.'

She is thinking of Rosanna in the garden, the coming and the going – like people weaving patterns in a folk dance, looking as if they'll collide but always swerving away, looping back. Finding a gap to disappear into. Always someone has to disappear. It seems to be a rule.

The pear tree. She can close her eyes and take herself there, beneath its branches, in the everlasting summer.

'Yes,' Don says quickly, with a sharp, sidelong glance. 'Anna was very helpful in all our house-searching.'

'Anna,' she says, bringing herself back. 'Yes, yes, she was.'

'So you're moving to Cranbrook? Lovely, and not too far.'

Kathy passes a plate of olive canapés. 'And you've been in your house for – how long?'

'Oh,' Don says, 'more than thirty years now. We moved there when . . .'

The pause stretches out while everyone waits. It's the sort of harmless-sounding question that can easily trip them up. This is his own fault, she thinks almost with relish, for getting them into this situation. Their oldest friends, their real friends, know about Rose; it's understood, no one needing to mention her name. With new acquaintances they have to skirt around this unstable ground that won't bear their weight.

'. . . when Anna was three,' Don finishes.

'Aaah, so all your memories of her childhood are there. It'll be a wrench to leave, Cassandra, I'm sure?'

Kathy's sympathetic tone sends her into a foment of rage. She feels her limbs tensing against the sofa's embrace. *I understand*, says the crooning voice; *you don't need to tell me. I know what you'll be leaving behind.*

*No, you don't. No one knows. No one can begin to know.*

She has to grant Kathy this, though – during that stilted conversation, a decision has made itself. On the way home, in the car, she announces to Don: 'I can't go through with it. We'll have to pull out. I can't live anywhere else. I'm staying here.'

Anna and Martin spent Sunday morning, as usual, at their health club: Pilates and a swim for Anna, weights and the sauna for Martin. Over a snack lunch in the bar, they considered seeing a film later. Anna was looking up times in the listings magazine when a man in his fifties, a gym acquaintance of Martin's, came over to their table.

'Hi, Jeff. How's it going?' Martin greeted him.

'Good, thanks. Thought we might meet up next week, if you're free one evening?'

He was about to engage Martin as his financial adviser. They arranged a time; then Jeff turned to Anna. 'He's in great demand, your husband. I'm lucky to get a look in. Are you in the same game?'

'Partner. Martin's my partner,' said Anna. 'No, I'm not. I work at an estate agent's.'

Jeff raised his eyebrows. 'So the two of you should have your fingers on the pulse, between you. Which one?'

'Burton Brown, in Holborn, at the moment.'

Jeff nodded, and Martin said, 'But it's not just *at the moment*, is it? Anna's doing a maternity cover, but we hope they'll make it permanent.'

'We? I haven't decided yet. I might turn it down,' Anna said.

'Really? Nice to have the choice.' Jeff settled as if for a long chat, stretching his legs. 'You've got something better in view?'

'Not really.' Anna gave a tight smile, not meeting Martin's eye; they were prickly with each other today, and she knew the reason. Martin had turned huffy on their way here, when she told him of her arrangement to help Ruth next Saturday.

'Again? I don't see why you want to get involved,' he said, and she had retorted, 'I know.' Privately, she hadn't forgiven him for his casual misinformation about Rose, for telling Ruth that Rose had died. He couldn't begin to understand the gap in her life, a dark place of incomprehension and reproach, a sore ready to weep again whenever she picked at it. Knowing how unreasonable it was to blame him, since she never spoke of it, only made her harden towards him.

At last Jeff said he ought to be going. 'Till Thursday, then, eight o'clock. Nice to see you, Anna.'

As soon as he'd gone, Martin turned back to the film listings. 'What was that about,' he said, not looking at Anna, 'saying no to Burton Brown?'

'Well, I might. I'm not sure.'

He put the magazine down; his face registered puzzlement, then exasperation. 'You can't be serious!'

'Why not?'

'It's a good position, you know it is. You like the work, and they'll give you the training you need to make a career of it. You're lucky to have a chance like that drop into your lap. What more do you want?'

'I don't know.'

'Oh, come on, Anna. You'd wait a long time for a better offer – I thought you'd bite their hand off. It's a good salary, convenient for home, it could lead to other things. Are you saying you'd rather drift from job to job, carry on as you were? You're not being rational.'

'Not agreeing with you, you mean.'

'You haven't given one good reason for not accepting.'

Anna tried to find one. 'I don't want to tie myself down, that's all.'

'For God's sake! You're thirty-three, not a student on a gap year. Tie yourself down? Why look at it like that? Aren't we all tied down in one way or another? How d'you think we pay for the flat, our membership here, our holidays, weekends away, the car? You'd miss all those things soon enough if you didn't have them.'

'It's just – things happen without me choosing them. I didn't choose Burton Brown. It happened that way, that's all. If I say yes, it turns into something I can't get out of.'

'All I know is that you're throwing away a chance most people would jump at. I don't understand you, Anna.'

The words hung in the air for a moment. She looked at him.

'That's right. You don't.'

Martin threw out his hands in a gesture of *I do my best.* 'So this is about more than the job. It's about everything.'

'Maybe.' Anna had the feeling that this conversation had already been written; that it was running ahead of her, pre-scripted. And being a script, it would end in a row, an ultimatum, a point of no going back.

'You were quick to put Jeff right when he thought we were married,' Martin said quietly.

'I don't like people making assumptions. But we can't argue here.'

'I don't want to argue anywhere. A relaxing Sunday was what I had in mind. Looks like that's off, then.'

He was on his feet, shouldering his kit bag, turning his back on her. Suddenly self-conscious, Anna became aware of all the people around, the jangly music in the background that couldn't have been quite loud enough to drown their conversation. She threw a jaunty smile at the barman in a pretence that nothing was wrong. Following Martin through the swing doors, she knew from the set of his shoulders and the speed of his walk that she'd done it now, spoiled their day – more than their day – and no wonder.

What now? Perhaps he expected her to scuttle after him, but instead she lingered in the foyer, reading notices about exercise classes and New Year offers on beauty treatments. When he realized she wasn't coming, Martin would probably march back to the flat, unless he'd chosen a film and would go ahead and see it by himself.

She thought of phoning Bethan to see what she was doing, but was reluctant to admit to rowing with Martin. Bethan and Cliff, both so sunny-natured, never seemed to quarrel, though she supposed they must. She left the foyer for the rawness of outside; it was a grey, miserable day, a hint of drizzle in the air, no trace of yesterday's transforming sunshine.

Ruth. Ruth was the person she'd like to go to now. But that was impossible; Ruth would be at Holtby Hall, and Anna wasn't sure where that was, knowing only that it was out in the Essex countryside. Even if she Googled it, she'd need to drive there, and didn't want to add to Martin's annoyance by taking the car without asking. Although she'd passed her test while still in her teens, she hardly drove now; living in London, there was little need. When they used the car it was invariably Martin who took the wheel, mainly because if Anna drove he was a bossy and fidgety passenger. Anyway, how could she run to Ruth and say she'd had a row with Martin, expecting Ruth, of all people, to sympathize?

I'm on my own, she thought, when it comes down to it. That's how it has to be.

She waited for a bus. If one came quickly, she could be back at the flat before Martin. She would pretend nothing had happened; that was usually the best way to get over a disagreement. But if he wasn't there, she'd have a quiet afternoon by herself, reading or watching TV.

As soon as she entered the flat, she knew it was empty. She was half disappointed, half relieved. If Martin came in, he'd probably shut himself in the spare bedroom that served as his study, hardly emerging for the rest of the day. She imagined a scene in which she apologized for saying those things, put her arms round him and kissed him, led him into the bedroom. But the fact remained that he was unlikely to thaw until she was safely bound by a contract of employment with Burton Brown.

He wants to control me, she thought, and her resentment hardened.

Now, with the afternoon to fill as she pleased, she felt only apathy. When the phone rang, she picked up quickly, expecting Martin's voice.

It was her father. 'Anna, love? I'm glad you're there. Have you got a minute?'

'Hi, Dad. Yes, of course.'

A pause, then: 'I'm a bit concerned about your mum. She's started to behave a bit oddly.'

'Oddly, how?' Anna's voice came out tight with anxiety.

'Well – she's suddenly taken against the idea of selling the house. Says she doesn't want to move after all.'

Anna assimilated this in silence, surprised only by her lack of surprise. She tried to find suitable words. 'But it was her idea, wasn't it? What – pull out now, when your buyers are keen?'

'Well, I think that's the point. It's suddenly hit her. Yes, we're all ready to proceed, solicitors engaged – and how can we disappoint them, the Baverstocks? They're all set. They've paid for their survey, looked into schools, made plans.'

'She'll come round. This is a wobble.' Anna offered the assurance she knew her father wanted. 'It's a big thing to adjust to.'

'I hope you're right,' said her father. 'But at the moment, she's adamant – wants me to ring both estate agents and call the whole thing off, tomorrow morning.'

'Is she having second thoughts about the Cranbrook house? Is that it?'

'I don't think so. She can't bear the thought of packing up and moving, that's what she says.'

'I don't blame her for that. It *is* daunting. I've said I'll help, any time she wants.'

'Thanks, love. I know you will. But there's more to it than that. She . . . doesn't seem quite herself, in other ways.'

'Like what?'

'Well – switched off from everything. It's hard to say, exactly – so, I thought maybe you could come down, see if you can find out what's at the bottom of it? Maybe one evening next week?'

Anna looked at her watch. 'I'll come now. I'm not doing anything.'

'Oh, thanks, love. I'd be glad of that. Martin too?'

'He's not here. I'll come on my own.'

'Ring me from the train, then, and I'll pick you up. Oh – don't say it was my idea, will you? She's not here now – she's popped next door. I'll make up something, tell her you phoned and were at a loose end.'

'OK, Dad. See you soon.'

Purposeful now, Anna draped her damp swimsuit and towel in the airing cupboard, changed out of her exercise clothes, put on a little make-up, and checked that her wallet and Oyster card were in her bag. She wrote a note to Martin saying *Gone to visit my parents*, adding, in case he misunderstood and thought she'd run home for sympathy, *Dad phoned – worried about Mum*. As an afterthought she wrote *Staying overnight*. She put a nightdress and washing bag into a holdall, together with a smart top and trousers for work tomorrow.

Waiting for the Piccadilly Line train at Russell Square, she heard the phone conversation over again, noticing this time the unfamiliar tone of her father's voice: a note of helplessness, of trying to deal with something beyond his grasp.

Home. Part welcoming, part stifling, it was always the same. It was the one certainty in Anna's life. Until the autumn, and her mother's astonishing announcement, she had taken for granted that it always would be. Common sense said that her parents should have left Sevenoaks years ago, but common sense hadn't, till now, been strong enough to let them pull free.

It was impossible to imagine other people living here. How could they? The house was Rose, and Anna belonged to it; so did her parents. Of course her mother would never be able to clear the rooms and close the door behind her for the last time. It would signify a final parting with Rose, consigning her to the past. Never would her mother do that, until it was forced on her by age or disability.

Whenever Anna went back, the house claimed her, stripping away the years. It told her she'd always be her parents' daughter, Rose's younger sister, always thirteen, allowed to the brink of adolescence but no farther. She was trapped there, pinned like a specimen on a collector's board. The family was caught in waiting, no longer complete. They didn't dare speak too loudly; they were careful with each other, too careful. There was no escape from that huge, unexplainable absence, a black hole that had sucked them in and shrunk them to a singularity, a full-stop.

Anna hadn't been home since Christmas. Her visits to her parents weren't frequent, not because of any deliberate avoidance, but because it was always easy to find something to do rather than set out for Sevenoaks. She was more likely to see them in London on one of their trips to the theatre or an exhibition, or to meet her mother for Saturday shopping at John Lewis or House of Fraser. Her father had recently retired, and her mother had worried that he wouldn't have enough to do; but in fact Don filled his days happily with a range of interests and outings, golf, and various DIY projects. Sandra had her part-time job – every weekday morning as receptionist at a health centre – and spent Wednesday afternoons in the local Oxfam shop. To all outward appearances, they led comfortable, purposeful lives.

Both parents were transparently pleased that Anna had settled with Martin, so presentable and well-grounded, even if her mother would have preferred him not to have a divorce behind him, and two sons. Anna's father liked to give himself credit for her new stability; it was through him that she and Martin had met, eighteen months ago.

Anna had recently split up with Simon, an aspiring but idle artist, with whom she had lived since her student days in Southampton. When they parted, her finances were in a mess; she asked her father for advice, he passed on the name of an adviser recommended by his accountant, and Anna made a telephone call. Martin sounded approachable, and offered to come round to see her one evening. After a dispiriting search, she'd found a tiny flat she could afford, at a stretch, in Lewisham. It served as a base, at least, while she looked for something better.

At first, she thought Martin was considerably older than her. He was businesslike in a dark suit, sitting on the only chair she had, while she wore jeans and a baggy sweater and sat on a bean-bag that was spilling its stuffing. She'd forgotten he was coming and hadn't even tidied up; the flat was full of cardboard boxes and carrier bags still waiting to be unpacked. He was too smooth to interest her at first glance, although she registered his even features, flawless skin and well-cut dark hair. His shirt was white and crisp; she imagined a wife at home, ironing it for him. He talked and talked about fixed-term investments and TESSAs as if Anna knew what it all meant. Quickly bored, she tried to assume an expression of at least vague intelligence. She wanted him to sort it all out for her; she didn't want to take an interest or make decisions. Eventually he glanced at her just as she was stifling a yawn. He broke off in mid-explanation, smiled, and said, 'I've lost you, haven't I?' He had beautiful teeth, and so kindly and genuine a smile that she started to look at him differently.

'Sorry,' she said. 'I'm clueless about all this.' He must think it a daffy, ingenuous thing to say: *Look at me, so charmingly disorganized.* She wondered what he thought of her drab flat, with posters Blu-tacked to the wall, and bare boards showing at the edge of the carpet. He must think her a slob, not to have made more of the place. Along with the dutiful wife, she imagined a brand-new executive house with a double garage, and someone to do the cleaning; she added a couple of kids, a boy and a girl, who went to private schools and had violin lessons.

Taking out a sleek diary, Martin told her that he'd go away and draw up details, and come back in a few days. She leaned over discreetly to look at his handwriting as he entered the new appointment: small, firm and precise.

When he came back the following week, on a humid July evening, he was less formal, in rolled-up shirtsleeves, with no tie. He wore glasses this time; Anna thought he looked good in them, almost better than without. He'd brought a folder with her name under a plastic label on the front, MS ANNA TAVERNER. She hadn't specified Ms; he'd got that right by himself. She sat beside him while he talked through the details. Even with all the windows open, it was sweltering in the flat. It was so humid that Anna felt the air clinging to her like sweat if she moved. She had showered and changed after work, but before Martin had finished explaining the various documents in the folder she felt dampness clamming her face. Even his white shirt was wilting a little around the collar, and in the V of its unbuttoning his skin glistened beneath a film of perspiration. He was slightly built, barely an inch taller than Anna, with a well-proportioned, compact body that looked fit and toned. Occasionally he took off his glasses and rubbed his wrist across his forehead. His eyes were hazel-brown. Anna decided that she liked having him in her flat and would try to keep him there a bit longer.

'Would you like a drink?' she asked abruptly. It would have to get cooler soon; she was desperate to get out of the room, to splash cold water over herself.

He looked relieved. Anna went into the kitchen, washed her face and hands and fetched the bottle of Chablis that had been chilling in the fridge. They drank all of it and she opened another. By the time he left, after she'd made him strong coffee, Anna knew that he was divorced, living alone, and had two sons; that he was thirty-nine, eight years older than her; that he'd been brought up in Worcester, but his parents now lived in Spain; that he usually wore contact lenses but found them uncomfortable during the pollen season; that he read mainly political biography and popular science, but liked Ian McEwan and Ian Rankin. She spent much of the evening looking at his hands and forearms and his mouth as he spoke, wondering what it would be like to go to bed with him.

Ten days later, she found out. He took her out for dinner; she wore a dress and put her hair up, such was the novelty of going out on what she could call a *date*, a proper date with a grown-up man. Afterwards they came back to her flat, drank coffee, talked; then Martin looked at her and said, 'Well.' It was a question. 'I suppose I should be going.'

'You don't have to.'

They undressed each other in her bedroom. Anticipating this, she'd shoved all the clutter into cupboards, and had changed the bed linen that morning. It was highly satisfactory. As she'd expected, Martin made love as well as he did everything else.

'What was your first impression of me? That first time you came round?' she tried to get out of him, after he'd stayed twice more.

'I thought, here's someone who's bloody clueless about money.'

'No, seriously,' she persisted. 'You don't end up in bed with all your clients, I suppose?'

'Far too time-consuming. Besides, most of them are male and not even slightly tempting. You're fishing for compliments.'

'That's right.'

The alarm went off, ignored by both of them. Martin stroked her shoulder with a fingertip.

'I thought you were interesting.'

'Oh? Interesting in what way?' Anna could see only a muddle of hopes and doubts, desires and vague good intentions.

Martin considered, then said, 'There's a lot you keep hidden.'

'But doesn't everyone? Don't you? Surely no one wants to be so transparent that everything's on the surface?'

'Perhaps what I mean is – you haven't found your way yet.'

'Have you, then?'

'Maybe. There's the boys. There's work.'

'And is that enough? Don't you wish you were with them all the time? Don't you have regrets?' It was the nearest she had come to asking about his failed marriage.

'Course. Hasn't everyone?' His eyes were closed. 'Regrets that would eat me up, if I let them. I don't let them.'

'But how do you stop?'

For answer Martin rolled over and began kissing her, and her arms tightened around him until the alarm shrilled again and the demands of the day took over. When she thought about it later, she wondered if he saw her as a distraction, or as his salvation. Maybe, in return, he could save her from herself. Or was that expecting too much?

She wanted him to have seen something unique in her, something unknown, as yet, even to her. She thought she loved him; *I am in love*, she told herself, when she ached at the thought of not seeing him for two days, when she yearned to find him beside her when she woke, his eyes warm as he smiled, sleepy and short-sighted. *Whatever 'in love' means.* It felt like playing a role, living up to something she'd read about, seen in films, as if being in love was a constant, a state to be achieved and hung on to. Everything about this new relationship surprised her: the speed of it; that she could get involved with someone like Martin; that he chose to involve himself with her. She caught other women's glances at him when they were out together, and was part thrilled, part ashamed of the inner voice that exulted: *He's with me! Look! I've got a proper man!* It couldn't last. She kept expecting him to end it, to announce that he'd found someone more confident, more elegant, part of the grown-up world he seemed to inhabit so easily.

'Well, Anna! He seems a really nice chap. I liked him a lot,' her mother said, in a phone conversation after Anna eventually took Martin to meet them for a restaurant meal. The sub-text was clear: *Here's the one for you to settle down with. Hang onto him, now that you've got rid of that other layabout.* Anna felt a surge of resentment towards Martin and a tug of loyalty to Simon, so gawkily thin that his ribs showed; shabby Simon, dressed always in shapeless T-shirts, sweaters with unravelling cuffs, frayed jeans with packets of weed in the pockets.

❖ ❖ ❖

Her father was waiting at Sevenoaks station.

'Thanks for coming, love.' He was more cheerful than he'd sounded on the phone.

'Thought I might as well stay.' Anna indicated her overnight bag. 'That's OK, isn't it?'

'Yes, yes, any time you like.' Don led the way to his car; when they were both belted in, Anna asked, 'How's Mum today?'

'Seems a bit more her normal self. You'll probably think I'm worrying about nothing. But I didn't tell you about last night – we had dinner with Malcolm and his wife, from golf. She started being funny about names. First she insisted on being called Cassandra, when no one's called her that for years. And when Kathy asked if we've – if we've got grand-children, she called you Rosanna.'

'Oh,' Anna said flatly. 'What else? What did she mean?'

'I don't know. Later on she talked about you quite normally.'

'Did she? What did she say?'

'Oh – that you're living in London, happily settled with Martin.'

Silenced by this, wondering where Martin was now and whether he'd seen her note, Anna turned to look out of the side window. It was almost dusk, and the swell of the North Downs rose beyond the town like a grey cloud-bank. She said, 'Did you say anything to Mum about it?'

'No. I didn't want to stir things up.'

'Sounds like it just slipped out. Rosanna instead of Anna.'

'Maybe you're right.' Her father sounded relieved. 'I'm making too much of it, I expect.'

65

*Didn't want to stir things up!* So typical of Mum and Dad, Anna thought, and of me too. Let's pretend everything's fine, then maybe it will be. But Rosanna, Rose–Anna. Did that make her two in one? Or only half?

Becoming an only child had been a difficult adjustment, after years spent in Rose's wake. Faced with the casual enquirer, hairdresser or friend-of-a-friend, Anna found it too complicated to embark on, too painful. Asked if she had brothers or sisters, she learned to answer, 'No, there's just me,' which wasn't even a lie. At the time, everyone from school knew, of course, and local people – Rose's disappearance had been all over the front page of the *Sevenoaks Chronicle*, until interest faded and there was nothing more to report. It slipped into the background, no longer requiring comment.

The *just* always echoed in Anna's ears. Just me. You'll have to make do with me. I know Rose was always more important, more special. Every time she thought she was grown-up enough to dismiss these feelings, they crept back to nudge at her.

This road, Ashurst Avenue, alongside the recreation ground with woods and fields beyond, had been Anna's route home from school for years and years; Rose's, too. For a moment Anna saw Rose running across the grass, long hair flying, tears streaming down her face; Jamie catching up, grabbing her arm, turning her to face him. Whenever Anna returned to Sevenoaks, Rose was everywhere and nowhere; she was used to that. But Jamie Spellman. Where was he now? She didn't want to think about that.

'We haven't talked any more about what she said – you know, wanting to call off the move,' her father said. 'Perhaps you're right, and it's only a glitch. Best to do nothing – leave her to think it over.'

'But how do *you* feel about it, Dad?'

'Me?' He shrugged. 'I'll do whatever makes your mum happy. She was the one who started this off, after refusing even to think about it, all these years. The Cranbrook house would've been fine, and it seemed we were on our way. But if she wants to stay put, it'll save us a lot of bother, that's for sure. I don't like letting people down, though. Our vendors and our buyers, both lots.'

'Perhaps it won't come to that.'

'I think, unless she raises it, we won't mention this. I thought we might talk about the birthday plans. It'll give a reason for you coming down unexpectedly.'

'Great, only I haven't really thought much about it yet,' Anna said, with slight reproach. 'Oh well, I can improvise.'

Her mother would be sixty at the end of July – unbelievably, to Anna – and at Christmas Don had proposed throwing a party. For Don's own sixtieth, he and Sandra had spent four days in Paris, but with Sandra's birthday so close to the anniversary of Rose's disappearance, celebrations had always seemed out of place. The approaching birthday and anniversary were both big ones: Sandra's sixtieth, and twenty years since Rose had gone.

'That's another weird thing,' said Don. 'When we talked about it on our own, she said, "Oh no, I don't think we should make a fuss. We didn't do anything for Roland." '

'*Roland?*' It took Anna a moment to assimilate this. 'But Roland's— What did you say?'

'I wasn't sure at first what she meant. It would have been two years ago, Roland's sixtieth. Did she mean we should have marked it in some way? We never have, before. And then she tried to pass it off, as if she hadn't meant to come out with it.'

Roland, Rose. The two missing members of the family. But Roland had died years before Anna was born; she and Rose had sometimes talked of him as the uncle they'd never had. They knew him only by his photograph: long-haired and gaunt-faced, stranded in the sixties where his life had ended at the age of eighteen. It was the family curse, Bethan said, visited on them by a bad fairy at a christening. All the more reason, Anna thought now, not to provide a new generation. But Mum – this did sound worrying. She wasn't nearly old enough, surely, for mental decline of a kind Anna didn't want to put a name to.

'I don't think I told you at the time – you were in Southampton,' her father said, 'but she hasn't mentioned Roland for years, apart from when George Harrison died.'

'George Harrison?'

'Yes, this was – what – ten years or so ago. The newspapers were full of it, and your mum – well! You'd have thought it was a personal bereavement. She bought all the papers and spent ages poring over the features and obituaries. She even cried – though she tried to hide it.'

'Well, I suppose she's of that generation that got swept up in Beatles hysteria. Perhaps she was one of those girls who screamed themselves silly. I don't ever remember her talking about it, though.'

'That's what I thought. I was pretty gutted myself when John Lennon was shot – it was the end of an era – but she didn't react in the same way to that. With George, though – she practically went into mourning. And finally I got it out of her that Roland had specially liked George Harrison. He played the guitar.'

'I know that, Dad!'

'I mean *Roland* played guitar. He was in a band, but I don't think it ever came to anything. Well – there wasn't time.'

'You never told me any of this,' Anna said, with an edge of reproach. 'About Mum acting weird.'

'No, well – you weren't at home, and it was so peculiar, but she suddenly snapped out it, and binned all the papers. It was if George Harrison's death had brought everything else back – Roland, and . . .'

'Rose.' Anna filled the pause.

The final turn into Knole Crescent, and she was back home, as if she'd never been away. There was the house, half-tiled and ivy-clad, behind a low box hedge. Anna – and Rose, even more – had scorned it as hopelessly old-fashioned as a child, envying her friend Melanie, whose house was open-plan with huge windows, but in the local estate agent's brochure it had been *a substantial Edwardian family house, semi-detached, in a quiet location close to the town centre and its amenities . . . many original features . . .* She knew now how desirable this style of house was; prospective buyers had exclaimed, Dad said, over the original tiles in the porch, the fireplaces, the generous proportions and secluded garden. And so they should.

In the warmth of the hallway, Anna and her mother exchanged kisses, while Don put the car away in the garage.

'Well, this is an honour!' Sandra greeted her. She was dressed in sharp-creased trousers and a cable sweater, scarf knotted at her neck; flat shoes in patent leather, discreet make-up. She didn't do scruffy, even for Sundays at home. Her hair, once as thick and richly brown as Anna's, was now tinted ash-blonde to disguise creeping greyness.

'Hi, Mum. OK if I stay the night?'

'Course you can! The bed's made up.'

Home received Anna, reassuring and cloying. It peeled back the years, telling her that the quality of light in this hallway, the particular smell of the house – some kind of polish or spray mixed with lingering Sunday lunch – would never change. From outside, the sounds of her father closing the garage, one of the doors dragging over the concrete of the hard-standing, then the slam and clunk, the turn of the key; sounds she never thought about for a moment when she wasn't here: all of them so deeply ingrained in her memory as to capture home in its entirety. Here she was her parents' daughter, the younger sister, the only child, while the other Anna, the Anna who tried to be grown up, stayed in London.

Stupid. Stupid.

In the kitchen her mother had Classic FM on the radio. She made tea; Anna asked about the evening with Kathy and Malcolm. When her father came in, she tried not to meet his eye, feeling like a conspirator.

Her mother carried the tea on a tray to the sitting room and drew the curtains, shutting out the night. Anna raised the subject of the forthcoming birthday, and her mother laughed ruefully at the idea of having a rail pass, qualifying for concessions. 'Don't knock it,' said Don, two years ahead.

'Well, what do you think, Mum? About your party? We could find a really nice venue, somewhere unusual.'

Anna expected protests of the *I don't want a fuss* kind, and sure enough her mother said, 'Oh, I don't know. I don't like big parties.'

'It doesn't have to be a big party, Mum. It could be for you and Dad and your special friends.'

Sandra thought for a moment, then shook her head. 'No. I don't think so. I can't be the centre of attention. Maybe I'll go off on my own somewhere.'

'Off on your own?' Anna pictured her mother running away from a party, abandoning her guests.

'Yes. On a holiday. I've never done that before.'

'I thought we might go somewhere together.' Don looked a little hurt. 'Venice, perhaps. We've often talked about it.'

'We can do that as well.'

'What sort of holiday have you got in mind, then, Mum?'

'Oh, I don't know, yet.' Sandra might have been shrugging off an irritation. 'It's only a thought. There's plenty of time to decide, now that we're not moving.'

Anna glanced at her father before saying, 'Yes, Dad told me you were having doubts.'

'It's not doubts. It's definite. You can go if you like,' said her mother, with a defiant look at Don as if it was all his idea. 'I'm staying here.'

Anna was silent, conscious only of a wash of relief. She knew that she ought to back up her father, find reasons and persuasion, but she couldn't think of anything worth saying. Things would have to change eventually; but not yet. Not yet.

# 5

No one had referred to Rose's room for years, but that was how they all thought of it. Anna's bedroom – as it still was to her, though she hadn't lived here since her sixth-form days and it was now the guest room – was opposite, at the front of the house. Her parents had the big double that overlooked the garden; a former box room had been knocked through and converted into an ensuite bathroom.

Anna dumped her holdall on the bed; paused, and crossed the landing, turning the handle on Rose's door, careful not to make a sound. She stood on the threshold, looking in.

For the first three years this room had been kept as a kind of shrine. Her mother kept the bed made up, and changed it once a week; pointlessly she washed sheets and duvet covers that were already clean, airing them on the washing line. Rose's clothes hung in the wardrobe and her shoes were lined up neatly on the rack, apart from the crochet sandals which Anna had hidden under her bed. She never wore them, but was too guilty to sneak them back, knowing Mum would notice. A framed photograph of Rose stood on the chest of drawers, as if it had the power to bring her back; behind it, a vase of flowers, usually roses, breathed their perfume into the air until they became fat and blowsy, dropping petals. Mum cut flowers from the garden, while they lasted; later, when winter came, she bought roses or lilies from the florist. It became such a habit that no one commented.

If anyone came to stay, Anna's grandparents at Christmas, or friends – she couldn't remember it happening often – Anna would have to sleep on the sofa downstairs, giving up her own room. No one could sleep in the sanctity of Rose's room, in Rose's bed. In the first days, weeks, months, Anna used to go in to stand in awe, or to gaze at Rose's books and music and wonder what Rose had been reading or thinking or listening to, the last time she slept here. Rose's absence was so strong that it became a presence, looming, oppressive.

At first, the door was kept open always. Mum would go in at nightfall to draw the curtains, and would open them again early each morning. The first phase of withdrawal was signalled by the closing of the door; a small thing, but it made the whole of upstairs feel different – narrower and darker. Sometimes, feeling furtive, Anna would open the door and peep in to see if everything was still the same. It was, but there were no flowers; the curtains stayed open, and the bed linen was unchanged from one week to the next. When her parents were out, she lay down, greatly daring, on Rose's bed. Once she fell asleep there, only waking when she heard the slam of the car door outside; she sprang up, smoothed the bedspread and plumped away the indentation of her head on the pillow, fearful of being discovered.

Then, when Anna was sixteen, the shock of returning from school one day to find the radio on in Rose's room and her mother busy with bags and boxes. The bed had been stripped; clothes were piled in heaps on the mattress.

'What are you *doing*?'

On her knees, pulling a box out from the floor of the wardrobe, her mother must have been so absorbed that she hadn't heard Anna unlocking the front door, or coming upstairs. She looked up, startled; her expression was that of a child caught doing wrong, quickly replaced by an air of tutting impatience.

'Having a good clear out. What does it look like?'

'Those are Rose's things!'

'I know whose they are. She doesn't need them any more, does she? It's a waste of a room. We may as well make use of it.' Mum flashed Anna a defiant look. She might have been rebelling against a diktat imposed by someone else. 'If you want any of these clothes, you may as well have them. You're about the same size now.'

'No!' Anna affected shock, although she had on occasion borrowed items from Rose's wardrobe when her mother hadn't been around. 'It's not right, wearing her clothes.'

Rose had so many. No one had seen her leave, that hot August day; Anna, last to see her, had given details of what Rose was wearing – jeans and a green vest top – and she and her mother attempted to work out, by elimination, what Rose had taken with her. A rucksack was missing, and the sketchbook, and the tapestry bag Rose used for her purse, keys and other small items. Rose's favourites were still in the wardrobe: the skinny black jeans, the denim skirt she'd customized with patterned patches, the green Indian top

74

with flowing sleeves that Anna had helped her choose from a market stall. She hadn't even taken the gemstone necklace Anna had given her last birthday; finding it in the muddle of a drawer, Anna had felt the sting of rejection.

Her mother shrugged and went on sorting. The cardboard box contained school books: exercise books in various faded colours, folders, ring-binders. She gave them no more than a cursory glance, then said to Anna, 'Pass me one of those bin-bags, will you?'

'You can't throw those away!'

'Why? What use are they to anyone?'

'They've got Rose's writing in them!'

'So?'

Anna gazed helplessly at her mother, not recognizing this strange, curt mood. Mum wore an expression that was quite unfamiliar: chin high whenever she turned to speak to Anna, her eyes almost scornful. Now she picked up an exercise book and flipped through its pages without interest before reaching for the roll of bin-bags by the door.

'Don't!' Anna protested. 'I want to keep them. Here, let me look.' She tugged at the edge of the box; her mother pulled it back, and for a moment there was a ridiculous tug-of-war which ended with the box tearing limply, the top layer of contents spilling out.

Mum shrugged. 'Go on then. Take one or two if you must, but you can't tell me you want all this history, maths, geography, RE.' She frisbeed them at Anna, one after another. 'Have whatever you want, but hurry up. I need to get this done.'

Anna took this to mean that she wanted to finish the job before Dad came in from work. If anything, Anna thought, he'd be pleased; it hadn't been his idea to keep the room as a Rose-museum. But what would he make of such a drastic reversal? Uncertainly at first, Anna delved into the box. No, there was no point keeping them all; she rejected the maths and science books, filled with neat figures and writing and diagrams, sprinkled all over with the praise of red ticks and comments, *Good work, Excellent, Well done!* A thinner exercise book must have been Rose's first, from her infant class. *Rose Taverner. Writing Book,* was written on the cover in a teacher's careful hand, and Rose had copied her own name underneath, in wobbling letters. Anna took that one, a history book from the first year of secondary school, and the folder containing notes and essays for A-Level English.

Mum showed no interest in her selection, bundling the other books and folders into bin-bags.

'You're not throwing it all away?' Anna asked. 'The clothes and everything?'

'No, I thought I'd give them to the church jumble sale.'

Neither of Anna's parents was a churchgoer, but her mother helped Lesley, who lived next door, with the jumble sale and the Christmas craft fair, and with a plant stall at the summer fête. That first autumn, Lesley persuaded Mum to go to services with her, suggesting that she might find comfort. Mum was welcomed, and prayers offered for Rose and for the whole family. Dad never went with her, and neither did Anna; she thought it hypocritical, only turning to God, whoever or whatever you thought God was, when you wanted something. But neither God's intervention nor more practical measures had brought Rose back, and the church attendance lasted only as far as Christmas.

Anna thought of strangers wearing Rose's clothes. She

might see people in the street wearing garments she'd re-cognize, like the denim skirt with patches. Strangers in Rose's skirts or jeans – it would be like wearing a dead person's clothes. Maybe they actually *were* a dead person's clothes.

On the first page of Rose's infant exercise book there was a crayon drawing. A group of figures, four of them, with stick limbs, bulbous heads and smiles like half-moons. They were drawn in descending order of size, going down to a baby on the ground, resembling an Easter egg with a face. Rose had drawn herself with long black hair and a smile like a banana. Overhead was a blob of yellow sun, and even that was smiling. Underneath, the teacher had printed four names, and Rose had copied them underneath in wavering purple. *Daddy Mummy Rose Anna.*

❖ ❖ ❖

Now, daring to sit on the bed, Anna thought: of course Mum won't leave. Why did we ever think she would? There was only one chance to leave, and Rose took it.

The clothes and the books had never got to the church jumble sale; they were still here, bagged up, in the cupboard and the wardrobe. They'd made it as far as the car boot before Sandra had changed her mind and carried them all back inside.

In recent years Sandra had taken up fabric-work – 'creative embroidery', as she called it. Her desk, sewing machine and workbasket were here, her silks and buttons and whatever she needed for her current project – a frame maybe, or stuffing for a cushion. Whether she sat for hours in Rose's old bedroom merely in order to put the room to practical use, or whether she saw it as unspoken communion, Anna often wondered. It had made her father uneasy at first, but his way was to humour her mother in everything she did. To challenge or question would mean bringing the taboo subject into the open.

Anna took off her shoes, lay down on the bed and stretched out. If she heard footsteps coming up the stairs, she would scuttle back to her own room.

Her mobile rang in her bag. She picked it up: Martin.

'Hi – are you at your parents' now? Are you OK?' He never used endearments like *darling* or *sweetheart* – neither did she – but his voice held no reminder of their earlier exchanges. 'Is Sandra ill?'

Anna remembered the note she'd left. 'No, it's all right. She's just . . . Dad thought she was behaving oddly. She wants to call off the move.'

'No! Well, the two of you can talk her round.' He sounded sure of that. 'So you'll be back tomorrow? Actually I need to speak to Don about his investments, but I'll ring again on the land line. See you latish, then, tomorrow – I won't be in till gone eight. Send me a text.'

'Will do. Bye then. Take care.'

Anna ended the call, and the silence of Rose's room settled around her. Moments later she heard the phone ringing downstairs, and her father answering.

*Is that it?* Rose whispered. *Your man, your relationship? Is that good enough? Are you really settling for that?*

Standing, Anna slid her feet into her shoes. 'Shut up, Rose,' she said aloud. 'Leave me alone.'

❖ ❖ ❖

## September 1988

Anna was trudging along Ashurst Avenue, her school bag heavy on her shoulder. Usually, when she walked with Melanie until they parted at the corner, it didn't seem so far, but Mel had gone to the dentist this afternoon and Anna was on her own. She was conscious of every step, the road stretching ahead and the sun beating down so hard that it must surely be scorching her scalp where her hair parted. The new school uniform she was so proud of, navy skirt and blazer and a white shirt, was hot and itchy. Her tie was in her rucksack, but she kept her blazer on because carrying it over her arm would be more of a nuisance than wearing it.

Ashurst Avenue had a row of identical brick houses on one side, and a wide expanse of recreation ground on the other. At the nearest corner as Anna approached, a play area was fenced off for children: a climbing frame, seesaw and swings. From the pavement, mud paths, trodden hard and grooved by cycle tyres, swooped into a dip and up again to the grass. At the edges of the park there were hidden places behind the trees where the grass was left uncut. People picked blackberries there at this time of year, and conker shells scattered the path, showing their pale insides. Anna scanned the ground for conkers, and picked up a big glossy one to hold and turn in her hand before slipping it into her pocket.

In her bag was a bottle with orange juice left from her lunch, and a Milky Way. And there was a magazine Melanie had lent her, with things in it Anna would look at later, out of Mum's sight, upstairs in her room. 'Look at this,' Mel said in the form room at break, opening it at a double-page spread, with a delighted giggle in her voice. There was a photograph of a naked couple, soft-focus, wrapped round each other. They were standing, and you could see the whole of the woman's back and her bottom, round and soft like a peach, but all you could see of the man was his arms and hands and part of one leg, and his sideways face as he kissed her neck. His eyes were closed, his arms dark and hairy against the paleness of the woman's skin.

Anna felt hot and clumsy, looking at it. Her hands were too big.

'Where did you get it?' she asked Melanie.

'It's Jamie's. He doesn't know I've got it. I took it from his room.'

Mel's brother was in the fifth form, like Rose. If only Anna didn't feel so small and new – she felt as if she'd shrunk, since being in the top class at primary school – she'd have thought herself clever and important for being in the same school as them, wearing the same uniform, having some of the same teachers.

She flipped back to the cover. 'But it's a girls' magazine!'

'A lot of boys read girls' magazines,' Mel said knowledgeably. 'They do it to find things out. Go on, read what it says!' she urged. 'It tells you all about – you know – how to do it. How to be good at it.'

Anna had only recently realized that *It* was something you had to be good at; Mum's version, when she had explained it to Anna, was that you did It to get a baby. She looked up at the commotion of two boys barging into the classroom, Jason Wiles and Andrew Morrison, shoving each other, knocking a chair aside in a play-fight. Melanie and Anna exchanged glances; Melanie scrolled the magazine quickly and stuffed it into Anna's bag, under the desk. 'You can take it home,' she whispered. 'Make sure you bring it back tomorrow.'

If Anna read the magazine in secret, in her bedroom, Mum would know. Her X-ray eyes would see through the wall, and she'd be cross and frosty; Anna could tell Mum didn't like what she called *that sort of thing*, from the way she went all tight and sniffy when it happened on television. Anna could never imagine her doing it with Dad, but maybe they'd only done it twice, once for Rose and once for her. If Mum found out about the magazine, Anna would feel dirty, bad – but still she did want to read it, have it all to herself, look at that picture again. She felt it burning through her school bag, scorching where it touched her. Her secret. Then she had a better idea. She could look at it now, in the park; later she'd hide it under her bed till tomorrow, in case Mum decided to look in her school bag to check she'd got everything, or to put in an extra muesli bar for her packed lunch.

The soles of her lace-up shoes slapped the mud path as she crossed into the park. No one was here. Anna sat on the bench and took out the orange juice and the Milky Way, which had gone squidgy in the bottom of the bag, and arranged them like a small picnic. Then she took out the magazine. Although there was no one in sight she had to glance around to check, in case a disapproving adult – a neighbour or someone Mum knew – should loom out of the bushes: *Just what do you think you're doing, young lady?*

Stalks of dried grass brushed her bare legs; the wood of the bench was warm through her skirt. She fumbled the pages of the magazine. It was so hot today that – if she thought no one would see – she could have taken her clothes off and let the air brush her skin. She imagined the warmth of wood against her bare bottom. The hot, tingly feeling made her limbs feel fuzzy. She felt daring and secretive for having such a thought.

Someone was coming. She rolled the magazine tight as a tube and thrust it into her bag, unwrapped the Milky Way and started eating it, swallowing too quickly; the sweetness caught in her throat, making her cough. She heard a girl's voice, high and distressed. Two people were coming fast along the footpath that led into the park from the far side, a boy and a girl. Over the hedge Anna could see them from the shoulders up, their shirts bright white against the hedgerow. The girl was running, the boy chasing her: they were only playing. When the girl burst out into the park, Anna saw the swirl of long hair and her wavery way of running. Rose.

Rose mustn't see her. Anna pushed the chocolate wrapper and the bottle into her bag, and was about to dart off behind the hawthorns and carry on walking home when she noticed that Rose was crying. Really crying. She ran across the park without seeming to notice Anna.

'Rose! Wait!' the boy shouted. A tall dark-haired boy. Jamie Spellman, whose magazine it was. Mel's brother. Anna had seen him with Rose before but hadn't known him make Rose cry. Perhaps Rose was upset because he wanted to try out those things he'd read about. He wanted to practise on her, in a private, secret place out there in the fields where they could lie down together with no clothes on while his hands went all over her. Where they could do *It*. It must be his fault.

She was heading for home, coming Anna's way, running

blindly with an arm raised to cover her face. Jamie was gaining on her. He sprinted close enough to grab her arm, and turned her to face him.

'Leave her alone!' Anna shouted hotly. 'Leave my sister alone!'

They both turned, startled. Jamie released Rose.

'Anna!' Rose's face was streaked with tears. In her frightened little-girl voice, she said, 'It's not Jamie's fault. I made him do it.'

'Made him do what?' Anna was still thinking of the magazine picture.

'Made him kill it,' Rose whispered.

'Kill *what*?'

'There was a rabbit,' Jamie said, scuffing a foot on the grass. 'It had that rabbit disease, what's-it-called, that makes their eyes go funny.'

'Myxomatosis.' Her voice muffled, Rose made it sound like *bixabatothith*; Anna almost laughed. Rose's eyes searched her face; she wants me to cry too, Anna thought.

'It was horrible,' Rose whimpered. 'The poor thing. Its eyes were all blobby and sore where it had been rubbing them. It was all mangy-looking. It didn't even try to run away from us. I picked it up.' She was rubbing her hands on her skirt, the backs and the fronts, rubbing off traces of rabbit, of disease.

'They only die,' Jamie said. 'The best thing you can do is kill them. Rose told me to, so I did it.'

'How did you do it?' Anna asked, fascinated. 'You haven't got a gun.'

'You don't need a gun, stupid. I hit it on the back of the neck,' Jamie said, with a flash of pride.

'I watched him. I didn't want to, but I did,' Rose said, her eyes filling again. 'He held its ears forward and he hit it—'

'Like *this*,' Jamie said, making a swift sideways chop with one hand. He looked at Anna to see the effect of his action. His eyes were pale blue, with clear whites. She imagined her own neck receiving the force of that movement that sliced the air like a karate chop.

'– and that was it. Dead. It didn't have time to squeal or anything. It twitched a bit, then went limp and soft. I hid it in the brambles. I couldn't bury it – the ground's too hard and I had nothing to dig with, but I found some flowers. Oh, Anna!' Rose draped her arm round Anna, leaning. Her hair fell around Anna like a shawl, the way it did when they played at being Rosanna. She was limp and soft like the rabbit; if Anna stopped bracing herself, they'd both collapse to the ground. 'The poor thing. Its eyes . . .'

'But you did the right thing,' Anna said. She couldn't imagine herself crying so much over one dead rabbit. 'You could have gone away and left it. That would have been worse.'

'And I knew how to kill it properly,' Jamie boasted. 'Not everyone would have known.'

'Let's go home, Anna,' Rose whispered.

'Our bags,' Jamie reminded her. 'In the bushes.'

Anna picked up her own bag, and Rose and Jamie collected theirs, left side by side in the long grass. Rose had apparently forgotten about Jamie. He walked with them as far as the turning where he lived; then he said, 'Are you all right now?'

'Yes,' Rose said, although she was still sniffling.

'See you tomorrow then,' he said, and Anna noticed he'd

gone a bit red. He came close to Rose and kissed her cheek; she closed her eyes and accepted the kiss with the faintest quiver of revulsion. Jamie saw Anna watching, turned even redder and walked off quickly.

'Has he done that before?' Anna asked, as soon as he was out of earshot. 'Was that why you went down the footpath? You left your bags in the bushes. Do you go there every day, to do kissing and stuff? Rose? Rose? What else does he do?'

'Oh, shut up, will you?' Rose flared. 'I don't care about stupid Jamie. I don't want to see him ever again.'

Because he killed the rabbit, she meant. That struck Anna as unfair. She thought of Jamie's hand breaking the rabbit's neck, and the same hand touching Rose's arm, tenderly, as he kissed her. Why did she let him touch her, if she hated it? Anna wouldn't have minded being kissed by Jamie. He had such lovely dark eyebrows, and there was the way his school shirt bagged out over the slender curve of his back. Anna knew that girls giggled and blushed when he passed them in the corridors at school. Rose had told him to kill the rabbit and he did, knowing how to do it quickly and efficiently. He could have said no, or told her to do it herself. She wouldn't have been able to. Anna imagined her holding the rabbit, her hand poised to strike, her face tight with the effort of willing. You couldn't do it half-heartedly; you'd have to do it, or not. Rose wouldn't have been able to, and she'd have to put the rabbit back in the long grass to go on suffering, with its terrible bulging eyes.

An ice-cream van came along the road, playing a snatch from *Greensleeves*, and Rose's mood changed. 'I'll treat you,' she told Anna. 'I've got money. What would you like?'

The ice-cream man was quite young, with a sun tan and

blond hair, and he was chewing gum. When Rose went up to the van his jaws stopped moving and his eyes fastened on her with interest.

'Hello, darling, what do you fancy?' he asked her, and she giggled.

'What have you got?' she said, tossing her head and flicking her hair back. Her eyes were bright and shiny but no one would guess she'd been crying.

'Well now, that depends.' He propped himself on one elbow. When he smiled his mouth went up at one side but not the other. 'Something with a bit of crunch? Or a long slow lick?'

Rose's expression was half shocked, half delighted. 'What do you want, Anna?'

'A Funny Face,' Anna said, pointing at the picture on the glass window.

'Oh yeah? I thought you already had one,' the ice-cream man told her, straight-faced, then looked at Rose with his lopsided grin and half a wink. She made a prim face, but Anna could see her mouth twitching at the corners and knew she was only pretending to look disapproving. 'Yeah, I know,' the man said to Rose, leaning forward on his elbows, 'it's hard to make your mind up, with so much on offer. Take your time.'

'A plain choc-ice, please,' she said. Three younger children came up behind, jostling, holding up their money. The ice-cream man whistled *Greensleeves* as he passed over the Funny Face and the choc-ice, and when Rose gave him the money he took hold of her hand as well and pretended he was going to pull her inside the van. She giggled and snatched her hand away. The man grinned at her, then looked at Anna and pulled a long, miserable face. 'Cheer up, ducky. It might never happen,' he said in a Donald Duck voice.

They walked away unwrapping their ice creams. When the van passed them the driver gave a cheerful *toot-toot*, and waved at Rose.

'Rose!' Anna reproached. 'You're so two-faced, you are! One minute you're blubbering all over me and the next you're *flirting* with that stupid man!'

'Some people,' Rose said, picking off the chocolate edging and eating that first, 'would have said thank you for the ice cream.'

'Thank you,' Anna said sullenly. 'But I thought you were so upset just now? Were you putting it on?'

'For goodness' sake grow up, Anna,' Rose said. 'It was only a rabbit.'

They didn't speak for the rest of the walk home. Anna ate her Funny Face almost without noticing, she was so cross with Rose. When they got indoors, Mum said, 'What's wrong with you two?' and narrowed her eyes at each of them in turn.

'Oh, nothing,' Rose said. 'Annie's in a bit of a mood, that's all.'

❖ ❖ ❖

# 6

Monday, and Anna was back in the office, behind her desk close to the front window, where she could see passers-by as they looked in at the properties displayed there. Sunila, the branch manager, was at a meeting at Head Office all morning, so it wasn't until after lunch that she called Anna into her upstairs office to tell her that the trial period was more than satisfactory, and the post could become a permanent one, if Anna accepted.

Anna agreed and thanked her, and Sunila said, 'Excellent! That's great. I'll get on to HR straight away and they can organize the contract. I'm really pleased you'll be joining the team properly.'

As she went downstairs, Kiran and Sophie were looking at her with expectant smiles. Kiran made prompting gestures. 'Yes?'

'Yes,' said Anna, and at once both were out of their seats, hugging her, talking of celebrating after work on Friday. Anna laughed with them, feeling, for the moment, happy. Now she would have colleagues, a routine, a regular salary. She liked them both: Sophie, with her cynical one-liners, and Kiran, fresh from university, ambitious and urbane, with a taste for sharp suits and ties that made him the butt of teasing.

The moment was broken when the young couple who'd been taking an interest in the window display came inside, and Kiran sprang to attention. Anna and Sophie, exchanging smiles, went back to their desks.

Anna took out her mobile and began texting a message for Martin: *Job now permanent.* She could have it all, just as Bethan had said: the home, the job, Martin – he'd assume she'd taken his advice and was seeing it his way, behaving like an adult at last.

What was she doing? These things were assembling themselves around her; she wasn't choosing them, only surrendering control. She cancelled the message without sending it.

Last night she had dreamed her Rose dream again, the one where Rose came back. She came back only for Anna to push her away. The dream played itself like a film Anna had seen many times, familiarity only intensifying its horror. They're in a plane together, sitting side by side. There are magazines, drinks, smiling attendants; she looks out at blue sky dotted with flat-based clouds of improbable regularity. Rose, in the window seat, is laughing, relaxed against the seat-back, turned towards Anna; she isn't afraid of flying. Anna is always afraid. Her stomach clenches; Rose's warm, laughing face makes something harden in her. Her intention is reflected in Rose's widening brown eyes. Rose shifts against the restraint of her seat belt and presses herself against the arm-rest nearest the window; her gaze holds Anna's. Anna has to close her eyes to do it. She stretches out both arms and pushes. She knows what will happen: the sides of the plane, the window, soften and sag like Dali wristwatches, rubbery, melting, holding Rose briefly as in a hammock, then thinning and splitting into chewing-gum strands with a mesh too loose to stop her from falling, spinning away into the immensity of sky and space.

A cry catches in Anna's throat. Her arm lunges into a futile, too-late, meaningless grab. No one has noticed what happened, but she feels blackness close in as the sides of the aircraft reshape themselves around her. She sits tight and alone. No one knows what she has done, but she feels the terrible irrevocability of the outstretched arms, the push. The intention. She must hide her secret, but guilt chokes her and crushes her into her seat.

Gasping for breath, hooked out of her dream like a fish, she surfaced into her body, into her bed. Usually Martin's sleeping warmth was close by; she could snuggle close and be calmed, even though he was quite unaware. Last night she reached out for him but found only the cool sheet, her hand sliding over the edge of the bed; she registered the shape of the wardrobe, the unfamiliar position of the window, and realized that she was in her old room at home. Her heart was thumping, the dream still vivid.

Rose had done this. Rose would never let go.

Letting herself into the flat, Anna thought of telling Martin her news. Now he'd approve of her; she'd go off to work every morning, and her salary would appear in the bank account every month. But she felt herself resisting. Had she bought herself a safety net, or was it, instead, a tightening mesh, strangling her when she tried to struggle free?

It was no good. Something was pushing her away from

her own life. Happiness was on the other side of an invisible barrier. Even when it seemed within her grasp, it was only there to mock. Happiness was something other people could do.

He'd be late back, she remembered; she'd better do something about food. Meanwhile, another decision made itself, and Ruth was the person she chose to tell, on the phone.

'I'm moving out of the flat. Martin and I are splitting up.'

She heard Ruth's intake of breath; then, 'What? You can't mean that!'

'I do.'

'But why?'

Anna searched for a reason. 'Things weren't working out.'

'But you seem – he seems – so, so—'

'Don't say happy. We're not. I mean weren't.'

'When did this happen?'

'It hasn't, exactly. Not yet. I haven't told him.'

A beat of silence, then Ruth said: 'So it's your idea, not his? Anna, whatever's gone wrong, it can't be that bad. Don't do anything in a hurry. You'll only regret it.'

'But I am. I'm moving out.' Anna felt obstinacy hardening inside her.

'But why? You don't mean – Is there someone else?'

'No! I need to be by myself, not part of a couple.'

'Oh, I meant— So, you're saying you want to live on your own, find a place, but Martin doesn't know? Have you done anything about it?'

'No,' Anna admitted. She had thought only as far as

staying at home in Sevenoaks while she found somewhere to live; but that would seem like tamely giving in, becoming a teenager again. Also, it would mean telling her parents, a prospect she didn't relish. And total immersion in her parents' concerns and muddles would never help to clarify her thoughts.

'You could stay here,' Ruth said. 'If it helps. Patrick's room's spare while he's in Edinburgh. Don't do anything drastic. Come and stay for a few days, or a week. Give yourself time to think.'

'Are you serious, Ruth?'

'Course I am.'

'But – why?'

'You're helping me, aren't you?' said Ruth. 'I can do this in return. It'd be an easy enough commute, wouldn't it?'

'Yes, straight in on the Central Line. When shall I come?'

'Tomorrow, after work, if you like. But – think about it first. You might change your mind.'

'I won't,' Anna said.

How quickly new plans were making themselves! It lent her a kind of recklessness. She would trust her instincts, see where they led. But this feeling of light delirium lasted only as long as it took to go into the bedroom and choose clothes to take to Ruth's, packing them in her wheeled case. After all, she still hadn't done anything for herself; she was simply falling in with another person's suggestions.

'Why the suitcase?' Martin asked when he got in, and went into the bedroom to throw off his tie and jacket. 'I thought you said your mum was OK?'

'She is. But first I've got good news.'

She told him about her conversation with Sunila, the

92

contract being drawn up. Martin looked delighted. 'That's brilliant – well done!' He embraced her, kissing her ear; then, sensing resistance, looked into her face. 'What made you decide?'

'It seemed too good a chance to miss.'

He gave her an *isn't that what I told you* look, but refrained from saying it. 'We must celebrate. Dinner on Saturday? I'll make a booking – where shall we go? You choose.'

'Thanks, but . . .'

He looked puzzled now. 'What's up? The suitcase – where are you off to?'

'I'm going to stay with Ruth.'

'With *Ruth*,' he repeated, incredulous. 'Why? What's going on?'

'You needn't make it sound like a conspiracy. She just . . . invited me to stay.' Baulking now at telling him the rest, Anna despised her own cowardice.

'You and Ruth aren't exactly best friends. Why this, all of a sudden?'

'I like her,' Anna said defensively. 'And she likes me. And I'm helping her.'

'Helping how? I can't see how, during the week. What's the point of going there now?'

'I think she needs the company, to be honest.'

'Well, that sounds nice and cosy.' Martin had turned away, reaching for a glass, taking a bottle out of the cupboard. 'Fine, if that's what you want.'

'I wasn't asking for permission,' Anna said coldly.

'No, obviously I'm the last person you'd think of considering.' Martin clattered things about in the utensil drawer, looking for a corkscrew. 'You keep telling me I don't understand you, but if you don't give me any help, what do you expect? How long's this for?'

'Till the weekend, at least. We're doing more house-clearing on Saturday, and probably Sunday too.'

'So you don't want to go out on Saturday and now you're busy on Sunday as well. You might have said.'

'I just did say.'

In bed that night they turned away from each other, lying separate and apart. Anna stared into the darkness, irritated by the steadiness of Martin's breathing.

On Tuesday evening, at Ruth's, Anna unpacked her clothes in Patrick's room. The walls were midnight blue, patched with posters of his favourite bands; books and CDs over-flowed the shelves.

'He's phoned a couple of times from Edinburgh,' Ruth had told her. 'He's thinking of working with a friend for a while, selling hi-fi systems.'

Anna hadn't met Patrick often enough to feel at ease with him. Now that she was stockpiling grudges against Martin, it was convenient to add one that had nudged at her from time to time: his apparent reluctance to involve her with his sons, as if she were some passing girlfriend rather than his partner. Patrick had been sixteen when she first met Martin, old enough to have a pressing social life of his own, and to find excuses not to come with Liam on his regular visits. His wariness towards Anna, the new woman in his father's life, had gradually been replaced, as he matured, by indifference that bordered on hostility. Anna tried not to feel intimidated by him. He had Martin's good looks and dark colouring, and a smooth-skinned youthful sexuality that

94

seemed to acknowledge Anna and simultaneously despise her.

She knew from Martin that Patrick had done barely enough work to avoid being thrown out of the sixth form at the selective school he and Liam attended. Having been marked out as academically gifted from an early age, he'd achieved disastrous results in his A-Levels – deliberately, as Martin saw it. When most of his year group had been busy with UCAS applications, he treated the whole business with open scorn; university didn't appeal to him. Now, he was having what Ruth euphemistically called a gap year, again without much sense of purpose. While his peers set off on the Thailand–Australia–US trail, or for community projects in Africa or South America, Patrick had been filling his days with nothing very much, his evenings behind the bar at a local pub. When Martin fretted about his son's indolence – incomprehensible to someone as work-driven as he was himself – Anna had taken the line, 'He's only eighteen. Plenty of time to find out what he wants to do.'

'I wouldn't mind, if he hadn't squandered the last two years,' Martin would argue. 'He's turning his back on all the chances he's been given.'

'At least he's around. At least he phones you sometimes, tells you where he is.'

Martin didn't get this reference. 'Yes, when he wants money.'

Now, hanging her clothes in the limited space Ruth had cleared in Patrick's wardrobe, Anna felt uneasy. It wasn't like staying in a guest room; wasn't neutral territory. It was stepping aside from her own life to invade Martin's, the half where she had no part, no business to be prying. She should have said no to this, made her own arrangements. Maybe she'd only stay a night or two. But then what? She'd have to find herself a flat.

'Anna!' Ruth called up the stairs. 'I'm opening a bottle of wine.'

They ate pasta with ham and mushrooms, and salad. With Liam there, the reason for Anna's visit couldn't be discussed, for which she was grateful. Liam didn't remark on her presence, beyond asking, 'Is Dad coming?'

'No, darling, not today. Anna's staying with us for a bit.'

Afterwards, when he'd gone into the sitting room to watch TV, Ruth made coffee. Now, Anna thought, there would be questions: questions she'd struggle to answer. But Ruth, instead, returned to the subject of Patrick.

'Martin thinks I'm too soft with him – but, honestly, try telling an eighteen-year-old what to do! And Patrick can be so obstinate. Well, they both can. The more Martin tries to cajole or persuade him, even threaten, the more determined Pat is to do exactly as he likes.'

'Who does he go around with?'

'He's made new friends at the pub – older boys, mainly – well, young men. Now he's gone off to Scotland to be with this girl, Rhiannon. I'm not sure if she's his girlfriend or just a friend.'

'It doesn't sound so terrible,' Anna remarked. 'It's not what Martin wants for him, but Martin can't run everyone's life.'

Ruth looked at her; realizing that this could have come over as *Let's talk about me*, Anna added, 'Patrick's sharp enough to find out what he wants, and find a way of doing it.'

'Mm. I expect you're right. I feel like a go-between, trying to keep the peace.'

Anna couldn't stop herself from saying, 'Why did you invite me to stay? I mean – you've got enough to think about.'

'It was the obvious thing to do,' Ruth said.

❖ ❖ ❖

The winter of the year Rose disappeared, Grandad Skipton was diagnosed with a heart condition, and died at the start of December. It was such a strange and terrible Christmas, that first one, that Anna was glad when it was over, relieved when the school holidays ended. Rose had always made Christmas special, taking charge of the present-buying and the tree-decoration in a bossy way that Anna secretly rather liked. Without Rose, the prelude to Christmas was flat and ordinary, the festive days an ordeal.

But first there was Grandad's funeral. Anna cried a little, awed by the occasion: the black clothes, the hushed voices, the solemn moment when the coffin was carried in. Grandad Skipton wasn't her favourite grandfather; he had always appeared rather stern and forbidding, compared to Grandad Taverner with his jokes and cuddles and games of Scrabble and Monopoly.

By the graveside Anna's mother stood arm in arm with Gran as if braced against an earth tremor, while the coffin was lowered into the ground. Anna watched at first in fascination and then in horror, as the realization struck her that death was final, that this was what it meant. *Rose, Rose* . . . Could Rose be dead, *really* dead, like Grandad? But what would be worse? Rose boxed into a coffin and buried under such a weight of earth as the heap that was ready to smother Grandad? Or Rose dead somewhere but yet to be found, floating in water, perhaps, or tangled in a ditch? That made Anna shiver, the thought of Rose with eyes open, dead staring eyes that would swim out of her dreams to stare and stare at her.

Anna's mind clouded, and panic shivered through her. Tears rolled down her face; she thought she was crying soundlessly, but Dad had noticed and put his arm round her, holding her close.

'I know, love. I know,' he whispered. And maybe he did.

❖ ❖ ❖

Cassandra knows that the others in the reception office at Meadowcroft think of her as prim, staying aloof from their gossip. She presents herself smartly, always in a skirt and jacket, with careful make-up, neat hair and discreet jewellery. She would never keep a patient waiting at the hatch while she finished a conversation, the way Pauline and Jilly sometimes do; she makes a point of getting there first, with a bright 'Can I help you?' in a way that reproaches the others. She answers the phone, deals with appointments and referrals, sends out reminders about vaccinations, health checks and prescription reviews. Over the years she's been here, the doctors have got younger and younger; she and the other receptionists are old enough to be parents to some of the newer ones. That doesn't deter Pauline and Jilly and the other part-timer, Louise, all well into their fifties, from making silly remarks about handsome Dr Sharp, the latest to join the practice. Lately their attention has switched to the new physiotherapist, who rents a treatment room in the annexe and sees private patients on three afternoons a week.

'I wouldn't mind him running his fingers down my spine,' Jilly says, with a suggestive giggle; she clutches her lower back, miming extreme pain. 'Ooh! I felt a definite twinge just now – maybe it's a sports injury?'

'I don't think you get sports injuries from slumping on the sofa,' Pauline teases. 'Bit old for you, isn't he? I thought you liked them young.'

'There's something to be said for experience. He looks like he knows his way around.'

Cassandra can hardly stop herself from tutting. She hates it when they talk like that; so unprofessional. They'd soon complain if they heard the pharmacist and his assistant, both male, talking about women that way.

She hasn't seen this man, the physio. Only his name.

Pointedly she gets on with her work. She keeps her head down. Every morning she is first to arrive, opening up the office, turning on the computers, sitting in her place by eight-twenty, ready to receive the first phone calls, the requests for appointments. At one o'clock, not a moment later, she puts on her coat and scarf and tells the others she'll see them tomorrow. She suspects that they talk about her when she's not there. *So buttoned-up,* she imagines them saying; *never one to share a laugh and a joke.*

She found her escape route in the property pages in the local newspaper, soon moving to websites and setting up email alerts. Don was astonished when he found her studying floor-plans and Google maps on the computer at home. 'It makes sense,' she told him. 'You've always said we should look for somewhere new. Perhaps it's time. A change is as good as a feast.'

'As a rest,' Don corrected her. 'That's the saying.'

'But I don't want a rest. I want to do something.'

'A feast, then, OK,' Don said, laughing, and she showed him the houses she'd bookmarked. So easy, at that stage, like choosing from a paint chart. *I'll have that one, or maybe this . . .*

Of course it wasn't really as straightforward as that. So much to think about. But Don saw it as a change for the good, a project to work on together. Anna – Anna was doubtful at first, Cassandra heard it in her voice. But this was Anna's new area of expertise, and she had contacts – heard that the Cranbrook house was coming up for sale before it appeared on RightMove or any other website. She spoke to the agent, arranged an early viewing. All this activity made Cassandra realize how inertia had settled over her like a cloak. Don and Anna were eager to throw themselves into purposeful activity on her behalf; all she had to do was let herself be swept along. Surveys, solicitors, searches – it would happen. Things only had to be set in motion.

Now, though?

No. She's got to stop this before it goes any further. She can't do it, can't break out from the walls she's built around herself. She doesn't deserve it, anyway; the airy space of a new house, the sense of life starting again. She can't abandon the life she has: it's her sentence, her curse, it's all she knows. She must stay here for Rose; she must wait. One day – when, when? – one day, she knows, Rose will walk in, casual, unflustered, still eighteen, as if she never really left, but stepped aside into a parallel world where time behaves differently.

And an obstinate part of her insists that she won't be

driven into hiding because of that man. She won't abandon Rose. She'll brave it out; she will carry on as she is. But – is she standing up for herself, or being defeated? It's a puzzle she can't sort out.

'Look, love,' Don tries. 'I know it's a big thing to face – packing everything up, getting used to a new place. We'll cope, with Anna to help. There's no rush. A few months from now, and you'll wonder what you were so anxious about. You'll be out in that lovely garden every spare minute.'

'No. No.' She shakes her head like a dog shaking water from its ears. 'It's no good trying to persuade me. I can't do it.'

# 7

Anna woke on Saturday to the sound of steady rain outside. She lay for several minutes thinking about the day ahead – another day of clearing and tidying at Rowan Lodge – and wondering what Martin was doing. He usually spent Saturdays with Liam, but this week it would be Sunday, as Liam was going on a friend's birthday outing today. With time to himself, Martin would more than likely catch up on work, spending hours at his computer, maybe breaking off for a session at the gym.

She found herself oddly touched by his loneliness before telling herself that she had no right to know, having walked out on him. That had been her intention, but Ruth was making her stay here seem normal, unprompted by anything drastic. She hadn't encouraged Anna to talk about Martin, speaking of him only in affectionate terms or in connection with the boys. This odd three-sided relationship was starting to feel comfortable, as if Ruth had always been part of it. No mention was made of when Anna would leave, or what she'd do next. It was enough to go from day to day.

After dropping Liam at his friend's house, Ruth and

Anna headed out to Rowan Lodge. In the drizzle of a mild but unpromising morning, the countryside looked grey, featureless, the gateways rutted and striped with puddles, the hedges blackly severe. The fields rose through mist to the ghosts of distant trees. Rowan Lodge looked forlorn behind its fence, but Ruth, resolutely cheerful, pointed to blunt green spears poking through bare earth by the gate. 'Daffodils. There are dozens along this edge.'

Inside she turned on the heating and made tea, and they returned to their clearing, Ruth sorting blankets and bed linen, Anna starting on the kitchen. They'd come prepared with boxes and old newspapers for wrapping, and progress was brisk; Ruth had put aside a few kitchen items to keep, and Anna packed the rest for the charity shop. The drawers contained mostly spice packets and sachets, sauce and mixes well past their sell-by date, and a range of cooking implements, some unrecognizable. One drawer was stuffed full of papers: receipts, and instruction manuals for the cooker, microwave and washing machine. Anna put these on the worktop, knowing that Ruth intended to find homes for the appliances via Freecycle.

Next came a manila folder of recipes cut out of magazines, and underneath that a framed photograph, face down. Anna turned it over. The frame held a grey mount, with oval cut-outs allowing four small photographs to be inserted. One was a wedding photo, an image blurring in Anna's eyes then swimming sharply into focus: Martin and Ruth. Ruth wore a simple white gown, scoop-necked and long-sleeved; Martin – longer-haired than now, and less consolidated somehow around the jaw – was smiling broadly. There were separate pictures of Liam and what must be a gap-toothed Patrick, each aged about five. The last, larger than the others, was a family group – Martin holding baby Liam, looking down at him, Patrick standing close to Ruth, her arm reaching over his shoulder, his hand raised to clasp hers. Here in Bridget's garden, perhaps? There was a hedge behind: Martin wore jeans and a polo shirt, Ruth a long patterned skirt and vest top, Patrick was in shorts.

What had happened? Why had Martin left? He looked so happy in the photograph, so proud; a loving father.

'I'll start loading these boxes in the car.'

Ruth's voice behind her made Anna jump; fumbling, she almost dropped the photo frame. Too late to hide it, to shove it back in the drawer or pretend she hadn't been looking; Ruth had seen.

'Oh,' Ruth said flatly. 'I didn't know Mum still had that.'

As she looked at Anna, awkwardness spiked the air, the consciousness of how it could so easily be between them.

After a pause, Anna said, 'Why did it end?'

'You don't know? Hasn't Martin told you?'

'I haven't really asked. It just didn't work out, that's all he's ever said.'

'Hah. Didn't work out.' It was the first time Anna had heard Ruth speak of Martin with any bitterness. 'He left me for someone he met through work. Hilary. She was married too. They'd been seeing each other in secret for nearly a year. You know the sort of thing – he'd be working late, seeing clients in the evenings, staying away at conferences. I never guessed. Till suddenly he announced he was leaving us to live with her.'

'But—' Anna felt her mouth dropping open. 'Martin did

that? What happened to this other woman, then? When I met him he wasn't with anyone. Or if he was, I didn't know.'

'Things didn't work out,' Ruth said, with an ironic twist of her mouth. 'Hilary went back to her husband. And – Martin didn't come back to me.'

'But, what, do you mean—' Anna faltered. 'You'd have taken him back? After he lied to you and deceived you? Left you and the boys for this Hilary who couldn't even make up her mind?'

'I don't know whether I would have or not. He met you.'

'But I didn't—'

'I know.'

The silence of the kitchen settled like dust: too quiet, too still. Anna's mind blurred. The idea flitted into her mind that Ruth had brought her here to kill her. Helpfully, Anna had placed six knives, lined up in order of size, on the work-top. *Don't be stupid.* There was no glitter of madness in Ruth's eyes; she looked, if anything, as if she regretted saying so much. Her eyes, so blue and guileless, always seemed ready to film over with tears.

Anna swallowed. 'I don't understand. I don't know why you don't hate me.'

'What would be the point?'

'And I don't know why you don't hate Martin.'

'I did, for a while,' Ruth conceded. 'But, well, he made an awful mistake. He knows that.'

'Is there – have *you* met anyone?' Anna asked. 'In five years there must have been opportunities.'

'Not really. Not the way you mean.' Ruth pushed the drawer shut. 'I don't know if I've got the confidence to start out again. Martin and I married so young, and I thought he was the only person I'd ever want, or need. I've been out with people occasionally, but nothing serious. There's someone I know through the garden project, a good friend. But Martin's the only man I've ever slept with. I suppose that makes me hopelessly old-fashioned.'

She looked at Anna for a reaction; Anna said nothing.

'I wasn't actually a virgin bride,' Ruth went on. 'In fact I was pregnant with Patrick when we got married. I suppose we were too young, both of us barely in our twenties. But after so long, I don't know that I want to get used to anyone else.'

Anna needed to be on her own to assimilate this. She could only think that Ruth had loved Martin with a loyalty he hadn't earned. What he deserved was her, someone as fickle as he was, someone who'd flit off and abandon him on a whim.

She was still holding the photo frame, unsure what to do. Hanging onto it looked like an attempt to claim what was rightfully Ruth's.

'I'll take that,' said Ruth, reaching out for it.

❖ ❖ ❖

## Summer 1986

Rose was on the swing, reading. She had a look of intense concentration, her mouth slightly open. One hand fiddled with a strand of hair, corkscrewing it round her finger, releasing it when she was ready to turn a page. The hand that held the book was wrapped round the swing rope; she turned herself in slow half-circles, one way and then the other, her sandals trailing on the bare, scuffed patch underneath. Anna was nearby, crouched over the small section of border the girls had been allocated for their experiments in growing. She was waiting for Rose to notice what she was doing, a little resentful of Rose's absorption in her book.

It was a day of heat and stillness, of pleasure that was part boredom; the passing of time was measured only by the house's shadow slowly elongating itself across the grass, the chattering of starlings and the drone of a light aircraft already assimilated into memory. This end of the garden, the girls' end, beyond the pear tree and the swing, was in full sunshine, and Anna felt heat strike at the back of her neck as she crouched over the baked earth.

Anna's patch of ground was divided from Rose's by a line of pebbles. Rose had grown marigolds, but Anna's seeds had failed to come up, and now she was making a pattern with stones and shells collected on their seaside holiday. Earth-dust caught in her nostrils, mingling with the sharp scent of marigolds from Rose's more productive half. She was humming quietly to herself, a repetitive tune without words. She wanted to transform the shells and stones into something magical, the way Rose would, but already it was becoming pointless; she was merely scraping dust about. To be real and purposeful, it needed Rose's attention, and the elaborate detail she would bring to the pretence.

Rose gave a sharp intake of breath. Anna looked up. Rose was holding the book close to her face as if she were short-sighted. She couldn't get the story in through her eyes fast enough.

'What?' Anna demanded. Rose didn't answer. 'What are you reading about? Rose?'

Rose's book was called *Lord of the Flies*. Anna didn't know what it meant, and the cover, just words, gave nothing away.

'Rose?' she said again.

Rose's eyes swam back from some other place, as if it took an effort to remember where she was.

'What?'

'I said what are you reading about?'

'Oh Anna, it's horrible,' Rose said. Her mouth twisted; Anna thought she was going to cry.

'Is it sad? What's happening?' Anna prompted.

'Listen – this is really horrible. There are these boys on an island, right? In two gangs. They're all up on a cliff. Listen. One of the boys levers a big rock off the top, and then this . . .' She started to read, in a hushed voice, so that Anna had to creep closer to hear. '*The rock struck Piggy a glancing blow from chin to knee; the conch . . .*' She glanced up. 'That's a special shell he's holding . . . *the conch exploded into a thousand white fragments and ceased to exist. Piggy, saying nothing, with no time for even a grunt, travelled through the air sideways from the rock, turning over as he went. The rock bounded twice and was lost in the forest. Piggy fell forty feet and landed on his back across that square, red rock in the sea. His head opened and stuff came out and turned red. Piggy's arms and legs twitched a bit, like a pig's after it has been killed. Then the sea breathed again in a long slow sigh, the water boiled white and pink over the rock; and when it went, sucking back again, the body of Piggy was gone.*' Rose lowered the book and looked at Anna, her eyes wide, then she shut them tightly. 'Isn't that awful?'

'Is he dead?' Anna had moved closer, and was poking at the long grass at the edges of the concrete the swing was set in. Something had come into the garden, something dark and furtive that chilled the bright day.

'Of course he's dead, stupid. Weren't you listening? Oh . . . oh, that's so awful. I can't stop thinking about it.' Rose dropped the book, folded her arms tightly and hugged herself.

*His head opened and stuff came out and turned red.* Anna imagined it, the boy Piggy falling like Humpty Dumpty, smack on the rock. Falling and falling to the violent *crack*, the shock of not falling any more, the slam of bones and skull against rock. The stuff that came out would be like creamed rice. And then he'd be sucked away by the sea and the other boys wouldn't have to look at him any more. He'd be eaten by fishes, all gathering round for the rice pudding, red, like when you mix it up with raspberry jam. Piggy, what had been Piggy, would be there in the water with nothing inside his head, nothing behind his eyes. Anna put down her stick and started to cry, quietly sobbing at first, then letting her voice rise. Mum would hear from indoors if she wailed loudly enough.

At once Rose was off the swing, crouching beside her. Her arms went round Anna, cuddling. 'Anna! Annie! I'm sorry. I didn't mean to scare you, honest. It didn't really happen. It's just a story.' She sounded frightened, and Anna knew why: if Mum came up the garden to see what the crying was for, and Anna told her, Rose would be in trouble. 'Don't cry, please,' she begged.

Even at nine, Anna knew how to make the best of a winning hand. She sniffed pitifully. 'All right. If you come and read me a story at bedtime. A nice one. Not like that.'

'Of course I will. I'm sorry, sorry.' Rose's mouth was against Anna's hair as they rocked together. Her hair fell around them like a tent.

At tea time, when Dad came home, Rose couldn't eat her pudding. They were having jam sponge with custard, usually her favourite, but she was only pushing it round her plate and trying to hide it under her spoon.

'What's the matter?' Mum asked. 'Have you been eating sweets?'

'No,' Rose said pathetically. 'I'm just not hungry.'

Anna knew why she couldn't eat it. It had red jam sauce and Rose was thinking of that stuff that came out of Piggy's head. Anna was eating hers up without any trouble, because she knew the stuff that came out was like rice pudding, not like this yellow sponge. She scraped her bowl, keeping a careful watch on Rose's. If Rose didn't want it, it oughtn't to be wasted.

At bedtime Rose read Anna a story about a girl who turned into a seal, and left her mother and father to swim out to sea with the other seals, her real family. Rose read stories much better than Mum or Dad did. She read them in a quiet voice that made you listen, and she believed in them; you could tell by the way her eyes went swimmy.

Much later, Anna heard her screaming from the depths of a nightmare, and Mum's feet hurrying along to her room.

❖ ❖ ❖

# 8

## Sandy, 1966

Roland was their father's favoured one; Sandy couldn't remember a time when she hadn't thought that. He had come first. He was a boy. In the album there was a photograph of his christening: the new family posed in the garden, her mother seated, the white-swathed baby in her arms, her father standing behind. What struck Sandy about this picture was her parents' almost identical smiles, inviting the world to share their good fortune. *Look – look what we've done. This is what we've dreamed about, and now here he is, made flesh.*

The war had ended five years before Sandy was born, but there was so much reminiscing about air-raids, gas masks and rationing that she felt it had only just slipped from sight. She knew her parents' war stories: how they'd met in 1943, on a bomber base in Lincolnshire; it was quite romantic, as recounted by her mother. Dad had been in Bomber Command, flying Lancasters; Mum was a WAAF typist. They met at a dance, fell in love; there was a photo of them, Douglas and Patsy, both smart and correct in their best blue, her arm curled round his. They dreamed that

Douglas would come through the terrible dangers of flak and fighters that faced him several times each week, and that one day, when the war was over, a shared future would be their reward: a wedding, a home of their own, a baby. A son. Sandy knew without anyone telling her that her father had specially wanted a son.

Turning the album pages brought her to her own photograph, with *Cassandra's Christening* printed underneath in white, on the thick grey page. There she lay, alone on satiny cushions, in the same white dress Roland had worn, her eyes gazing soulfully away from the camera. There were pictures of Roland and herself together as they grew up: on beach holidays, or in school uniform. But it was to Roland's christening and babyhood that her eyes were always drawn. *They didn't have me, then. They were happy without me, before I existed.*

She didn't hold it against Roland, though, that he'd come first. He was her hero, her pride, her friend and her enemy, her supporter, critic and confidant. At eighteen he was tall and lean, thin-faced, with thick dark hair that fell to his collar – like a girl's, their father said disparagingly. Several of the girls in Sandy's form were silly about Roland, eyeing him at the bus stop as he waited with other sixth-form boys. Her mother had always said that there was something about men in uniform, joking that it was Dad's RAF blue that had attracted her. Yes, Sandy could see the uniform thing when she looked at Roland, and more particularly at his best friend, Phil Goss. They wore their school blazers, ties and white shirts under sufferance, yet there was a sort of disciplined grace about them; in their Cuban heels and narrow trousers they were as tall and leggy as racing colts. Out of school hours, with two other friends, Roland and Phil were the Merlins, enclosed in the special bond that held them and the music they made. Then, they had another kind of beauty: raw, thrilling and suggestive. Especially Phil.

Coming second, and being a girl, had its compensations. Roland was the one who carried the expectations of their parents, especially their father. Roland was one of the brightest students in his year, expected to sail through A-Levels and get a place at Oxford to read mathematics. This had been planned for so long that everyone took for granted that it was Roland's ambition, rather than their father's.

Roland, Cassandra: romantic names, suggesting myth and high drama. They had been chosen by Mum, who once told the children that their father had favoured David and Susan. At infant and junior schools Sandy had liked her unusual, important-sounding name and was glad she wasn't Susan, of which there were three in her class. But when she reached secondary school, Cassandra sounded hopelessly old-fashioned, even prissy, and she made herself known as Sandy.

Like Roland, she passed the 11-plus and went to grammar school – in her case the rather unambitious St Clare's, whose girls were aimed at secretarial jobs or positions in the armed forces, only a minority going on to university. Careers advice was limited, with the assumption that the girls would be trained as assistants to male bosses. Sandy accepted this, imagining herself poised and sophisticated, hair in a cool chignon, typing letters and managing her boss's appointments diary. She would go to college and learn shorthand-typing and filing and how to answer the telephone. None of this excited her, but it would be a passport to London, to the fashionable streets and trendy shops; it would provide money to spend on clothes and outings. 'It's a good grounding for a girl, shorthand and typing,' her mother told her. 'You can work anywhere, with those skills. And you can always go back to work part-time when you've had children.'

By the fifth form, when the era of Swinging London asserted itself with intoxicating energy, all this felt dull and unenterprising. Sandy began going around, in school and out, with Elaine, who had recently joined the form. Elaine was chestnut-haired and striking, with an air of worldliness and independence. Not only had she been out with boys, but she was more fashion-conscious than anyone Sandy knew; she usually had a magazine in her bag, scorning *Jackie*, Sandy's choice until then, in favour of the more sophisticated *Honey*. At breaks and lunch times they pored over the problem pages, Elaine taking a lofty attitude towards the naivety of the letter-writers; they studied hints on hair, make-up and skin care, and absorbed fashion details. Merely to know names like Biba and Mary Quant, to use them casually in conversation, brought the colourful, carefree magazine lives within reach.

Their school skirts became progressively shorter, and they wore slingbacks with stacked heels instead of the regulation lace-ups or bar shoes. Soon only the frumpiest and most biddable girls wore knee-length skirts and sensible shoes. Their form teacher threatened lines and detentions, but had little power. According to Elaine, Miss Thompson was a frustrated spinster. Rumour said that she'd been engaged during the war but that her fiancé was killed in the

D-Day landings. This impressed Sandy, but Elaine was dismissive: 'It happened all the time. She'll never find anyone now, not at her age.' Miss Thompson, Sandy estimated, must be around Mum's age, over forty, invariably dressed in dowdy two-pieces and porridge-coloured stockings. 'No wonder she's jealous,' Elaine said, with a toss of her abundant hair.

Hair was another point of contention. *Long hair must be plaited or worn in a ponytail*, the rules said. Rather proud of the length of hers, Sandy had at first worn it in two plaits, but only the first-formers did that, looking like sweet little Swiss girls. The current mode was for long straight hair falling like curtains from a central parting. Even St Clare's had to move with the times, and some of the younger teachers now wore their hair long and loose, with skirts well above their knees.

Sandy examined herself in the long mirror inside her parents' wardrobe door. If she narrowed her eyes and pretended to be looking at someone else, then yes, she was passable, though not as striking as Elaine. Her features were unremarkable; her hair, long and brown with fair glints in it, was her second best attribute. She had recently overtaken her mother in height, and her slim body had a grace she never felt when in company and overcome by self-consciousness.

Her number one asset was Roland. Having a brother in a rock group saved her from dullness.

Every afternoon, on the bus home, it felt as if the world was theirs. Elaine and Sandy bounded upstairs, making for the back seats. Time was their own here; freed from lessons and bells, they'd earned this interlude of giggles and gossip. With shoes kicked off and ties stuffed into their pockets, they shared chocolate bars or crisps as they reviewed their day: who had dropped an easy catch in rounders or had been an unbearable know-all; who'd displayed a greying vest or pudgy flesh in the PE changing room; which teacher had got flustered, outsmarted by Elaine or another of the mouthier girls. Here no one could dent the confidence Sandy borrowed from Elaine. Their cackling laughter drove nervous shoppers to the front seats, and kept mothers with toddlers on the lower deck.

Their bus took them past Grove Park, the boys' school: beyond Victorian stone buildings, the cricket field stretched green and smooth alongside the road. Sometimes there was an after-school match, only of interest if the players were sixth-formers, tall and rangy in their whites, with open-necked shirts and rolled sleeves. They made Sandy think of the First World War poem she'd read in English, all about *Play up! Play up, and play the game,* as if warfare was an extension of school cricket. The association made these boys appear sacrificial, bareheaded in the sunshine, submitting themselves to the discipline of the game. Sandy was hoping for a glimpse of Phil, but couldn't see him; there was Roland, though, standing in the outfield, hands on hips, looking intent. Possibly he was composing: that was what he did, all the time.

Sandy saw Elaine gazing towards him, and laughed.

'Bad luck. You've got a rival.'

'Who is she?' Elaine leaned forward. 'I'll scratch her eyes out, the cow.'

'Whoever he writes all those songs about.'

'Yeah? Who?'

'Dunno. He's not going out with anyone that I know about.'

'Perhaps there isn't anyone. Perhaps she's an imaginary muse,' said Elaine. 'Hey, p'raps it's *me*! He wants to seduce me with songs. Immortalize me.' She turned her head for a last look as the bus pulled away; a bowler was preparing to run up. 'Ooh, don't you love it when they rub the ball against themselves like that? Do they have any idea how sexy it is?'

'Oh, you!' Sandy nudged her. 'You wouldn't take much seducing, if you ask me. I thought it was Roland you fancied, not just anything in trousers.'

'Anything in cricket trousers. *Mainly* Roland. And preferably out of them.'

Giggles and gasps passed between them, irrepressible as bubbles.

'You haven't *told* him?' Elaine leaned against Sandy. 'You wouldn't?'

'Don't need to, do I? You're as subtle as an elephant,' Sandy said, though in fact she did, often, make teasing remarks to Roland, to embarrass him. When that happened he went gruff and mumbly, his eyes shifting away. He didn't believe her. He was modest like that.

After the funeral, whenever Sandy climbed the second flight of stairs her steps were heavy with dread. The door to Roland's room was closed, and that was unbearable. But if it had been open, that would have been as bad. Worse, if anything could be worse.

He wasn't here. Wouldn't be here ever again. That thought hammered at her brain, failing to penetrate.

He was gone. Wasn't coming back. Ever.

The house was full of a silence that pressed against her

ears, filling her mind to shrieking point. Silence tugged her into its depths; silence was a cloak she huddled into. It filled her mouth when she tried to speak; it buzzed in her ears. It turned her words into meaningless gabble. It slowed her movements, weighted her limbs. It turned everything – eating, dressing, brushing her hair – into pointless attempts to fill the hours that stretched ahead. The relief of sleep led only to the renewed shock of waking, knowing that it wasn't a dream, that the room next to hers was empty of Roland.

She could never undo what she had done.

❖ ❖ ❖

# 9

On Saturday evening Ruth was going to a party in Chingford. 'You could come too?' she offered, but Anna heard the doubt in her voice and said, 'Thanks, but I'm happy to stay here with Liam.'

This made it easier all round, because otherwise Liam would have had to go to the party, which, he'd made clear, he didn't want. Anna made omelette and salad for him and herself while Ruth got ready. It was someone's birthday party, one of her Holtby Hall acquaintances; her present was already by the front door, a bottle of Laphroaig in a gift bag with a tag saying *To Aidan, with love from Ruth*. When Anna saw this and raised her eyebrows, Ruth laughed and said, 'Aidan's a friend. It's not what you're thinking.'

The phone rang while Ruth was showering. 'I'll get that,' Anna called, and answered.

It was Martin.

'Did you want to speak to Ruth?' Anna said coolly.

'No, to you, about tomorrow.' Martin sounded as if nothing had changed; maybe not much had, but Anna felt as if a gulf of time had opened up between them. 'I'll be there for Liam by nine-thirty, and I'll fetch him back about six. Then I can bring you home, OK?'

Anna was wrong-footed; this hadn't been discussed, unless he and Ruth had made some arrangement. 'But I'm not coming back,' she told him, 'yet.'

'Not coming back?' He sounded startled. 'Why not? You've been there nearly a week now. You're not planning to move in, I take it?'

'No.' It came out on a questioning upward note.

'So what's the problem? You don't want to outstay your welcome.'

'Nice of you to put it like that,' Anna said, all too conscious that nothing had been discussed with Ruth.

'Is there something you're not telling me?'

'I don't know.'

'You don't know? Look, Anna, I haven't got time for this. Come home tomorrow and we'll sort things out. What's bothering you? It's nothing we can't solve. You know that.'

'But how can you be sure? You just said you hadn't got time.'

A pause; she heard a slow exhalation of breath, then: 'What have you arranged with Ruth?'

'Nothing! I just need—'

'*I* need you *here*, Anna! Don't you think you owe me an explanation, at least? Walking out like this?'

'I haven't said I've walked out. I'm not ready to decide anything yet.' Anna bit her lip; she heard how infuriating she must be.

'Decide?' Martin sounded curt now. 'Decide what? I really don't know what you mean.'

'No . . . I don't know, either.'

120

Another pause. 'I'm doing my best, but you're not making it easy. I can't for the life of me see what's upset you, and you don't seem able to explain. Or maybe you can't be bothered. You're not being fair.'

'Sorry. I know. I can't—'

How to explain that she liked it this way, this limbo-state, this period of suspended animation? Or was it a jumping-off point to something new?

'Look,' he said, 'I'll be there tomorrow. Come back with me, and we'll sort this out. We can, I promise.'

His kindlier tone almost made her waver.

'Please, Martin – just let me have this break. I like helping Ruth, and it'd be good to get the house-sorting finished. See you tomorrow, OK?' she said, and rang off. Her eyes were filling with tears; she blinked them away.

'Who was that on the phone?' Ruth said when she came down, her coat open over a wrap dress in a dark indigo print. Used to seeing her in jeans and sweatshirt, Anna was struck by her delicate attractiveness; her fine skin, her simple, flattering hairstyle, sleek and straight in a chin-length bob that swung as she moved. She wore a light perfume that had something of the sea about it.

'Martin,' Anna told her. 'He'll be here for Liam at nine-thirty.' Ruth looked at her as if expecting more; Anna added, 'You look lovely.'

'Thanks! OK. I don't suppose I'll be late back, but don't wait up.' She bent to kiss Liam, who gave a wriggle and grunted goodbye.

'Have fun, drive carefully, and don't talk to strange men,' Anna said, at the front door.

She poured herself a glass of wine, and juice for Liam.

He was lying face-down on a bean-bag, channel-hopping in a way that annoyed Anna intensely when Martin did it. Abruptly, she found herself missing Ruth, although they'd spent all day together. She wished they could sit down in the kitchen and share the wine, and talk: address the matter of how long she could stay, and what to do about Martin.

It wasn't fair, of course – how could it be? Ruth was the last person to ask for sympathy and advice. The idea was forming in Anna's mind that she might nudge Martin and Ruth back together. Wasn't that what Ruth wanted? Martin had made an awful mistake, she'd said. And was continuing to do so? He'd admitted to regrets – wasn't there an obvious solution, one that would suit everyone? Maybe that was behind Ruth's invitation, Anna thought: it wasn't for company and support, but because she wanted Martin left on his own.

'Is there someone else?' Ruth had asked on the phone, and Anna had denied it, but now she recalled Ruth's 'No, I meant . . .' and heard what she'd missed at the time; Ruth had been asking if there was someone else for *Martin*. She had him down as a serial adulterer.

Well, let Ruth think that; but in that case, why would she want him back? And – Martin wouldn't, would he? He was too busy with work, for one thing. Anna didn't want to believe that he could be deceptive, that he could lie, and go on lying. But he'd done that before, when he was married to Ruth – why not now?

And Ruth's motive in telling her about Hilary? Unless Ruth was totally guileless, and Anna thought she was too clever for that, it could only be to put Anna in her place, to diminish her importance in Martin's life. How could they be friends? Yet here she was, curled up on Ruth's sofa, in charge of Ruth and Martin's son. The only decent thing to do was remove herself from the scene, leaving Ruth and Martin to sort themselves out.

*Stop it, stop it. This is doing my head in.*

She tried to follow what Liam was watching on TV, but found it incomprehensible; she sipped her wine, picked up the book Ruth had left on the low table, *The Selfish Gene*, and read two pages before putting it down and going upstairs for her mobile. In Patrick's bedroom she called Bethan's number, not sure whether this was a good idea or not.

'I've got news,' she said, when Bethan answered. 'Guess.'

'You're pregnant!'

'No.'

'You're getting married?'

'*No.*'

'You took the job!'

'Yes, I did. But it's not that.'

'Go on then, you'll have to tell me.' Bethan sounded buoyed up, full of laughter.

'Where are you?'

'Home, in the kitchen. We're about to start cooking. Come on, spill!'

'I've split up with Martin,' Anna said, relishing the way it sounded: cool, decisive. Against the cosy picture of Bethan and Cliff making a meal together she saw herself as free and independent, about to rearrange her life.

'*What?*' Bethan shrieked. 'Are you mad?'

'No. It wasn't working out.'

'Did you have a big row or something?'

'No. It just seemed a good time to finish it.'

'For Christ's sake, Anna! What is it with you? You solve one problem and find another. Have you met someone else, is that it?'

'No I haven't!' Anna said hotly. 'Is that the only reason for ending a relationship?'

'So you're *hoping* to meet someone else.'

'I'm not! Honestly. I used to fantasize about meeting some man who'd transform my life and me with it, but that's naïve. I've grown out of that now.'

'I thought you *had* found him. Anna, you're off your head.'

'I'm not! Just now I want to be on my own.'

'We need to meet up. Have you moved out of the flat, or what?'

Anna explained about staying with Ruth; Bethan gave a humph of disbelief.

'I'd better go – Cliff's parents are coming, and I've got all these onions to chop. Look, how about Friday – oh no, I can't, it's our sales conference. I'll give you a ring tomorrow. Don't do anything stupid, OK?'

'OK,' Anna said, meaninglessly, and rang off.

She went downstairs with her laptop and settled in the sitting room with Liam. Intending to catch up with emails, she was soon sidetracked into one of her regular distractions: entering Rose's name into Google, Facebook and Friends Reunited, convinced against common sense that Rose would suddenly bob up, cheerful and offhand, as if she'd never been away. When she did this in the flat, she minimized the screen if Martin came into the room, not wanting him to see. Rose's name was never mentioned between them. When they'd first met, he'd listened and been sympathetic, but the subject was now closed. Her fault, or his? He'd never met Rose, so she may as well never have existed.

And he'd told Ruth that Rose was dead. That confirmed Anna's suspicion that he'd think she was wasting her time, clinging to false hope.

If Rose came back, everything would be different. For Anna, for their mother. Life would pick up; not where it had left off, she couldn't expect that, but on a steadier and more purposeful course. Anna told herself this, yet the Rose of her imagination was fixed for ever at eighteen. Anna had drawn level, then overtaken, and Rose was stranded at the age of young girls she saw in the street and on the Underground. Not many more years would go by before Anna was old enough to be the mother of the Rose she remembered. She recognized this, but couldn't adjust her vision, couldn't see Rose as a mature woman in her late thirties, almost forty in fact; a woman who'd had lovers, maybe children – a life of which Anna knew nothing.

If she had a life at all. Maybe Martin was right. Maybe eighteen was as far as she'd got.

On Facebook there were images, links, groups and campaigns to join, threads of conversations; Anna found herself flitting from one thing to another, settling only briefly here and there. She accepted a friendship request from someone she'd only vaguely heard of; she signed a petition about the NHS; she read postings that ranged from pointlessly mundane to self-aggrandizing. On an impulse she posted a statement on her own page: *Anna Taverner is still looking for her sister.* She could always scrap it later if she decided against making so public a declaration; meanwhile it felt like putting a message in a bottle, and about as much use.

Friends Reunited was more promising. At least here, when she entered Oaklands School and 1990, she saw names that had a connection with Rose, among them Christina Marchant. On the message board she found another name she recognized: Khalida Malik, clever, bound for Cambridge, who'd had an equally brainy sister in Anna's year. Khalida had posted a query: *Did anyone ever find out what happened to Rose Taverner?*

Anna caught her breath so sharply that Liam turned round and looked at her blankly before returning his gaze to the screen.

Someone had replied, *No, but she used to go out with Jamie Spellman. He might know.*

Jamie Spellman. Anna would rather forget Jamie Spellman, and one of the most shaming episodes of her teenage years, but he kept coming into her thoughts.

Anna's friendship with Melanie Spellman hadn't lasted; Mel had left school at the end of year eleven, and soon afterwards the family had moved away. But Jamie – he'd known Rose as well as or better than her girl friends. He'd been questioned when Rose disappeared; inevitably, there had been speculation that Rose was pregnant, but he had claimed that if so it couldn't have been by him. Still, he might remember *something*; something he hadn't told the police, something that hadn't seemed important at the time, but that might be significant to Anna.

Clicking back to Facebook, she typed in *Jamie Spellman*. A choice of four came up; one was in the States, one showed only a black silhouette, the third was from London but looked too old; and the fourth was also in London, with a photograph of someone too far away to be recognizable, in a long winter coat standing in what looked like a park, but that *could* – God! – it could be him. Anna felt herself flushing. She clicked ADD A FRIEND, then SEND A MESSAGE, and typed, *Are you the Jamie Spellman who went to Oldlands Hall in Sevenoaks?*

As soon as she'd sent it, she wished she hadn't. Would he respond? And what if he did? Into her mind, alarmingly vivid, came a scene she had tried to forget: the hot grass, children's voices from the play area; thrilling, excruciating. What choice did she have but to relive and keep reliving? To abandon her teenage self would mean abandoning Rose, too.

Leaving Facebook, she clicked to the Missing People website she often visited, though it filled her with a confusing rush of hope and despair. So many people disappeared; more were added each month. So many lives abandoned, families left like Anna's in the torment of uncertainty. The weekly appeal currently showed a young woman in her twenties, missing since Christmas. There were stories too of discoveries, of people turning up at home, sometimes after a gap of twenty or more years. To Anna, their relatives were the lucky few, the jackpot winners. Without telling her parents, both of whom would have objected for different reasons, Anna had listed Rose here as a missing person, uploading a photograph. People would see it. Someone would know.

She glanced at Liam. It felt underhand, looking at this web page in his presence, as if the sad lives shown on the screen might somehow infect his.

When Anna first found the site, it had included an Unidentified People page, which she had visited regularly, passing the caution that *Some images may be disturbing.* They always were, because here were details of dead people, washed up on beaches, found in woodland or half buried in quarries. For some, the only image was of a black silhouette with a large question mark, but most were reconstructions, derived from decomposed bodies or even skeletal remains. They turned before Anna's gaze, offering themselves full-face, three-quarter profile, side on. They had a waxy, corpse-like look, these faces, and strangely staring eyes, as if the artists – if that's what they were called – hadn't been able to forget that they were trying to summon people back from the dead. Often pieces of clothing were shown: jeans, T-shirts, distinctive trainers or badges.

Bodies, remains, shreds of lives. A whole gallery of them. Anna had found it guiltily irresistible to scan through those lost, dead faces, with their suggested trailings of hopelessness and despair. The more she looked, the more astonishing it seemed that most people managed to hang on, going from day to day with enough obstinacy and dogged hope to give shape to their existence. Yet, now that the website no longer included this section, she wanted it back. Every image that wasn't Rose had seemed to raise the odds of Rose being alive.

But all the missing people. What if you lost everything? What if you cut yourself off from everyone who cared about you? How would you live, and go on living?

Always there hung over these searches the glaring possibility that Rose had been killed. She could have been dead for almost twenty years. She might never be found. Or – any day that felt normal or dull – there could be a police phone call to say that remains had been found: bones, shreds of clothing. Sometimes Anna thought that nothing could be worse than the horror of that, but, yes – worse still was the likelihood that nothing would ever be resolved. The truth about Rose might remain for ever unknown, as impenetrable as on the day of her disappearance.

Anna and her parents never spoke about it, but she knew that each of them believed something different. To her father, Rose was dead: abducted, on that hot August day, and murdered, in a random act of violence. To her mother, Rose had betrayed them all by leaving, for some reason wanting to punish them. Anna had thought she shared her father's view, but now something insisted – superstition, mis-placed hope, denial? – that Rose must be alive. Somewhere she had to be alive.

Sharing any of this was too risky. Her father would see it as a foolish clinging to hope that had long since withered. To her mother, the idea that Rose had died was simply unthinkable, a different kind of betrayal, a giving-up; but colluding with her would be unfair, leading only to ever-lasting disappointment. Martin, on the rare occasions when Anna had mentioned Rose, offered no opinion at all; how could he? It was before his time, and – Anna thought – beyond the grasp of his imagination. Rose wasn't around, never had been, and there was no more to say. Yet, to Ruth, he'd said that Rose had died, as if he knew something Anna didn't; as if he were humouring her by letting her dream on.

That was one of the justifications Anna gave herself for leaving: that he couldn't know how it felt to have a shadow sister, and that she had no way of telling him.

\*   \*   \*

Returning to Facebook, she found to her surprise that there was already a reply from Jamie Spellman. He'd accepted her friendship invitation and sent a message: *Anna, yes, that's me. Where are you now? I'm in Islington, married with two kids, working in graphic design. Still nothing about Rose? That's awful.*

For a second she wondered how he knew, then remembered that she'd entered *looking for her sister* as her status update. She began a new message. *I'm living in Hatton Garden, and in a relationship.* She hated that phrase, so altered it to *with a partner*, not sure whether either part of the sentence was true any more. *I'm trying to contact people who knew Rose,* she entered, adding, on impulse, *Could we meet perhaps? One day next week if you're free?*

She clicked SEND, then instantly wished she hadn't. Too late. Would he? Could she?

With access to his profile now, she went to his page and looked at the photos posted there: several images of his children, a baby and a boy of about four, and of a pretty dark-haired woman, presumably his wife. Only one of Jamie himself, in which he still looked vaguely arty, with his ankle-length coat, tousled hair and plimsolls. Still, married with two kids – what could be more conventional? And at home on a Saturday night, at his computer, probably listening out for the baby crying upstairs. He'd grown up, of course he had. With some people you thought they never would, that they'd stay as glossy and smooth-skinned as they'd been as teenagers. Jamie would be nearing forty now, the same as Rose.

The reply came back quickly: *Could do Tuesday lunch time, 1-ish,* and naming a pub near the Barbican.

Anna sent back *Great! I'll be wearing a black coat and red scarf,*

130

and added her mobile number. Almost having forgotten where she was, she came back to the warm room, Liam and the TV. Already she felt nervous. Could she go through with it? Meet Jamie, face him, talk to him normally, as if he were only someone she'd known once, her sister's boyfriend? She'd have to. Re-examining things, turning them over and looking at them with fresh eyes, might mean facing worse than this.

In the morning, Anna took care to be out by the time Martin collected Liam for a day at the RAF museum at Duxford. Deciding against accompanying Ruth to Holtby Hall, she took the Underground train and returned to the flat. She aimed to slip in and out, leaving no note, so that unless Martin gave detailed scrutiny to the contents of her wardrobe he wouldn't realize she'd been and gone.

She let herself in, hearing the silence; sensing, almost, her own absence. Exasperation mingled with a kind of longing as she moved around the flat – tiptoeing, hardly breathing: why? She touched Martin's things: the book on his bedside table, *Stalingrad*; his towelling robe on the hook on the door. The bed was neatly made. Did he miss her in his sleep, turn to her in the night and find her gone? She slid open the wardrobe door and touched the sleeve of one of his shirts, lifting the cuff to her mouth to inhale the clean ironed smell. Always immaculately turned out for work, Martin used an ironing service. Irrationally, Anna felt annoyed by this evidence of continuing meticulousness. *He doesn't need me. Never has. He doesn't even notice I'm not here.* His life was going on exactly as before: he could concentrate on reading, go to the gym, organize his laundry.

What had she expected? Signs of derangement and despair? Would she have preferred him to be helpless without someone to pluck rumpled garments from the floor and restore them lovingly to their hangers?

She thought of mornings when she'd watched Martin dressing, choosing a tie, knotting it in front of the mirror. He never looked more desirable to her than when he was soon to leave, about to present himself to strangers. Sometimes – before she'd started at Burton Brown – she had tugged at his sleeve and pulled him to her, murmuring, 'Don't go. Be late for your meeting. Come back to bed.' He would yield for a few moments, then shake her off, laughing, saying that there'd be plenty of time later.

*Stupid. Stupid. Get on with it.*

Briskly Anna began choosing clothes, folding them into the empty case. A jacket for work, a short black skirt and three tops; a pair of smart shoes as an alternative to the boots she'd worn all week; jeans, fleece and T-shirt, trainers, hairdryer. Enough to be going on with.

The ringing of her mobile startled her; she hurried back to her bag on the sofa, and fumbled for it.

Bethan.

'Anna? It's me. Is this a good time? Where are you?'

'Oh – hi, Beth. I'm back at the flat.'

'Well, thank Christ for that. You've seen sense at last.'

'In a bit of a hurry, though. Look, I'll call you in the week, OK? And – thanks.'

Too easy, and without even lying. But Anna felt furtive now. Hurriedly she zipped her case, took a last look around to check that she'd left no trace of her visit, and closed the door behind her.

❖ ❖ ❖

## Late July 1989

Anna was looking for something to do. Mum and Dad had gone out to visit friends, leaving Rose in charge, so she felt almost duty-bound to play up. Rose had been writing an essay for most of the morning; they'd eaten their lunch together in the garden, and now Rose had fallen asleep on the lounger, her face to the sun. A bottle of sun-lotion lay on the grass beside the book she'd been reading. Her skirt was hitched up, her bare legs stretched out, smooth and shiny with sun-cream, browner than Anna's would ever go. It wasn't fair. Mum had told Anna to take care in the sun, not to burn; her skin went red and blotchy if she stayed out too long, and more than once, waking in the night, she'd scratched her arms and the back of her neck into soreness. Rose never burned. She only had to step out into sunshine and her skin turned the colour of tawny honey.

Rose asleep looked to Anna like someone in a painting. She could be under an enchantment, waiting for a handsome prince to kiss her awake. She might have been made of different stuff from Anna. Anna was all blotches and clumsiness and hot prickling embarrassment, while Rose – Rose had what Melanie's mother called *poise*. Poise meant that she could sit in a chair and wrap one leg round the other and look like a model in a magazine, or she could stand in a way that compelled you to look at her. If her long hair was untidy, it might have been arranged like that for a photo-shoot, the way models sometimes looked as if they'd just got out of bed. Anna tried hard to acquire poise for herself. She practised elegant ways of sitting, giving herself pins and needles.

Now Anna was bored. She'd finished her homework this morning, because it meant she could sit in the same room as Rose and pretend that her RE project was as important as Rose's history essay. She'd spent most of her time colouring the pictures, and knew that the writing part was skimped, and that Rose would never skimp. Still, they both had books out and pencil cases and were working, ready for school tomorrow. Rose had said they might go out for a walk later, but *later* was some way off; Anna wanted something to do *now*.

She wandered indoors. The house felt so different on a hot day, cooler than outside, the curtains moving gently to the air from open windows. A fly buzzed loudly on the kitchen windowsill. Anna rescued it, guiding it outside, then went upstairs. Instead of going to her own bedroom she stood in the doorway of her parents'.

It felt somehow grand and forbidding, this room; bigger and much tidier than hers or Rose's, with the bed always made, covered by a cream bedspread you couldn't bounce or sprawl on or you'd never get it as precisely draped again, its edges falling exactly to the floor. Her parents had a bedside table each, with an alarm clock and a weighty book on her father's side, a small jar of pills and a more feminine kind of book on her mother's. Anna didn't go in there much, but wandered in now to sit at Mum's dressing table, which always intrigued her. When Mum sat on the low padded stool, looking at herself in the mirror as she put on make-up, it seemed a glamorous thing to do, like an old-fashioned film star, except that a film star would have light bulbs all round her mirror.

'Of course not, you're much too young,' was what Mum said when Anna asked if she could wear make-up. Rose did, but not much – mainly dark grey stuff round her eyes, and mascara, and concealer which she dabbed on any emerging spots, though it was rare for her to have them. These items she kept in a bead-spangled pouch that sat on top of her chest of drawers, next to a small mirror on a stand. Mum had a special make-up drawer, which was altogether more mysterious. Anna slid it open, sitting on the cushioned stool.

The drawer smelled of perfume and powder, heady and cloying. Inside was a zipped bag, containing lipsticks, eye-shadow pencils and round containers of blusher. There was a powder compact with a dusty mirror inside, and a pot of rouge or lip-gloss, its surface worn into a smooth, glistening dip. There were tubes of hand-cream, foundation and moisturizer and hair-removing cream, slim jars of nail varnish in boiled-sweet pink, all the paraphernalia of being grown up and female. So much of it, so much to learn and remember! You'd think Mum went out every day looking like a painted doll; in fact Anna had never seen her wear more than powder and lipstick.

Anna picked up a sachet of face-mask and read the instructions. There were several in the drawer, so Mum wouldn't miss one. With nail scissors she snipped off the corner, and at once the contents began to ooze out – like thick cream, only tinged with green, and giving off a sort of clayey plastery smell, not unpleasant. You had to smooth it over your face and neck and leave it to dry, the instructions said. Anna fastened her hair back more securely into its scrunchie, and used one of Mum's grips to keep her fringe out of her face. She put a dollop of creamy stuff on her

135

chin, and began to spread it with her fingertips. It felt like covering her face with custard. Over her eyebrows she spread it, up to her hair-line, and all over her nose and cheeks and jaw, till all that was left was her mouth, which suddenly looked very pink and mobile, and two circles around her eyes. A clown face looked back at her from the mirror. She stared, almost frightened, and giggled at herself.

There was a blob on the blue carpet. She dabbed at it with one finger, making a pale smudge that worsened when she tried to scrub it away with a tissue. She used the tissue to wrap up the empty sachet, which she must remember to take downstairs and hide in the bin.

She felt the odd sensation of the mask hardening and tightening on her face, pulling her skin. She'd intended to put on make-up, the whole works – foundation and eye-shadow, blusher and mascara and lipstick – but now she couldn't. What else did Mum keep in these drawers? Listening out for Rose's tread downstairs – if she came indoors, there'd be time to bolt into the bathroom and wipe the stuff off her face – Anna closed the top drawer and pulled out the middle one. Mum's scarves were in there, silk and chiffon and fine wool, bright plain colours and pale patterns. Nothing interesting.

The bottom drawer looked boring too, full of card folders. They held dull-looking papers, accounts and bills, apart from one near the bottom that had a label saying *Certificates*. To Anna, a certificate was something you got at school, for swimming or winning a race on sports day or for reading lots of books, but the ones inside were made of flimsy folded paper.

The word *Deaths* caught her eye first. Who had died? But

it was her father's name written there, in old-fashioned loopy writing: Donald Leonard Taverner, and the words at the top were *Certified Copy of an Entry of Birth*, she read. *Pursuant to the Births and Deaths Registration Acts, 1836 to 1947.* It was her father's birth certificate. How stark and impersonal, *Birth* and *Death* in the same phrase, as if nothing in between counted for much. The date on it was 1948, ages ago. Underneath was an identical certificate for Cassandra Mary Skipton, dated 1950. It was weird to imagine her parents as tiny babies, new-born, with no idea of growing up and coming together to be Mum and Dad. Next came a marriage certificate, with both their names and the date 1969, and another birth one. Anna's eyes registered the details in shocked delight: *Anna Rose Taverner, 1977.* She knew it was hers, but it made her think of someone else: a helpless baby, red-faced and repellent in the way new babies were when she saw them squalling in the supermarket, refusing to be shushed.

Wasn't there one for Rose too? She couldn't see it here. Anna flattened the papers and put them back in the wallet-folder, then lifted out the one underneath, which had a white label but no title. Inside were more papers, official-looking like the others, but A4 sized and on thicker paper.

The top one must be Rose's birth certificate, but it looked different from Anna's. It had her name, Rose Patricia Taverner, and the first date was her birthday, 10 March. The widest column said *Name and surname, address and occupation of adopter or adopters*, and underneath that was Dad's name and then Mum's.

Anna's heart gave a dizzying thump. Her mind blurred. There was something here she was failing to grasp.

*Adopter. Adopters.*

Dad's name and Mum's.

It meant Rose wasn't really her sister. Was that what it meant?

*Adopters.*

They weren't Rose's parents. She hadn't been their baby. She was someone else's.

Her eyes had gone funny, not focusing properly; she had to hold the certificate close to her nose to read it again, and again, to be sure.

Yes. At the bottom it said *CERTIFIED to be a true copy of an entry in the Adopted Child Register maintained at the General Registry Office*, and the date – November 1972 – had been written in by hand.

Adopted Child. Rose Patricia Taverner.

Rose wasn't her sister. Rose, with her different skin, her differently shaped body, was no relation at all. Anna felt that somewhere inside herself she had always known that.

But – she looked around dizzily at the room, which seemed to have changed since she sat down – it couldn't be true, or it would mean they'd lied. Mum and Dad were liars, and so was Rose.

Looking up at the mirror, Anna was startled by the clown face staring back, the mask cracking into lines and flakes. Her hands trembling, she took out her own birth certificate again, doubtful now about what she'd seen. It frightened her, that there were official papers about all of them, about Mum and Dad and herself, papers with stamps and signatures without which you might not properly exist, papers saying that one day you would die. Papers that made someone not who you thought they were. Her own certificate – with the full names of Mum and Dad written in, Donald Leonard Taverner and Cassandra Mary Taverner, formerly Skipton – looked like a confirmation that she *was* who she thought, but could she trust it? It was only a piece of paper. She held it in one hand, Rose's in the other, comparing them. She had been born, it said here, on her own birthday, to her own parents. Rose, though, had come from somewhere else.

Anna was shivering. It didn't make sense. It couldn't! Rose would have said. She had always been there, ahead of Anna, bigger, doing things first, knowing everything. Rose wouldn't lie. If she did, she wouldn't be the same Rose. But then: who *was* she?

Hearing Rose's voice, she came back to herself with a jolt; how long had she been sitting there, gazing at words that jumbled themselves into nonsense, words that danced and teased in front of her eyes? She'd been listening out for Rose, but she must have forgotten; now Rose was calling out from the top of the stairs, soundless on bare feet, and the bedroom door was open and Anna sitting there in full view.

'Anna? What're you— Oh—'

Rose had stopped, leaning against the door-frame, a hand to her throat. Then she started laughing. 'Where did you get that?'

Anna fumbled the papers – too late to push them out of sight – before realizing that Rose meant the face-mask.

'You made me jump! Your face, it's like a Halloween ghost!'

'I was just . . .' Anna faltered.

'Did Mum say you could? She didn't, did she? You're bad, Annie, using Mum's stuff, when you know I'm in charge of you! Are you trying to get me into trouble?'

'No, I . . .' Anna looked down at the certificate in her left hand, then held it out. 'Look. Look, I found this. What does it mean?'

'What?'

Rose came in and reached for the paper. Anna saw her small frown as she read, her eyes scanning from side to side. She gave a small sharp intake of breath, but said nothing. The room was bedtime-quiet, the only sounds a dull ticking of the clock on Dad's bedside table, and a car in the road outside.

'Where did you find it?' Rose said, and her voice came out croakily, as if squeezing past a blockage in her throat.

'In there.' Anna pointed to the drawer.

Rose stared; she knelt, and began rummaging through the drawer, pulling out the other folder, bending close over each certificate in turn. Her loose hair tumbled over her shoulders; impatiently she pushed it back. She seemed to have forgotten Anna. Resentful, Anna said, 'You should have told me. Why didn't you?'

Rose turned and stared, her gaze unsteady. Still in that strange harsh voice, she said, 'Why do you think?'

Something was wrong here. Anna had started it and now there was no way of stopping.

'I don't know,' she whimpered, and felt tears trickling over the caked mask.

'Go and wash your face,' Rose ordered.

Soon Mum and Dad would know, and be cross. Anna hoped Rose was putting everything back exactly as it was, so that they could pretend nothing had happened and go out for their walk and never refer to what those papers said.

Obediently she went to the bathroom and ran cold water, dabbing at her face with the flannel. The mask softened as she wiped, but still clung to her skin; when she thought she'd got it all off and peered closely at herself in the mirror, she saw white bits in her eyebrows and in the corners of her nose. More and more chalky stuff flowed out as she rinsed the flannel, squeezing it under the tap.

When she left the bathroom, Rose's bedroom door was closed. There was no answer when Anna called her name, then knocked, but Anna went in anyway. Rose was lying on the bed, staring up at the ceiling. The certificate was still in her hand.

'You've got to put that back! Mum'll be cross.'

'Anna, you don't understand. You just don't understand. Go away and leave me alone.'

Anna went downstairs and out to the garden, and sat sideways on the recliner, staring at the lawn. The house's long shadow was falling across the grass, and the heat had gone out of the day. She *did* understand. Rose wasn't her sister. They weren't related. They weren't even slightly sisters.

She was an only child now. Rose had turned into a stranger, an unknown girl who for some reason lived here, like the poor sister in a fairy tale. Except that Rose would never be happy in that role. She'd taken first place for herself, leaving Anna to be the downtrodden one.

Rose didn't emerge from her room until Mum and Dad came home, soon after seven; Anna found herself creeping around the house as if someone were seriously ill. As soon as their voices were heard in the hall, Rose came down. On the third stair from the bottom she stood very still in a way that made them and Anna turn to look at her. Slowly she unfolded the adoption certificate, holding it out to show them. In her new, grating voice she demanded, 'Why haven't you told me? Why haven't you ever told me?'

Mum went pale. Never before had Anna seen that actually happening to someone: their face going so grey and rigid that you'd think all the blood had drained right down to their feet. She looked like a waxwork of herself. Dad said, 'I think we'd better all sit down,' and he put an arm round Rose's shoulders and guided her into the sitting room. 'Anna too. Come on, love.'

It was like they were having a meeting. At first Mum was silent; then, when she spoke, her voice was changed, and smaller, as if the air had been squeezed or jolted out of her. Tears trickled steadily from her eyes, and she snuffled into a handkerchief. Rose didn't cry, but she kept saying, 'Why didn't you tell me? Aren't I old enough to know?'

'We were going to tell you when you were eighteen, love,' Dad said. 'We talked about it and decided that was best.'

'But why? It wasn't like you couldn't have a baby of your own. Anna's not adopted, is she? I saw her birth certificate. Why would you adopt me when you could have your own baby?'

'Rose,' Dad said, his arm round her, 'we love you and Anna both the same. You're both our daughters and we love you very much.'

'But why would you . . . ?'

Over and over it they went, round and round. Rose and Dad did most of the talking; Mum watched their faces. When she did speak, her voice was full of tears. 'Rose, darling, we chose you because we wanted you more than anything. We wanted a little girl to love. And we do love you, we always have, from the first moment we saw you, and ever since.'

'So who am I?' Rose's eyes couldn't settle on anything. 'Who am I?'

Dad was still cuddling her, and now beckoned Anna and Mum to join in, so that they were all clasped together in a ridiculous team hug. Anna couldn't remember that happening before, ever; hugging didn't come easily to their mother. Mum seemed to have become smaller and younger.

'You're who you always were,' Dad was saying. 'Our beautiful Rose. Your mother couldn't look after you herself, so she gave you up for adoption.'

'Gave me up?' Rose repeated, indignant.

Anna's thought had snagged on the phrase *your mother*. Suddenly it meant something different, something new. Not Mum, but a stranger. A strange, remote, other mother who didn't want her own baby.

'I want to know who she is. I want to meet her.' Rose seemed to be speaking from a long way off.

'No, darling, please,' said Mum, her voice still tight and tearful. 'It's better left. Better not to stir things up.'

Always, whenever Anna looked enviously at Rose, there had been the comforting thought that one day she would metamorphose into something similar; ugly duckling into swan. Well, no, not *ugly* – even at her most despairingly self-critical, Anna saw no ugliness in the face that looked back at her from the mirror. Dullness, ordinariness, yes. Her hair was thick and brown like Mum's, her eyes more grey than blue, and although she could find nothing wrong with her features there was nothing remarkable about them, either. She had the sort of face no one would look at twice. People would look straight past her and gaze at Rose.

Now, she wondered how she could ever have believed that Rose was her blood-sister. Rose's eyes were brown, her hair dark and springy, with natural kinks. She had different skin. Different genes. Different everything.

Anna told Melanie, and from then on it was a game to imagine who Rose's real father and mother might be. Mel thought that the mother must be a ballet dancer who'd escaped from Russia. And her father? He might be a rock musician, a film actor, a member of the royal family. Or, more luridly, a murderer; he was in prison serving a life sentence, and didn't know he had a daughter. Anna's theory was that Mum had snatched Rose from her real mother, stolen baby Rose from outside a shop, maybe, or from a hospital, and had somehow got an adoption certificate to make it look legal. Why, otherwise, would Mum be so furtive about it, so guilty?

Whatever the truth, Rose had acquired a new glamour. Intrigue wafted about her like perfume. A mysterious other life had been bestowed on her, full of possibilities; Mum and Dad had only borrowed her. Anna felt critical of herself, by comparison. It felt rather unenterprising to have just one set of parents who lived in an ordinary house in Sevenoaks, and to know exactly who she was.

Rose soon became matter-of-fact. With time to assimilate her changed identity, she announced that she didn't want to meet her birth mother after all; wasn't even the slightest bit curious. At home everyone continued to treat her carefully,

144

and Dad told Anna to be considerate of Rose's feelings, after such a shock. Rose had special status. The idea grew and grew in Anna's mind that Rose was her parents' favourite.

'They chose her,' she complained to Mel. 'They didn't choose *me*.'

'Oh, but that's just silly!'

If they'd been able to choose, wouldn't they have picked someone cleverer, more beautiful, more special? Anna watched closely for signs of preference, for Rose being allowed to get away with things, or receiving excessive praise. But Rose carried on much the same as she always did. She had interminable conversations with her friend Chrissie; she read lots of books, ready for starting in the sixth form. She painted and drew in her bedroom; she did a big self-portrait in pastels, hair tumbling and kinking over her shoulders, eyes gazing a question. She painted herself reflected in a series of mirrors, her face echoing back and back until it became a postage stamp, unrecognizable.

Often Anna thought of that moment in the bedroom, frozen into stillness in her memory, when she'd held out the paper, and Rose's hand had been stretched out to take it. The last few moments of not-knowing, of being proper sisters, before Rose turned into someone else.

❖ ❖ ❖

# 10

## Sandy, 1966

The Skiptons lived in a town house on the eastern side of
Croydon: a narrow, modern terrace, three-storeyed. Sandy
and Roland's bedrooms were on the top floor, divided by a
square of landing. Roland's room was the larger of the two,
and he spent hours alone in there on his homework, or
practising his guitar and perfecting his compositions. Only
rarely would he let Sandy in; usually the door was closed.

In the Merlins Roland sang only backing vocals; Phil,
with his raw, plaintive voice, was their lead singer. In his
bedroom Roland sang softly, or hummed, going over and
over a snatch until it flowed. His hero was George Harrison
of the Beatles. Sandy preferred Paul – that face, those eyes
that gave him an almost preternatural beauty! – or even
John Lennon, with his acerbic wit. But then her interest
was rather different. Roland admired George for his quiet
strength, his willingness to let the more outgoing John and
Paul take the lead, and above all for his virtuosity with the
guitar. When the new Beatles album, *Revolver*, was released
in August, Roland bought it immediately and played it
over and over on the portable gramophone in his room. It

included three George Harrison songs: *Taxman*, *I Want to Tell You*, and Roland's favourite, *Love You To*, with its Indian sitar accompaniment like nothing heard before on a Beatles record. Roland learned all three, singing them in a fair approximation of Harrison's soft Liverpool accent and flattened tones, though his guitar couldn't replicate the thrilling sound of the sitar. When Sandy was allowed in to listen she closed her eyes to Paul McCartney's voice in *Eleanor Rigby*, which unfolded its scenes of loneliness and waste like episodes from a novel.

Their father had been tolerant of the Merlins at first, when the four boys – Phil and Roland, with Mick the drummer and Dempsey on bass guitar – formed the group during the summer after O-Levels. As a holiday occupation, Roland's father saw it as a reasonable, even commendable way to pass the time. But they stayed together in the sixth form, helped by Phil's older brother Brian, who drove a van and became their unofficial manager, hoping to get a recording contract. They appeared at youth centres and dances, attracting a local following. Girls at school spoke of them as if they were a real, established group, to be mentioned alongside their famous idols.

Now that Roland was in the upper sixth, his father disapproved. 'It's taking up valuable time. Getting in the way of your school work. You should be knuckling down – you only get one chance.'

'I can do both.' Roland would never be drawn into argument.

'You might think so, but you'll let yourself down. All this caterwauling – where'll it get you?'

Roland had a quiet stubbornness that meant he drove

himself hard but pretended not to. In front of his friends, especially Phil, he kept up an attitude of not caring, of giving only scant attention to his studies. In reality he worked hard for his successes. When his O-Level results came, the string of nine grade As was marred for him by a B in Latin. His results were among the best in his year group, but he wouldn't celebrate, wouldn't be congratulated; in his own terms, he'd failed.

With Sandy's O-Levels approaching now, she was relieved not to have the same spotlight turned on her. She was fairly sure of getting good enough grades for a secretarial course without putting herself through the anguish of trying for the top and failing.

There was too much going on to let school dominate her life.

Occasionally, at weekends, Phil came round to work on songs with Roland. They were the Lennon and McCartney team of the Merlins, sparking ideas off each other. On one memorable occasion, when Sandy had lingered in the bedroom doorway, Roland told her, 'Go away, Sand, we're working,' but Phil bestowed a smile on her – oh, something to treasure for days and weeks to come! – and said, 'It's all right, Sandy. Come in if you want.' And she sat on a floor-cushion, mesmerized, ignored, as they put a song together: haltingly, pausing to note down chords, as words and music slowly came together. More than once Phil stopped playing and asked her opinion, and her happiness was complete.

Beautiful Phil. Sandy gazed and gazed, storing every detail in her memory – the fall of light hair that curved into the back of his neck, bony hunch of shoulders, sweep of lowered eyelashes, hands caressing his guitar – so that she could recall every detail later, in bed. Those few words of acknowledgement were a blessing; she wanted no more. She had fallen in love with his voice, with the range of expression it conveyed, from searing anger to a barely whispered intimacy that touched something deep inside her.

When she saw the group on stage, what attracted her most powerfully was Phil's remoteness, his absorption: his eyes half closed as he cradled the microphone, the creak in his voice that was almost a sob. Who was he thinking of as he sang Roland's lyrics? Someone, surely. Phil made the words his own, flinging them at no one in particular, not looking at any one girl in the audience. Roland stood behind, sometimes sharing a mike stand with Dempsey as he leaned in to sing backing vocals. Or, when the lead guitar took off thrillingly on its own, rising above bass and drums in notes that rose like bell chimes to the ceiling and gathered there, Roland seemed lost in an ecstasy that was almost painful, and Phil would turn to look at him, acknowledging his moment. Sandy could never be part of this, other than as an observer, and that was its attraction. It was an exclusively male thing, bonding them into brotherhood. To perform was to expose themselves to an audience, to lay bare their passions, invite ridicule and sneers. There was bravery in that, Sandy thought; bravery and defiance. On weekdays they were ordinary schoolboys, but as the Merlins they were transformed into something bigger. Energy pulsed from their voices and their instruments, vital, exhilarating.

'I want to be their road manager,' Elaine said.

'They've got one.'

'Assistant, then.'

'You wouldn't, if you saw the back of their van,' Sandy told her. 'All beer cans and chip papers and plugs and leads and sweaty T-shirts.'

'Oh, take me there!' Elaine inhaled deeply. 'I'd love it. I'd get drunk on it.'

Elaine's chance came at the end of the autumn term. As a daring innovation that year, the fifth form was allowed to hold a dance jointly with the boys from Grove Park. Elaine, who was on the fifth-form council, pressed for a live group rather than a DJ, and the Merlins were booked.

The resulting performance got the group banned from St Clare's and also from church youth clubs nearby. In the form room the Merlins were spoken of in the same breath as the Rolling Stones; Phil injected a new strut and swagger into his act, imitating Mick Jagger's feral magnetism. Bookings rolled in; Sandy gained prestige at school. Meanwhile Elaine was summoned to the headmistress's office to account for herself.

'Have you any idea how damaging this is to the school's reputation? I might have expected you to have more sense of what's appropriate. You've let me down badly.'

This was relayed to Sandy with full dramatic effect; Elaine could do Miss Mowerby's rigid, upright posture to perfection, and the way she spoke through closed teeth.

'*I understand that these young men made blatant references to sexual intercourse,*' Elaine went on, flaring her nostrils.

'She didn't say that!'

'She did. That's what this is all about. Roland's lyrics. Oh, he's such a hero, your brother! You should have heard me, all innocence.' Elaine made her eyes big and round. '*No, really, Miss Mowerby? Are you sure? I had no idea!*'

150

What had caused this outrage was Roland's latest composition, *The Power of Love*, written for the occasion. Sandy had listened to him improvising in his bedroom, but hadn't heard the full version until Saturday night, and even then couldn't make out most of the words; with the amplifiers turned up, it was poundingly fast, crashingly rhythmic. But one of the staff, who must have paid close attention, reported suggestiveness and indecency. It didn't sound like the sort of thing Roland would write.

The evening after Elaine's summons, when he was bent over physics homework at the desk in his bedroom, Sandy asked him. Unmistakably pleased with himself, he opened the desk drawer and pulled out a folder, from which he took a page covered in words and chord notations. He handed it to her and carried on working.

*It's electrifying, terrifying,* she read,
*Energizing, so surprising,*
*Titivating, elevating,*
*Awe-inspiring, mesmerizing,*

*CODA: It's the power of love,*
*I've got the power of love.*
*Feel the power of love,*
*The power of love, love, love, love, love.*

*It's concentrated, triple X-rated,*
*Soul-uniting, neon lighting,*
*Heat-provoking, engine stoking,*
*Unbelieving, heavy breathing,*
*Lusting, trusting, pelvic thrusting –*

*CODA to:*
*That's the power of love − love − love − love − LOVE.*

On Saturday night Phil had belted these words into the school hall at full volume, the rhythm speeding towards the climax of crashing chords from Roland, finishing on a guitar vibrato that trembled in the air. There was a moment of silence, then squeals and shouts from the floor. Phil looked too exhausted to acknowledge the audience, all energy ground out of him. Sandy was struck by the fact that it was happening here − *here*, in the hall where prayers took place every morning, where the girls silently filed in, form by form, their shoes squeaking on the polished floor, to stand for the hymns and kneel for the prayers. Never before could such a sound have penetrated the primness of St Clare's.

Now, studying the words, she giggled, and looked at Roland's bent head.

'How do you know about all this stuff? You can't have . . . you know—'

'Go away, Sand,' said Roland, head down. 'I'm working.'

On the following Friday, the *Echo* carried a short piece headed VICAR BANS LOCAL GROUP, and a photograph in which the band members were just about identifiable. *Lead guitarist Roland Skipton, 18, penned the offending lines,* said the article, and Phil was quoted as saying, '*We're only giving a picture of the lives and feelings of teenagers today. Songs about holding hands and writing love letters are old hat.*'

Roland's father was appalled. 'Did you stop to think of the disgrace to the family?' Just in from work, he confronted Roland in the kitchen, brandishing the local paper. 'If anything like this ever happens again, ever, don't expect to look on this as your home. Go and . . . go and live in the back of a van with your precious Merlins or whatever you call yourselves, and see where that gets you.'

'Douglas, for goodness' sake!' Patsy protested, a hand on his arm. 'It hasn't come to that.'

He shook her off, glaring, and renewed his attack on Roland. 'No one would think you had mock A-Levels coming up. How will this get you to Oxford?'

'Oxford's your idea, Dad. I don't remember being asked what *I* want.'

'Your mother and I work hard to give you the best education, the best chances. You seem determined to squander them, spend your time making up filth—'

'For Christ's sake cool it, Dad,' Roland muttered. 'It's only a bit of fun.'

Sandy – listening, frozen, not daring to speak – wondered how he could say that. His songs weren't just fun: they were *him*. They had a passion and intensity that surprised her, usually kept so well hidden. She looked from one to the other, dismayed to see her father red-faced and even close to tears.

Their mother's tactic was to wait for the outburst to be over, then take the role of peacemaker. 'There,' she soothed, when Douglas had repeated that Roland was a disgrace, and stomped upstairs. 'He's said his piece now – we can forget all about it. Let's not upset ourselves any more, not with Christmas coming.'

Nothing must be allowed to spoil Christmas, those few days closeted with family over puzzles, Monopoly and TV. An aunt and uncle came to stay; camp-beds were brought out and the bed-settee unfolded at night, and there was a pleasurable air of making do. Entertaining her younger cousins allowed Sandy to join in games she'd usually condemn as childish, sprawling on the floor to shake dice, playing hide-and-seek and Murder in the Dark.

Roland disdained all this. He stayed in his room, claiming that he needed to revise for his exams; he appeared for meals, said little, and gave the air of being so absorbed in his studies that he couldn't disengage his brain to indulge in games or frivolity. It was a ploy that wrong-footed their father: Roland was doing exactly as bidden, so how could he criticize? Distraction, lack of sociability, even rudeness would have to be excused. The Merlins weren't mentioned, and Roland hardly left the house; but Sandy knew that Phil was visiting relations in York, and that the band had no bookings until mid-January.

Elaine was being allowed a party on New Year's Eve, when her parents were staying away overnight. Excited phone calls were made; friends from school were invited, especially those with older brothers. Elaine made it clear that Sandy was responsible for getting not only Roland there, but the other three Merlins as well. Knowing that she could never reciprocate by having a party of her own – her mother's idea of a party would entail jelly and ice cream, pass-the-parcel and the blowing-out of candles – Sandy tried hard, though the most she got from Roland was 'Might do. If Phil's cool with it.'

Roland had a secret girlfriend, Sandy was certain. It was written all through his more soulful lyrics: *I think of us together, but you know I'll never tell, And I dream you won't despise me, for loving you too well . . . In my dreams you say you love me, though I've fallen, long ago, But I wake up and it's raining, and there's no way you can know.* When Phil sang these words, she could let herself think – giddyingly – that these were *his* feelings, but of course they came from Roland.

Her determination to find out who Roland dreamed of in this way came partly from *schadenfreude*; it would do Elaine no harm to find that she couldn't always have what she wanted. Sandy loved Roland as he was, moony and withdrawn but with the amazing extrovert side he revealed only in performance. If he started going out with Elaine, it would create an awkward triangular relationship, with herself caught between them.

On the Thursday between Christmas and New Year, her parents went to the theatre, a treat they gave themselves once a year. They left early for the train to London; Roland was out, but returned with a bottle of vodka he'd bought, and was soon sprawled on the sofa, listening to *Revolver* at full volume, glass in hand.

'Try some, if you want.' The bottle was open on the coffee table. 'A lot of girls like it with orange.'

Sandy fetched a glass and tried a little neat vodka. It tasted at first almost medicinal, then tingled on her lips and tongue and down her throat, making her cough. Within minutes she felt warmed and relaxed. She and Roland had never done this before; it made them allies, passing the bottle, pouring spirit into each other's glasses, swigging like connoisseurs. Sandy sat on the floor, leaning against the sofa. Soon most of the vodka was gone – Roland far outpacing her – and she felt floaty, as if nothing mattered much. *Revolver*'s final track, 'Tomorrow Never Knows', was a weird one: all fragments of tunes that loomed and faded, giving a swimmy, drunken effect that exaggerated the swirl in her head. John Lennon's voice, as he sang about letting go and floating upstream, might have been strained through a filter, coming from far off.

'I don't get this,' Sandy said, tilting her head back to look at Roland upside-down. 'What does it mean?'

She could ask, knowing that in his helpful brotherly way he would enlighten her. He wasn't like the girls at school; to admit ignorance to them was to be pathetically childish.

'Who knows? I don't. But to me it's . . . finding your real self.' He was leaning back, eyes closed. 'It's like, you know, you can go from day to day doing what you're told, thinking what you're taught to think. If that's all you do, how can you know who you really are? You're the only one who can find out, by letting go of everything you think's important.'

'With drugs, you mean?' Sandy searched for the right word. 'Acid?'

'If you can get it. But that shows you what's already in your head. You only see what's in there when you get rid of the clutter.'

Sandy tried to turn her gaze inward, to examine her own mind, but found only the buzz of thoughts that zipped back and forth, colliding with each other. Was there something deeper, running like a river beneath the daily trivia floating on the surface? What if she found nothing there? Her main thread of thought was about Saturday's party and whether she should spend her Christmas money on the orange and purple tunic she'd seen in Chelsea Girl.

'Roly,' she asked – he'd hated being called that since he

left primary school, but sometimes she forgot – 'you will come on Saturday, won't you? You and Phil and the others?'

'Probably, unless something else turns up.' He pulled himself up from the sofa and went to the gramophone, squatting next to the open lid.

'And – what about *her*?' she asked him, greatly daring. 'Will she come?'

'Who?' He looked at her in genuine surprise.

'You know. *Her*. The girl you write all those songs about.'

'Ah.' Roland slid *Revolver* back into its sleeve. He turned away; she saw the edge of a smile.

'I can't believe you make it all up. It's so real. There *is* someone, isn't there? I can tell by your face.'

'Might be. Might not.'

'Come on,' she wheedled. 'What's the big secret? Why won't you tell me who she is?'

'You haven't guessed? No, I don't think you would.'

'Guessed what? Is it Elaine?'

'*Elaine?* No.' He was laughing at her, not unkindly; maybe he was laughing at himself. 'You've got no idea, have you?'

Sandy shook her head. It was like this at school, when remarks went to and fro over her head like taller people passing at netball, arcing the ball over her head while she grappled hopelessly at the air. Roland took some while choosing another record; when it started she recognized his favourite Rolling Stones single, *Paint It Black*, with its troubled, urgent rhythm.

'Come on, then,' she tried. 'You've got to tell me now.'

'All right then. But you might not like it.' He looked at her. 'And for God's sake don't tell Mum and Dad. Promise?'

'OK, but why's it such a big secret?'

Roland gave his inward, private smile. 'Because – it isn't a she.'

'What d'you mean?'

'What I said. It isn't a girl. It's Phil.'

'What is? I don't get it.' She sat up, cross-legged. 'It's Phil who writes the songs? But I know he doesn't. I've heard you making them up.'

'Oh, Sand, you're so naïve! Listen. There isn't a girl, real or imaginary. I write the songs. About Phil. And he sings them back to me. Do I have to spell it out?'

'You mean you— Oh, but that's—' Sandy bent forward to clasp her knees, head reeling; *that's disgusting* was what she'd been about to say. 'D'you mean you – you and him . . .'

'No. Whatever you're thinking, the answer's no.' Roland went back to the sofa and flopped down on his back, gazing at the ceiling. 'Some things I keep to myself.'

'So it's just the songs? You haven't told him? Why not?'

Roland's mouth twisted into a smile. 'Why d'you think? I don't want to spoil it. He'd run a mile.'

'I don't blame him. It's perverted.'

'It isn't, Sand. It's the most beautiful thing there is. I thought you might try to understand.'

'I *am* trying. It's a bit much to take in.'

She wasn't sure she believed him; was he making this up, to tease her? In a way, yes, of course it was obvious that he and Phil were close, in the way footballers were, or the Beatles, or the boys that pushed and armlocked each other at the bus stop, ignoring everyone else – it didn't have to mean they were *like that*. It was only recently that Sandy had become aware of homosexuality, through jokes passed

158

around at school; jokes she hadn't understood. 'Did you hear about the two Irish queers?' That was one of Elaine's, relayed in the form room one rainy break time. 'John Fitzpatrick and Patrick Fitzjohn.' A beat of silence, then shrieks of laughter from the other girls, hands clapped to mouths: 'Elaine, you're awful!' Nonplussed, Sandy had looked from one to the other, concealing panic beneath a hesitant smile. 'You don't get it, do you, Sandy?' mocked Susan Morgan. 'Someone explain.' Someone did, with gestures; aghast, Sandy tried to pretend she'd known all along, but convinced no one. 'She's so *naïve*,' she heard Susan hissing to Elaine, as they took their maths books out of their desks. Now Roland had called her that as well. It seemed to be the worst kind of condemnation.

'But it's against the law. You could go to prison.' She knew that much, from Elaine.

'That's because the law's stupid. How can it be against the law to love someone?'

Her own brother was telling her he was *one of them*, and not ashamed, and calling it beautiful, and talking about love, not the sexual things people joked about. At least, if they saw her now, Susan and the others would have to credit her with sophistication: drinking vodka and discussing such matters with her rock musician brother. What did *they* know, after all? All their posing was nothing but talk.

'Are you *sure*, though? That you're – you know – like that?' she ventured. 'And sure Phil isn't?' Maybe she could get used to the idea; if Phil were like Roland he'd be more unobtainable than ever, but she would never need to be jealous of another girl.

Roland gave a humourless laugh. The vodka was nearly

159

finished now; he drank straight from the bottle, upending it for the last drops. 'Yes, and yes, I am sure. It's girls with Phil. He's the one who fancies your friend Elaine, if you want to know.'

Sandy closed her eyes, feeling this as a physical pain in her chest; it was only right that she should share Roland's hurt. Hazily she thought of it as a diagram, like the vectors they did in maths at school, with angles and arrows: I love Phil, and Roland loves Phil as well, but Phil fancies Elaine, and Elaine loves Roland. No one loves me. It lacked symmetry; it toppled under its own weight. In her mind, these diagonals made a rickety kite; tweak any corner and it would twist out of shape.

❖ ❖ ❖

# 11

All through Tuesday morning Anna found it hard to concentrate on work. She kept glancing at her watch, as jittery as someone anticipating a first date.

What could Jamie Spellman tell her that she didn't already know, or that he hadn't told the police twenty years ago? This would be nothing but a pointless ordeal. The obstinate part of her argued that there must be *something* Jamie could give her, something of significance only to herself.

At least ten minutes earlier than necessary, she was in the cloakroom, brushing her hair, checking her appearance in the mirror. She had dressed plainly, distancing herself as far as possible from the gauche teenager of their last meeting: hair swept up and held in a comb, her black suit, silver ear-studs. What change would Jamie see in her? But to follow that train of thought meant summoning memories that threatened her resolve.

The pub was busy, a large male group clustered round the bar, all tables occupied, but as Anna entered and stood inside the door she saw Jamie looking her way, getting up from his seat at a corner table. Even though she'd seen his

Facebook photos, she was surprised: he was older than she'd imagined, a grown man with the teenage Jamie's quick glances. Far too old for Rose, she found herself thinking; a different generation.

Threading her way towards him, Anna wondered about the etiquette for meeting someone under these circumstances. A kiss would be too familiar, a handshake too ridiculously formal. Jamie solved the problem by stepping forward, putting a hand on her arm and guiding her towards the seat he'd saved. 'You made it,' he said, a remark that needed no answer. 'What can I get you?'

Anna asked for a glass of house white, and busied herself with unwinding her scarf, taking off her coat and draping it over the chair-back. He returned with the drinks surprisingly quickly, given the press at the bar: Anna's wine, and a second half of beer for himself to follow the unfinished pint already on the table. He sat forward, looking at her. In contrast to her studied formality, he was casually dressed in jeans and a collarless shirt with a white T-shirt showing at the open neck. His face was thinner than she remembered, lined around the eyes; short untidy hair and a stubbled jaw gave him a rakish appeal, especially when he smiled. Anna felt herself blushing, and was immediately angry with herself. There was friendliness in his glance, and sympathy, cutting straight through the aloofness she had tried to summon.

'So. Rose. Still nothing.' He was serious now, looking down at his clasped hands. 'Awful. So you've no idea?'

'We don't know any more than we did then.'

'All these years. You know, I used to think you looked a bit like her, but now I can't see it at all.'

162

Anna took this to mean that while Rose was beautiful, she was ordinary. 'There's no reason why we should look alike. Rose wasn't – isn't a blood relation.'

'No, she was adopted, wasn't she?'

'You knew that? Did Rose tell you?'

'Yes, she talked about it, but Mel told me first.'

'Oh, of course. How is Melanie?' Anna asked, glad to be sidetracked for a moment.

'Yeah, she's fine. Married, with a baby boy. She lives in Horsham now. You're not in touch, then?'

'No. It's my fault, I expect. I've never been good at keeping up with people.'

'But something's made you start looking for Rose again, after so long? Why now?'

'Well . . . it's like nothing's really changed for twenty years. My parents too – they're still in the same house. They'll never be able to leave. My mother, at least. It's like we're all stuck. Waiting. Me especially, only I don't know what for.' It seemed an oddly intimate thing to be saying to someone she hardly knew. 'Does that sound silly?'

'No. No, it doesn't.' Jamie took a deep swig of beer. 'Her real mother – presumably the police followed that up? Rose didn't run away to be with her?'

'No. That seemed a likely explanation at first – I mean, better than some of the other things that could have happened. But the police checked, and there'd been no contact. Rose said she didn't want to meet her birth mother, didn't even want to know who she was. There was no way she could know the mother's name, let alone how to find her, without going through the adoption agency. She'd had her eighteenth birthday the March of that year, so she could have done it then. But she didn't. The agency confirmed that there'd been no contact.'

'So – why this? What did you think I could tell you that might be any use?'

Anna shook her head. 'I don't know. I really don't know. I just thought there might be something you'd remembered. Something she said, even hinted at. She must have told you things she didn't tell anyone else.'

Jamie looked doubtful, but said nothing. He drained his first glass and began on the second, almost absent-mindedly.

'For instance – you stopped going out with her, before you both took your A-Levels, didn't you?' Anna prompted. 'And you thought Rose had met someone else, but no one knew anything about that.'

Jamie gave a one-sided smile. 'She was the one who finished it. I wouldn't have.'

Anna remembered a morning in the kitchen, her mother saying something about Jamie, and Rose's casual, 'Oh, I'm not going out with him now,' as if Jamie meant nothing to her at all.

'Well, love, it's sensible to concentrate on your A-Levels,' was their father's response. 'You only get one chance.'

It was Anna who had been dismayed; how *could* Rose? Anna had thought Jamie was a fixture. But Rose had refused to say any more; she sat eating cereal, looking so demure that Anna knew that this wasn't her reason at all; doing well in her A-Levels had nothing to do with it.

'If she didn't actually tell you she'd met someone new, what made you think that?' Anna asked, daunted by the impossibility of unravelling this at such a distance.

'Gut feeling.'

Anna thought back to all the questions, the police at the house, the sympathetic WPC, the gentle but persistent probing. Who were Rose's friends? Her boyfriends? Of course they'd interviewed Jamie. Had she made any new friends recently? Who had she been seeing since the end of term? No one knew of Rose having another boyfriend in those last weeks. Chrissie would surely have known if she had.

'Someone from school?' Anna suggested. 'Someone in the sixth form?'

Jamie made a *search me* face. 'She went all mysterious. Made like she had a secret she couldn't tell me. She was like that – well, you'd know well enough. She loved drama.'

'So what did she tell you?'

'Nothing at all. It was like she was dangling something in front of me, then snatching it away.'

'Who could he have been? Why would she keep it secret? Even her best friends didn't know. Or – *was* it a he? You're not thinking—'

'No, no.' Jamie smiled, ducking his head as if the joke was too private to be shared. 'It was a *he* all right.'

'How can you know?' Anna asked sharply. 'What did she tell you?'

'Nothing. It was—' He looked directly at her for a moment. 'Something about her. She wanted me to think she'd moved on from schoolboys into a different league.'

Anna had picked up a beer-mat, turning it in her fingers. The words jammed in her throat, but she had to ask. 'There was an idea that Rose might have been pregnant – but was it true, what you said, that it couldn't have been you, if she was?'

She was definitely blushing now; she could feel the hot rush to her face. Jamie must have noticed; he looked embarrassed too, angling himself slightly away from her.

'Mm. I never got that far. God knows I tried hard enough, but it never happened. I'll tell you one thing, though. I think she was sleeping with *him*.'

'What makes you say that? She can't have told you?'

Jamie took another swallow of beer. 'No. But the last time I saw her, a couple of weeks after we'd left school, there was something different about her. A sort of pride, a sort of – awareness. It was like she was flaunting it, wanted me to know. It's nothing I could prove. A feeling, that's all. That's why it's no real help. But I'm not making it up. At that age – I don't know about you, but I had antennae for that sort of thing. Knowing when someone wanted to put me down. And she *was* putting me down, making like she wanted to spare my feelings.'

'But this was after you'd stopped seeing her? The split happened earlier, didn't it – before the exams?'

'Mm. She came round to my house, to dump me, basically. We were in my bedroom. We used to go up there a lot – listen to music, do homework, sometimes, or just lie on my bed, and a couple of times in it, but she'd go so far and no further. That time, she sat on the end of the bed, facing me – God, I remember this so well – and she wouldn't let me touch her. She told me it was over. She didn't want to go out with me any more.'

'And that was it?'

'Yes. I tried to change her mind – to tell you the truth, I cried. I was completely gutted. It was the first time for me – first love, and now the first time I'd been dumped. It hit me incredibly hard – things do, at that age. My world had caved in. D'you know what I mean?'

Anna nodded, thinking of the pear tree, the absence of Rose; the dread-filled days that followed. 'So you told the police all this?'

'Well, some,' said Jamie, putting down his glass, 'and I won't forget that, either. I don't know if I was chief suspect, but I certainly felt like it.'

Could Jamie have invented the new boyfriend, as a way of diverting attention from himself? But Anna rejected this. She believed what he'd said; besides, why agree to meet, if he had something to hide? He might have had reasons for obscuring the truth then, but not now.

'But you must have kept seeing her at school,' she said. 'All through the exams.'

'Yes, and it was a wonder I managed to do anything at all. I remember in the art room, our life-drawing exam, the model. I kept looking at Rose, but she never even glanced at me. There was a leavers' ball, but I didn't go to that. Rose and I bumped into each other in town once, and had a couple of drinks in the pub. We'd both applied for art foundation at Ravensbourne, so we'd be seeing a lot of each other, at least I thought so. But that *was* the last time. I tried to talk her round. Told her I still loved her. See, I can say these things now. It hurt like hell at the time.'

'And what did she say?'

Jamie made a wry face. 'She laughed.'

'Laughed?'

'I don't mean nastily. In a sort of . . . older sister way. Like she'd grown out of me. Said she'd always like me as a friend, but no more.'

'Always,' Anna repeated.

Jamie looked at her. 'I know. There hasn't been any

167

*always*, has there? It must have been a huge thing to get over, losing your sister.'

'Yes, it—'

There was sympathy in his gaze, and a warmth of understanding. Anna found herself thinking wildly: we could go off somewhere, find a hotel. We could console each other for Rose; forget Martin, forget Jamie's wife and kids. It would be different, now. We both know so much more. She looked down at his hands, and imagined them unfastening her clothes. A rush of desire tingled through her.

Jamie put down his empty glass. 'You live with a partner, you said?'

It felt like a rejection. *Get a grip, for God's sake.* She composed her face, and told him a bit about Martin, the flat, her new job, making it all sound happy and permanent; in return she asked about his family, his work. Time was running out; they both needed to get back to their offices.

'I don't know if I've said anything the slightest bit useful.' Jamie shrugged himself into the long coat she'd seen in the Facebook picture, turning up the collar.

'I don't know either. But thank you.'

'Good luck. I hope you find what you're looking for.'

It was bitterly cold outside, sleety rain starting to fall. Anna wrapped her scarlet scarf around her neck and pulled out her umbrella. They stood on the pavement, about to go their different ways. Last time they parted, she had yelled at him to fuck off.

'When you cried,' Anna said on an impulse, 'how did she react?'

'Oh . . .' Jamie gazed across the road, shaking his head slightly. 'She was sympathetic, but – well – triumphant.

That's the only way I can put it.' He looked at her with the self-deprecating smile that allied them as Rose's victims. 'You know how to get in touch, if there's anything else.' He kissed her on the cheek: a perfectly ordinary, sociable kiss, but it sent guilt and shame flooding through her. It was Rose's fault. Of course. Everything was Rose's fault.

'Thanks. It was nice to . . .' she faltered.

Jamie nodded. 'Sure. Keep in touch. Why not send Mel a message? She's on Facebook. She'd love to hear from you.'

'Great. I'll do that,' Anna said, knowing she wouldn't.

As she walked towards the Underground, her feeling was of relief: she'd done it, got through, apart from that ridiculous moment of self-indulgence. If she met him again, it would be less difficult, now that their younger selves had been pushed out of sight. If this had been their first meeting, she'd have liked him instinctively for his honesty and directness. Before, it had been impossible to see him as he was, with Rose in the way. How did anyone survive being a teenager? Exposed, relentlessly, at school, to everyone's scrutiny and speculation; opinions and tastes shaped round those of others, endlessly adapting to what was considered cool, or not; the air prickled with the electric tensions of admiring, envying, despising, rebuffing, jostling for supremacy. But Rose *had* survived, Anna was sure. Rose was a survivor. Didn't everything about her say that?

She delved into her bag for her Oyster card, wishing she'd asked Jamie why he loved Rose. Was that a question to be asked, or answered? Too late, anyway – it wasn't something she could raise in a Facebook message.

What puzzled her was why Rose had kept her new love a

169

secret, even from Chrissie, her best friend. Chrissie had seemed to Anna too big and sporty to attract boys, or to want to bother with them; Rose was the daring one, eager to rush into experience. Rose was too open – too *boastful* – to keep a conquest to herself. She would have paraded her new relationship in front of Christina, made a drama of it. Surely Christina must have known? But if she had a snippet of knowledge, even a guess, she had chosen not to pass it on to the police, or to Rose's parents.

It must have been someone Rose shouldn't have been seeing. Someone older, even someone married? Was that possible?

Or – had Rose simply invented a new lover, as a way of fobbing Jamie off, or of taunting him?

Turning her mind to practicalities, Anna bought a sandwich and a smoothie on her way back to the office, where she made three phone calls before resuming work; she'd stay on late to make up for her extended lunch break. Christina Marchant should be easy enough to track down; she sent a dutiful card to Anna's parents every Christmas. A Directory Enquiries search brought up the Weald Close address and number: so Christina's parents were still living there. Anna made a second call, identifying herself as a school acquaintance of Christina's, and Mrs Marchant obligingly passed on details. 'Christina Talbot she is now, dear. Lives in Bromley, near the civic centre. Got a pen handy?'

The third call produced Christina herself, a little out of breath, as if she'd had to run for the phone.

'Anna Taverner? What, you don't mean there's news – has something—?'

'No, no.' Anna had underestimated the shock her name

might provoke. 'I just wanted to talk to you. I wondered if we might meet.'

'Oh! Well . . . I suppose so. Talk about Rose, you mean?'

Anna wouldn't have recognized her voice. She might have been anyone.

'Yes – not because I've found out anything new. I haven't.'

'Are you still in Sevenoaks?'

'No, in London, but I can come down to Bromley if that's easier – one evening, or at the weekend. Are you free on Sunday morning?'

'We go to church, so the afternoon's better. Easiest if you come round here, as long as you don't mind the children and the baby. About three-thirty – is that any good? But I don't think I can—'

'Great,' said Anna. She wrote down the address Christina gave her, folded the paper and tucked it into her wallet. Yes, she remembered now that the latest Christmas card had mentioned a new baby: Mum had said something about it. At least Christina would be easier to face than Jamie, but whether this was progress, or only a pointless plod over old ground, Anna couldn't tell.

❖ ❖ ❖

**June 1993**

It was the summer of her fifth-year exams. Wimbledon fortnight. Anna had taken her first French paper and was walking home from school alone, past the park and the row of houses that bordered it. '*Agassi leads, five games to three, third set,*' drifted through an open window. Her feet were slippery with sweat inside her sandals. She thought of getting home, making herself a cold drink with ice, and sitting in the garden with a token effort at revising for tomorrow's history. Or she might watch the tennis, if the Agassi match hadn't finished.

Someone was coming along the path towards her. She saw dark hair, long legs in denim jeans, white shirt flapping undone over a tanned stomach: it was Jamie Spellman, Rose's old boyfriend. Less friendly with Melanie now, Anna hadn't met Jamie for two or three years. He must be twenty-one now, the same as Rose. She looked at him appraisingly as he came nearer, and saw him return the scrutiny, keen-eyed. He hadn't realized who she was. She tossed her head and flicked back her hair, enjoying this new power of attracting male glances, encouraging or dismissing them as she chose.

Jamie stopped in front of her.

'Anne! Thought I recognized you.'

The ghost of Rose stood between them.

'You look so different,' he said, his eyes sweeping down her body, then up again.

'Surprise, surprise. I'm sixteen now. I was a little kid when you went out with Rose. And it's Anna, not Anne.'

'It seems such a long time ago. And you still don't know anything?'

Anna shook her head, finding it hard to breathe or swallow. She turned away from him and walked slowly down the dip of grass into the park. He followed, and they sat on the bench. She looked at the length of his thigh, and a torn slit in his jeans through which she saw lightly tanned flesh.

'You used to come here with Rose, didn't you?' she

remarked.

'Yeah. There was that time with the rabbit. It really freaked her out. You were here, weren't you?'

'Yes.'

'She was weird like that, Rose. Gorgeous but weird.' He looked at her. 'You're not bad yourself, these days. You know that?'

*Not bad* was the best Anna could ever hope to achieve, in Rose's shadow. An idea presented itself. She stood up, shouldering her school bag.

'Where are you going?'

'Come on. Let's go for a walk.'

Would he follow? Was she good enough bait? He got to his feet, but said doubtfully, 'Where to?'

'Where you used to go with Rose. Take me there.'

Anna's heart was pounding as they crossed the field and went through the kissing gate to the footpath. She knew where it led, behind a row of back gardens and into an open field. The field was full of ripening barley, rippling to the breeze's touch like a head of blow-dried hair. Between the stands of barley, where the tractor had left tyre-tracks, the ground was hard and deeply cracked. At the edge of the field ran a stream, fringed by trees. Jamie walked ahead, then waited for her; he took her hand and led her through a faintly trodden gap between shrubs and brambles into a hidden grassy place.

'Here. Here's where we used to come.'

Thorny twigs snagged Anna's hair; she reached up to free herself. The stream, a torrent in winter, was a sluggish trickle between mud banks. There was a Coke can lodged against a root, and sweet papers scattered in the grass.

Other people came here, not just Jamie and Rose.

'What did you do, you and Rose?' Anna asked. She dropped her bag and went close to him, lifting her face to his. 'Show me.'

She saw his eyes widen in surprise; he smiled. 'This,' he said, and put his arms round her, moving his mouth to press on hers. She leaned into him, closing her eyes, tasting the saltiness of his lips. He was tentative at first, but then his arms tightened and his tongue was inside her mouth, a huge thing, probing, searching. No one had kissed her that way before – in fact it was hardly kissing, more of an invasion – and she wasn't sure that she liked it, but Rose must have done it so she'd have to learn. She moved her hands down from his shoulders to his hips. He was pushing himself against her, and she felt the surprising, immediate hardness of his penis against her stomach. She shifted her hand to explore; he gave a little gasp, and drew back.

'Are you really, you know, up for it?' he said, incredulous.

So she didn't have to, and that made her reckless. 'Course.' She gave what she imagined was a knowing, worldly smile.

He seemed doubtful. She felt a thudding of relief, and disappointment too, because he might laugh and reject her; already her skin was prickling with the shame of that. But he gave a sigh and held her close and started to kiss her again, a hand finding its way inside her shirt. After a few moments he hooked a leg round one of hers and tipped her off-balance, and they sank to the ground together. His hand was warm on her thigh, edging up under her skirt, pulling at her knickers. She helped him, getting them over her feet and throwing them aside, and he unzipped his jeans. He

174

moved himself to lie on top of her; a knee came up to push her legs apart. His breath was harsh in her ear as his hand moved in to touch where no one had touched before. Catching her wrist, he guided it down and closed her fingers over his penis, a hot rubbery thing that throbbed with a life of its own. After a few moments he groaned into her ear, pushed her hand away and rolled onto his side to fumble in the pocket of his jeans.

'What are you doing?'

'What do you think?' His voice was husky. 'You don't want to end up in the club, do you?'

Waiting, lying still, she remembered how he'd demonstrated killing the rabbit, his hand chopping the air. She heard a crackling sound and smelled rubber before he rolled over her again, breathing against her neck.

'Do you always have one of those in your pocket?' she asked him, amazed. 'Just in case?'

He didn't answer. He pushed her legs wider apart, fumbling with his fingers. It wasn't going to work, she was convinced. But she felt a sharp pain as he pushed into her, a pain that was repeated as he went on shoving. At first his weight was over her; then he raised himself on his hands, with his eyes closed and his mouth open. She thought: I'm doing it, actually doing it! But she hadn't expected it to be so brutal. He was hurting her with each thrust, so much that she felt he must be damaging her inside, but he didn't seem to notice. The ground was hard and bony under her shoulders and hips. She thought: I'm Rose, doing what Rose did, same person, same place. She supposed, while she waited for it to be over, that Rose must have liked it.

Abruptly it was finished. Jamie groaned and collapsed

against her, all impetus gone out of him. Maybe, she thought, this would be the romantic part, where they'd lie together and talk. He'd kiss her and stroke her hair and look into her eyes. He would say sorry for hurting her and promise it would be better next time. She remembered how tenderly he'd kissed Rose; she knew he could be gentle.

But all he did was slither away from her to strip off the condom and throw it into the stream, which struck her as a disgusting thing to do. Then he pulled up his pants and jeans. He seemed to have returned from somewhere else.

Anna almost said, 'Is that it? Is that what all the fuss is about?' But she felt too battered to say anything at all, and suddenly ashamed. She found her knickers and put them back on. In films, people took off all their clothes; she hadn't so much as removed her school tie. But none of this had been much like films. She wondered if she were bleeding; it felt like being wounded. Still, she'd done what she wanted, and there was a sort of triumph in that.

Jamie stood up, brushed bits of twig and dried leaves off his clothes, and reached out a hand to pull her to her feet – the first time he'd taken any real notice of her since they lay down together. 'Are you OK? It was your first time, wasn't it?'

So he had noticed. She waited for him to add something more, but when she nodded he only smiled and said, 'It gets better with practice,' and she saw that she'd given him the triumph of shagging a virgin. He'd be telling his mates about it tonight, while she revised her history. It was the price of her triumph.

Fair enough – she'd used him, too.

Now she asked him what she really wanted to know. 'Was it like that with Rose?'

He didn't look at her. He swiped at a trailing bramble with his foot and trampled it flat.

'I never did it with Rose,' he said.

Anna stared at him. 'But you came here with her. You told me!'

'Yeah, that's right. We used to – you know – snog, grope a bit. Have a fag. Or just talk.' Now he looked at her directly. 'It was nothing to do with me, her doing a moonlit flit. I mean, if she was pregnant, it wasn't me. We never did it. She wouldn't.'

Realization thudded hollow in Anna's chest. She'd been cheated of her victory. She snatched up her bag and shouldered it, stumbling out into the sunlit barley field. The glare was too bright, hurting her eyes. *All* of her hurt.

He'd been pretending she was Rose. He must have. And she'd been pretending too, but she'd never be Rose: only stupid, deluded, gullible Anna.

'Anne!' He was following. 'It was your idea – don't pretend it wasn't! Wait up!'

'I'm Anna. *Anna!*' she yelled back, furious. 'Fuck off, will you?'

Hot tears welled in her eyes as she ran back along the footpath, slowing to a jog-trot as she reached the park. There were children on the swings and two young mothers sitting on the bench, chatting; they looked at her curiously as she crossed the field. She thought of the phrases Mum used for what she'd done. Thrown herself away. Cheapened herself. Behaved like a woman of loose morals.

*I hate you, Rose. Look what you've made me do. I hate you.*

❖ ❖ ❖

# 12

Cassandra is in reception, making an appointment for a patient. She scans her computer screen while the woman waits, holding her child, a whiny girl of ten or so, by the hand. The girl is kicking her foot against the skirting board below the reception hatch in a bored, irregular rhythm.

'Don't do that, Kira,' says the mother at last, but it's too late – the thudding has got inside Cassandra's head. She feels a tightening, a mounting tension that makes her eyes waver and the screen blur.

'Thursday the eleventh, ten-twenty?' she says. The words come out in the proper order, measured and polite, but it might be someone else saying them. The woman nods, and Cassandra writes the date on an appointment card. The pen seems to be a living thing, trying to slither out of her grip. As she hands over the card, the woman's gaze rests briefly on her face, disapproving, unsmiling. Perhaps it mirrors her own expression.

She can hardly breathe. She swivels her chair and looks down at her hands, sees the tremor in them, the un-controllable shake as she tries to hold them steady. She seems to be looking down on her hands from somewhere high above. If she doesn't get out of here, fast, she'll throw up, or faint. There's a prickling in her armpits; she can smell sweat, smell her own fear. It clams her hands, clams her thoughts.

There are people waiting at the hatch; a peevish-faced elderly woman is looking at her. She can't face them, can't get out a coherent word.

'Jilly, could you?' she manages. 'Sorry, I'm—'

She pushes her chair back so abruptly that she stumbles and almost falls. Jilly's face and Louise's are pale blobs, floating in mist.

'Are you all right?' someone says.

'Yes. No.'

Regaining her balance, she walks giddily towards the door at the back of the office that leads to the staff loo and outside.

In the toilet cubicle she leans against the wall and fights for breath.

*I can't go back in there. I can't. I've got to get away.*


Christina Talbot's house was a big thirties semi in a tree-lined street a few minutes' walk from Bromley South station. The large, muscular girl – strapping, Mum used to call her – was now a plump woman with brown hair streaked blonde, and loose clothes that didn't conceal a bulky waist-line. Surely, Anna thought, she's older than Rose; older than Rose could ever be. Christina had a balding husband, who was outside doing something under the bonnet of an estate car, and three children, aged from about ten down to the baby. Anna struggled with the concept that Rose, by now, could have made a life like this for herself.

The two older children were watching TV in a sitting room, the floor strewn with toys, bits of Lego and building bricks. 'Sorry about all this.' Christina was holding the baby in her arms. 'We'll go through to the back, it's quieter.' She led Anna through to another room, a kitchen/dining room, almost as cluttered.

'How old is he? She?' Anna asked, looking at the baby; she hadn't been interested enough to pick up this most basic information from the latest Christmas card.

'Six weeks. This is Oliver.' Christina was smiling, looking at Anna for some further response.

'He's lovely,' Anna said awkwardly. She never knew what to say about babies, seeing them as messy, demanding, cumbersome things. She hoped to feel differently about Bethan's.

'If you hold him, I'll put the kettle on,' Christina said, handing him over.

Wondering at her readiness to give the baby to a stranger, Anna adjusted to his weight, and smelled milk, lotion and warmth. He was bulky in his nappy and his layers of soft clothes; his breath made small bubbles at one corner of his mouth and his eyelids were the delicate mauve-pink of the inside of a shell. Anna stared, fascinated, disturbed. Illogical resentment flashed through her at the thought that Martin had done this, had held his own baby sons, Patrick and then Liam; he'd done it without her, in his other life, long before he knew she existed.

Christina laughed at the way she held the baby so gingerly. 'You haven't got kids of your own, then?'

'No.' It still struck Anna as a surprising possibility. 'Actually, I've never held a baby before.'

'You've never – ?' Christina's eyebrows shot up. 'You're – how old? Early thirties, you must be? And you've never held a baby?'

'Thirty-three. No, I've always been afraid to. And there aren't any children in our family.'

'No?' Christina said it sympathetically, though Anna had simply been stating a fact. 'No, I suppose not, what with—'

She was doing the same as everyone else, stepping delicately around Rose's name, although Rose was the sole reason for Anna's presence. Christina busied herself making the tea, glancing at the baby every few seconds. Once, as he stirred, his eyes flickered open, misty blue and unfocused. Anna expected him to squirm and wail as he realized she wasn't his mother, but he only wriggled against her arm. Tension prickled Anna's neck. He was too new, too vulnerable; she might carelessly hurt him. There must be countless ways of harming a baby. She saw herself letting him fall from her arms, his bare head striking the table leg, the floor. So easy. What if her arms went limp, her hands released him? By imagining, was she willing it to happen?

'Take him,' she told Christina. Her voice came out tight and strained. 'Take him back, please.'

'What's wrong? Is he wet?' Christina's voice was calm, no maternal instinct alerting her to danger.

'No. But . . .' Anna's arms were tense. Now the baby did waken, opening his mouth like a yawning cat; he began to whimper and wriggle, the fingers of one hand curling on her sleeve. His eyes opened. He knows, she thought. He knows he's not safe with me.

'OK. Give him here.' Christina took him, giving Anna

181

an amused look, in which Anna read *You'll learn soon enough, when your turn comes.*

'Sorry. I knew he'd cry. I don't know how to hold babies,' Anna said. She felt a quite uncharacteristic urge for a cigarette, something to occupy her fingers and calm her nerves. She hadn't smoked since she was a teenager.

Christina didn't comment. She soothed the baby, cradling his head against her neck. 'Tea's ready,' she told Anna. 'If you pour, I'll take him upstairs and see if he'll go down.'

'Right. Thanks.' Anna's hands were shaking as she lifted the teapot. Her vision blurred giddily. She wanted to be comforted and soothed; she sipped her tea while it was still too hot. The door to the other room opened, releasing a burst of thudding music. Feet ran upstairs; Anna heard a girl's voice, Christina's quick '*Shhh!*' and a toilet flushing. The other child, the boy of eleven, came into the kitchen and took a can of Coke from the fridge, glancing at Anna but not speaking. She didn't speak either. The calendar on the wall hinted at the demands of being a parent: *Matthew dentist. Oliver clinic 10.45. Ellie gym club.* When did Christina find her own time? Anna couldn't see a single indication of something Christina might do for herself.

Returning, Christina told the children to turn the TV down and tidy up, and sat gratefully at the table. 'God, they keep you busy. What about you? No kids, but are you married or anything? You said Anna Taverner, but lots of girls keep their own names these days.' Her glance flicked to Anna's ringless left hand.

'No. I'm single,' Anna said, wanting this to be true, thinking that she could have spent today looking at flats.

'Well, you've got plenty of time to start a family. People have babies later and later, don't they?'

Anna suppressed a sigh. Babies, breeding, the unavoidable next item on anyone's agenda.

Christina offered biscuits from a packet, then took one for herself. 'It's a bit addictive, once you start,' she said, leaving Anna unclear whether she meant babies or biscuits. 'Anyway. You want to talk about Rose.'

'Yes.'

'I really don't know what I can tell you. I always thought she'd come back, but, well . . . Still nothing, after all these years?'

'We don't know any more now than we did then.'

'I went through it again and again in my mind, after,' said Christina. 'I told your parents everything I could think of, and the police, but it wasn't much help. I didn't know that she'd met anyone in particular. She wasn't on drugs or anything like that. She never talked about problems at home. I was her best friend – I'd have known. You probably remember, I was on holiday the week before she went. If I'd been around – well, maybe things would've been different. But it's no use wishing, is it?'

'Do you know why she broke off with Jamie Spellman?'

Christina considered for a moment, then shook her head. 'Not really. I don't think there was a row or anything. There were other fish in the sea, that's all I thought it was. She didn't want to be tied down.'

'But did you know of any other fish? Did she dump Jamie for someone else? He thought she did.'

'We went through all that, didn't we? No. Not that I knew of.'

'She'd have told you, wouldn't she?' Anna persisted. 'Was there someone she talked about, anyone she fancied?'

'No, sorry, Anna. I can't think of anything to tell you that you don't already know. I'm sorry if this is a wasted journey. Surely, really . . .' She hesitated, her glance sliding away from Anna's.

'What?'

Christina sounded apologetic. 'I know there's never been a – a body, but, I mean, we're sort of assuming she chose to stay away, aren't we? Surely the most likely thing is that she's dead. I said just now that I kept thinking she'd come back, but that was then. Not now. I'm sorry.' She looked at Anna, then away, towards the window. 'Poor lovely Rose. She had so much to look forward to.'

'No,' Anna said, too loudly. She wouldn't hear Rose spoken of in the past tense. 'She's not dead.'

'But how can you know?'

'I just do.'

Christina looked at her warily. Anna saw her struggling between a desire to humour and the urge to express common-sense logic. Common sense won. 'But – d'you really think she could have left home of her own free will and not got in touch, all this time? I mean, we all have rows with our parents, at eighteen. They don't usually last twenty years.' She was sitting with an ear turned towards the stairway in case the baby cried. 'Wouldn't you do better to accept it – move on, get on with your life? You can't wait for ever.'

'Accept what?'

Christina wouldn't say it again. She made a *you know* gesture, a small tilting of her head.

Anna looked down at the table. *Move on* – meaningless, grating, with its implication of criticism. *Get on with your life.*

'Tell me about Rose,' she urged. 'I don't just mean about her leaving. Anything you remember. What was it like, being her best friend? I want to know.'

Her belief in Christina was wavering; she noticed the beginnings of lines around her mouth, the carefully styled hair, the pearl ear-studs. What could she possibly have to say about eighteen-year-old Rose, from this distance? She was too old to be Rose's friend, almost middle-aged; a mother, respectable, dutiful, a church-goer. Anna tried to recall the teenager with the loud laugh, the sixth-form tennis star with the powerful double-handed backhand. This matronly Christina was pushing the younger version out of view.

'Well,' Christina said, 'she was so pretty I was jealous – she didn't even need to try. Clever. Artistic. Moody sometimes. Still, I suppose we're all moody sometimes.'

She smiled, offering the biscuits again. Anna couldn't imagine Christina being moody – she struck her as permanently cheerful, straightforward. Anna realized that she disliked Christina, maybe always had. Ever-reliable, ever-practical, always right, Christina had been a foil for Rose; deliberately chosen, perhaps, to highlight Rose's dramatic tendencies.

'Yes, I know that.' Anna tried not to sound impatient. What she wanted was specific memories. Arguments, incidents. Insights. Christina wasn't going to be much good at that; she was frowning, in the way of someone not much used to analysing.

'When you think about Rose, what do you remember?' Anna prompted.

'I remember she did my biology drawings for me,' Christina said. 'I did biology A-Level but I was hopeless at the diagrams. I used to give Rose whatever I had to copy and she'd do lovely clear drawings, really quickly, while we chatted at break or lunch time. Alimentary canals, that sort of thing, or heart valves, all just right. My teachers never knew, but they must have wondered why I couldn't do it in tests.'

This was better. Anna smiled encouragingly.

'I remember how she was with boys,' Christina said. 'With her looks, she was never short of them. She'd go out with someone and be keen, then suddenly it was finished. She'd never say why. Just, "I don't like him any more," when she'd been all over him yesterday. She could take them or leave them. That's why I don't think she ran off with someone. She wasn't in a hurry.'

'What did she talk about doing, when she left school?' Anna asked. 'She had her place to do art foundation. But after that – did she say?'

'Yes. I remember the police asked me, but I wasn't much help. She said so many different things. She talked about art college in London, or sometimes it was Glasgow, or Paris. Or she'd just paint, or travel, or get a local job and save some money. It was different from one week to the next.'

'What else? What else do you remember?'

Christina thought for a moment. 'I remember how she used to get upset about things. Work herself up into a real state.'

'You mean the hyperventilating? What things?'

'There was once in history. It must have been when we

186

were in the fifth, because I didn't do history A-Level like she did. Our teacher was showing us a video about the concentration camps. The gas chambers and the experiments and all that. It was grim. We all sat there stunned and quiet. I was sitting next to Rose, and suddenly she jumped up and ran out of the classroom. She knocked a chair over and the teacher shouted at her to come back, but she didn't stop.'

'Then what?'

'The teacher told me to go after her. It was Mr Evans – did you know him?' Anna nodded, and Christina continued, 'I thought she'd be in the girls' loos, crying. She wasn't, so I looked in the field, and the library, all round the place. Couldn't find her anywhere. It turned out she'd run out of school.'

'Where did she go?' Anna asked. She'd never heard anything about this.

Christina shook her head. 'I don't think she ever said. I phoned that same evening – I was quite worried by then. But she only laughed. "Got me an afternoon off school, didn't it?" she said. I supposed she'd been round the shops or something. And when I said, "It was awful, wasn't it, that film?" she went, "Oh, that," as if she'd already forgotten. Back at school next day she made a joke of it, said she'd suddenly had to dash for the loo.'

Anna knew Rose's trick of being in tears one minute, flippant the next. She had always hated that – the way Rose would upset her with something gruesome, then dismiss it as nothing. But she also remembered that Rose had woken screaming from a nightmare about *Lord of the Flies*, after saying it was only a story.

'Then there was the time she stopped eating,' Christina said.

Anna had forgotten. Now a scene flipped up in her mind of Christina at home, shouting at Rose through her closed bedroom door.

'You had a row with her,' she says. 'I remember that.'

'Yes, about starving herself,' Christina says. 'Did you realize how bad it got?'

'I can't have done,' Anna says. 'I can vaguely remember Mum saying Rose was on some silly diet.'

'It was worse than that. She stopped eating altogether. Perhaps she managed to hide it from your parents.'

'When was this exactly? Can you remember how old she was?'

'There was a famine in Ethiopia,' Christina says. 'When would that be – 'eighty-six, 'eighty-seven? We were about fifteen. Anyway, I know that was why.'

'She stopped eating because there was a famine in Ethiopia?'

Christina nodded. 'She stuck up a picture inside her locker. A starving kid – big eyes, pot belly, little stick legs, the sort of thing we were seeing on TV. So every time she opened her locker she'd remember not to eat. We used to keep our lunch in our lockers, and most morning breaks we had chocolate or crisps, to keep us going till lunch. But now if she was tempted, she saw this picture. I remember telling her, "This is stupid. If you want to help, send some money, but what use is starving yourself?"'

'What did she say?'

Christina thought for a moment. 'Something like, she wasn't trying to starve, but she couldn't bring herself to eat with those pictures on TV every night. I thought she must be eating at home or your parents would know, but then I found out. She was just pretending to eat at odd times.'

Anna remembered Rose in the kitchen, turning up her nose at the smell of cooking; saying, 'Not for me, Mum. I'm not hungry.' Then, later, making herself a sandwich and taking it up to her room. Mum, worried: 'I don't know what's the matter with her. Some silly diet, I suppose.' Dad: 'Diet? Have you seen the size of those sandwiches? Leave her, she'll get over it.'

'Yes, it went on for – oh, I don't know – a week or two,' Anna told Christina. 'She made excuses not to eat with the rest of us.'

'That's right. She told me,' Christina says. 'She'd take food up to her room and then throw it away, smuggle it out to the bin. She got to the stage of being proud of it. I know, because she told me she hadn't eaten for nearly a week – all she'd had was water. The first whole day was awful, she said, then she stopped even feeling hungry. I told her it was completely bonkers – wasting food, throwing it away, to show sympathy for people without any. She just wasn't logical. I remember a row in the form room. Some boys were mucking about one lunch time, throwing sandwich-crusts about, and one of them stuffed a tuna roll down the back of the radiator so it'd stink later. Rose went ballistic – really had a go at them. She was all, "How can you waste food? Don't you know there are people starving in Ethiopia? Children, babies?" Well, you know boys that age. One of them offered to send his crusts and the other one pretended to get the roll back to put in the Oxfam box. Rose was beside herself – crying, yelling. I think she'd have hit them if I hadn't held

189

her back. And yet she was chucking her own food in the bin every night. In the end the boys got quite scared. They went outside and Rose cried all through lunch time. I stayed with her, and told her she was getting hysterical because she wasn't eating. I think it was that same night I came round to your house.'

'You shouted at her,' Anna prompted.

'That's right, I did. I'd had enough. She wouldn't let me into her room for ages, but eventually she did and I gave her what for. I told her she'd die if she didn't eat, I said she was being stupid and melodramatic. I said if she cared that much about the famine, then for the love of Christ we'd do something useful – clean teachers' cars at lunch time and earn money to send, or join in the church fundraising. She went all quiet, then said, "Sorry," just like that, and next day she was back to normal. Well, almost. It took her a couple of days to get used to eating. But she took the picture out of her locker and never said another word about that week of not eating, or the famine. We never even did the car-cleaning. She didn't mention it again, not once. So I didn't, either.'

'And we had no idea, at home. How can you not know someone you live with is deliberately starving herself?' Anna gave Christina a searching look. 'What else didn't we know?'

Christina only shrugged. 'It's such a long time ago.'

Anna had always thought that Rose told her horrible things to frighten her, to wield a sort of power; that she didn't feel things as deeply as she pretended, and that she did it to get attention and sympathy. But there could have been another reason for Rose's abrupt switchings-off; maybe it was the only way she had of distancing herself.

'I know you used to look after her,' Anna said. 'When she had those panic attacks.'

'Oh yes. Remember that time on the playing field, when she was hyperventilating? You wanted to dial 999. You were terrified, weren't you? I'm not surprised. I was, at first.'

Anna warmed to Christina for seeing her fear, for not remembering her as a pest.

'Was she – would you say . . .' Anna wasn't sure how to put this. 'The intense way she felt about things, the way she'd suddenly switch moods – do you think she was mentally ill? Did she need help?'

'I don't know.' Christina swept crumbs from the table into the palm of her hand, and stood up to scatter them in the sink. 'Where's the line between being over-sensitive and being disturbed? And I've only picked out those examples. You could make anyone sound peculiar, doing that. I've left out all the normal teenage things about her.'

'Like?'

'Like – well, for one thing, the way she'd got passing notes in lessons down to a fine art. She only did it in the lessons she didn't like – maths was one. She'd look like she was paying attention, be writing things down or even have her hand up to answer a question, and all the time there'd be these notes going along the rows. Sometimes two or three at once. I don't think she ever got caught, not once.'

'And she still got As all round.' Anna liked this idea of a subversive Rose.

'Yes, sickening, wasn't it?' Christina was refilling the kettle. 'She always worked hard in spite of that, but she didn't have much respect for the teachers. Apart from her art teacher. He was different.'

'Mr Greaves. Jim.' Anna had been taught by him too, in the sixth form. 'Yes. He came round to the house, after, to see Mum and Dad. Rose used to talk to him the way she wouldn't to any other teacher. He liked her too, you could tell. He knew about her being adopted. He thought she'd gone to her real mother. But she hadn't, we know that.'

Could there be more to Mr Greaves than anyone had thought? Anna wondered now. Rose's special teacher, her confidant? He'd talked to the police; he'd been worried, upset, but could that have been an act? Surely not. He'd been a special teacher to Anna, too, and she would have sworn he was genuine. One of the worst things about Rose's disappearance was that it made everyone seem underhand, manipulative.

Opening the fridge door, Christina paused and said, 'I've just remembered someone else she liked, that last year. A new science teacher, physics. Mr . . . wait – Mr Sullivan. D'you remember him?'

'Mm – vaguely.' Anna's mind produced an impression of a young man walking along a crowded corridor, intent, tall enough for his head and shoulders to rise above the throng of navy-clad pupils. Sabrina Fawcett, in Anna's form, had fancied him, she remembered; he didn't take their class for science, but occasionally he'd come into the lab for something, or they'd see him in the prep room, in his white coat. Any personable young male was bound to stir up teenage lust in the hothouse atmosphere of a mixed comprehensive, but science wasn't one of Anna's favourite subjects, and like many of the girls in her year she'd been more impressed by Mr Spicer, Paul Spicer, who taught PE and whose tanned legs were often on view as he strode about in shorts and trainers. But wouldn't Rose consider herself too mature for a crush on a teacher?

'He was form tutor to one of the other sixth-form groups,' Christina said, 'so he was there whenever we had assembly. And he was at our leavers' ball.'

'Tell me about that,' Anna prompted. She remembered Rose taking ages to get ready, and Dad taking her photograph in the garden, before she left. For once, Mum's offer of dressmaking had not been spurned. She and Rose between them had customized a sea-green dress Rose found in a charity shop, taking it in to fit Rose's slender figure, making a wide cummerbund of black fabric. To Anna it looked glamorous enough for a film star, and Rose had done her hair loose and in deep waves that tumbled over one shoulder, leaving one side of her neck bare. It was one of the last photographs.

Christina brought the mugs over. 'Oh, this takes me back,' she said, smiling. 'You'd have thought it was the Oscars, the fuss we all made. I think it was the first time there'd been a leavers' ball like that – before, it'd been a barbecue and disco. We talked endlessly about dresses, and the boys got themselves DJs, and one or two of the girls even had their make-up done professionally. Then there was a great flap about going with a partner. The really one-up thing, for us girls, was to come with a boyfriend from outside school – someone cool, someone older. People paired up for the night, borrowed each other's brothers, that sort of thing. I didn't have a boyfriend and I nearly didn't go, but then a boy from our form asked me. David Wiseman, his name was.'

'Rose went on her own, didn't she?'

'That's right. She could have had ten different partners if she'd wanted, but no, she wasn't going to do the same as everyone else. She wanted to look as if she was still choosing. She wanted other girls to be jealous because their boyfriends would wish they were with her.'

'Did she tell you this? Or is it what you thought?'

'Bit of both. That's how she was.'

Anna looked away, towards the notice board and a post-card pinned there, a drawing of hands clasped in prayer and, in italics, *Be assured, if you walk with Him and look to Him, and expect help from Him, He will never fail you.* She remembered the mention of church this morning. When Christina had said *for the love of Christ* a few minutes ago, she had meant it.

'Course,' Christina was saying, 'for most of the evening it made no difference if you had a partner or not. There was disco music, and people danced in groups or with no one. But now and then – towards the end especially – there was a slow smoochy number, and that's when Rose went over and asked Mr Sullivan to dance. Actually it was my fault – I dared her to, as a joke, not thinking she actually would. The teachers were mainly there to keep an eye on things, but some of them joined in – you know, uncle-at-wedding sort of thing' – she mimed a sitting bump-and-grind – 'apart from one of the PE teachers who was a fantastic dancer. Total star, he was.'

'Mr Spicer. Paul Spicer.'

'That's the one.' Christina gave a sudden grin that revealed the ghost of her eighteen-year-old self.

'So Rose danced with Mr Sullivan?'

'No, she didn't. She went over to the group of teachers but he said no, and she had to walk back again with a whole group of us watching. So instead she grabbed a boy who was standing nearby and started smooching with him.'

'Did you tell this to the police?'

Christina gave her a sceptical look. 'What – that a teacher refused to dance with a sixth-form girl at a school bash? Hardly a crime, is it?'

'Maybe she saw him again.'

'But there's no reason to think that. I teased her a bit about it, but that was all.' Chrissie shrugged. 'To be honest, I can't remember that either of us ever mentioned him again, after the dance.'

'I wonder where he is now?' Anna was already fidgety, wondering whether the school would pass on details; whether, even, Mr Sullivan still taught at Oldlands Hall. He would have been only a few years older than Rose, which would put him in his forties now; about Martin's age. 'Do you know his first name?'

Christina thought for a moment. 'Michael, I'm pretty sure. Yes. Michael Sullivan. But Anna, you can't hound the poor chap about a schoolgirl who fancied him twenty years ago. Most likely he doesn't even remember.'

'Maybe you're right.' *And maybe you're not*, Anna added silently. 'Are you in touch with anyone else from school?'

'A few of us get together sometimes. We've talked about Rose now and then.'

The girl, Ellie, came through from the next room, looking suspiciously at Anna, looping her arms round Christina's substantial middle and leaning against her in a way that implied she'd been ignored for too long. 'Mattie won't let me watch CBeebies,' she complained.

Christina said, imperturbably calm, 'All right, love. I'll be there in a minute. Why don't you read your book?'

'Don't feel like it.' Ellie's whiny voice made Anna want to slap her.

Getting up from the table, Christina took the mugs and teapot over to the sink. 'I'll give you my email address before you go.'

Anna took the hint, looking at her watch. 'Yes, I'd better head back. Thanks, Christina. It was kind of you.'

'If only any of this could bring her back. I still miss her – that is, I miss her as she was then. Maybe I wouldn't even know her, now.' She found pen and paper, wrote rapidly, tore the sheet off the pad and handed it to Anna, who scrutinized her handwriting: round, regular as knitting, a circle floating above each i.

They went to the front door together.

'Thanks again.' Anna was eager to be gone.

'Keep in touch. I'll pray for you,' Christina said, surprising Anna, who raised a hand in farewell and walked away quickly. She remembered Christina making that offer before – praying for Rose, as if she had a direct line that led to the solving of everyone's problems. A lot of good that had done.

Still, Anna had come away with a new lead. Christina may have thought she'd said nothing of importance, but she'd given Anna what she wanted: a name. Michael Sullivan.

And a scene. Walking back to the station, Anna played it in her mind, embellishing it. There stands Rose, beautiful and imperious in her sea-green dress, her glossy hair falling over one shoulder and bare arm; she is full of the assurance Anna grants her that she can attract anyone she chooses.

And there across the hall – mentally, Anna decorates it with draped gauze and paper flowers, recalling her own leavers' ball – is Mr Sullivan, Michael Sullivan, with a group of teachers, most of them older than him. He's already noticed Rose, of course; how could he fail to? Each time she glances in his direction their eyes meet, and it's like a signal, a promise, crackling between them through air heady with perfume. Next to Rose is Chrissie, plumply pink in a too-tight, too-pale, too-fussy dress that makes her look like an overweight bridesmaid, her hair big in the layered waves that were popular then. 'Go on,' she urges, nudging Rose, giggling. 'Ask him. You know you want to.' Chrissie isn't used to champagne; her voice is shrill with it, carrying to the group nearby. Rose looks again at the teachers over by the stage. 'Yes, I will,' she says clearly, and crosses the floor in a slow, deliberate walk, one hand grasping a fold of her dress so that it swishes behind her. Someone wolf-whistles. Michael Sullivan must know she's coming for him, but his expression is unreadable – however hard she tries, Anna can't see him; she pictures a tall figure in a dinner suit, but can't bring the face into focus. Rose smiles her invitation, but Michael Sullivan doesn't respond, and she has to say aloud, 'Will you dance with me?'

What does he say? Anna can't hear; sees only the slightest shake of his head. Rose turns, as abruptly as if he's slapped her in the face. She walks back to Chrissie and the others across what now seems a vast expanse of polished floor, a skating rink ready to send her feet skidding from under her. She holds her head high, but her cheeks are glowing and her eyes are hot with tears.

'Turned you down, did he?' mocks one of the boys.

Rose turns her rejection into a joke, sidling up to him. 'I'll have to make do with you, Darren.' She swings him into the dance, swaying to the rhythm, laughing into his face to show she doesn't care.

Not once does she glance over at Michael Sullivan. But, but. She is Rose, and her memory records every humiliating detail.

❖ ❖ ❖

# 13

## Sandy, 1967

The funeral was all wrong, with nothing of Roland in it. Everyone wore sombre clothes and spoke in platitudes: *So terribly sorry* and *He had so much to live for.* Several boys from Grove Park were there, solemn in uniform, not sure how to behave; the whole family came, great-aunts and -uncles Sandy only distantly remembered, and cousins awed by the enormity of what had happened. There were hymns and readings chosen by Roland's parents, and the service was conducted by a vicar who hadn't known him. It shouldn't be like this, Sandy thought, all wrapped up in formality; she pictured, instead, a huge bonfire on the beach where Roland had been found, and candles, and stars, and everyone singing the songs he had written. He should have stayed there, cremated on the sand like Shelley, his ashes floating to the sky. Instead, this raw grey day, and the winter churchyard, hedged about with yews and cypresses and centuries-old tombstones so weathered that you could hardly read the inscriptions – this wasn't a place for Roland. It was too early in the year for even the first snowdrops. The new grave was a gash in the turf, the heap of soil next to it respectfully covered by a tarpaulin, as if the sight of fresh earth might render the *ashes to ashes, dust to dust* phrase too literally to be borne. They can't do this, Sandy thought; can't put him in the ground, next to all the dead people. It was outrageous: too final, too stark.

When the first spadeful of earth spattered over the coffin, she watched intently, searing the moment into her brain. Someone was sobbing behind her and Elaine wept copiously into a large handkerchief, but Sandy was too clenched up inside to cry. Phil was ashen-faced, eyes hidden behind dark glasses, and Dempsey looked like a frightened little boy.

'It's always worse when it's a young person who's died,' she heard one of the great-aunts say, as they walked back to the cars.

Sandy played *Revolver* over and over again. She had moved Roland's portable record player into her room, and some of his favourite LPs, but it was mostly *Revolver* she listened to. *Eleanor Rigby* was now unbearably sad, and the final track eerily prophetic. When she closed her eyes and listed to George Harrison singing *Taxman* or *Love You To*, she could almost bring Roland back, seeing his intentness and absorption as he bent over his guitar. She played and played the record until she knew every song by heart.

After all, the mock O-Levels turned out to be something of an anchor. She could have been let off doing them, but was adamant that she wanted to: otherwise, what else but to shut herself up with her misery? The mocks gave her a structure, a challenge. Instead of attending school full-time, she was allowed to come in just for the exams. She knew, from the respectful glances and hushed voices of the other girls, that she'd acquired a sort of glamour; she'd passed to the other side of something they could only imagine. In the corridor she saw younger girls nudge each other and whisper, 'That's her, Sandy Skipton – you know, the one whose brother . . .' She pretended not to notice. During breaks she hid in the library.

In the English Literature exam, her composure deserting her, she sat head in hands, tears dripping onto the blank page. Delia summoned the invigilating teacher, and Sandy was escorted out of the room, but insisted on writing her answers later that day in the library, with Miss Roberts the geography teacher in attendance. It was Thomas Hardy's fault, making her think about Sergeant Troy who was thought to have drowned, but reappeared a year later.

Only in books. In real life drowned people stayed dead, and you had to know that, even if you couldn't make yourself believe it.

'You're being terribly brave,' Miss Roberts told her, at the end.

It was harder when the exams were over and they went back to the normal timetable. Sandy avoided Elaine and attached herself instead to Susan and Delia, without caring much for either of them. If she could endure the remaining weeks of term, and the proper exams – what did they matter, now? – she could leave school. Where she would go, who she'd be, she had no idea. It struck her for the first time that wherever she went, she'd have to take herself with her.

Roland had hardly spoken to Sandy since New Year's Eve. He shut himself in his room, keeping the door closed; he appeared only for meals, saying little. His A-Level mocks would start as soon as term began. Their mother fretted that he was working too hard, that he ought to take breaks and go out with his friends, but his father took the view that there'd be time to relax when the mocks were over. The Merlins weren't mentioned, and no sound of singing or guitar-strumming came from Roland's room, so maybe he really *was* working all hours.

On the Wednesday of that first week in January, the TV news was full of Donald Campbell, who had been killed attempting to break his own world water-speed record. Sandy, supposedly re-reading *Far from the Madding Crowd* in the front room, watched mesmerized as footage of the crash was shown again and again: the jet-powered speedboat like a dart on the chilled greyness of Coniston Water, slowly rearing above the surface, then flipping into a somersault amidst a welter of spray. Campbell's words were heard over the radio: '*She's going . . . she's going . . .*' Then silence, and turbulence slowly subsiding to nothing. The lake had swallowed up the speedboat and the man inside it and had claimed back its stillness, the water mirroring dark mountains and cloud.

'Great way to go,' said Roland's voice behind Sandy; he stood gazing at the screen, mug in hand, then slipped out of the room before she could answer. She thought of the mystery of being alive one moment and dead the next; would you be conscious of your death, would you *live* it? They hadn't yet found Campbell's body, only parts of the wreckage, but no one doubted that he had died, crashing at more than two hundred and seventy miles per hour.

Those were the last words Sandy could remember, with

any certainty, Roland saying to her, other than the odd monosyllable as they passed on the stairs or met in the kitchen. On Saturday morning he went out early and never came back. Why he chose to go to the Isle of Wight, no one was sure – maybe he remembered a childhood holiday spent there. He had been seen on the passenger ferry, and later walking along the coastal path from Freshwater Bay. His train and ferry tickets were in the pocket of the rucksack he left on the grass above the beach. Currents had carried his body some way along the shore to where it had been washed up and found by a dog-walker. The autopsy revealed that he'd drowned after taking LSD, and at the inquest the coroner returned a verdict of death by misadventure. For the second time Roland's name appeared in the *Echo*: LOCAL SCHOOLBOY FOUND DROWNED. The mention of *mind-altering drug* horrified Sandy's father, who would have preferred that detail to be glossed over. Sandy heard him on the telephone berating the editor, but the damage was done, and she had to feel sorry for him. LOCAL SCHOOLBOY WINS PLACE AT OXFORD was what he'd set his heart on.

❖ ❖ ❖

# 14

Anna and Ruth now had an arrangement to take turns shopping and cooking. As tonight was Anna's turn, she bought food for supper at the M&S shop at Victoria: chicken breasts, salad, focaccia and a pineapple. Walking up from the station with her carrier bag, she thought of the evening ahead: Ruth would be tired from her day's gardening, Liam probably doing last-minute homework. Anna would make the meal, and tell Ruth, maybe, what Christina had said. Later she'd do a Google search for Michael Sullivan, and see if that led anywhere.

But she found Ruth in the kitchen sharing a bottle of wine with a man she introduced as Aidan. Anna looked at him with keen interest. He was older than she expected, fiftyish, with a tanned, weathered face, and short hair silvered with grey. He'd been working with Ruth at Holtby Hall and wore cargo trousers and a dark green fleece unzipped over a T-shirt. They shook hands – he held hers in a firm grip – and she noticed that his eyes were a light and piercing green.

'Aidan's come back to eat with us,' Ruth said. 'I hope you got my text?'

'No!' Anna hadn't looked at her mobile since arriving at Christina's house. 'Fine, though – there's plenty for four.' She began taking out her purchases, putting them ready by the hob.

Aidan fetched an extra glass from the cupboard and poured a glass of wine for Anna. So he knows his way around, Anna thought, and wondered if he spent nights here, before remembering that Ruth had told her she'd never slept with anyone but Martin.

'Aidan's the architect in charge of the project,' Ruth explained.

Anna was unwrapping the chicken, assembling spices. 'Is the house being restored, then, as well as the garden?'

'The house is eighteenth century and in quite good nick,' Aidan said, with a hint of a Newcastle accent, 'but there's a separate stable block that's being converted into a visitors' centre and restaurant—'

'– which Aidan's designed,' said Ruth, with evident pride.

'And Ruth's project, the walled garden, is making great progress. You should come and see for yourself some time,' Aidan told Anna.

'On a Sunday,' said Ruth. 'We're always there on Sunday.'

Just friends, were they? As they told her more about the work in progress, Anna noticed the way sentences passed back and forth between them, and frequent glances at each other. Lucky Ruth, she found herself thinking; clever Ruth, to have found herself this accomplished and, yes, attractive man. Was there a more girlish note than usual in Ruth's voice as she laughed?

It felt companionable in the kitchen, the three of them:

Anna browning the chicken in a pan and cutting up the pineapple, Aidan making salad dressing and Ruth setting places, Liam drifting in to ask when the food would be ready.

Anna was bringing the warm bread to the table when they all heard someone coming in at the front door. Ruth looked up, startled. Anna's first thought was that it must be Martin – did he still have his own key?

But it was Patrick who came into the kitchen, bleary and dishevelled in a loose coat, saggy jeans and a paint-marked sweatshirt. He looked at the gathering – uncomprehendingly at Anna and Aidan, then, 'Hi, Mum,' and ''Lo there, bruv,' to Liam.

'Pat!' Ruth went to greet him with a big hug, which he returned perfunctorily. 'Why didn't you say you were coming? I'd have met you at the station.'

'Wasn't sure what my plans were,' Patrick said. 'God, I'm tired. There were engineering works all over the place – diversions – buses – you name it. It's taken for ever.'

'Come and sit down, sweetheart. This is Aidan – you haven't met before, have you? And, er, Anna's staying for a bit. How long are you home for?'

'It's not happening after all. I've chucked it in.'

'Oh, but what about Rhiannon? You were so—'

'That's all finished as well. She's staying on in Edinburgh.'

Ruth brought another chair to the table and ushered Patrick into it, caught between concern for Patrick and the pleasure of having him home.

'You're here to stay!' Liam looked delighted.

Patrick shrugged. 'Yeah, till I decide what to do.'

'Oh . . .' Ruth's eyes flitted to Anna and back to Patrick. 'The thing is, Anna's in your room. If I'd known, we could have—'

Patrick hunched his shoulders. 'No sweat. I'll sleep on the sofa.'

'Glass of wine?' Aidan had fetched another glass and now proffered the bottle, but Patrick shook his head.

'I'll have a beer, thanks.'

Now what? Anna was all too aware that she could get on a train and be back with Martin in less than an hour. But logistical problems with rooms and beds couldn't be allowed to determine the course of her life. Briefly she wondered about B&Bs, hotels; but more immediately there was the meal to consider. She looked down at the four pieces of chicken now nicely browned and ready to eat; she'd have to cut them up and make five portions. But Ruth said, 'It's OK, Anna. Pat doesn't eat meat, he's vegan. I'll find something in the freezer.'

'Don't fuss, Mum. I got something while I was waiting at Birmingham. Eat yours first.'

'The thing is, sweetheart, Anna's not just here for tonight. She's been here a couple of weeks.'

'Why? Where's Dad?'

'Well . . .' Ruth looked sidelong at Anna, who 'Martin's at home. He's at the flat and I'm here.' She felt herself blushing.

'She and Dad have split up,' Liam said, as if stating the obvious.

'Is that right?' said Patrick, startled into looking properly at Anna for the first time.

'We're . . . spending some time apart, let's put it like that.'

207

'What,' Patrick said, with a knowing smile, 'is Dad having it off with someone else? So you two are teaming up? That's a new one.'

'Pat, please! Don't talk like that. Anyway – let's eat, and afterwards I'll sort something out for you if you're hungry – you must be, surely.' Ruth sat down again, and Anna served the meal. How crowded the kitchen felt now, the air spiked with unasked questions. As ever, Anna felt unsettled by Patrick: by his cool, dismissive gaze, and his look of a younger and more rumpled Martin, his eyes the same shape, the same hazel-brown. Whatever he thought of this set-up, and of his mother apparently having a new man, he revealed by no more than a sceptical raising of eyebrows. Always he made Anna feel wrong-footed, as if she should have known he'd turn up.

'Of course you must have your own room,' she told him. 'I can sleep on the sofa.'

'No worries. You can stay there. It's no difference to me,' Patrick said, unsmiling. He fetched a second beer from the fridge, flipped open the ring-pull and drank deeply.

Anna caught Ruth's eye. What now? Everything had changed in the last half-hour; she couldn't stay on here, that much was obvious. Even staying for one more night was making herself a nuisance. Meanwhile, the conversation was skirting around everything that was important. Aidan asked Patrick how he'd liked Edinburgh, which he apparently knew quite well; Ruth tried to find out what his plans were, but got only brush-off answers. When Ruth found vegetarian sausages in the freezer and cooked them with tomatoes and oven chips, Patrick ate ravenously; as soon as he'd cleared his plate he said that he had phone calls to make, and went up to Liam's room for privacy. His rucksack, a large shabby one studded all over with badges and with bed-roll attached, squatted in the front hall, reminding Anna that she was the squatter, that if she wasn't here Patrick could take over his own room, unpack his things and no doubt present Ruth with a quantity of dirty washing.

Anna made coffee, and Aidan left soon afterwards. Ruth went to the door with him, and came back into the kitchen a few minutes later, a little flushed.

'You're a dark horse, keeping him to yourself,' Anna teased Ruth, to avoid the trickier subject of Patrick.

'Aidan? But I'm not, and I haven't. We're good friends, that's all,' Ruth said, running water to wash the glasses. 'No, I don't mean *that's all*. We're good friends, and I want to keep it like that. Real friendships are so important.'

'I suppose.' Anna had never been much good at holding onto friends. 'They come and go.'

'No, Aidan won't go. He's a constant in my life.'

'Ruth, about Patrick,' Anna said uncomfortably. 'You must be pleased to have him back – but I'd better leave, hadn't I?'

'I don't know what to suggest,' Ruth said, after a pause. 'Only – Anna, why don't you go back to Martin? That's by far the best thing for everyone. I mean, it's great having you here, I'm not trying to push you away, but you need to sort things out. You know Martin wants to. And surely you do, too.'

'No. I can't go back.' Anna turned away, stacking plates in the dishwasher. 'It's too easy. It'd feel like giving in.'

'Giving in to what? I can't believe you seriously want

to end it.' Ruth's eyes met Anna's; Anna looked away.

'I can't stay with him just because it's convenient.'

'Is that all he is to you? Don't you love him?'

'I don't think I know what that means.'

'So you don't,' Ruth stated.

Anna searched for words, reasons. 'I don't know what people mean by it – love, luurve. People talk about it all the time, as if you either love someone or you don't. Like passing your driving test, or getting a certificate that no one can take away from you. But it's always changing – you've got to be with someone, or you can't stand the sight of them, or they make you laugh, or irritate the hell out of you – that's what it's really like.'

'All that, of course.'

'Maybe I don't love him as much as you do.' Anna surprised herself by coming out with it; Ruth too, who looked at her open-mouthed for a moment before turning away. I've offended her now, Anna thought; I've called her bluff.

'I can't make out what you want,' Ruth said, after a pause. 'And I don't think *you* really know.'

'Maybe I don't. It isn't that I want anyone else,' Anna said. 'I only want . . .'

'Mm?' Ruth waited, expectant.

The phrase *to find out who I am* had come into Anna's thoughts; she stopped before saying it aloud, and said tamely, 'Oh, nothing.' The truth was that she was being greedy, as well as impractical; she wanted the situation held in suspension for as long as she chose, with Martin ready to have her back or be discarded, at her whim. She wanted Ruth as well, wanted their friendship to grow; she wanted Ruth to say, 'Anna's a constant in my life,' the way she had spoken of Aidan. She wanted a real, lasting, grown-up friendship for once, even if it sprang from the unlikeliest of beginnings.

That night, in Patrick's bed for what she decided would be the last time, Anna couldn't sleep. Alternatives chased themselves through her head, pursued by *but, but, but*s. And something else slipped into her mind: the face of the physics teacher, Mr Sullivan, seen in profile as he stood, hands in pockets, looking intently at something. She fretted and fretted at this memory until it came back to her, teasingly, threatening to blur and fade if she looked too closely; but at last she placed it. Her last year at school, the sixth-form art exhibition. Some of the teachers, as well as students' parents and friends, had come to the celebration evening; she'd been surprised to see him there for no better reason than that he was a science teacher and she hadn't expected a scientist to be interested in art. He'd been studying her painting, *Shore*, and when he saw her standing quite close he'd made some vaguely complimentary remark about it, she couldn't remember what, and had seemed embarrassed to be caught examining it so closely. She wondered briefly if he'd make her an offer – teachers sometimes did buy student art – and, if so, whether she could part with it. But she hadn't spoken to him again; hadn't, in all probability, so much as thought of him between then and the conversation with Christina, not knowing of Rose's interest. Still his face refused to come into clear focus, and she couldn't make the two incidents – this, and the leavers' ball – add up to anything significant.

While she was puzzling about this, a different answer

came to her: so perfect a solution that she almost got out of bed to ask Ruth immediately. She would suggest moving into Rowan Lodge. For a while, at least, till Ruth was ready to sell.

'Is that really what you want?' said Ruth, surprised, in the morning. 'It's a bit out of the way, and you haven't got a car. You'd need to get to the tube station every morning.'

'I'll get taxis, or walk. Or buy myself a bike. I can finish the sorting, even do some painting for you, if you want. I like painting. And tidy up the garden.'

'It's not a bad idea. It might stop you from doing anything drastic. And I don't like the thought of the place being empty.'

'I'll pay rent,' Anna offered. 'I'll be your tenant. Do it properly.'

'No, you needn't. Especially if you're making a start on the decorating. You can be caretaker.'

Anna felt exhilarated by this new plan, thinking about it as she sat on the Underground train; it was in her mind all day at work. She saw herself chopping logs in the garden, and sitting by a fire's blaze with the curtains drawn.

'You'll be lonely,' Ruth had warned.

But loneliness was what Anna wanted. She would invite Ruth round for dinner, maybe with Aidan; she would cook wonderful meals, de-clutter the place, transform it with light plain colours and vases of budding twigs. She could play at having a home of her own. It was a ridiculously cosy vision, she knew, more *Ideal Home* magazine than real life, but irresistible nonetheless. And, she decided, she would paint – not only walls, but pictures. With space and time to herself, she would retrieve her brushes, buy new supplies. She felt herself stretching and expanding into this new vision of herself.

In a quiet moment at her desk she entered *Jim Greaves* and *James Greaves* into Google, but nothing on the list pointed to Mr Greaves the art teacher, who must have retired long ago and was perhaps of a generation not to use the internet. She tried *Michael Sullivan*. There were more than eight million references, the list beginning with an author, a lawyer, an attorney in Massachusetts, links to Facebook and Wikipedia. She tried again with *Michael Sullivan Science*, limiting the search to UK websites.

There it was, on the tenth of many pages, on the website of a school in Plymouth. *Head of Science: Michael Sullivan, B.Sc. M.Ed.*

❖ ❖ ❖

## July 1991

'I've booked us a holiday,' said Anna's father. 'A week in Norfolk.'

Anna saw from the tightening of muscles around his mouth that he expected opposition. He was just home from work; Mum was preparing dinner, and Anna, ravenous, was looking for something to eat without being told off for ruining her appetite. She stood by the open fridge, a wrapped slab of cheese in her hand.

There was a silence, as if he'd said something blasphemous. Anna glanced at her mother. Holidays were Rose: didn't he know that? How could they even think of going away without Rose?

'What do you mean, a holiday?' she asked.

Her mother only stared, frozen in mid-movement, saucepan lid in her hand, releasing a steamy potatoey waft into the already hot kitchen.

'A cottage, a nice little cottage in Norfolk.' Dad produced a brochure from his briefcase and leafed through the pages. 'Here, see? Blakeney, the Crow's Nest.' He held it out towards Mum, then, in the face of her obvious hostility, showed Anna instead. 'This one here. Won't it suit us down to the ground? It's perfect.'

'Don't stand with the fridge door open, Anna,' said Mum, in a tight, strangulated voice.

Surreptitiously nibbling at a piece of cheese she'd broken off the wedge, Anna bent to look. The brochure page showed a selection of holiday cottages, each with a brief description. The Crow's Nest was sandwiched between two others in a terrace, with a blue front door that opened in two halves like a stable; there were checked curtains at the windows, and a jug of wild flowers on the windowsill. She thought of the carefree people who might stay in such a place, a family trailing in with sand on their shoes, and pieces of seaweed to hang from the window-hooks. There'd be a dog that surged indoors with them, beating its tail against their legs. A happy, whole family.

'You needn't think I'm going anywhere,' said her mother, draining the potatoes with much clattering of lid against saucepan.

'But I've paid the deposit. We don't want to lose that.'

'You can go, you and Anna. I'm not budging from here.'

Anna saw her father's compressed lips, her mother's eloquently turned back. She hated it when they were like this.

'Where is it, where's Blakeney?' she asked, to break the deadlock.

'North Norfolk. Blakeney, right up near Cromer.' Her father was turning the pages, finding a map. 'See? It's not that far to go but it'll give us a proper break. We could all do with one.'

Mum said nothing, but lined up the three plates and slapped a slice of pork pie on each. 'Help yourselves to salad and potatoes,' she said tightly. 'Oh, I forgot the mayonnaise.'

'You can go out on boat trips from Blakeney Quay,' Dad continued, as if nothing was wrong; he took off his jacket and hung it on the back of his chair before sitting down. 'Sometimes there are seals on Blakeney Point. And there's the bird reserve at Cley Marshes. Lovely, that bit of coast. I went on holiday there as a boy.'

Anna piled potatoes and salad on her plate and started eating; her father cut up his slice of pie, but Mum sat opposite him, not even picking up her knife and fork.

'Will there be television?' Anna asked.

'Yes, look.' Her father pointed to the row of symbols underneath the photograph. 'But there'll be better things to do than watch the box. We'll take binoculars and—'

Anna saw that her mother was weeping silently, tears running down her face, her shoulders shaking with suppressed sobs.

'Oh, now, love!' Dad reached across the table to take her wrist, but she jerked away. 'This was meant to be a nice surprise.'

'I'm not going.' Mum jolted the words out between juddering breaths. She got up to snatch a tissue from the box on the windowsill, and stayed standing. 'What if – what if she comes back, and no one's here? What if there's news?'

'We won't be far away. It's not like leaving the country. Three or four hours and we can be back home if need be.'

'No. No.'

'We've got to do things,' Dad said gently, and he pushed his plate away. 'Got to at least try.'

Anna saw how red and puffy her mother's eyes were; she gave way to a storm of weeping, as if the tears had been stored inside her, waiting for release. 'I – I – can't.' The words croaked out of her. 'I won't. I can't go on holidays without her and have Christmas without her and birthdays without her – I can't stand it! I won't.'

'But, love.' Dad got up and took her elbow and put his other arm round her, guiding her back to the table. 'What choice do we have? We can't do nothing for the rest of our lives. We've got to get on with things. Annie needs a holiday, don't you, love?'

'Yes,' said Anna, thinking of the pretty cottage, and wondering whether some of the happy familyness might spread itself to everyone who stayed. She hated it when her mother cried. It meant that her parents weren't able to put things right, not for her, not for themselves. She'd taken only one mouthful of pork pie and her stomach craved more, but how could she go on eating, with the kitchen suddenly full of raw grief?

Rose, always Rose, she thought savagely. What about me? Don't I count for anything? Sometimes she hated Rose for doing this to them. Like an evil fairy she had them under her spell, a curse that said, *You'll never enjoy anything again. If you ever catch yourself laughing, you'll think of me and feel guilty. Always. For ever and ever. You'll never be free of me.*

*　*　*

They went to Blakeney. It was Anna and Dad siding against Mum, so they won. Anna was used to these sidings and alliances, shifting according to need. In the past there had been more flexibility: Anna and Rose against both parents, or Rose with Mum, or Rose with Dad. Always Rose had been on the winning side, instinctively knowing who to choose as her ally.

This time, it wasn't much of a contest. Mum had no fight left in her; she only cried. The victory felt hollow; there could be no sense of triumph, with such an inadequate opponent. Her father's trump card was to arrange for Granny Skipton to come and stay at home while they went to Norfolk; Gran, on her own now, liked to help whenever she could. Dad would phone twice daily from the Blakeney Hotel, and they could set off for home at any moment, if something – the unspecified *something* that always hung over them – should happen.

Holiday, they called it, but it felt more like a test they'd set for themselves. They had to endure the week away to prove that they could do something called a holiday and make at least a pretence of finding enjoyment in it. Anna thought of previous holidays – to Sussex, to Devon or Cornwall, once to North Wales. It seemed now that Rose was the only person who counted, her mood determining whether the others were happy, or purposeful, or bored. It was Rose who devised complicated beach games, the diverting of streams or the creation of artworks from shells and stones. Rose took charge of Anna, who always did what Rose wanted. Rose had never been to Blakeney, but she was a phantom fourth presence, emphasizing the charade.

Mum behaved like someone convalescing from a long illness, taking her first shaky steps in the open. Dad stowed everything in the car and led her out to the passenger seat. She spoke in a small, wavering voice that made her seem very young or very old. In the back seat, plugged into her Walkman, Anna read a magazine and wished she'd stayed at home with Gran. A boring village in Norfolk – it wasn't a proper holiday. Mel was in Majorca, with her parents and Jamie, and had stirred up Anna's envy by talking about the sea-front, the heat, and the boys she was sure to meet. When she returned she'd be tanned, glossy and smug. What could Anna bring back, to compete?

But she found, in spite of herself, that she loved Blakeney. She liked the pretty cottage, on the steep street that led up from the harbour; she liked her room, with its creaking wooden floor and blue gingham curtains; liked waking up there, with sunshine streaming in, and the big sky beyond the cluster of roof-tiles and chimneys. People said that the sky was bigger in Norfolk, which she thought must be nonsense: how could it be? But so it appeared, arcing overhead in a great bowl of cloud-flecked blue that swept away towards the promise of beach and waves. The air carried an enticing tang of sea, a faint saltiness she could taste on her lips. A strange, bubbling cry lifted over the marsh: a curlew, her dad said. Sometimes the sky was dappled with cloud that might have been dabbed there with a giant white-tipped paintbrush. Dad called it mackerel sky, and Anna imagined an artist at work, making a scene of countless pale fish that shoaled towards the eastern horizon.

Rose had never been here, and that meant Anna could claim it for her own.

They went for walks, they ate crab salad lunches and fish-and-chip suppers, they went on a boat trip but saw no seals; Anna did some sketching. Her mother wore at first a mulish expression, making it clear that she was here under sufferance. Morning and evening she walked to the Blakeney Hotel to phone home. Anna pretended not to notice. At first time passed slowly, with no one of her own age to be with. The next cottage was occupied by a family with two younger children, a little boy, and a spindly girl of about eleven, who looked at Anna in awe. One evening the parents invited hers to drink wine in the little cobbled garden that fronted the row of cottages. They tried hard, these neighbours, but Anna's mother was tight-lipped and aloof, saying almost nothing for fear of saying too much.

'Is Anna an only child?' Anna heard the mother asking, and at once her own mother said 'Yes,' rapping the word out, forestalling further questions. Anna darted a look at her, and almost said, 'That's not true.' But it *was* true, literally, and maybe now it was true in every way.

Anna was discovering her own muleishness. Her mother's attitude of mute suffering made her impatient. Anna decided that she would do as she liked, go off with Dad or on her own; if Mum chose to stay indoors and drape herself in misery, that was up to her.

Bird-watching saved them, Anna and her father. Out on the shingle beach, or on the Cley Marshes bird reserve, where they paid to go in for the day and sit in the wooden hides full of knowledgeable people kitted out with binoculars and telescopes, she and Dad built up a list of the birds they'd seen. Oystercatchers and lapwings, Sandwich terns and greylag geese, black-tailed godwits and green sandpipers. Anna forgot that she'd rather be in Majorca with Mel, giggling over dark-eyed Spanish boys. This was absorbing; this was a world of its own. She settled into the way of it. You'd find your place, seated on a wooden bench in the hushed darkness of the hide; then you'd let down the flap in front of you – carefully, not letting it clank – and gaze out at the expanse of water and reeds in front of you. At first you might think the pool was unpopulated, except by a group of ducks dozing with heads under wings or feeding desultorily. Rewarded for patience, your eyes would pick out movement in the sedges, or a white shape would move out into view, or there'd be the thrilling flight of a small flock of waders, arrowing and swooping, wing-patterns glancing and flickering as they changed direction, then landed as lightly as windblown leaves, and became identifiable as dunlins. Anna saw them on the seashore too, small busy birds that raced along the water's edge and darted into the waves.

She pored over her father's bird book, amazed that the birds and wildfowl that dropped out of the sky or blew in from nowhere should match so precisely the illustrations in the guide. These wild creatures were part of a pattern that was known and recorded. Other people had sat and watched, compared and noted, and now here were the birds, feeding, flocking, roosting. They looked and behaved exactly as the book said they would.

❖ ❖ ❖

On her way to Waitrose, Cassandra sees Rosanna in the street.

She stops dead; someone behind tuts and swerves, looking sharply at her for an apology she doesn't make. Her attention is on the young woman ahead, walking slowly along the row of shops, talking into a mobile phone. Only her back view is visible, but it *is* her, Rosanna – the turn of the head as she talks, the hair, the set of her shoulders. Even the way she places her feet.

Now Cassandra is hurrying in pursuit, shoulder bag slapping her side, shoes clopping on the pavement. The young woman talks on, oblivious, until Cassandra's hand on her arm makes her turn sharply.

And at once it's all wrong, she is someone different. Too old, or too young – Cassandra's mind crashes into disappointment and confusion – with the wrong features entirely, and glasses, and too much make-up. Expectation in her glance turns to puzzlement and then annoyance.

'Oh . . . sorry. I thought you were my – my – daughter.' Cassandra feels herself turning hot, or pale; she's not sure that her words have come out in the right order.

'OK.' The girl shrugs her off, sidesteps, and walks on, laughing as she continues her phone conversation. She doesn't care; why should she?

Cassandra finds it hard to breathe. She steps into the florist's doorway to recover. Of course she knew Rosanna wasn't here; what was she thinking? Everything is blurring, swimming. The sense of dread holds her rigid; if she tries to move, she'll fall down and not know how to get up again.

The shop door behind her has opened, releasing a waft of warm air heavy with the perfume of lilies: sweet, cloying. It fills her senses. She closes her eyes and is in the churchyard, numb with cold and disbelief. White hothouse lilies, so wrong in the chilled air; the ground gashed open to receive him. Everything wrong, everything out of joint. Then, and always.

*I didn't mean to, I didn't mean—*

'Are you all right, my love?'

A face floats in front of her. She wills herself to stand steady, to answer. 'I'm perfectly all right, thank you.'

'You don't look all right, sweetheart.'

It's another young woman of Zanna's age. Outrage makes Cassandra pull herself erect. Has it come to this, women of her daughter's age calling her *my love* and *sweetheart*, as if she's senile? But the woman's face is so full of genuine concern that she finds herself on the verge of tears.

'It's just that I keep losing them,' she blurts. 'They come back and then I lose them again.'

'Lose what? Look, why don't you come in and sit down for a minute or two?'

Cassandra shakes her head; she fumbles in her shoulder bag for a tissue and her fingers meet the smooth leather of her purse, which she pulls out in triumph.

'No, I'm fine, see – here it is after all.' She holds it up. 'Thank you. I'm perfectly all right now.'

Unsteadily she walks away. Knowing that the kind woman is still watching from the doorway, she raises a hand in jaunty farewell. A tear courses down her cheek, and she swipes it away. Such a mess, such an utter mess she has made of her life. Roland was only the first. He set the pattern, or she did, and there's no getting away from it.

This is her punishment. She must wander and wonder, searching strangers' faces in the street, catching her breath at the lift of a chin, a hunch of shoulder, a way of standing. Always hoping, always crushed with disappointment.

❖ ❖ ❖

# 15

## Sandy, 1967, 1966

It felt incongruous for spring to come as usual, for the days to lengthen and green shoots to push out of the earth, as if nothing had happened. Sandy felt like a stowaway, with no right and no choice but to be carried along with the vast indifference of the world's turning. No way of getting off, unless she followed Roland, and she wasn't brave enough for that.

The ringing of the telephone had ceased long ago to be of any personal interest, but one wet evening in March she heard her mother answer downstairs, then call her name.

Unbelievably, it was Phil.

'Need to meet you,' said his voice, husky, almost whispering.

'Why?'

'Just say yes.'

'What for?' She was jolted out of her torpor.

'Can't talk now. Meet me Saturday?'

'Yes – yes. Where?'

'At the station. Early, say eight. Can you make it the whole day?'

What could he have in mind? The possibilities turned and tangled in her mind. Surely, surely, it could only be something to lift the guilt from her. Part of it, at least. He had been as close to Roland as she was, or closer; he knew things she didn't. Where had the LSD come from? That hadn't been ascertained, from Phil or from anyone else. Seeing him in the churchyard, pale and motionless by the graveside after everyone else had moved on, the thought rippled through her: *He loved Roland.* Surely Roland had been wrong. She might have spoken to Phil, or gone and stood mutely beside him, but her father had taken her arm and led her away towards the line of cars waiting beyond the lych-gate. Afterwards there was a funeral tea at a nearby hotel; Roland's headmaster, two teachers and a few of the boys had been there, but Phil must have slipped away.

She set out to meet him on Saturday without telling anyone. If the death of Roland hadn't been the sole reason for the outing, she'd have thought it an impossible fantasy, setting off for a whole day with the boy she had doted on. The day when Roland had left home was too recent for her to inflict such anguish on her parents again, so she invented an alibi: a shopping trip with Delia, and tea at her house afterwards. Sandy's mother was pitifully pleased that she was starting to go out again.

At East Croydon station, Phil asked at the ticket office for two returns to Portsmouth. Sandy realized what she could have worked out earlier: that they were setting off on a kind of pilgrimage, following Roland.

'We're going to the Isle of Wight?'

He nodded, handing pound notes through the ticket-office window. She rummaged in her shoulder bag for her purse; she had two half-crowns and a few pence.

'I haven't got enough,' she told him. 'I can't pay you back.'

'Don't expect you to.' Phil pocketed the tickets and his change. 'It was my idea.'

'We used to go on holiday there when we were little. We stayed at Shanklin.'

'I know,' said Phil. 'Rolls told me.'

What else did he know? What other memories had Roland shared with him? Everything, now, every casual remark Roland might have made, was loaded with significance, as if he'd left a trail to be followed.

Announcements crackled over loudspeakers; they both listened. 'That's ours,' Phil said. 'We change at Clapham Junction.'

The first train was full of people in weekend mood – families, pairs of women, other teenagers. She knew that she and Phil must look like boyfriend and girlfriend, but they hardly spoke; it didn't seem right to chatter, and she couldn't ask him anything important. In adjoining seats, they didn't have to look at each other. Soon Phil took *New Musical Express* from his canvas shoulder bag, and studied it closely until their stop. Wishing she'd brought a book, Sandy made do with a copy of the *Daily Mail* someone had discarded.

The next train, from Clapham to Portsmouth Harbour, was less crowded, and now she could only think about Roland making this same journey. The return ticket in his rucksack – along with his toothbrush, spare T-shirt, razor and notebook, and a paperback copy of *On the Road*, apparently just bought – gave ample indication that he hadn't

226

planned to kill himself. Maybe he'd have phoned, later that evening. *I needed to get away. Had to be by myself for a day or two.* Had he changed his mind? Deliberately let the sea take him?

At Portsmouth it was hard not feel a little adventurous, following signs for the Isle of Wight ferry, then boarding the boat. There were only a few passengers. Sandy and Phil sat by a salt-stained window, watching as the ferry pulled out past wharves and cranes, car parks and building sites, a Victorian pub, and on into the greyness of sea and sky. Then it felt more symbolic to brave the cold wind out on deck than to shelter inside. Sandy wound her scarf twice round her neck and thrust her hands deep into her pockets; strands of hair lashed her cheeks. A hovercraft sped ahead, low on the water, throwing up spray like a snowplough. The island already filled the horizon, long, low and hazy, and as Ryde came more clearly into view she saw buildings stacked up a low hill surmounted by a church spire. She remembered the years-ago family holiday, the special feeling of being on an island, where the daily business of life couldn't reach. She thought of Roland standing here, perhaps remembering too.

Wouldn't he have jumped over the side if he'd wanted to drown himself? Quicker than walking into the sea, more decisive. What would it feel like, to care so little for your own body that you could abandon it to be swirled by currents, bloated with sea-water, battered by waves? When did your body cease to be *you*?

'Do you think he's still *somewhere*?' she asked Phil. 'Or just – gone?'

Phil considered it, standing very still, hair blowing across

227

his face; then he shrugged. 'I don't believe in an afterlife or any of that shit. So – I guess he's just gone. Finish.'

She wanted to ask more, to find out if the one thing she hoped for was true – that in spite of what happened at Elaine's he did love Roland, and that Roland had died happy, knowing that. But of course not, because if that were true, Roland wouldn't have set out by himself. Wouldn't have given himself to the sea.

They looked out at the Solent, at a big cross-Channel ferry and a large tanker in the distance; then Sandy asked, 'Are we going to the actual place? How will we find it?'

Phil turned his back to the wind, huddled into his inadequate coat, arms tightly folded. 'I know where. Went with Rolls.'

She looked at him in surprise. 'Not . . . ?'

'Not *that* time, no. Christ – wish I had. Last summer. While you and your parents were on holiday. The weather was hot and Rolls said why not take off, the two of us, go to the sea. I thought Brighton, but he said no, let's get a ticket to ride, like the song. I said, ride where? and he said *Ryde* – he felt like going to an island, leaving the mainland. So we did. This, exactly – same train, same ferry. Over there we bought fish and chips, then hitched lifts. Didn't know where, but we ended up at Freshwater Bay. Then walked along the downs.'

Sandy was silent, sensing more; after a pause Phil continued, 'We didn't talk much. Rolls had gone quiet, the way he did when he was working out a song. I knew he'd show me when he was ready.'

'And did he?'

'Yes. Only not then. He didn't finish it till weeks later.

That was when it all started to go—' There was a catch in Phil's voice; he took a moment to recover himself. 'Anyway. That day. We sat on the grass and shared a joint. Then we went down to the beach, this long stretch of beach. We could see the white cliffs that lead round to the Needles.'

'Roly didn't say anything,' Sandy said. 'Not to Mum and Dad, not to me either. When we got back from Devon he said he'd been hanging around at home.'

'Well, he was like that. Kept things to himself.'

Sandy gazed at a screaming gull that seemed balanced on the wind, its wings outstretched. Roland and secrets – the gull's cry was an accusation, memory a blunt kick of pain, familiar to her now.

Ahead, Ryde was coming into focus, with individual buildings discernible, and people waiting on the pier, braced against the wind.

'So why come back?' Sandy asked.

'Dunno really. Thought of it and just had to. That funeral bollocks – I hated it. So stiff and dry.'

'Me too. It felt all wrong. Nothing to do with him.'

Phil turned away from her to lean on the railing. 'So – this, instead. For Rolls.'

❖ ❖ ❖

With less than an hour until midnight there was no sign of the Merlins, and in Elaine's view Sandy was responsible for ruining her party. The music was loud, the room packed, the air thick with smoke; what had started out as fruit punch had been generously boosted with spirits from Elaine's parents' cocktail cabinet. Various boys were present, but none of them counted for much, as far as Elaine was concerned. To show that she didn't care, she was flirting vigorously with a boy Sandy had never seen before. She was wearing a new dress, very short, in cream crochet, her enviable legs clad in turquoise tights; her hair shone conker-coloured in the glow of shaded light-bulbs.

Pretending, pretending, that's what parties were about. You had to act as if you went to them all the time; if this one was a disappointment it would be someone else's fault, never yours. While desperately hoping the right boy would notice you, you'd try to convey that you could select anyone you fancied. It was imperative to convey that none of this mattered, that you could be somewhere else if you chose, that your presence would bestow cool wherever you went. Always you were waiting for something, without being sure what; you only knew that it wasn't happening yet, but might arrive from elsewhere.

Things became hazy. People overflowed into the garden, though it was bitterly cold outside; the sweet smell of pot mingled with cigarette smoke. Then Phil and Roland were here after all, with Dempsey. Someone changed the record to a Kinks album, and the mood was instantly more excitable; Dempsey began strutting and posing, clearing a space around him. Roland, in black shirt, shades and a trilby hat, made for a group drinking in the kitchen, but Elaine headed him off, grabbed his hand and pulled him into the front room and the dancing. Roland wasn't extrovert like Dempsey, but still a good mover; he danced in an ironic, self-mocking way, face deadpan. Sandy found herself partnered with a lanky shy boy, someone's brother, but it was too hot and crowded now, smoke stinging her eyes. She escaped outside, looking for Phil, hoping for maybe a few words from him, an acknowledgement.

When the cold drove her back indoors, she saw that Elaine's second string had been demoted to DJ, and with Roland firmly in her grasp Elaine requested something slower. At first Roland played along as she snaked her arms around him and pressed her hips against his, her hand moving down his spine. Then, abruptly, he pushed her aside with a vigour that sent her stumbling into the arms of a surprised Dempsey. 'Woo-*ooo*-ooh,' someone hooted, as Roland elbowed his way out of the room. Elaine recovered enough to smooch with Dempsey instead, in a jokey way, but five minutes later she was in tears in the kitchen, cutting between Sandy and the shy boy who were moving towards a first fumbling kiss.

'Did you see?' Elaine raged, grabbing Sandy's arm. 'Did you see what your brother did?'

The boy backed off, easily deflected. Sandy and Elaine retreated to the top stair, Sandy consoling, Elaine sobbing angrily, her mascara running in sooty streaks. 'Shoved me away like I was a piece of dirt! – oh, why did I want him to come? The whole party's ruined now. I don't even want to *be* here.'

'Shh, shh. Forget about it. There are lots of other boys.'

'Gah! You *know* Roland's the only one I care about! He acted like I'm hideous or something – disgusting . . .'

Her distress, childlike and oddly endearing, made Sandy want to offer her something.

She whispered, 'There's nothing wrong with you, Laine, really there isn't. It's him.'

'How d'you mean?' Elaine snivelled.

'It's not girls, with Roly. He's – you know—'

At once Elaine stopped sobbing and looked at her wide-eyed. 'Are you kidding me? Christ, you're not, are you? Your brother's a poof? My God!'

'You mustn't tell anyone.' Sandy was alarmed by Elaine's quick understanding, her abrupt change of mood. 'Look, wait – it's a secret, right? I only told you because—'

She grabbed Elaine's arm; Elaine flung her off, lurched to her feet and hurried downstairs, regardless of her spoiled make-up and smudgy eyes. Sandy scurried behind as she headed out to the garden, pushing past a couple who sat entwined on the doorstep. Phil and Roland stood smoking by the fence.

'Hey, you two! So!'

'Laine, wait—'

'This is a surprise,' Elaine went on, loudly enough to turn heads. 'Not really fair to us girls, though, is it? Oh, sorry – am I interrupting something? It's darker down the far end if you want privacy. Only mind the faggots by the shed.'

Roland's eyes flicked to Sandy; she looked down.

'What're you on about?' Phil said easily, tapping his cigarette; glowing ash dropped to the lawn.

'Come back in, Laine,' said Sandy, pulling at her. 'You've had too much to drink.'

'Correction. I haven't had enough.' Elaine was swaying as she turned on Roland. 'Bit sneaky, isn't it, all those songs about girls? But, no, I get it. Your fans wouldn't be so keen if they knew you were going at it with each other.'

Phil laughed. 'What's this all about? What's put this into your head?'

'It's obvious, now,' Elaine said, her voice harsh. 'Can't think why it took me so long.'

'You're talking rubbish, little girl. Have your tantrum – I'm heading off. This is just a kids' party.' Phil dropped his cigarette and ground it with his heel, then strode towards the side gate, not looking back. Roland stood in indecision, watching him go.

'Lovers' tiff?' mocked Elaine.

'Roly, I didn't mean . . .' Sandy faltered.

Briefly his gaze met hers.

'Don't worry, you'll soon make up,' Elaine told him. 'I expect you know how.'

In answer Roland grabbed hold of her shoulders with both hands, and pushed his face against hers in a rough semblance of a kiss; as she squealed and resisted, he held her hard against him. 'Is that what you wanted?' he said, snarling the words into her face; then he almost dropped her, turned and walked away fast. Moments later raised voices could be heard from the street.

'He's mad, your brother – barking mad.' Elaine bent forward, clutching her stomach. 'I feel sick—'

'Get a drink, everyone – it's nearly midnight!' someone yelled from the kitchen, and moments later cheers and yells almost drowned out the sound of Elaine retching into the shrubbery.

Standing by, Sandy could think of no way of unsaying what she'd said, of putting right the damage she'd done with those few disastrous words.

❖ ❖ ❖

Phil's insistence on doing things in order meant buying fish and chips at a café in Ryde, eaten in reverent near-silence. Then they hitched a lift in a van as far as Yarmouth, where a wide creek bristled with masts; they walked from there, thumbing, until a farmer towing a trailer stopped and took them on to Freshwater Bay. Sandy's parents had impressed on her the dangers of hitch-hiking and she'd only done it once, with Elaine, but Phil took for granted that it was the only way of getting about. She was safe enough with him; it wasn't like hitching alone.

Freshwater Bay was a small settlement: a couple of hotels, a lifeboat station and a few houses in a dip between hills. To the west, downland rose high, dropping in sheer chalk cliffs to the sea. Phil and Sandy walked in the other direction, along a path close to the edge of lower, sandy cliffs. The wind gusted into their faces. Below them, waves rolled greyly in, breaking into foam on the long stretch of sand. Not much used to walking, Sandy had to scurry to keep up with Phil, who strode head down, not looking back. Irritation rose in her. Why couldn't he have *told* her they'd be doing this, so that she could have worn boots, instead of light slip-on shoes that rubbed her heels and were already clagged up with sheep turds? This whole thing was pointless anyway; Roland was in the churchyard at home, and the unfamiliar surroundings seemed only to emphasize that she wouldn't find him here, or anywhere. Nevertheless a kind of exhilaration grew in her as she looked down at the beach, the wind snatching at her hair and thrumming in her ears. The light dazzled, and the salt-laced air charged her with energy, making her feel she could shrug off tiredness and run and run.

Now Phil waited for her to catch up. Finding a sheltered dip, he slid down to sit on the grass; she dropped her bag and squatted next to him. A footpath led down to the beach, with a handrail for the steeper sections, and steps of bleached wood. A notice warned that swimmers should take care of strong undercurrents.

Phil reached into his canvas bag and took out a roll of plastic with soft brown stuff in it, a packet of cigarette papers and a lighter. 'A spliff, first. Same as before.'

He tapped and rolled, and sealed the paper, seemingly expert. Sandy hid her surprise; maybe he thought she did this all the time? When Phil had taken a couple of drags, he passed her the joint, the tip compressed, slightly moistened by his lips. Briefly she relished the intimacy of sharing. He'd done the same thing with Roland, and she knew he would prefer Roland to be here now.

'Cassandra's a great name,' he said. 'Better than Sandy. She told the future, didn't she? About the Trojan War. Only no one listened.'

Sandy tried not to cough as she inhaled, feeling the sweet hot rush into her lungs, anticipating the light-headedness that would surely follow. 'So what did you do next? When you came here with Roly?'

'We swam.' Phil grinned at her, taking back the joint. 'We ran in with our jeans on. People looked at us like we were mad, but it was hot enough to dry off in the sun. We came back up here and had another spliff. Then hitched back to a pub and had a few drinks till it was time for the boat back.'

'But that can't be all!'

'It's not all.' He looked down; Sandy saw the tremble of

his lips. 'It's my fault. My fault he's dead.'

'How can it be? It's *mine*.'

Phil nodded. 'Yeah. That too. We messed things up, between us. Messed *him* up.'

'At the party?'

'And before.'

'You mean he told you?' Sandy guessed.

'Told me—?' Phil looked sidelong at her, then understood, shaking his head quickly. 'No. No. But he gave me the song. The one he started when we were here. It was the night before the party. We'd been practising with the others, in our garage. Brian was going through stuff, ready for our next gig. After, the others left, and Brian was out in the van, and Rolls gave me a bit of paper. "Finished it last night," he said. "Don't read it now," he said, "read it later." And he went off home.'

'And?'

'I read it.'

'You didn't like it?'

Phil shook his head slowly. 'I sure as hell wasn't going to sing it. Even if no one else knew. Most of his songs, any of the romantic or sexy ones, anyway, were about girls. At least, I thought so. This was different. It was about . . . *us*, that day. Only there was no *us*, as far as I was concerned. We were good mates. We had a great day here, but not like he thought. I'm not – you know.'

'So what did you do? What did you say?'

'Nothing. Hadn't thought what to say. I hoped he'd know, and just drop it. But—' He swallowed with an effort, spoke again. 'Then the party, and Elaine barging in.'

'So that wasn't news to you, what she said? About

Roland?'

Phil gave a sort of wincing huff. 'No. No. If it was only the song, and me saying forget it – well, that's not like *everyone* knowing. I mean, thinking they did. Joking. Saying things.'

'And – was that the last time you saw him? When you were shouting at each other outside Elaine's?'

'Yeah, I – told him we were all finished. The Merlins, everything – I didn't want any more to do with it. With him. Told him I'd torn up his stupid song, and all his songs were rubbish anyway. Then I went off to another party and got smashed. Day or two later I thought maybe it wasn't such a big deal, we could forget it – I hadn't said anything to the guys. So I phoned, and your mum answered. She went to get him, then came back and said he was out. She's a hopeless liar, your mum. Rolls was blanking me. I'm not surprised, the things I called him.'

'Oh – Phil.'

He gave a hopeless shrug. 'Thought about coming round to see him, but – well, I didn't. Then it was too late.'

She said, 'And *did* you tear up the song?'

'No.' He placed a hand on his canvas bag. 'It's in here. At least I've got that. It was the last thing he wrote, or I suppose it was.'

*If only, if only.* If she hadn't said, if Phil hadn't, if Elaine hadn't – Roland would be alive. If, if, if. She would never escape from *if only.*

Sandy got up and walked towards the path, and the flight of steps down to the beach below. She stood on the top step with a sense of nearing the end of Roland's journey, the end of his life. What had been in his mind as he walked down to the sea's edge? Had he known what he was going to do? Or had he just come here to think, to get away from Phil, from her, from everyone?

With a sense of inevitability she began to walk slowly down to the beach. A young couple, well wrapped up, called a cheerful greeting as they passed, the man throwing a ball for a black Labrador that leaped joyfully into the water. The tide was half in, or half out; Sandy couldn't tell which. She walked out to the tideline, feeling the gritty crunch under the soles of her shoes. The wind came off the sea, March-chilled; goose-flesh prickled her arms. It must have been far colder for Roland, in January. She pictured him standing here, alone, lost, unreachable; then she felt a shivering at the back of her neck as Phil came to stand close.

'The LSD.' She turned to him. 'Where did he get that? Had he taken it before? Do you think he knew what he was doing – I mean, did he want to drown, or, you know, just let his mind go and float, like John Lennon said?'

Phil puffed out his breath. 'Wish I knew. Bit of a pothead, old Rolls, but I never knew him take acid. It was something we all talked about, like we knew. But I don't think any of us had done it. Maybe he got it from someone at the party. Don't know about you, but I'd rather think it was an accident while he was on an acid trip. And I hope it was a good one.'

Sandy was silent, watching the waves, letting herself be mesmerized by their rhythm: the wash and lull, the hiss as they sucked back, pulling rivulets of grit in the undertow. You could be pulled in, let your eyes go swimmy and the sound wash into your ears, so that the waves infiltrated your mind. You'd think they were calling you, that you could drift away and dissolve, become part of the whole timeless rise and fall of the tides, pulled by the moon. Even without acid or alcohol you could start to think that.

She hoped the moon had shone, that the stars had dazzled and danced on the water, that his last moments had been wondrous. She hoped it had not been like dying. But the cold, the icy grip of sea-water in January – that would have been enough to kill him, and however you died you had no choice but to go there on your own. The thought of wading into the grey, heaving mass was enough to make her shiver and huddle more closely into her coat.

'So. This is it,' Phil said. 'We ought to do something, say something. To make up for that crap funeral.'

'His song. You've got it there. Sing it. Sing it for him. It's what he wanted.'

Phil looked at her in dismay. 'I can't!'

'You can. Isn't that why you've brought it?'

Slowly, his lips pressed together, Phil reached into the side pocket of his bag and brought out a folded sheet of paper. He studied it, not letting Sandy see.

'I can't. Couldn't,' Phil said, with a crack in his voice. 'It's too . . . and there's no tune.'

'But it's his last – please, Phil, could I at least see? It's his – his handwriting. It'll be like he's here.'

Phil was biting his lip. He refolded the paper, stood silent for a moment, then pushed it into her hand and turned away.

Roland had written in fountain pen, broad-nibbed, with the black ink he always favoured. Long downstrokes with swooping tails gave character and determination to his words. Sandy knew his writing so well that it was like hearing him speak. Words, chords pencilled in at the sides. *Only a Day*, she read:

*The earth turned on its axis/*
*Creating night and day/*
*And clocks ticked through the hours/*
*In the usual way/*
*But something changed for ever/*
*On that incredible day/*

*CODA: Only a day/*
*Only a day/ (overlapping)*
*Only a day/*
*Yes it was only a day/*

*We travelled to the island/*
*Then we came down to the bay/*
*And the words were lost inside me/*
*The things I never could say/*
*Too big a risk to tell you/*
*You might have laughed it away/*
*You'd think I was only teasing/*
*That it's some new game to play/*
*I'd better stop pretending/*
*That you could want me that way/*
*And I knew I'd never have my fill/*
*On this or any other day/*

*CODA: Only a day, etc . . . Do you remember that day (Riff)*

*Then a feeling passed between us /*
*That words could never convey /*
*And I know I wasn't dreaming /*
*No need to shrug it away /*
*In my mind you're standing with me /*
*Looking down at the bay /*
*And I'll keep us there for ever /*
*The way I wish we could stay /*

*CODA: Only a day / Only a day / Only a day . . . (repeat to fade)*

Sandy gazed and gazed at the words, thinking of Roland writing them alone in his room. From what Phil had said, he must have finished it the night they'd talked – the vodka night, as she thought of it. He'd gone upstairs and finished his poem, while she slept in the next room. Maybe because of the conversation they'd had. It was his last song. A song full of joy and love that had led to his death.

'Roly,' she whispered, and looked at the poem for one last time before refolding the paper. She went after Phil, who was walking slowly along the tide's edge, head down.

'Thank you,' she said softly. 'It's beautiful. Keep it.'

Phil held the page in his hand for a few moments, looking at it, before putting it carefully back into his shoulder bag. Sandy stooped to pick up a pebble, choosing a flinty one; she weighed it in her hand, feeling its smoothness and its one sharp edge, then threw it into the sea, as far and as hard as she could. Phil did the same. He didn't look at her, but she saw his eyes shiny with tears.

She touched his sleeve; then his arm went round her and they stood together without speaking. At first she thought only of the comfort of another body warm against hers, sheltering her from the wind; her face was against his jacket, his arms held her, and here was the one person who knew exactly the blend of pain and guilt, anger and bewilderment that held her and wouldn't let go. It was too cold to linger; they retreated up the beach, still linked, to a notch in the sandy cliff that offered shelter. There they huddled together, embracing like survivors. Their first kiss tasted of salt, his tears and her own; then hands reached and grasped and slid inside clothing, and her breath quickened with his. Her head swam with the certainty that Roland was here too; that they were doing this for him.

❖ ❖ ❖

# 16

Ruth thought that the weekend would be soon enough for Anna to move to Rowan Lodge, but Anna insisted on going the next evening. Ruth drove her there, taking her bags and some kitchen equipment, regretting now that they'd emptied the cupboards so efficiently and given so much to charity shops. An old bike was strapped to the roof of the car; Ruth said that she hardly used it any more and certainly wouldn't miss it. When they arrived, she checked the oil tank and got the boiler going, turned on an electric fire and showed Anna the central heating controls. 'Are you sure you'll be all right? The phone's disconnected, but call me on your mobile if we've forgotten anything.'

'I'll be fine,' Anna said, although at that moment she was wishing more than anything that she could go back with Ruth and sit in the warmth of the kitchen over a pot of coffee. She'd forgotten how dark it was here at night, without street lights, and so few other houses nearby. Still, she'd chosen this; she couldn't change her mind now. The house was frigid with winter and neglect, but – to Anna's relief – held less of Bridget's presence than it had on her first visit. She didn't want to share with Bridget.

'Coffee, tea, bread, milk, yoghurt, cheese, butter.' Ruth unpacked a cardboard box. 'It seems a bit like camping, but I can always come over tomorrow night and take you to the supermarket in Epping.'

'You've got enough to do,' Anna told her. 'I don't want to be an extra burden.'

'You're not. I'll miss you! It's been fun having you to stay.'

'Thanks again, for everything.' They went to the door together, and hugged; Anna felt suddenly tearful as Ruth went out to the car. Backing out to the lane, Ruth waved, and pulled away up the hill. Although it meant letting precious warmth out of the house, Anna stood watching from the open door until the car's rear lights were quite out of sight.

Silence and darkness settled around her like a cloak. She remembered telling Jamie that she was waiting for something, though she didn't know what. Maybe this was the way to find out. In spite of her doubts earlier, she felt oddly comforted, contained in her own stillness. I can't live in London, she thought. I need trees, quietness, space, a garden. I should have known.

Her attention was caught now by the stars: how startling they were, how brilliant, with no intrusive streetlamps to blot them out, no lit buildings apart from the cottage behind her. It felt like a gift, a dazzling display, a blessing on this new phase of her life. There they were in their slow wheeling, which Rose had said you could almost see if you stood for long enough, east horizon to west. And there to the south stood Orion, the bold, unmistakable pattern of belt and sword and raised arm that Anna had known since childhood. He towered high, dominating the southern sky. Turning, Anna saw patterns and clusters, more and more stars pricking through until she felt she could fall into them, and her neck ached with tilting. There weren't many more constellations she could identify: the Plough, the wide W of Cassiopeia, and – yes – the Pleiades, the Seven Sisters, in the horned shape of Taurus. She remembered that.

*How many stars can you count?*

*Seven. Seven Sisters.*

*No, more than seven. Don't look straight at them. Look to one side, so you can catch them out.*

But the more you look, the more you can't see, and the Rose of her imagination was there beside her, so close that Anna ought to be able to reach out and grab her by the wrist and not let go. Rose, who always knew more, always several steps ahead.

'Where are you?' Anna asked, and was startled to realize that she'd spoken aloud, and that she was alone in the dark, with Ruth gone, and the empty house behind her.

Going in, she turned the key in the door and slid the bolt across – no multi-point locking here – then made up her bed, with the sheet and duvet cover Ruth had lent her. She'd decided that it would be too creepy to sleep in Bridget's double bed, and was installing herself instead in the smaller room overlooking the garden, the one Ruth had used whenever she stayed. Sometime this week, one lunch time, she'd go back to the flat and collect more of her clothes, CDs and toiletries. Smuggle them out, perhaps, bit by bit, till she had all her belongings here? But if this was a final separation from Martin, as it seemed to be, she ought to tell him, and make it definite. She would have to find the words for that –

words that wouldn't yet come, but how could it be done without them?

Staying here for a while would make it easier. She thought of herself, Ruth and Martin as marker-pins on a map, forming an elongated triangle. At a proper distance from each other.

❖ ❖ ❖

## August 1990

The Wednesday of Rose's leaving divided everything into Before and After. It was the day when normal life stopped being safe, predictable, even boring, and became something too big and terrifying to endure.

Time thickened like treacle. Anna floundered through it in a daze. Everything was too brightly coloured, too loud, too bewildering. There were things like meals, and bed, and deciding what clothes to wear, but it all felt irrelevant. There was another girl doing these things; looking, to any observer, like the usual Anna.

A whole day went by, and another. It began to feel normal to have police in the house – at first two male sergeants and a WPC, later the WPC on her own. Photographs were produced, a description written. There were questions, questions. How had Rose seemed? What had she been wearing? What did they think she'd taken with her? Anna and her mother tried to work out what was missing from the wardrobe, but could only say what Rose *hadn't* taken: not the crochet sandals, not the appliquéd denim skirt, not the floaty green top. Her bag had gone, with her purse in it. No one knew how much money the purse had held. Anna told them that Rose had been drawing that morning, but her sketchbook seemed to have gone with her.

The house was suspended in time, waiting. The air felt still, too still. *Something awful's happened.* The thought kept nudging at Anna's brain. *Something so awful I can't think about it.* At the same time she expected Rose to come back, surprised to find everyone anxious and agitated. The straining of ears and will to hear Rose's key in the lock, her usual clattering entry with bags and art folder, was a physical ache.

Dad went to school to collect Rose's exam results. The envelope sat on the mantelpiece for three days before Mum opened it so that they could tell her if she phoned. She'd got her three As; there should have been celebrations. The phone kept ringing: both lots of grandparents, Rose's friends, the police. Every time the phone rang, Mum's eyes seemed to darken, her body to shrink into itself, but usually it was only someone asking for news, or the police confirming that there was no news. There was nothing.

'A girl with three A grades has got enough brains to keep herself out of trouble,' Dad kept saying, repeating it like a mantra.

After a whole interminable first week, the police phoned. There was a body that might be Rose. The body of a teenage girl, washed up on a beach near Whitstable. Anna's parents were required to go and identify it.

That evening lodged in Anna's memory, thrillingly awful. Mum and Dad getting ready to go, talking to each other in shaken, subdued voices, speaking for the comfort of keeping some things ordinary: 'Are you ready, love? Got your keys? Hadn't you better take your coat? It'll be cold later.' Beneath the talking, each of them was shut up with the horror of what was to come.

Anna didn't go with them. Gran and Grandad Skipton came over, to stay with her while Mum and Dad were driven to a morgue or hospital or police station; Anna wasn't sure where they had to go. She watched the police car drive slowly down the road and out of sight, and stayed there at the window, breathing on the glass, pulling the curtains round her like a shawl. She wanted to hold tightly to the last minutes of Rose still being alive. She knew from television how it would be. Someone quiet and respectful would pull back a sheet, and there would be Rose's drowned face, bruised and swollen from being in the water. Dad would say in a quavering voice, 'Yes, that's her, that's Rose,' and Mum would break down in terrible racking sobs. Rose would be covered up again, the sheet touching her eyes, her mouth. The fabric would shape itself to her face, covering the bruises and the swelling. She would be unblemished again, untouched. She would be one of those stone effigies in cathedrals, the folds falling gracefully from her limbs. Time would lose its meaning, and she'd be fixed like that for ever, a girl of stone.

Anna's reflection stared back at her from the blackness of outside. It swam and blurred and became Rose's drowned face, with staring eyes. Anna tugged the curtains together to shut her out. She went back to sprawl on the carpet, the TV on for company. None of them could settle, but Gran and Grandad were trying to pretend that things were normal, for Anna. 'I can't ask them, I can't,' Anna had heard Mum whispering to Dad. 'It's Roland all over again. I can't put them through that. It's too terrible to think about.'

But the grandparents had offered, and now here they were, moving about the house slowly, as if too much vigour might propel Rose out of the shadows where she'd been lurking, and into some otherworld.

When the phone rang, Gran jumped visibly. She and Grandad looked at each other; Gran said in a whisper, 'I'll go.' She went through to the hall, closing the door behind her. Anna turned her eyes back to the TV, to a cartoon that normally she'd have sneered at as babyish. A dog with ears flapping like streamers was loping along a road in big bouncing strides, not seeing the steamroller coming along behind. The steamroller caught up, flattening the dog into a cut-out shape on the road, like Mum's paper dress patterns – a meaningless cartoon death that was forgotten next moment when the dog stood up and shook itself back into shape and carried on running. Anna didn't look round when Gran came back into the room. As long as she kept staring at the screen, she could hold back the moment of knowing.

'It's not Rose. It's not her. Oh, lovey.' Gran stooped and gathered Anna into her arms, expecting her, Anna supposed, to cry with relief. Anna felt no urge to cry. She struggled free and ran out into the back garden. When she looked up at the sky there were stars pushing through the blackness, more and more of them as her eyes adjusted, till the sky was a pincushion pricked with dots of light. The stars were bigger than she was. She wanted to shout to them, leap up and catch one. The Seven Sisters were somewhere out there, the Pleiades, blurring and dancing together, uncountable.

There was still a poor drowned girl lying under that sheet, someone's daughter, someone's sister perhaps, but she wasn't Rose. She had taken Rose's place. Her death confirmed that Rose was alive and running.

❖ ❖ ❖

# 17

The narrow, carpetless flight of stairs and the lingering smells of fat and smoke from the café underneath would have deterred Anna, but the young couple – a girl of about eighteen and her amiable-looking boyfriend – followed her up without comment. The flat on the second floor consisted of a living room with a kitchen at one end, a bathroom and one bedroom; the furnishings were worn but clean. The bedroom window, north-facing, looked out on an expanse of rain-washed brick wall, drainage pipes, and – if you craned your neck – a glimpse of grey sky.

'Oh, it's lovely,' said the girl, who had the air of being ready to be pleased with anything offered to her. 'Isn't it, Jace?'

'Yeah,' said Jace, slipping his arm round her waist. Anna looked at their bright faces and knew that they were picturing themselves here, cosily watching TV from the sofa; they were thinking of all the sex they were going to have in this bleak narrow bedroom. For a moment, remembering herself and Martin in the Lewisham flat that first time, Anna envied the transparency of their desires. Were they runaways? Did anyone know they were in Leytonstone, looking for a flat?

This girl – Kylie, had she said, or Keeley or Kayleigh? – looked wan and undernourished. Well, the café downstairs might be handy for feeding her up.

'We can afford it, can't we?' said the girl, looking appealingly at Jace, her arms draped round him.

'Course we can,' said Jace, and Anna saw in the swell of his chest how he wanted to be the man, the provider. 'We like it,' he told her. 'A month's rent for deposit, right?'

Anna nodded. 'Good. We'll go back to the office and sort out the paperwork.'

She was intrigued by such brushings against other lives, always at a point when changes were being made or contemplated, where a new house or flat promised transformation into a different person – happier, more confident, more successful. People imagined that they could leave their old lives behind, moving into new selves with a change of habitat. Often they mentioned their reason for moving – a change of job, a wish to be nearer central London – but with some there was furtiveness, making her suspect that they were evading responsibilities, or trying to escape.

Whenever a missing person reached the headlines and relatives pleaded for information, Anna felt herself reluctantly linked to these desperate seekers, like members of a club. Around them, watching like a host of angels in a medieval painting, were the missing. They talked and whispered together, debating whether or not to return to the human world, bestowing joy and tears of relief on the ones who waited, trapped in limbo. Whenever one of them did come back, Anna felt resentful. The parents or sisters or partners in waiting ought to have served their full sentence alongside her. They had cheated; their lost person, returning, had taken a place that was rightfully Rose's, as if only a limited number of hostages could return from the underworld.

Over the years, Anna found in every teenage girl a potential Rose. It had become a habit, gazing at them, wondering where they came from, where they were going, who cared for them and what they expected from their lives. As Anna matured, girls of eighteen looked younger and younger, until, now, they were a different generation, a separate, exotic breed. Girls in groups, girls on the Underground, girls out shopping together, girls aware of their sexiness and the glances they attracted. With their glossy hair, their smooth skin, their supple bodies, their distinctive fashions, they assumed a confidence Anna couldn't recall in herself at that age. They intimidated her, the way they kept coming, year by year, wave upon wave of teenage girls pushing her aside. They jostled and giggled, elbowing Rose's ghost out of their way.

Waking in her room at Rowan Lodge, Anna was puzzled first by the absence of another body, then by the flowered curtains, the window in an unfamiliar place, the silence.

The room was cold; she felt the chill at her neck and shoulders as she stirred, looking at her watch. A quarter to eight. About to scramble up in panic, she remembered that it was Monday, and her day off, as she'd worked on Saturday. She huddled the duvet around her for a few minutes more, then got out of bed, wrapped herself in her dressing gown and pushed her feet into slippers. Opening the curtains, she rubbed at the windowpane with her sleeve and stared in surprise at the garden trees all ghostly with frost, the grass whitened and crisp. For a moment she thought that it had snowed overnight; but no, it was hoar-frost, misting the air, blurring the horizon so that the parkland beyond the garden rose whitely into cloud. So still; so quiet. She caught her breath at the unexpected beauty. Tracks left by some small animal crossed the lawn and headed under the shrubs; a blackbird landed on a tree-branch and particles of frost descended in a shower.

'Are you mad?' Martin had asked, when she phoned to tell him she was moving here. 'Why maroon yourself in a godforsaken hovel miles from anywhere, when you could be at home?'

'It's hardly a hovel. And I *want* to be miles from anywhere.'

'Miles from me, at any rate – that's obvious. Why not do the whole thing and take yourself off to a Buddhist monastery?'

'Great idea! Thanks. I'll try to find one.'

Martin huffed. 'What's behind all this? If you've met someone else, for God's sake why not say so?'

'I haven't!' She felt stung by this. 'If I had, d'you think I'd move him into Ruth's mum's house?'

'Anna – it's quite beyond me to predict what you are or aren't likely to do. Let me know when you've had enough and I'll come and fetch you home.'

She felt impatient with him. Why was he being so tolerant? How far would he let himself be pushed, before saying *That's it, then – we're finished*, and cutting off the possibility of return? Was that what she was waiting for – Martin to make the decision, so that she didn't have to?

Ruth had been concerned that Anna would find the

254

cottage too isolated, but instead she relished her solitude. Between them they had finished clearing the main bedroom and had bought paint; Anna planned to get on with stripping the wallpaper today, but after making toast and coffee she decided to go out walking instead; the frozen beauty of the landscape was a gift that needed acknowledging. Among Bridget's remaining books she had found a large-scale Ordnance Survey map; she had only trainers to wear, no walking boots or wellies, but the ground was too frozen to be muddy.

For more than two hours she walked, frosted grass crunching underfoot, her breath clouding in the air. She found her way along bridleways and across fields, and along hedgerows where startled pheasants whirred clumsily into flight. She paused to study her map, scanning for the next stile, the next marker post; she walked along a single-track lane where a horse and rider were the only traffic to pass, steam rising from the horse's clipped flanks. A thin, wheedling call of birds caught her attention and she looked across the whited-out fields to see a flock of birds flying low, their wing-tips rounded and dark, flicking black-white-black as they wheeled and landed. Lapwings. Peewits. They reminded her of the holiday in Blakeney, the pleasure she'd taken in the abundant birdlife and had since forgotten. Only the distant motorway hum reminded her that she was less than an hour from central London. It was years since she'd done this, and she realized that it filled a need she'd been unaware of: to be alone, walk among trees, see the sky uncluttered by buildings; to feel space around her and in her.

Unhurried, she returned along the edge of a ploughed

field that was frozen into hard ridges and furrows. She let herself into Rowan Lodge, and the warmth that had built up in her absence, and felt oddly at home.

After changing her damp socks – her trainers had proved inadequate – and putting on the kettle, she prepared to start work on the bedroom walls, paying her debt to Ruth. It was only when the postman arrived, bringing two letters and a catalogue addressed to Bridget, that she remembered it was Monday, and there was nothing to stop her from phoning the Plymouth school. She made herself wait until lunch time, hoping to reach Michael Sullivan in person rather than leaving a message. It might not be the same person anyway; it wasn't an unusual name, as her Google search had proved. If she drew a blank with him, she'd try harder to find Jim Greaves.

Damping the wallpaper, pulling it off in shreds and tatters, she rehearsed what to say, but still, when at last she made the call and a receptionist answered, found that her voice had gone husky and hesitant.

'Who shall I say is calling?'

'Anna.' Her surname would give too much away; she didn't want him (if it was him) to be alerted.

'Anna from . . . ?'

'From Heinemann Publishing,' Anna improvised.

The receptionist said that she'd try the staff room, and there was an interminable wait before a male voice answered.

Anna sounded to herself like a fifteen-year-old schoolgirl. 'Are you the Michael Sullivan who used to teach at Oldlands Hall in Sevenoaks?'

'Yes, yes I am. Who is this?'

'It's Anna Taverner.'

A pause, then: 'Anna Taverner?'

'Yes. I think you knew my sister Rose.'

'Has something happened?'

Anna was thrown by that. 'Happened? I expect you know that Rose disappeared, twenty years ago. I know you were at the school then.'

'What's this about?'

'I'm trying to trace her. Nothing's been heard of her in all that time. I wondered if you might remember something – anything – that might give me a lead.'

There was such a long silence that Anna would have thought she'd been cut off, except that she could hear staff-room chat and laughter in the background, and the chink of crockery.

Then Michael Sullivan said, 'I'll have to get back to you. I can't talk now. Can you give me your phone number?'

Sitting on the bedroom floor, on the sheets of newspaper she'd spread over the carpet, Anna went over and over this brief conversation, weighing every nuance.

*Has something happened?* What had he meant by that? Was he simply asking whether Rose had been found? In which case he didn't know. But there had been no preamble, no *Oh yes, I remember,* or *What a terrible business* or *So, still nothing, after all this time* – which had been Jamie Spellman's reaction; nor was it the fear of hearing something grisly, which had been Christina's. He hadn't denied knowing Rose. *I think you knew my sister Rose,* she'd said, and he'd replied with that quick, defensive *What's this about?* That wasn't the response of someone who had known Rose merely as a pupil he hadn't even taught. Someone who hadn't thought about Rose for two decades.

He knew something. Otherwise why offer to get back to her? *Would* he return the call? Anna saw herself waiting and waiting, clutching her silent mobile. Of course he wouldn't ring back. He had something to hide.

What now? She imagined herself phoning the police, of squad cars racing to the school, leading Michael Sullivan away in handcuffs for questioning. Ludicrous. What did she have against him? That he'd refused to dance with Rose, and had looked at a painting five years later?

She kept hearing his voice: a deep voice, softly spoken, with the trace of a southern Irish accent. She remembered that: an attractive voice, she'd have said. But she felt chilled now, hearing his words over and over again, alert to how incriminating they sounded. She heard all the things he hadn't said.

What was he doing now? Had he gone back to his classroom, to teach his next lesson quite normally? Or was he panicked into flight, knowing that his cover had been blown?

She could take a day off work and catch a train, find her way to the school, and confront him. She imagined herself storming into a classroom, yelling *Where is she? What have you done to my sister?*

She'd give him twenty-four hours. If he didn't phone back she would set off for Plymouth.

The shop has a new display of shoes for babies and toddlers, a whole side window full of them, arranged on shelves and stands with yellow ducks and chicks and daffodils scattered among them. There are sturdy little boots, bar shoes, trainers; ballet pumps, shoes with appliqué flowers on the toes; shoes in poster-paint colours. On her way from the car park to the post office, Cassandra stops outside, with a little gasp. She feels like a child in a sweetshop, gazing hungrily. The fluffy toys call to mind a larger yellow duckling she made from felt, years ago, a memory she pushes away. But the shoes! They tug at her; she feels a wrenching ache that is almost pleasurable. She wants to hold and touch them. She wants all of them.

A woman with twins in a buggy stops too; she smiles at Cassandra. 'Adorable, aren't they? So tempting. Pricey, though. More than I can afford.' And she moves on, a young woman of Anna's age, busy with her babies and her bags of shopping.

*I* can, though, Cassandra thinks. I can afford a pair and I'm going to buy some, for Zanna. Why shouldn't I?

She pushes open the door; there's a cheerful donging, and an assistant looks up from the counter. There are yet more shoes inside, three shelves full, for very young children. Cassandra walks wonderingly along the shelf, touching, stroking. She picks up a miniature white boot; holds it to her cheek, inhales the smell of new leather. How to choose?

'Aren't they gorgeous?' The assistant has come to stand beside her. 'Are you looking for something special? Is it for a grandchild?'

Cassandra's mind blanks for a moment, then she says, 'Yes. Yes, it is.'

'Little boy or little girl?'

'Girl,' says Cassandra.

'Lovely. What sort of colours do you think she'd like? Are

you looking for a dainty little-girl shoe, or something more chunky, like these boots? Oh, I *love* these. I bought a pair for my nephew.'

Eventually Cassandra chooses a pair of purple bar shoes, the smallest size, with white stitching, and button fastenings in the shape of a green and white daisy. The assistant wraps them in layers of tissue paper, and puts them into a small blue carrier with silky cord handles. 'You can always exchange them if they don't fit.' She is waiting for the card machine to print out its receipt. 'What's she called, your granddaughter?'

Cassandra smiles. 'She isn't born yet.'

'Oh – and will she be your first? How exciting.'

Cassandra hugs the secret excitement to her. It's like being a member of a club, a secret grandmother club, a new phase of her life. When she gets home with her purchase – only now does she remember that she'd been heading for the post office with Don's parcel, which is still in her bag – she lifts out the shoes and places them side by side on the kitchen table. She imagines small feet in them, standing squarely; sturdy little legs, and white ankle socks with frilled edges. But how will she ever see? She won't know, and it will be a new loss; everything is loss. She fastens the daisy buttons on one of the shoes, and holds it to her mouth; tears prickle her eyes.

Then it occurs to her that she'd better hide them. Up in the bedroom, she tucks the bag to the back of the wardrobe shelf she uses for storing presents.

❖ ❖ ❖

# 18

## Sandy, 1967

Sandy never spoke to Phil again. He phoned, once, and she put down the receiver quickly, terrified by that time that her parents would find out. *He mustn't know. He must never know.*

Travelling back from the strange pilgrimage, she had wanted to copy Roland's song into her notebook, but Phil wouldn't let her. Instead, back at home, she wrote down the title, and the phrases she remembered. She also had Roland's handwritten song lyrics in the folder she had taken from his room, and his desk diary. The brand-new diary was empty apart from exam dates and the Merlins' few bookings for January and February. There were no Merlins any more. Phil had told her on the train that he couldn't think of continuing without Roland, and that Mick and Dempsey were forming another group.

The first time she missed a period, when the date marked on the calendar was two days past, the thought darted across her mind that it would be weird if she was pregnant – weird, but surely not probable. Hardly even possible. Some of the girls at school said that you couldn't get pregnant by doing it just once. And . . . the *doing it,* herself and Phil, in a haze of sorrow and desperation, could hardly be the same act that the girls giggled about in the cloak-room, discussing how close they had come, how tempted, how insistent their boyfriends had been. There was a pill now that could stop you getting pregnant, and the papers said that this would lead to a huge rise in immorality if unmarried women were allowed to have it. You could simply take a pill each night and never have to worry again. You could go off and sleep with ten different boys, Susan Morgan said, in her airy way of speaking, as if from vast experience.

As the days passed, and the fear of pregnancy lodged itself firmly in her mind, Sandy longed for the cramping pain that would signal the start of a period, usually such a nuisance. Her body couldn't betray her like this. If she stopped thinking about it, everything would be all right. Instead, each day that passed added to the sick feeling of inevitability. How had she let it happen? She was so ignorant, so naïve, as everyone said. There were ways of dealing with it, weren't there? Jumping down stairs, or drinking gin? But remedies like that belonged in lurid stories like *Up the Junction*, a copy of which had gone round the fifth form like a virus, increasingly battered as it passed from hand to hand. Sandy pretended to find it risqué and exciting, but was shocked by the currency in which Nell Dunn's girls traded – sex in exchange for a couple of beers – and by how utterly unromantic the sex was, in doorways and the backs of vans. They were cynical and reckless, those girls; bad girls who knew what they were doing but took risks all the same, and faced the consequences. There was no magic wand that could solve the problem of a pregnancy.

Rube in the story had gone to a dubious older woman for help, and something horrible had been done with a syringe, but still Rube had ended up screaming in pain, and everyone knowing.

Another day went by without the longed-for bleeding, another week. Eventually a second X on the calendar passed without incident. *Something will happen*, Sandy told herself. *It will be all right.* Her body might have been someone else's, holding on smugly to its secret workings.

Her mother, discovering that the supply of sanitary towels in Sandy's dressing-table drawer was undepleted, broached the matter. They'd better make a doctor's appointment. Periods could be missed for a variety of reasons: stress and upset, she said, were among the most likely. It wasn't surprising that Sandy was suffering from delayed shock.

Dr Jennings said the same thing, but also that pregnancy was the most common reason: had Sandy had sexual intercourse?

Her mother smiled tolerantly. 'Well, I hardly think—'

'Yes,' said Sandy.

Dr Jennings tapped the tip of his biro on his notebook. Ah. In that case, a pregnancy test would be the first step to take.

'*Cassandra!*' her mother said outside the surgery, in a horrified whisper. 'Were you telling the truth? Can you really have been so – so – Where did this happen? Who's the boy?'

Sandy had prepared for this, concocting a vague story about a party, gatecrashers, herself drinking too much to be quite sure of what she was doing. She added reckless details, seeing each new shock register on her mother's face. There might have been more than one boy; she hadn't found out names; she'd been drunk on vodka and must have passed out.

The test was positive. She knew, by then, that it would be. Disastrous though this was, she felt oddly distanced from her situation, as if reading about someone else, or watching a film. Her mother was tearful, her father cold and appalled.

'Let me get this absolutely clear.' They were having what her mother called a family meeting, sitting at the dining table; things had to be sorted out, decisions made, and it would be her father who did the deciding. 'You've behaved so disgracefully that you're unable to tell us the name of the boy responsible? A well brought-up girl like you, showing no more sense than that? Not a thought for the consequences?'

He sat rigid, hardly looking at her. Sandy had seen this when he berated Roland for neglecting his studies. This was worse, far worse. Her mother kept giving him anxious glances; she was frightened of him, Sandy saw, when he was like this, as if he'd turned into a stony-hearted stranger. Rarely had Sandy been the one to receive the brunt of his anger. Now, as she realized Roland had done, she was finding a retreat inside herself, so that his words floated over and past her. *You don't know how it was. You don't understand. It was for Roland.* She couldn't begin to explain; had no wish to try. The scene on the beach with Phil – his voice breaking over Roland's words, the pebbles they'd thrown into the sea, and their coming together, so roughly, so tenderly – was stored in a secret place in her mind, enclosed and sealed like a glass dome she'd been given once in her Christmas stocking, a wintry scene that blurred into a snow shower when she turned it upside-down and then righted it. Theirs was a dome of sea-murmur and wind-salt and tide-washed sand. Maybe it was oddly fitting that their sorrow for Roland should create a new life.

'So you've nothing to say for yourself, not a word of apology or regret?' Her father's voice wavered alarmingly. 'There doesn't seem to be a shred of decency in you.' He balled his fists on the table. As he stood up, she saw that his face had reddened and his eyes had gone puffy. 'I can't bring myself to look at you. I can't bear it. I'll never get over losing my son, my boy . . . never . . .' His mouth quivered; he struggled for control. 'And now you . . . this . . .'

Sandy and her mother sat silent and dismayed while his footsteps hurried upstairs, and the bedroom door slammed.

'Oh, darling, he doesn't mean it!' Sandy's mother got up from her chair, giving her an awkward hug. 'It's terrible news for him, on top of everything else. We'll have to make allowances.'

A plan was made. Sandy's parents' priority was that no one should know; Sandy would be removed from view before her pregnancy became evident. The family must not be tainted. A place would be found in a home for unmarried mothers; the baby would be given up for adoption, and Sandy would pick up her normal life and try to forget her disgrace.

With this all determined, the torment of uncertainty removed, she began to feel curiosity rather than revulsion about what her body was doing; even pride, that it could work so silently and smoothly to create a new human being. About the end of the process she could hardly think at all.

Meanwhile she went to school, revised for her O-Levels, kept her secret. She hated the thought of people guessing, talking behind her back, speculating. She would feel like one of those *Up the Junction* girls.

The library became her sanctuary. Every afternoon, when lessons ended, she spent an hour there before it closed, usually with Delia, who did homework until her mother collected her by car on her way home from work. At first Sandy did this to avoid the jostle and chatter on the bus, but gradually found pleasure in those afternoon hours: light slanting through high windows, the alcoves between tall shelves, walled on both sides by book-spines in dull colours; the creak of floorboards as Miss Stopford, the librarian, moved around the bays with her trolley. Sandy worked methodically, taking notes, underlining headings, sorting through algebra exercises. There were few people in the library at this hour, herself and Delia and a handful of sixth-formers preparing for A-Levels. Sometimes they would glance up and acknowledge her with a faint smile before returning to their books. It made her feel like one of them, part of an exclusive club, for whose members the narrowing tunnel of revision and exams was the only future that needed considering. Occasionally she thought of telling Delia her secret, but always stopped short. If no one knew, she could pretend it wasn't happening, that the funnel of exams was the only thing that concerned her, and after-wards there would be freedom.

Occasionally, inevitably, she saw Phil. On a bright June morning, sitting on the lower deck of the bus on her way to her first maths paper, she saw him waiting at his stop with two other boys: blazerless, his tie loosened and collar open, eyes narrowed into the sunlight as he gave a grimacy smile at something one of the others said. He didn't see her. But, her eyes fastened on the street ahead, she was acutely aware of every sound as the three of them boarded, clumping up the stairs to the top deck. When the bus pulled up at the Grove Park stop she turned to watch as they jumped down and headed through the school gates; she saw the sharp angles of his shoulders, the swing of his walk, his hair falling straight, almost to his shoulders. He carried the same canvas bag he'd taken to the Isle of Wight, with his marijuana and Roland's lyric in the side pocket. Now the bag seemed more familiar to Sandy than its owner. He was as remote as when she revered him as the lead singer of the Merlins, the beautiful boy she had gazed at in church halls and youth clubs, whose voice had seared itself into her brain. It was impossible now to believe that he had any-thing to do with the life growing obstinately inside her. Envying him the careless arrogance of being young and male, she watched until the bus pulled away and he was lost from view.

❖ ❖ ❖

# 19

**Spring 1995**

In her last year at school, Anna spent hours in the art rooms. She liked the quiet concentration, the smell of dust and acrylic paint, the sense of working for something other than exams. In addition to double periods twice each week, she was drawn there at odd times when she had a free lesson, to work on her project, browse through art books or stare out of the window. It didn't feel quite like school, somehow, up there on the top floor where two rooms took up the whole of what had once been an attic. High windows were set into the eaves, and beams running across were used to hang mobiles or textile work. The art department was the domain of Mr Greaves and his younger colleague, Alys Hardcastle. Mr Greaves – Jim, to the sixth form – was a painter first, teacher second, and it was no secret that he preferred his A-Level groups to the raucous younger classes with their wide extremes of talent and ineptitude, compliance and bolshiness. Five years ago he had taught Rose; he was one of the few teachers Rose and Anna had in common. Rose liked him, mainly because he didn't so much teach as guide, encourage and understand.

It was seeing Rose's A-Level exhibition that had made Anna in turn choose art. Unlike Rose, she didn't have any particular ambition, even though the department was very successful with its sixth form in particular.

For her special study, Rose had chosen two Viennese painters, Gustav Klimt and Egon Schiele. She filled notebooks with sketches and designs, commentaries and interpretations: her books were beautiful in their own right. She made fabric collages in homage to Klimt, using machine and hand embroidery; her drawings from life class imitated those of Schiele: graceless, graceful, knowing, with sinewy bodies, expressive hands, and eyes sometimes blank and sometimes boldly challenging.

Rose's other project was all about mirrors. She painted a new and more complex version of her own portrait, endlessly refracted. She surrounded an oval mirror with a huge question mark, so that the viewer saw his or her own image framed and interrogated. She made collages from mirrors she bought in charity shops and smashed into splinters; the face of the onlooker was reduced to fragments and glimpses. In her own version of a Magritte painting, *The Son of Man*, in which a man looking into a mirror sees his own back view instead of a reflection, she substituted herself, seen as a smooth sweep of dark hair. In the series that grew from this, the girl saw herself reflected as a baby, a mask, a blank, a skull, a wizened old woman, a grimacing gargoyle. In one there was no reflection at all, only a calm, featureless sea with a strip of light at the horizon that was almost blinding. She titled the project *Selves*; it was specially commended by the examiners, who praised its boldness and innovation.

Five years later, when Anna's turn came, she chose

269

Charles Rennie Mackintosh, led perhaps by Rose's interest in the early twentieth century and Art Nouveau. She knew she wasn't stretching herself as she produced notebooks lovingly lettered in the distinctive Mackintosh style, copied chairs from the Willow Tea Rooms, drew furniture designs of her own. It was beautiful and stylish, but remote from her. 'Why did you choose this?' Jim Greaves asked her; she said something about liking the linearity, the cleanness, and how startlingly modern the Mackintosh designs must have looked in their own time. More of herself went into her other project, in mixed media, which she called *Missing*. Mr Greaves never said a word to her about Rose; she knew he didn't need to. She made collages of torn paper, cut paper, showing fragments of possessions: an address book, a mascara wand, a key, a handwritten note, layering and layering them. She made a lino-cut of a single footprint and formed patterns with it, overlapping, heading off the edge of the paper. She took photographs, asking friends to pose; she did a whole series of paintings, back views of teenage girls walking or running away, full of details suggestive of railway stations, motorway services, lay-bys, ferry terminals. She made a mosaic of tiny faces, with the letters of the word MISSING placed randomly among them; another collage was made from bus and train tickets.

Her favourite was a painting she called *Shore*, on a tall, narrow piece of Daler board that emphasized its long per-spective. A low tide lapped at the left-hand edge; footprints, sharply delineated in the foreground, walked along wet sand above the tideline; far in the distance the person leaving the prints was a tiny, undistinguishable figure, grey in the haze of a sea-mist. Jim Greaves preferred the pastel drawing of Rose's bedroom, empty of its occupant, waiting; it reminded him of Mary Cassat, he said. He liked the composition, the fall of light, the purples and greens smudged into the shadows.

Anna threw herself into this work at the expense of her other subjects. It was better than talking, better than explaining. There was no direct reference to Rose in either words or images. In her commentary, she wrote only in general terms. *People go missing. People are missed.*

After the examiners came, there was a Friday evening viewing for the students' families and friends, with wine and canapés, before the exhibition opened to the rest of the school. Anna didn't invite her parents, and her mother was reproachful and hurt when she read about it in the local paper.

❖ ❖ ❖

Anna's mobile rang late in the evening, past eleven. She was getting ready for bed, deciding what to wear for work tomorrow.

'It's Michael. Michael Sullivan.'

'Yes?' She clutched the phone, and the room revolved around her.

'Look, there are things I can tell you.' He seemed to be speaking in a deliberately low voice, as if someone else were present, someone he didn't want to overhear. 'But – can we meet? I can't do it on the phone. Are you still in Sevenoaks?'

'No, in Essex. But I work in London.'

'Is there any chance you could come down to Plymouth?'

'I could get the train,' Anna said, wondering why she was

agreeing; but yes, of course she'd go. She would do whatever he said, go anywhere, for one morsel of information.

'Is Saturday any good?'

'Yes, I'll come. I'll look up trains.'

'Send me a text message, and I'll meet you at the station.'

'OK. I'll do that.'

Michael gave her his mobile phone number; then he added, 'You might want to bring an overnight bag. It's a long way.'

When she rang off her heart was racing; she felt dizzy. What did he have to tell her that couldn't be told over the phone? And the overnight bag? It was possible to get to Plymouth and back in a day, surely. His suggestion sounded dubious, as if he planned to lure her off somewhere. But, in a face-to-face meeting, she could press him, look for clues in his expressions and body language. Whatever he planned to tell her, she would find out more, and more. She plugged in her laptop and looked up trains, finding one that would get her to Plymouth for half-past twelve.

It was no use trying to sleep. She tried, gave up, went down to the cold kitchen and made herself coffee. Saturday was an interminable distance away. It was a screen, a curtain that would soon be swept aside. When she got to the other side, she would have something to fill the twenty-year void. More practically and immediately, she would have to convey this change of plan to Ruth, who was expecting to spend Saturday wallpapering her mother's bedroom, with Anna as assistant.

She phoned from the office next morning. 'Ruth, I'm really sorry but I won't be able to make Saturday after all.'

'What, are you working again?'

'No, but I've said I'll meet someone.' It sounded feeble, a fobbing-off; and, after all, she'd agreed to do the decorating as part of their arrangement.

'Oh.' Ruth sounded put out now.

'Look, I know Sunday's no good for you, but I'll get on with the wallpapering then, OK?'

'Have you done it before?'

'Er, no.'

'Well, it's not that easy when you start, especially on your own. I'd rather you didn't. It'll have to wait.'

'I really am sorry—'

'It's a man you're meeting, isn't it?' Ruth broke in.

Anna hesitated. 'Yes. An – old acquaintance.' She was reluctant to explain; it might turn out to be nothing more than another disappointment, another dead end. She was about to say, 'It's not what you think,' but Ruth spoke first.

'I hope you know what you're doing, Anna.'

Yes, Anna thought; me too. But she had to do this, and there was no one she could tell: not Ruth, not Bethan, certainly not Martin or her parents.

On Thursday, in her lunch break, Anna went to the flat to collect a pair of old boots she wanted for walking in the fields, and a few other items of clothing. Letting herself in, she heard a voice, a female voice laughing; she froze in the doorway, her key still in the lock, her instinct to back off quickly, but Martin had already seen her and was rising from the armchair. A sleek blonde woman sat on the sofa.

'Anna? I wasn't expecting you.' He came towards her, holding her gaze; she moved aside so that the armchair was between them.

'No, well. It's only a flying visit.' Her voice came out a little hysterically. This was the stuff of cliché, wasn't it, of soap opera – walking in on Martin with another woman? She could only think that it hadn't taken him long.

Martin made an awkward gesture. 'Er . . . you haven't met Lenka, have you? Lenka, Anna.'

The woman stood, smiling, extending a hand to Anna. 'Anna, hello. We've spoken on the phone, I think.' She spoke charmingly, with a Russian or Polish accent which, yes, Anna remembered hearing before. Lenka had left messages for Martin or asked for him to call her back; she was a financial analyst, whatever that meant. Her hand was cool, her grasp firm and assured.

'We're having a quick catch-up before a meeting at the Barbican this afternoon.' Martin indicated the coffee table strewn with papers, his laptop open. Lenka's dark jacket was over the back of the sofa; she was slim, almost skinny, dressed in a tailored white blouse tucked into a charcoal skirt, hair swept smoothly back into a comb. She was about Anna's age, and the kind of impeccably groomed woman who made her feel gauche.

'Right. Well, I won't get in your way.' Anna went through to the bedroom, and found her old boots in the back of the wardrobe. She couldn't imagine Lenka wearing clumpy boots; sheer tights and high-heeled court shoes were more her style. Unable to remember what else she'd come for, Anna grabbed, at random, two sweaters, underwear and several pairs of socks, which she stowed in the holdall she'd brought for the purpose.

Martin was trying to pretend this was normal. 'What are you doing for lunch, Anna? We've just grabbed a sandwich.

Can I get you something – coffee, fruit juice?' He stood in the bedroom doorway, and she noticed that he was wearing the indigo tie she particularly liked, one they'd chosen together on a short break in Florence. But she didn't want to look at him.

Lenka was putting her papers in order, slipping a folder into her briefcase.

'Thanks, no, I'm in a hurry. See you later. Nice to meet you, Lenka.'

Three lies.

Martin followed her out of the door and into the communal hallway; he turned her to face him, hands on her shoulders. 'Anna! When are you coming back? I need to know.'

She twisted herself away. 'I don't know. Does it matter?'

'Course it bloody matters!'

'I'll ring you some time. When you're not so busy.' She flicked her eyes in the direction of the open door.

'For God's sake! Don't be stupid—'

But she was already halfway down the stairs; she heard him go back in, the door closing behind him. Heading down Hatton Garden, she wondered what he'd tell Lenka; then she remembered, too late, that she'd intended to collect her favourite earrings, silver and jet, a present from Martin last birthday. She hesitated, feeling the loss of them, then walked on. She couldn't go back now without losing face.

❖ ❖ ❖

# 20

**Sandy, 1967**

Although Sandy feared that she would swell like a balloon, her pregnancy did not show until well into the summer, and even then she could conceal the bulge under a loose sweater or tunic. For the last two weeks before she went to Bridge House, she and her mother went to stay with widowed Aunt Vera in Paignton. The pregnancy was never referred to, though Aunt Vera – her mother's sister – must have known. Sometimes Sandy caught her mother and aunt talking together in hushed voices, looking up at her with bright fake smiles as she entered the room.

At the beginning of November her mother took her to a red-brick Victorian building in Maidstone. It had a bleak, institutional look, though nothing outside announced that Bridge House was a home for unmarried mothers. Sandy had resigned herself to this, almost welcomed it, as a way of shutting herself away from everyone's disapproval. But as she got out of the taxi in the forecourt, she was filled with dread, thinking of the workhouse in *Far from the Madding Crowd*, Fanny Robin's last hope. How would she get through this? Could she switch off her mind, simply endure from day to day until her sentence was served?

The matron, a woman in her forties called Mrs Pickard, was less formidable than Sandy had expected. Over a cup of tea in her office, she told them that the girls could have visitors on Saturday or Sunday afternoons.

'That'll be nice, won't it?' Sandy's mother said, in the crisply cheerful voice she was adopting for the occasion. She would come alone for visits, Sandy knew. Dad had refused to bring her, even though, as Mum didn't drive, it had meant coming by train and taxi. His farewell to Sandy had been stiff and awkward; he'd see her in a few months, he said. At the last moment he had given her a kiss, the first for weeks; she felt the tremble in the hand that gripped her arm before he hurried indoors, closing the door behind him.

'Don't fret, darling,' Mum had said, on the train. 'Things will eventually get back to normal. He's finding this very difficult.'

Mrs Pickard showed the way to the bedroom Sandy would share with two other girls, and the bathroom nearby. There were two drawers and a narrow wardrobe; a single shelf held two books and a stack of magazines. Sandy saw her mother's face registering the sparseness, her smile wavering slightly.

'I'll be all right.' Sandy wanted her gone.

'You can phone home, dear, whenever you want,' said Mrs Pickard. 'There's a public telephone in the hallway.'

So far Sandy had seen only two other girls, both heavily pregnant, coming out of what appeared to be a kitchen, each carrying a plate with a slice of cake on it. They looked at her with curious, hesitant smiles; Mrs Pickard introduced them as Tracy and Maggie. 'Most of the other girls are out at the moment. This is the time when they can go for a walk or to the shops.'

When her mother had left, Sandy unpacked her clothes in the bedroom and looked out at the autumn garden, hating the feeling of being new, and the lack of privacy – where would she find solitude? She had never shared a bedroom before, only occasionally when she'd had a friend to stay. But alongside her qualms there was a feeling of relief: here, no one would judge her. Everyone was in the same situation. They're only girls like me, Sandy realized, girls who've been silly or unlucky. Not the tarts and streetwalkers Dad said would live in a place like this.

There were sixteen residents of Bridge House, five of whom already had babies. One girl, who was keeping her baby son, left the home after a week of learning how to care for him. Most of the babies would be adopted at six weeks.

Sandy tried to avoid the babies. A year ago she would have thought they were sweet, but now they frightened her with their demands, their flailing hands, their messes and smells, their pink mouths that opened to wail in inconsolable distress. She didn't want to think of the thing inside her as a potential human being. Her parents had stipulated to the matron that the baby must be taken away at birth; they thought it best, and when the case worker asked if Sandy agreed, she said that she did. A girl in the next bedroom could be heard weeping over the imminent parting with her baby, making Sandy glad of her decision. Why put herself through such a prolonged ordeal, if it could be done swiftly?

'It's final, that's what it is,' said Tracy, whose own baby was due in a fortnight. 'Once you sign the consent form, that's it. You can't change your mind. You'll never see your baby again. Ever.'

The inmates spent most of each morning doing jobs around the house: cleaning, helping in the kitchen, or working in the laundry. 'Slave labour,' some of the girls complained, but the work was not demanding, and it passed the time. Exercise classes took place before lunch, which was the main meal of the day. Afternoons and evenings were mainly free, and the girls made their own tea in the kitchen. It was like another kind of school: the friendships and rivalries, the squabbles when one girl used another's make-up or was thought to do less than her share of kitchen chores. Sandy fitted into the daily routines. On winter afternoons, the curtains drawn against the early dark, the sitting room softened by a pool of light from a standard lamp and the glowing bars of an electric fire, Sandy felt that this would last for ever, her own life held in waiting for the emergence of the other she was carrying. For all the petty jealousies, the lack of privacy and the sparse surroundings, she felt safe here, where pregnancy was the norm, and all the girls shared the same doubts and fears.

In twice-weekly craft sessions they made 'bounty boxes' – shoe boxes covered in collage, lined with paper and filled with small toys and gifts. These boxes went with the babies to their adoptive parents. Sandy learned basic knitting, and sewed plain-and-purl squares together to make a patchwork blanket which could be used on a cot. Following a battered pattern book she made a duckling from yellow felt and stuffed it with kapok; she sewed on an orange beak and flipper-like feet, and embroidered black eyes with

279

lashes. When the toy was finished she felt an unexpected pride in it; almost, she thought, she'd be sorrier to part with this duckling than with the baby. She made a collage to cover her shoe box, collecting pictures of flowers and animals from magazines and postcards. Then, when the box was finished and its contents packed inside, she took no further interest.

Olivia sobbed quietly as she stuffed a felt dog for her bounty box, her fringe drooping over red and swollen eyes. Other girls tried to comfort her: 'Think of having your life back, being able to do what you want!' And, 'You can have another baby, when you're older. When you find the right boy.'

There was a lot of talk about boyfriends. Tracy's came to visit, a shy, spotty youth who looked far too young to be a father; Marion had a photograph of hers on the only shelf. One of the girls was pregnant by a married man, who did not visit.

'Have you got a boyfriend, Sandy?' They all wanted to know that.

The first time she was asked this, a reckless impulse made her reply, 'No. He died. Drowned.'

She didn't know why she said it, but it gave her a tragic air that made the other girls treat her with respect. Having lied once, she had to carry on lying, elaborating. Almost she began to believe in this version of her story. In her imagination it was Phil who had drowned, who had gone from her life for ever.

# 21

Anna hadn't yet made use of Ruth's bike, and was spending far too much each week on taxis to and from the tube station. She was living cheaply in other ways, offsetting the cost; but she'd have to think ahead, invest in a small car, perhaps. When the mornings and evenings lightened, she could use the bike, but for now she didn't relish the thought of cycling along the country lanes in darkness, with vehicles swooshing past.

She didn't much like arriving home after dark, either. For those few moments after the taxi left her, its headlights sweeping the hedgerows as it turned back up the hill, she stood alone in thick, stifling darkness. She had bought a pocket torch to keep in her bag, and always had her key ready in her hand; she resolved to ask Ruth about fitting a security light.

Indoors, she went through the ritual of locking and bolting, going round the house to draw curtains, turning on the radio. Then she could relax, put the kettle on or pour a glass of wine, change from her office clothes into jeans and a sweater.

On Friday night, late back, she was gearing herself up for

an early start in the morning. Her taxi was booked, her rail tickets ordered online, to collect at the station tomorrow. She heated a pasta dish and ate it with salad, quickly, hardly tasting it, and was washing up when the doorbell shrilled.

She tensed, aware of the darkness outside, her isolation. There was no spyhole on the door, no chain. It could be anyone. Someone might have been watching her movements, knowing she was alone.

*Don't be neurotic.* It was probably the neighbour she hadn't yet spoken to, or maybe Ruth.

Cautiously she slid back the bolt and opened the door a crack, ready to slam it again, to kick hard if a foot tried to insert itself into the gap.

It was Martin who stood there.

Her hand went to her throat. 'Oh! You scared me.' Her voice came out husky with relief. 'What are you doing?'

'Are you going to let me in? It's bloody cold out here.'

She stepped aside, closed the door behind him and stood with her back to it. He wore his black overcoat, a suit underneath, with a white shirt and dark red tie. She had always liked the dramatic contrast of red, black and white against his dark colouring; now it annoyed her to acknowledge how good he looked, how he brought masculine assurance into the hallway where she'd stood dithering moments before.

'What are you doing here?' she repeated.

'Come to see you – what does it look like? I've been visiting a client in Cambridge, so I made a detour.'

'It's late.'

'I know it's late. Sorry if I'm putting you out. Thought I might get some sense out of you, if I came round.'

'I see,' Anna said coldly.

'Look, are we going to stand in the hall or can we sit down and talk?'

'We can sit down, I suppose. If you're willing to enter the hovel, as I think you described it.' She led the way into the sitting room. Martin threw his overcoat over a chair-back, and sat down; she stood by the fireplace, facing him.

He said flatly, 'Ruth says you're meeting someone tomorrow.'

'Did she?'

*Thanks, Ruth.*

'You haven't wasted much time. Or – *is* this a new thing?' His coolness matched her own. 'How long have you been seeing him?'

'Fuck's sake! Considering Ruth knows nothing about it, I can't see why you're both jumping to conclusions. Unless it's because you *want* to think badly of me.'

'I don't want to think badly. I just don't know what's got into you. Whatever you're playing at, I don't like it.'

'Don't you? Well, get used to it. I'm not playing. That's one of the main reasons I like it here. Being on my own. Being able to come and go without having to account for myself.'

'I see. Don't you owe it to me to be clearer about your intentions?'

'What intentions?'

'Ah,' Martin said, maddeningly calm. 'Precisely. For instance – are you planning to collect the rest of your things from the flat, move out properly? Or carry on with this halfway arrangement?'

'You keep on about what I'm planning.' Anna leaned

against the mantelpiece. 'Why do I have to plan? Why can't I let things happen?'

'Because you're an adult, supposedly, with other people to consider. For God's sake, Anna – you want it all ways. You want to be independent, but you're stopping short of making a complete break. Maybe you haven't got the courage.'

'It's not courage,' she retorted. 'It's a simple matter of sorting out where I'm going to live.'

'Simple, is it? So I'm nothing more to you than a flat mate you'll abandon the minute it suits you?' He looked at her in exasperation. 'Can't you sit down? I'm getting neck ache looking up at you.'

She moved away from the fireplace, but turned towards the door. 'Would you like something? Wine, coffee?'

'No, I want to sort this out. Could you please give me a sensible answer for once? Either come back with me now, or collect your things and give me your key. If you *have* moved out, I don't want you dropping in at odd times.'

'Oh dear,' she said, her voice rising triumphantly. 'Did that mess things up with Lenka, just when you were getting cosy?'

Martin gave a theatrical sigh. 'Don't try to make something out of nothing. Lenka came round for a sandwich and a chat. You know that's all it was.'

'You don't exactly have a good record for faithfulness,' Anna flung at him.

He looked at her, brows lowered. 'And what's that supposed to mean?'

'Ruth told me about your affair.' Her turn to play the Ruth card. 'With a married woman called Hilary.'

'Oh, did she?' He glanced down, then up again, meeting her gaze. 'Well, that was years ago, and all I can say is I'm not proud of it and I wish I hadn't been so bloody stupid. But it's nothing to do with you and me.'

Anna shrugged. 'Easy to say that. It's who you are.'

So he wished it hadn't happened, did he? Which meant he wished he was still with Ruth? For a moment Anna saw it as a noble gesture she was making, clearing out, clearing their way.

'Let's not drag up the distant past,' Martin said. 'I can't see how that helps. Why don't you come home? I'll wait while you pack your bag.'

'*Home* – you mean your flat? It's never felt like home to me. I don't like living in London. I prefer it out here.'

He threw her a look of incredulity. 'You've never said that! Never a word. Am I supposed to be telepathic?'

'What'd be the point? You'd never move out of London. You're there and I'm here, and it suits both of us.'

Martin shook his head slowly. 'This is another excuse, isn't it?'

'It's not! I do like it here – it feels more like home than the flat ever has.'

'So – that's it, then? You're not coming back?'

Anna shook her head. 'I've told you, I can't go anywhere now, even if I wanted. I'm busy tomorrow.'

'You could cancel.'

'I couldn't. Look,' she said, capitulating slightly, 'I'll phone you when I get back, shall I, on Sunday?'

'Sunday?' Martin was visibly taken aback. 'You're away till Sunday? So you're planning to spend the night with whoever it is?'

'There you go, on and on about planning!'

'I'm wasting my time.' Martin sprang to his feet, reaching for his coat. 'Sorry to have taken up so much of yours.'

'OK. I'll do it, since that's what you want.' Anna felt suddenly reckless. 'Hire a car next week and come for my things.'

He stood for a long moment looking at her; she couldn't read his expression. Then he turned away. 'Fine. It's probably best. Come when I'm not there, will you?'

In the hall she relented enough to move towards at least a sociable farewell kiss – they could be grown up about this, couldn't they? – but he was brisk now, already out of the door, calling only a curt 'Bye, then.' He zapped his key-fob and the car unlocked with a loud obedient click; Anna closed the door and stayed there, listening, until the sound of his engine had faded.

The house felt empty now, with him gone. She closed her eyes, imagining a different scenario, if she'd gone to him and said, 'Don't go, Martin. Stay with me. Please, stay.' They could have snuggled together in the night-time chill of the bedroom; she could have told him where she was going and why; asked him, even, to go with her. Would he have agreed? He might have offered to drive her to Devon; he was always good at helping in practical ways.

It was pointless, wondering, and too late, now. She'd do this alone. It was a part of her life that Martin had never understood.

In bed, Cassandra is propped up against pillows, leafing through her gardening magazine. She flicks past advertisements for gazebos, conservatories and stylish wellingtons, pauses for longer over photographs of summer gardens, velvety lawns and rose-clad arches. Her attention is caught by a border planted in white, cream and blue; she reads the caption, reaches for the notebook on her bedside table and writes down *Sisyrinchium striatum*.

Don is getting ready for the morning, for an early round of golf with Malcolm; his shoes are clean, his bag of clubs propped against the wardrobe.

'Have you seen my cap? The dark red peaked one?'

'It's in there somewhere. Second shelf down, I think.' Cassandra doesn't look up from the irises, the foxgloves, the scrambling white rose. She is thinking of summer, of new gardening projects. She wonders whether a wrought-iron bench like the one in the photograph would look better under the pear tree than the heavy wooden one that's beginning to peel and flake.

'Who are these for, love?'

She looks up at Don, over the top of her reading glasses. He's lifting the paper carrier bag in one hand, the purple shoes in the other, holding them by the straps. Cassandra stares at them and feels herself blushing hotly.

'Is there some great mystery? What's going on?' Don gazes at her. 'It's not – you don't mean – oh, love, is Anna expecting?'

She gives a slight nod. It's the easiest answer, the obvious one. And, even, possible.

'Well, why on earth didn't you tell me!' He's beaming now, placing the little shoes side by side on the bed, leaning over to give her a hug and a kiss. 'Why the big secret?'

She returns his embrace. 'It's not certain yet – I shouldn't have—'

'But you couldn't wait to start shopping. Well, that's fantastic news! Grandparents at last, hey? Won't that be great?'

She envies him his uncomplicated pleasure, his wide grin. For as long as she remains silent, she can pretend it's true.

'Do you think she'll tie the knot with Martin, then? Will they be shopping for a ring? Living in Hatton Garden they've only got to pop downstairs.' It's a joke he's made before.

'That'd be nice.' Cassandra finds herself wondering what she might wear to a wedding. Anna would never go for a big fussy church occasion, she's sure of that much.

Don picks up one of the shoes and holds it in his palm. 'What if it's not a girl she's expecting, though? Too early to tell, surely? Would the shop let you swap these for boys' shoes?'

'Oh . . .' she says vaguely. 'It's a hunch.'

'One of your Cassandra moments, was it?' Don rubs his hand up and down her arm. 'Well, maybe you're right. We'll see. We must celebrate, all four of us. Go out for dinner. Shall I see how they're fixed for tomorrow night?'

❖ ❖ ❖

# 22

**Sandy, 1967, 1968**

Two weeks before Christmas, it was Sandy's turn to go to the nearby hospital. She went unaccompanied in the ambulance, as none of the home staff could be spared. On arrival she was taken charge of by brusque strangers. 'Well, what did you expect?' said the midwife, when she whimpered with the shock of labour pains. 'No one said it'd be easy, did they? You should have thought of that.'

She felt so ignorant. All the while, she had harboured the idea that her body couldn't nourish a foetus that the world didn't want; it would surely wither away, or slip out prematurely. More recently, when she felt it kicking, she imagined it balled up and angry, already resenting her. Often she had felt drained and ill, as if this alien thing was sucking all her energy into itself. At other times she felt a kind of perverse pride that her body could achieve such a feat.

Between her and freedom loomed the inescapable ordeal of giving birth. Marion said that it was like being ripped to pieces; you'd scream and scream, and long for it to be over. Others, newly delivered, spoke of nurses who took relish in the girls' fears and the pain they would have to endure, and talked in loud voices about adoption. Marion had been in a ward next to a woman whose baby had been stillborn, and who had shrieked at Marion in hysterical grief when she heard the nurse's tactless remarks.

I'm going to die, Sandy thought, gripped by the frightening power of contractions. Surely I'll die; something must be going wrong. No one could survive this. Hours passed, in a terrifying private place where she could only strain and sob, wait for the next wave of pain, give herself up to it.

'Push. You're not trying! You've got to push. It won't come out on its own.' The voice floated towards her from a long way off, and at last she had the sense of powerful instincts overwhelming her, an irrepressible force taking charge. She was carried on a current, strong and deep, and at last it was over. She had come through the straining and sweating and heaving; she was alive, and so was the baby; she heard its thin cry. She lay back exhausted; damp hair clung to her forehead; tears ran down the sides of her face and trickled into her ears.

'It's a girl,' said the midwife.

Someone propped Sandy up on pillows and washed her face, and she was given the little wizened thing to hold; only briefly, because it was to be fostered until adoption formalities were completed. She stared at her baby in astonishment. How had such a tiny thing not been squeezed and crushed to death? Its eyes were closed; it moved its fists; it was alive. A living, separate creature.

'Just for a few minutes, dear,' said the midwife, in a kindlier tone.

Sandy looked at the clenched face, the new skin, the scalp

streaked with hair. She'd never looked at a baby with such intentness, had never fully understood what it was to see a life at its very beginning. Certain for some reason that it would be a boy, she had planned to call it Roland.

Now this. A red-faced baby girl, gasping with the shock of being born, of breathing air.

'Her name's Rosanna,' she said. 'I want her to be called Rosanna.'

Sandy's parents had sold their Croydon house in the autumn, and moved, in December, to a smaller one in Tonbridge. Her father continued to commute to London, while her mother found work as secretarial assistant to a local vicar.

Having been reluctant to go to Bridge House, Sandy now found herself equally unwilling to leave it and the friends she had made there, to re-enter a world that wanted girls like her brushed out of sight. The birth had loomed like a punishment, an end of something; she'd given little thought to what she'd do afterwards, and now found herself dumped back into a life that felt only slightly familiar. Even the expected sense of freedom meant nothing, and had turned to anti-climax and lethargy. She had done something almost miraculous, bringing that whimpering thing alive into the world, but her achievement must be hidden away, never referred to. Her body, swollen and bruised, aching for the baby it had toiled so hard to produce, wept blood and tears and milk, but soon recovered, guarding its secret.

In spite of everything, she had done reasonably well in her O-Levels. Her mother, on her weekend visits to Bridge House – Sandy's father had not come, not once – talked

291

about secretarial courses and the shorthand and typing skills that would give useful entry to a variety of jobs. She enrolled Sandy at a local college, to begin a course as soon as she came home, or rather to the house that was now called home. Sandy also signed up for English A-Level, which she could take by attending a weekly evening class. She'd missed the first term, but the set books studied then were *The Tempest* and *Tess of the d'Urbervilles*; having enjoyed *Far from the Madding Crowd*, and seen the film, with Julie Christie so beautiful as Bathsheba, Terence Stamp imperiously handsome as Sergeant Troy, she felt sure she could cope with Tess. The other students were either adults, or teenagers who'd failed to make the grade for A-Level courses at school, so she didn't feel as outclassed as she'd been by the few high-flyers at St Clare's.

The new house, a thirties semi in a road near the station, had nothing of Roland in it; nothing of Sandy, either. Her parents had established themselves, their furniture arranged in much the same way as before, but to Sandy it felt temporary, as if she'd never really belong here. Maybe she wouldn't stay long. Once armed with shorthand and typing, she could find a flat of her own; even share with Marion, whose baby, six weeks old, was handed over to his adoptive parents in mid-January. 'It was so awful I can't tell you about it,' Marion wrote from Rochester, where she had returned to her parents. 'But I expect you know.'

On the TV screen, American aircraft bombed villages in North Vietnam; villages burned, terrified children ran from the smoke. In the Winter Olympics, ice-skaters twirled and glided, goggled skiers flew down ramps, commentators stood on snowy slopes. The Beatles went to India to study meditation with someone called the Maharishi, and were photographed sitting cross-legged, hung with flower garlands. Mounted police rode into a crowd of protestors in Grosvenor Square. Martin Luther King was shot dead in Memphis; students rioted in Paris. Cloistered in Bridge House, Sandy had taken little notice of television news and had only the vaguest idea what the Vietnam War was about, or who Martin Luther King was. She skated over the surface of her new life, tentatively at first, certain that the ice would splinter and she would be sucked through into the stifling dark. Something had been left behind; she must go back, go back. But everything was pulling her forward.

Sandy's parents gave the story to relatives and to their new neighbours that she'd had a long illness and convalescence: 'Yes, glandular fever takes a long time to get over, but she's making headway,' she heard her mother telling the woman next door. Lying was acceptable, apparently, under these circumstances. Usually Sandy found that she could use vagueness as a shield, saying 'I've been in hospital,' only if pressed. It was taboo to mention the pregnancy, the baby. No one talked about that at home, beyond her mother's occasional reference to *your trouble* or *all that business*. It had been a diversion, a swerving; now she was back on course.

The surface part of her mind concerned itself with Pitman shorthand, with vowel signs and line position and abbreviations. *We are in receipt of your letter dated 15th March,* she read. *I am writing in connection with the above unpaid invoice. Kindly sign and return the enclosed document in the pre-paid envelope.* She learned about different kinds of filing systems and how to keep a boss's diary. In the middle of the night she jolted

293

awake from the horror of earth spattering over Roland's coffin, the impossibility of him being put into the ground. She saw the cross-faced baby that had lived inside her; she dreamed that she had carelessly lost it, abandoned it to die, left it in the street for a stranger to find. In her dreams she searched and searched, with a heaviness inside her that told her she would never find what she was looking for.

She would be found out. Someone would see through to the tangle of guilt that twisted and coiled inside her.

❖ ❖ ❖

# 23

Knowing she couldn't concentrate on a book, Anna bought the Saturday *Guardian* to read on the train. The stands and kiosks at Paddington were decked out in red and silver: hearts and ribbons, candles and chocolates, the florist's frontage knee-deep in crimson roses. She'd forgotten that it was Valentine's Day tomorrow; for the first time in years, it was irrelevant.

But, making her way to the Plymouth train, she found herself recalling last year, when she had surprised Martin by booking theatre tickets and a late supper afterwards, and he'd surprised her by asking her to marry him.

'Are you joking?' she had answered, thrown by the timing as much as anything, because Martin was so sceptical of the torrent of slush that Valentine's Day had become. 'Have you had a glass of wine too many?'

But he assured her that he wasn't, and hadn't, and that he loved her, and why not?

'But what for?' she objected. 'What difference would it make? I know you could tell me all about the tax advantages of being married, but to me it's just a piece of paper we don't need.'

'So much for my romantic gesture,' Martin said. 'So you're turning me down? For my clodhopping way of introducing the subject, or because you really don't want to? Should I be distraught?'

'Course you shouldn't! It doesn't mean I don't love you. You know I do – at least, I hope you know. We're happy as we are, aren't we?' And they had held hands across the table until suddenly it seemed urgent to return to the flat.

Well, she thought now, finding her window seat, hanging up her coat; look how things change. They might have been two different people.

Valentine's Day, though. Martin's dismay when she told him she was staying away tonight – did he imagine she was heading for a steamy weekend in a hotel, with red roses and champagne and breakfast in bed? And with who? It was a ridiculous idea, almost laughable. But she regretted making him think more badly of her than he already did. For a second she thought of sending a text: *It's not what you think.* She took out her mobile, started entering the message, then cancelled and put it away again. What was the point?

Her attention was moth-like today, settling lightly then flitting off again. Somewhere past Swindon, she was looking without much interest at the *Guardian* travel section when her mobile rang; *Dad* showed on the screen.

'Anna? Just thought I'd give you a call.' His voice bubbled with excitement. 'It's great news, love. Can't tell you how pleased I am.'

'What news?'

'Sorry if I wasn't meant to know yet. Your mum let it out – she couldn't wait. It's the best news I've had in ages.'

'*What* news?' Anna gazed blankly at the fields and hedgerows flashing by.

'That we're going to be grandparents! It's great, Anna – fantastic. Well done, love. I thought, if you and Martin are free tonight – why don't we go out to dinner, the four of us, have a little celebration?'

'Dad, Dad! I don't know what you're on about. Where on earth did you get this from? Did Mum say something?'

A pause, then her father said, in a changed voice, 'She's bought baby shoes. I found them in the wardrobe.'

'They must be for someone else. It's nothing to do with me, Dad.'

'But she said—'

'Mum told you I was pregnant?' Anna lowered her voice, all too conscious of other passengers nearby; this wasn't a conversation to have in public.

'Yes, love. So . . . she's got it all wrong? Oh, dear dear dear.' His tone was flat now. 'Well – maybe you and Martin could come over anyway? Tomorrow, if tonight's no good?'

'Actually, Dad, I'm on a train – I'm on my way to visit someone. And – I'm not with Martin. I'm staying at a friend's house for a bit.'

'Is everything all right, love?'

She knew he'd picked up her dissembling. She would have to tell him, but not now.

'Everything's fine, Dad. I'll give you a call when I get back.'

Trying to make sense of this, Anna gazed out at undulating landscape, ploughed fields and meadow, woods, a church spire in a distant town. Could her mother really have told him she was pregnant? Or had he simply misunderstood, finding a present bought for someone else? She had heard of imaginary pregnancies, but could you have a phantom pregnancy at one remove? This sounded uncomfortably like mental slippage on her mother's part, and now Anna was guiltily aware that she'd had little contact with her parents since the brief visit; no more than the odd evasive phone call. She ought to go and see them; phoning wouldn't be enough. When she next saw them she'd have to tell them about her split with Martin; it couldn't be put off indefinitely. Rather than celebrating imminent grandparenthood they'd be devastated and upset, and that might propel her mother into further confusion.

She'd worry about that later. Today, first. There might be a revelation more important than any of that.

Not confident of recognizing Michael Sullivan, she had sent a text message to say that she was wearing a black coat and red scarf. When the train reached Plymouth and she went through the barrier, a man standing at the entrance looked at her intently and walked towards her.

'Anna?'

'Yes.'

They shook hands like people at a business meeting. 'Thank you for coming all this way,' he said, as if it was for his benefit.

No, she definitely wouldn't have picked him out of a crowd; she scanned his face without seeing anything to recall the young teacher of her memory. He looked a little older than Martin: taller, with hair greying a little and swept back from a high forehead; thin, mobile face, diffident smile; the kind of face that's unremarkable at first but becomes interesting with acquaintance. He looked entirely personable, but she wasn't going to trust him. Certainly she wasn't going to let herself *like* him.

She'd imagined they would go into the city centre, but instead Michael gestured towards the station buffet. 'I thought we'd get a coffee to start with,' he said.

Not sure what this meant – as a prelude to what? – Anna followed. There were a few customers in the café but she supposed they might as well talk here as anywhere else. At his suggestion she installed herself at a corner table while he went to the counter.

'Do you live in Plymouth?' she asked, when he returned with two lattes.

'No – I just work here. You? London, you said, but where exactly? What do you do?'

Anna gave only brief answers, conscious of the big questions hanging between them; in return he told her that he left Oldlands Hall the same year she did, took a temporary post in Bristol which became permanent, then moved on to the Plymouth school where he was promoted to Head of Science.

'Do you remember me from your time at Oldlands?' Ridiculously, she caught herself being deferential towards him, just because he'd been a teacher at her school.

'Yes, of course,' he said, 'though I never taught you, did I?'

'Why *of course*?'

He didn't answer, asking instead, 'So – what's prompted this?'

'It seemed like a long shot,' Anna told him, 'a very long shot. One of Rose's friends told me that Rose was keen on you, that last year. She told me about the leavers' dance, and

I remembered you coming to the art exhibition when I was in the upper sixth. I know, it doesn't sound like much. But, well . . .' She looked at him intently. 'When I phoned you it didn't seem such a long shot after all.' She paused. 'Do you know what happened to Rose?'

'Yes. Yes, I do.'

A beat of silence; she found her voice. 'How? You've known all this time and not said? How – how can that make sense?' She had the wild idea that he was about to confess to a murder, that this was his purpose in bringing her here. 'Is Rose dead?'

'No, Anna. Rose is perfectly well,' he said gently. 'I'm married to her.'

'You're—? No. That's impossible.'

The buffet swayed and blurred around her, the bright adverts, the cooler with racks of bottled drinks. His face had become a pale medallion hanging in front of her, the mouth moving, speaking nonsense. An announcement about a Paddington train floated at her, mixing itself up with Michael's words. He was playing an elaborate trick on her, seeing how much he could get her to believe. He was mad, deluded; he had to be. He'd killed Rose, or was keeping her captive somewhere.

'It's true,' he said. 'We've been married for fifteen years.'

'But – I don't understand,' she said helplessly.

'No, of course you don't. Not yet.'

They were interrupted by a bustle at the next table: a couple accompanied by a sulky teenage boy and a slow-moving elderly woman, settling themselves in the seats; the man bumped his wheeled suitcase against Anna's chair without apologizing. Anna looked at Michael, thinking that surely they couldn't continue their conversation here; but the younger woman called out, 'Platform two! I *said* platform two!' and the whole party got up and surged out again.

'Where is she?' Anna demanded, as the door swung to with a bang.

'She's at home.'

'Can I see her?'

'Yes, if you like.'

'If I like!' Anna knew that she wouldn't believe him until she did see Rose for herself; her thoughts whirled between longing and fear, eagerness and reluctance. 'Tell me,' she pleaded. 'Tell me everything.'

'Yes, I will.'

Anna listened, her eyes fastened on his face, anxious not to miss a word, a nuance. Words hung briefly in the air and melted like snowflakes, words she needed to gather and store, take out and examine: words too frail to fill a gulf of twenty years. How could words do that?

'In a way,' said Michael Sullivan, leaning forward, hands clasped, 'I helped her to leave. I didn't want to, but I did.'

'You helped her? Why? How?'

'She asked me to. You probably know I was in my first year of teaching when I met Rose. I had a sixth-form tutor group, not the one Rose was in, but I saw her most days in the sixth-form centre, coming and going. I was attracted to her from the start. Occupational hazard, for a young teacher surrounded by so many adolescent girls – but there was something about Rose . . . and of course I knew I had to be careful, I was very aware of that. Rose would always

301

smile and say hello, and then she started approaching me at odd times about her university applications – whether I thought she should take a gap year, things like that. I helped her as best I could. I was flattered – there were plenty of other teachers she could have asked, and it wasn't as if she was going for science subjects. Then the exams started. She got herself into a state, the morning of her art history paper – said she couldn't go in, couldn't face sitting in the exam room again. She was crying, shaking. I had to calm her down, persuade her it'd be OK. She went into the hall and did the exam, and next day she brought a present to thank me.'

Yes, Anna thought, recognizing the Rose she knew: the tears, the hysteria, the sudden change of mood. 'What did she give you?'

'It was one of her drawings. Postcard-sized, a female nude.'

'Quite a suggestive thing to give a young male teacher.'

'Yes. She told me she'd done it in life class, but the face was hers. I suppose I shouldn't have accepted it, but I did. I've still got it.'

'Then what? The dance?'

Michael nodded. 'On her last day at school she asked if I'd dance with her at the ball, in a sort of flirty *Please, sir* way. I laughed it off. Then, on the night, she looked so beautiful, in a green dress . . .'

Anna nodded. 'I remember.'

'I couldn't take my eyes off her. When she came over, I just couldn't, much as I wanted to – couldn't risk it, in front of everyone. I'd have given myself away. So I said no. I hoped she'd understand, but . . . to her it was a put-down. A public rejection.'

'So when did you see her after that?'

'When she followed me home. It was still July, term-time. I'd just got in one afternoon – I usually walked to and from school, I was renting a house near the library – when she turned up, wanting to come in and talk. I felt uneasy, and she knew – she teased me, said she wasn't a schoolgirl any more, she was eighteen, a consenting adult.'

'You mean you—?'

'No, no. Not then. I explained about the ball, and that was enough. She came round again on the first day of the summer holidays, and that time – yes. We spent the whole afternoon in my bedroom until suddenly she upped and left. I wanted to see her again, but also I was scared shitless, wondering what I'd done. Technically she was over eighteen and had left school, but still, if it got out I'd have been in serious trouble.'

'Even though she'd been practically stalking you? Where would you stand, legally?'

'I don't know. If it happened today, there'd be questions about grooming – though I hadn't. Anyway. The very next day I was due to leave for Thailand for the whole summer break, with Pippa, my girlfriend from university. And I didn't want Pippa to know about Rose. My head was in a spin, to be honest. I told her when I'd be back, and we planned to see each other. But in Thailand I felt sure I'd made a fool of myself, or was about to. She was heading for art foundation – well, you know that – and she'd meet other people and forget about me. Maybe she'd even hit on me for a bet. That's what I thought at the time.'

303

'So you were away when she went missing? But you said you helped her.'

'Yes. The first I heard about her disappearing was at the staff training day. Beginning of September. People were talking about it – it had been all over the local papers, apparently. Well, that threw me into a quandary. I wasn't the last person to see Rose by a long way, but all the same I should have gone to the police. Even if only to eliminate myself as a suspect – someone might have seen her coming to my house or leaving. And of course I was worried for her. Pippa had gone back to Hull – she was starting a teaching job there – and I was wondering what the hell to do when Rose phoned.'

'*Phoned?* Rose phoned you? So you were the one person who knew she was alive, and you didn't let on?'

'Anna, I couldn't. I struggled with that, believe me. She wanted me to help – she pleaded, said I was the only person she could trust. And before she'd tell me where she was, she made me promise not to tell anyone.'

'But, God, we were thinking of murder, kidnap, all sorts of horrible things – my parents – I don't know how we stayed sane!'

'I know. Or rather, I can only imagine. That's why I wanted her at least to send a card or something, or let me take a message – let your parents, and you, know she was alive and OK. But she wouldn't. Said they'd track her and try to make her go home. Said they didn't have a claim on her any more.'

'But why did she—?'

'She said it was her choice to leave, no one had made her. She wanted me to help, but only if I respected her decision.

304

Otherwise she threatened to put the phone down and that would be it. So – I agreed. I couldn't risk losing her, not knowing what state she was in. There was a weekend between the training days and the start of term, so I went to meet her straight away. She was in Bristol – she'd headed west, with an idea of going to Cornwall, but she got as far as Bristol and was almost out of cash.'

'So you promised to help?'

He nodded. 'I thought I'd persuade her to come back, get in the car and head straight home. But she was adamant. She'd left home and she wasn't changing her mind.'

'But – you haven't said what made her leave so suddenly!'

'No.' Michael hesitated now, looking at her doubtfully. Then he said, 'Anna – do you know about your other sister?'

When he'd told her, Anna was silent: filling in details, making the brief outlines into a scene, as if watching a film. It was the August day of memory and mis-memory, the day of the garden lounger and the toenail painting. The day she called a casual goodbye to Rose, not even bothering to go outside: she couldn't now recall the words of farewell, though it was the last time she had heard Rose's voice.

'Excuse me,' she said, getting to her feet. 'I need to find a loo.'

Anna saw herself plodding down the cul-de-sac, a small figure in shorts and a sun-hat, although she couldn't actually remember what she'd been wearing that day. Now Rose is alone in the garden with her book, and the sun's warmth that makes the day feel unhurried, holidayish. It is Anna's painting, the scene impressed in her mind – Rose in the dappled shade of the pear tree, her clothes pale, her skin and eyes luminous, as if the pear tree exists for no other reason than to cast flattering green shade over the sitter.

It's the garden of their childhood, of their games and pretending and fantasies; it has contained and absorbed them, but now Rose has outgrown it. She is whiling away her time, waiting. What's in her mind? She is thinking about next day, surely, and her results; but she can't be *very* worried, sure of her place at Ravensbourne. Anna couldn't shut out the knowledge that Rose's A-Level grades would all be As, eclipsing her own more prosaic B, B and C, five years later. Rose, as always, was better, cleverer, surging ahead, doing everything with more flair. And, surely, more urgently and enticingly, Rose must be thinking about *him*, about Michael; closing her eyes to recall the intimacy in his bedroom, clothes dropping to the floor, his eyes sweeping down her naked body. She is thinking of the things she hopes and expects to do again, more thoroughly, and soon.

The garden has a side gate; anyone can walk in, and someone does.

In Anna's scene Rose is drowsing instead of reading, finally falling asleep, letting the book slip from her hand to lie face-down on the grass. She wakes to the surprise of someone looking down at her, standing by the lounger. A young woman, twenty-something. For want of any other face to supply her with, Anna gives her a version of her own.

'Who are you?' Rose asks sleepily, and the intruder smiles and says, 'Don't you know?'

No. Of course Rose doesn't. She looks puzzled, and the young woman says, 'I'm Zanna. Rosanna.' She says it as if

Rose is meant to know already. 'I'm your sister.'

'My what?'

'Your sister. Sort of sister, anyway. Your mum is my mum too.'

'What? How can she be?' Rose is looking up at Zanna through sunglasses, which she now takes off for a better look. Her thoughts blur.

'She hasn't told you about me, has she? She's told me about you. You're Rose, and your little sister's Anna.'

Anna now wonders if she and Zanna might have passed each other in the street a few moments before; neither gives the other more than a quick glance, not recognizing that they're half-sisters.

'Oh! You mean my other mother,' Rose says.

'I don't. I mean Cassandra. I'm talking about the three of us – Rosanna, Rose, Anna,' says Zanna. 'It's odd of her to give us those names, like we're part of each other. Don't you think?'

'How do you know her?' Rose asks sharply

'I told you. She's my mother too.'

'This is rubbish! Complete rubbish.' Rose stands, pushing her feet into sandals so as not to give the stranger the advantage of height; in wedge heels, Rose is several inches taller. 'I don't know who you are, or what gave you such a stupid idea.'

'It's all true, if you'll just listen. The adoption agency put me in touch with her, with Cassandra. You're adopted too, aren't you? She told me that. So really Anna's my sister but you're not. Is Anna around? I'd like to see her.'

Anna couldn't decide on Zanna's motivation. Was she resentful, vengeful, or merely curious? And what did she think of Rose? Was she disconcerted to find someone so beautiful, so unlike her – because although Anna could picture her only vaguely, she must be cast as plain, unbecomingly dressed, with a clumpy, waddling walk, maybe, in order to make the contrast with Rose all the more striking.

'I see,' says Rose. 'You want to take over. You want to be me. That's why you've come.'

That's how Rose, with her gift for melodrama, would see it. Her mother has deceived her, has claimed back her first-born, Rosanna, her real daughter. They were characters in a folk tale, babies exchanged at birth. Rose was only a replacement, a foundling. They could so easily be swapped back, the only proper end of the story. Zanna is a cuckoo, huge, demanding, ravenous, bent on pushing her rival out of the nest.

'Come in, why don't you?' Rose goes on, as Zanna hesitates. Her voice is hard-edged, a little shrill. 'Have a good look round. Why don't you stay? You belong here. I don't. I can go.'

'No, I didn't mean – I only wanted—'

'Have you brought a bag?' Rose says, over her shoulder, striding towards the open French windows. 'Or is it simpler if you take over my clothes? You're a couple of sizes bigger, but the looser things might fit. I don't know about the shoes.'

How would Zanna react? It would be hard to resist the chance to see inside her mother's house, to see how she lived. But although Anna was curious about this young woman, this half-sister whose existence was unknown to her half an hour ago, her eyes were on Rose. Rose, whose sudden fury of energy brought her to life in Anna's mind, just as she had indeed been brought to puzzling, incomprehensible life by Michael's story.

Rose, with a plan shaping itself in her mind, would flounce around the house so quickly that Zanna can hardly keep up.

'Here's your room,' she says, with a dramatic flourish. 'You can move straight in. Give me half an hour. I'll take what I need and go.'

But perhaps it wasn't like that at all. Maybe Zanna, Rosanna, had been to the house before, with her – with their – mother. Because the mother here needed re-casting too: she would have to be played by someone other than the Sandra Taverner Anna thought she knew. She had become a woman with a secret daughter, a hidden past.

Rosanna, Rose, Anna. In her mind they lined up like Russian dolls on a shelf, decreasing in size, herself the smallest and least important. Rose had always been larger and brighter, but now there was someone else, someone powerful enough to elbow Rose aside, out of her life and into a new one. Or perhaps the shock had sent Rose tumbling off the shelf to smash into little pieces, and it was Michael who picked up the bits and put them back together.

'Are you OK?' Michael said, when she arrived back at the table and threw him a vague smile. He had changed too: no longer a suspect, but someone she would have to trust, because he was the one person Rose had trusted when she turned away from her family.

'I still don't see how it could have happened like that. How she – Rosanna – could turn up like that, without my mother knowing.' She slumped into her chair, though

309

Michael had zipped up his coat and it seemed that they were going somewhere.

'I don't think she did appear from nowhere. Rose got the impression that she and your mother had been meeting regularly for a year or so, away from home, of course. Maybe Rosanna followed your mother, or got hold of her address somehow. Maybe your mother gave it to her.'

'Rose was adopted too – you did know?'

Michael nodded, and Anna went on, 'She couldn't have contacted her birth mother until she was eighteen, and then only if the mother agreed. On Rose's eighteenth birthday I asked if she was going to, but she said no, she didn't see the point. But maybe that changed – you must know?'

'Yes,' said Michael. 'Rose *is* in touch with her mother. They don't meet often – a couple of times a year. There's a stepfather, and a half-brother and -sister, quite a bit younger.'

'So she's got a whole new family?' Anna's voice came out small and hurt. 'She left us all behind and started again?'

'I wouldn't say that. They're not close. And it wasn't easy for her.'

'What about Zanna now? Does Rose see *her*?'

'No, not since that day.'

'But have you, or Rose, considered that this Zanna might not have been telling the truth? She could have been ill or deluded for all we know, and somehow got hold of the idea that she was my mother's daughter.'

'Rose believed her,' Michael said simply.

'So – what then? Tell me how it happened, after you went to her in Bristol.'

'I felt responsible – if I really was the only person who

knew, it was up to me to try to make her see sense. I tried, I really did try, to persuade her that it wasn't so bad, and that she had to talk to your mother about all this. She flatly refused. She said that your father didn't know about Zanna, and she couldn't be the one to tell him. And she felt betrayed. She said that your mother had never wanted her – only wanted Zanna. Your parents adopted her because they thought they couldn't conceive, and then they had you.'

'But I'm sure that's not true!'

'It's what she thought. Or what she convinced herself.'

'That was one of the awful things, when she went. I remember one of my great-aunts saying *At least she's not your real daughter*, as if it would have been worse if it was me. But to them, she *was* their daughter. She must have known that, surely?'

'Maybe. But once she gets an idea in her head there's no shifting her.'

Of course, he knew Rose better than she did, now; Anna had to take this in. She said, 'Tell me what happened when you came to Bristol that first time. When she refused to go back.'

'She met me at the station. I hardly recognized her – she'd cut her hair short and ragged, her lovely hair, and she wore dark glasses, and looked pale and exhausted. That made me all the more determined to get her home. I bought her something to eat and talked at her for ages. She listened, but in a quiet, obstinate way. Nothing made any difference. She said she wasn't that Rose any more, the Rose your parents thought belonged to them. Maybe she never had been. And she kept reminding me that I'd promised not to break her confidence. That she had the right to leave home and start out on her own. So eventually, when I saw I wasn't going to win, I had to go along with it. She was used to a nice home, food on the table, parents who loved her, and you – she'd soon start missing all that, I thought. Maybe she did, but it didn't change her mind.'

'But she did need you.'

'I guess she'd have managed somehow, but I was glad of the chance to know she was safe, and had somewhere to stay. She'd slept rough, the first couple of nights. Then she got herself a job picking fruit, sleeping in a shabby caravan. I helped her find a cheap B&B in Bristol while she looked for work, and we found her a one-room bedsit and a wait-ressing job, and that was enough to keep her going. Every weekend I went to see her. I finished with Pippa – it had always been a bit on-off anyway. It was Rose now. And . . . you know how they say you can get used to anything, and it's true – it soon seemed quite normal to go off to Bristol every Friday after work, and head back to Kent every Sunday night. A teacher's starting salary wasn't great, but it was a lot more than she was earning. Six months later we found a little house, and then I thought of that as my main home and rented a tiny flat in Sevenoaks for term-time. I liked it at Oldlands, got on well with the head of depart-ment there, and at the end of my second year I was offered a promotion, so I stayed on, even though it'd have been easier to move to Bristol. But also there was you. Oldlands Hall was Rose's link with you.'

'She wanted that?' Anna said, astonished.

Michael nodded. 'Yes, she asked about you, and I always told her if I saw you around school or covered one of your lessons. And I came to your art exhibition.'

'Yes, I remember.'

He looked regretful. 'When I saw that it was all about *her*, it made me realize all over again what she'd done to you and your parents, how it wasn't something you could get over. I had another try. But she wouldn't budge, wouldn't make a phone call. She was afraid of going back.'

'But why? Afraid of what?'

'Of even thinking about her old life. It was like a box she didn't want to open.'

'Couldn't you have—?'

'Insisted? I tried, Anna, believe me. She threatened to run away again. Said she'd done it once and she'd do it again. I believed her. And I couldn't risk that, couldn't force her. It would have to be her own decision.'

Anna nodded slowly, knowing how Rose could be.

'I haven't told you – she changed her name,' Michael said. 'She called herself Rosalind, Rosalind Owen. I don't know why she chose Owen. She's Rosalind Sullivan now. But she's Rose to me, always has been.'

'Is it that easy, then, to change your name? What about papers?'

'She applied for a new copy of her adoption paper, saying the old one was lost. That's the equivalent of a birth certificate, so once she'd got that she could get a passport, register for tax, et cetera.'

'Rose always said she'd never get married,' Anna remembered. 'Marriage was too dull and conventional for her.'

Michael smiled. 'Well, we did, soon after our first son was born.'

'You've got a child?'

'Two boys, fifteen and eleven.'

Anna's head swam with this new piece of information. How many more shocks were waiting for her? How many more family members, relatives she'd been unaware of? She imagined them clustering round her like shadows, unseen till now. The thought flashed through her mind that Michael could be lying; that Rose was dead after all, and had been for twenty years. Raising both elbows to the table she rested her forehead on both hands for a moment, then rubbed her eyes.

'What I don't understand is' – she looked at him blearily – 'is why, if you kept your promise for twenty years, you're breaking it now by telling me all this?'

'Because Rose said I could.'

'She knows about me?'

Michael nodded. 'I told her, the day you phoned. I think we've had enough of secrets.'

'Why's she ready to let it all out, after so long?'

'You can ask her that yourself.'

'Are we going to your house? Is she at home?'

'Yes – is that OK?'

'Well, I . . .' The words crumbled in Anna's throat. 'I can't take it in, that it's going to happen. Today.'

'I know. Of course you can't.' Michael looked at his watch. 'We've got to get another train. There's one due in ten minutes.'

'To where?'

'Penzance. We live in Cornwall, a few miles from Land's End.'

'Land's End! So she kept going, then. Heading west as far as she could without taking to the sea.'

314

She wasn't sure why this came out flippantly, but Michael nodded and said, 'It'll mean staying till tomorrow. Are you OK with that? There's no way you could come to the house and still get back to London tonight.'

'I haven't seen Rose for twenty years,' Anna told him. 'I think I can spare one night.'

Michael's small Peugeot was in the car park at Penzance station. Fastening her seat belt, Anna wanted to protest that she wasn't ready, she needed more time; she felt sick at the thought of meeting Rose within the next hour. The car climbed a steep lane away from the town, with views over the harbour and across to St Michael's Mount, its causeway part covered by the sea. Soon the coastline was lost to view, hidden behind high banks each side of the single-track lanes. Dusk was falling; when the car crested another low hill, the sea spread out again in front, calm, deepest blue, with dark cloud streaking the horizon. A lane led steeply down to a settlement, too small to be called a village: a cluster of cottages in a cove, with cliffs on either side. In the fading light Anna saw low pines and ragged palms, a small stone quay with tethered yachts and dinghies. Reflected lights shimmered on the water. She had the sense of arriving somewhere she'd been before, as if the place had been waiting.

Now Michael seemed nervous too as he backed the car into a space behind a garden fence.

'OK?'

He gave her a sidelong glance before getting out; she nodded, not trusting herself to speak. The person she was about to meet wouldn't be Rose, but someone else. This would turn out to be a dream, the kind that segues into a different story altogether.

She followed him to the front of a white-painted cottage. A paling fence enclosed a tiny front garden, all stones, adorned with pieces of driftwood, netting and fishing floats. A pot of daffodils stood by the door. Anna thought of the Norfolk holiday: Blakeney, the holiday cottage, and her vision of the contented family who belonged there.

'We're here!' Michael called, opening the front door, which led straight into a small sitting room, furnished in shades of red, maroon and brown, with many cushions and throws. There was a reassuring smell of cooking and woodsmoke. The first person to appear, clumping down a spiral staircase, was a small dark-haired boy introduced by Michael as Euan; his face broke into an open smile when he saw Anna, quite without curiosity, as if she were a neighbour who'd called in. Anna wondered how much he knew about his mother's past. She could identify with that, Michael's revelations having shown her how little she knew about her own mother.

'Mum's in the boathouse,' Euan told his father.

'It's where she paints,' Michael explained. He gestured to Anna to come outside, and round the side of a low wooden building that fronted the quay. A board displayed a large mosaic fish, made of bits of broken china and mirror, and the sign SANDPIPERS GALLERY. IF CLOSED KNOCK AT COVE COTTAGE. In the interior, lit by an angled lamp at one end, Anna saw walls hung with paintings and sketches; she had a quick impression of seascapes, birds and studies of wild flowers.

But her attention was on the woman who sat inside at an easel, her back to them. As the door opened she stood, put down her paintbrush and wiped her hands on her jeans. She looked first at Michael, then at Anna, with a wary half-smile.

'Hello,' Anna said uncertainly. 'Rose.'

# 24

Later, Anna thought that it could hardly have been any
different, that first meeting. They couldn't have hugged
ecstatically, with squeals and gasps of 'God, I've missed
you!' The knowledge stood between them that Rose could,
at any time over the last twenty years, have picked up a
phone and dialled their parents' number; could have sent
them a letter, a postcard, a message via Michael. Anna's
main feeling, at the moment when Rose stepped towards
her, was of bewilderment. She stood rigid, unsure what her
face was doing. For a moment Rose moved as if to kiss
her, but stopped awkwardly. They stood facing each other.

Rose in her late thirties still had a girlish figure but her
face was weathered, with the beginnings of lines around her
eyes. Her hair was long, as it had always been, held back in
a loose plait (Anna found it impossible to picture her with a
short ragged crop, as Michael had described), and she wore
frayed jeans, plimsolls and a smocky garment of multi-
coloured weave, with a pendant of turquoise sea-glass on a
thong.

Anna felt a ludicrous impulse to ignore this woman who
seemed to be Rose, and instead to move around the small

gallery studying the paintings, or to bend and stroke the cat which she now noticed on a cushioned chair near Rose's easel – a grey long-haired cat that looked at her unblinking. What on earth to say? If she opened her mouth, twenty years' worth of recriminations and self-pity would scramble to get out.

It was Michael who spoke first. Anna feared that he'd offer to leave them alone together; after several hours in his company, she was more at ease with him than with Rose.

'Let's go indoors,' he said, and Rose nodded, and went around the gallery turning off lights and an electric heater. 'Come on, Fossil,' she said to the cat, which chirruped a reply and jumped down from its chair to rub against her legs. Rose's voice was deeper and less plaintive than Anna remembered.

They went into the house, where the boy Euan was now sprawled on the sofa with some kind of gadget in his hands, pressing keys with his thumbs. Seeing Anna's bag by the door, Michael said that he must phone the nearby guesthouse, there being only two bedrooms here. While he did so, Rose said, 'Take a seat, Anna,' and went through to a narrow kitchen. Anna looked at Euan, studying his neat features, straight dark hair and intent expression; trying to decide if he most resembled Rose or Michael, she concluded that he was not greatly like either. After a few moments Rose returned, carrying a tray loaded with glasses, a bottle of white wine and a can of soft drink. Their eyes met briefly as Rose set down the tray on a low table of roughly shaped wood.

What were they going to talk about, with Euan here? Michael said into the phone, 'Yes, ten-thirty latest,' and rang off; he turned to face the two women, rubbing his hands together in the manner of an awkward host hoping his guests will get on together.

Rose poured wine. 'I've got you a Sprite, Euan,' she said; the boy answered, 'Thanks,' his eyes on the small screen in front of him. When she'd poured wine and handed it round, Rose sat on a cushioned stool; Michael, on an upright chair by a writing desk, looked from Rose to Anna, holding his glass as if about to formulate a toast of some kind, thought better of it and raised it to his lips without speaking.

'It's a lovely cottage,' Anna remarked, for want of something to say.

'Yes, isn't it?' said Rose. 'It suits us perfectly, even though Michael has to do all that travelling back and forth. I fell in love with it at first sight. And there's my studio. I could never live anywhere else.'

'And your other son?' Anna asked. 'Is he around?'

'Oh, Finn's off on a sailing weekend. He loves sailing, always has. You probably won't see him. How long can you stay?'

'Only till tomorrow.' Anna thought of the train journey back, of work on Monday morning: so remote from Rose's settled life. Having been with her for barely fifteen minutes she knew already that Rose wasn't going to protest, *Oh, but that's hardly any time at all! Can't you stay longer?* Rose nodded, and sipped her wine. 'You won't meet Finn then. You'll have to get the train by about three, and he won't be back till after dark. He's gone over to Scilly with some friends.'

'And you? Do you go sailing?'

'Only now and then. Michael does. Maybe he could take you out tomorrow morning.'

Anna felt a strong temptation to get up and grab Rose by both shoulders and shake her; so composed, so pleased with her life, with her family; ready to be hospitable to Anna, but only as she might treat a passing visitor in whom she had little interest. Michael, who seemed aware of every nuance, said, 'It's you Anna's come to see, Rosy. Why don't I go and put the oven on, and you two can stay here and chat. You' – he addressed the boy – 'come and give me a hand?'

This *You* seemed to Anna a strangely perfunctory way of speaking to his son until she realized that of course it was *Eu* – a shortening of Euan. The boy got slowly to his feet, turning off his gadget with a tinkly sound, and Michael ushered him into the kitchen, closing the door behind them. Rose bent to stroke the cat, which lay purring at her feet, rolling over and showing the pale fur of its underside. 'You're a lovely boy,' she murmured. 'Oh, a beautiful boy.'

'What shall I tell Mum and Dad?' Anna said bluntly.

Rose looked at her properly for the first time, then quickly away, as if her eyes were hurt by too bright a light. 'You'll have to tell them, I suppose.'

'Well, course I will!' Anna tried to hide her impatience. 'You don't seriously think I could pretend not to have seen you, not to know you're alive? Rose, have you any idea what it's been like for them? For me, as well?'

On Rose's face she saw the expression she had noticed before, when Michael and Euan had been in the room; a look of shutting herself peaceably into some inner place. Knowing it was completely the wrong tactic, Anna couldn't stop herself from blurting, 'You're a mother now. How would you feel if one of your boys vanished without a word? Sailed off and never came back?'

'But I'm not your mother's daughter, Anna,' Rose said.

'Still! She – and Dad – adopted you, brought you up. Don't you owe them anything?'

'Yes, yes,' Rose said, almost irritably. She got up, stirred the ashy logs with a poker and added fresh ones from the basket, kneeling on the rug, and staying there. 'You can tell them I'm here. Maybe they might come and visit.'

'Don't you think you should make the effort to visit *them*?'

Rose seemed startled by this; she turned, her eyes widening in alarm, and for the first time Anna saw a glimpse of the sister she had known. 'Oh no. I never leave Cornwall. Never go far from here.'

Later, when Michael drove her up the lane to the guest-house, Anna asked him about this.

'No, Rose rarely goes farther than Penzance. There's a group of local artists that exhibit together, and two or three times a year we go over to Scilly on the boat, to deliver paintings to a gallery there. She hates crowds, hates big towns. Penzance is more than enough for her, driving the boys to school and doing the shopping. She has panic attacks – maybe you know that. She struggles to breathe.'

'I remember a couple of times at school. But it sounds like she's got worse.'

'Well, it's not so bad now, as long as she stays in her routine and the places she knows. She goes to a meditation class – that seems to help. And her painting, of course. She needs that. The odd thing is that she's quite happy for visitors to come into the studio, even ask questions. It's as if her artist role gives her a front, a persona. When we first lived in Bristol was when the attacks were at their worst.

That's why I could never push her. I was always afraid she'd run away, or do something drastic.'

'But now – now she must feel secure, surely? I mean, the worst has happened in a way – I've turned up, she's been discovered – but it's not really going to affect her much, is it?'

'Only in a good way, I hope.'

'It's not as if anyone's going to try to drag her back to my – our – parents. But I'll have to tell them, obviously. Apart from everything else, they'd love to know they've got grandsons. That's how they'll want to think of your boys. Do you think Rose will let them?'

'She'll come round, I'm sure, now that we've got this far.' Michael was turning abruptly into a gateway; the tyres crunched gravel. 'Here we are. Trelissick Lodge.'

They were in the driveway of a half-tiled Victorian house set among pines. Michael turned off the engine, and said, 'I'll come in with you, say hello to Mary. It's been quite a day for you, hasn't it, one way and another?'

'You could say that. Thank you for all you've done.'

'It's a huge relief, to tell you the truth. I can't tell you how much. I'm so glad you got in touch.'

He sat silent for a moment, Anna beginning to sense how much his devotion to Rose had cost him – as if Rose, typically, had handed over her burden of guilt for him to carry. If, that was, she had ever felt guilt.

'Does she ever—?' Anna began, but Michael was out of the car now, going to the door. Mary, a woman in her fifties, answered his ringing. After arranging to collect her after breakfast tomorrow, Michael gave Anna a kiss and a hug, with far more warmth than Rose had so far shown.

323

Showing the way to a large and rather fussily furnished room, Mary was inclined to chat, but Anna wanted to be alone now, to assimilate all that had happened and to think about the big new questions that buzzed around her head. She dumped her bag on a chair and opened the window to let in cold air. At once she was struck by the utter quietness and darkness outside. She was used to that at Rowan Lodge, but this felt different, with the sea less than a mile away; there was a faint saltiness on her lips, on her skin. She was looking, she thought, downhill towards the cove, but could make out only garden trees, dimly lit by solar lamps on the drive. She thought of Rose, moving around the cottage, looking through an open door to check that Euan was peacefully asleep, then getting into bed with Michael. Would they talk quietly together; would Rose be open with him now, and if so, would she express fear, or disappointment, or panic?

And where was Zanna now, Rosanna? This other half-sister, conjured from nowhere, who had walked into Rose's life with such dramatic results? Shivering now, Anna closed the window and drew the curtains. She remembered what her father had told her: that her mother had given the name *Rosanna* when someone asked about her children. Anna had thought at the time that the name Rosanna was a muddled conflation of her name with Rose's. But now . . .

Her mother had had another baby. Anna struggled to believe it. And if it were true, her father knew nothing of it; she felt certain of that.

How could anyone keep such a secret? What had it done to her mother, concealing such a huge thing for most of her adult life? And had she gone on meeting Zanna, quite unsuspected, for the twenty years of Rose's absence? Had she known of Zanna's unannounced visit that day, and kept it from the police, from Dad, from everyone? Secrets had bred secrets, spreading like a virus. And that made it unfair, surely, to blame Rose, who had been caught up like Anna in a suffocating mesh, but had found her own way of breaking free.

Earlier, at Cove Cottage, they had eaten their meal in a book-lined room between kitchen and sitting room, the four of them, knees almost touching under the small table, passing salad and granary bread to accompany the spiced chicken dish prepared by Rose. Only now did Rose ask Anna some of the things Michael had already asked on the train: what did she do? Was she married?

'I live with my partner, Martin,' Anna found herself saying; perhaps to have something to show Rose, an indication that she too was loved and wanted.

*Had* been.

'Oh, and how did you meet him? What does he do?' Rose asked.

When Anna explained that Martin was a financial adviser, she saw Rose dismiss him in an instant. Not interesting enough for her consideration.

Anna thought: I've always put Rose first. I've let my idea of Rose shape my life, my idea of what I want.

'If you'd like to phone Martin, Anna, please do,' Michael told her. 'You won't get a signal on your mobile.'

Anna thanked him, but said that there was no need. Now, though, lying in bed with the light on, her mind was too active for sleep. Wondering what Martin might be doing, she pictured him watching TV alone, a late film perhaps, or something he'd recorded; he was rarely in bed before mid-night at weekends. What would he be thinking?

She'd have to stop this. It was no longer any business of hers, what he did and didn't do.

Tears sprang to her eyes now, tears of weariness and a sense of both the shock and the anti-climax of this strange day that had carried her from place to place and now left her alone and flat. The gap between expectation and reality was too wide to be filled. Always, over the years, she had had a sense of being owed something big enough to compensate for the emotion she'd invested in Rose, and the need to find her, or at least find out what had happened to her – to have something to fill that void. She had imagined that her reward for faith and persistence would be handed to her all at once, like a lottery winner's cheque. Now the gap had stretched too wide to be filled.

Anna wept quietly for the loss of Rose, and of herself. She wept for the girl who had spent half her life in waiting.

In the morning Anna saw the cove properly in daylight, saw the curve of granite cliffs that enclosed it in a horseshoe shape, the coastal path rising on either side; she saw distant light on the sea, rays slanting between clouds. The sea towards the horizon dazzled and held the eye with its shift-ing and glancing colours. Seen from above, the cove was a tricky exercise in perspective drawing, with its odd angles of roofs and chimneys and steps cutting down steeply between houses, the lane winding round to sweep to a halt by the little quay.

She wanted to see Rose's paintings; to interpret and com-pare, finding herself lacking, no doubt, in comparison, glad of the ready excuse that she hadn't painted for years. When she mentioned that she'd like to see them properly, Rose unlocked the studio and turned on the heater. 'Here it is. See for yourself,' she said offhandedly, then made a desultory effort at sorting through papers and sketchbooks on her desk, occasionally glancing up to see what Anna was looking at. There were landscapes and seascapes, some in watercolours, most in acrylics. Anna preferred the odd little glimpses: a half-open garden gate, a clump of thrift clinging to the cliff, a rowing boat pulled up to rest on a pebbled shore. Then there were seabirds, all done in watercolours, looser in style. Gannets, purple sandpipers, oystercatchers with startling red-orange bills against their pied colours. Backgrounds were washed in, lightly indicated: lichen-coloured rocks, clumps of samphire, wet sand washed mirror-smooth or marked with the tread of webbed feet. They were proficient but unremarkable. To Anna, Rose's story needed a more dramatic outcome, worth the cost to everyone concerned: she ought to be a Barbara Hepworth, a Gauguin, producing ground-breaking work rather than pleasant souvenir pictures of the kind seen in countless shops and galleries along the coast. Anna felt, illogically, as if Rose had snatched the privilege of being an artist, taken the one chance available, and set up a cosy little industry. Through Anna's mind floated the more dramatic colours and forms of the work she'd once imagined herself producing.

'You can have one, if you like, to take away with you,' Rose said, not looking up.

'Can I? Thanks.'

It was the *take away* that echoed, as if Rose couldn't wait to get rid of her. Anna fought back *Stuff your pictures*, deciding that a gift from Rose was the very least she deserved – some kind of proof that she existed, perhaps. She spent some while before choosing turnstones: two plump birds, at rest by a humped rock; behind them, waves washing in, creaming into patterns of foam. Like all the paintings it was signed *Rosalind Sullivan*, a name that was beginning to mean something in Anna's mind. Only now did she notice that there were no people in Rose's work.

Rose sealed and taped it in bubble-wrap for Anna's journey home, then suggested that they should go for a walk while the weather was fine. 'You'd better borrow my walking boots. We've got the same sized feet – at least we used to have.' She looked momentarily discomfited by this *we*, by this admission of former intimacy. 'You won't get far in those heels.'

Anna pushed her feet into Rose's boots, spreading her toes, adjusting to the indentations of different feet.

On the cliff-path, Anna's black coat billowed and flapped, and her red scarf flew out like a banner. With Rose, Michael and Euan, she walked head down into strong gusts from the west, picking a way up the steep path, scrambling over boulders, standing like figureheads to look down into the next bay and the steel-grey sea, with waves breaking into white crests, far out. That meant it was rough today, Euan told Anna, with the air of imparting expertise.

'I don't know how you can live in London, Anna.' Rose's words were whipped away into the wind. 'I couldn't stand it.'

It was the kind of remark Anna had come to see as typical of her: exasperating but true. Anna thought how cocooned Rose was here, if she could be cocooned and at the same time exposed to the Atlantic – so removed from cities and commerce and the need to earn a living; because surely, unless Rose's paintings were far more successful than Anna had reason to suspect, she couldn't support herself by her earnings or contribute a great deal to the family finances. Yet Anna did agree.

'I don't know how to live in London, either.'

'Why do you, then?'

'Well – because it's convenient, I suppose. Has been, anyway.' Anna paused; she would have to abandon the fiction that she was living happily with Martin, and wished now that she hadn't mentioned his name. Then she saw that Rose wasn't listening, wasn't really curious. Convenience had never been much of a priority for Rose: her own, or anyone else's.

Time was running out. They had lunch at a pub in the next bay before walking back, gusted and buffeted, the wind behind them now; Rose called a warning to Euan not to go too close to the cliff-edge. Anna had spent very little time alone with Rose and saw now that she wasn't going to; that Rose had, possibly, engineered the windy walk and the pub lunch with other people around them precisely to prevent Anna from confronting her with things she preferred not to examine.

'You must come again, and stay longer,' Michael said. 'You and Martin.'

'Oh yes, do,' Rose echoed; but already Anna knew that if they met again it would be at her own or Michael's instigation, not Rose's.

It was Michael who drove Anna to Penzance station. Outside the cottage, Rose hugged Anna and said, 'Thank you for coming.' She seemed to mean it.

'Do you still paint, Anna?' Michael asked, in the car. 'You were so good.'

'No, I . . . gave up.'

The truthful answer would have sounded feeble. *I stopped because of Rose. I haven't painted since the sixth form. Rose was always ahead of me. Always better. Always showing me what I couldn't do. I could only copy, and fail.* To avoid explaining, she said, 'What about you? Why physics?'

'Study it or teach it?'

'Well, either. Both.'

'Because the laws of physics are the foundation of the universe,' he said. 'The laws of matter and energy, time and space. Physics explains everything.'

'*Can* everything be explained?'

'Perhaps,' he said. 'If only we knew what questions to ask.'

On the train Anna leaned against the seat-back and closed her eyes. Rose was receding faster than the train could travel, growing smaller and smaller as if seen through the wrong end of a telescope. Much farther, and Anna knew she would doubt that she had met Rose at all. In her bag the small turnstone painting, cushioned in its bubble-wrap, signed with Rose's new name, was the only real evidence; she had to restrain herself from taking it out and tearing off the wrapping to convince herself.

How did Rose do it? – inspire such devotion in the men who loved her? First Jamie Spellman, openly declaring his love; then Michael, shaping his life and career around her peculiar needs, commuting to Plymouth each day so that

Rose could stay in her remote sanctuary with sea and birds for company. Rose seemed to command unquestioning loyalty, and love far more extravagant than Anna felt *she* would ever have or deserve.

I've made such a mess of my life, Anna thought. Failed at everything.

Pale moorland rose now on either side, flashes of farms and church spires, a river; already the countryside looked less distinctively Cornish, and Rose was left behind. As soon as Anna had a signal for her mobile she tried calling, got voicemail, and left a text message instead: *Found Rose. On train back to London.*

❖ ❖ ❖

# 25

## Sandra, 1968

At the technical college Sandy met Donny Taverner, a mild-mannered, industrious boy who was studying electrical engineering on day-release. They first spoke in the cafeteria when, passing, he jolted her table, sloshing a puddle of coffee across the Formica top. She snatched away her pencil case and shorthand notebook; he apologized profusely and scurried about with paper napkins, mopping up. A week later, when she met him again, in the lift, he asked her name, and told her his. He was tall, dark-haired, with a rather beaky nose – nothing special, she thought at first, but she liked the way he looked at her with frank admiration. What she noticed was his hands – long-fingered and expressive like Roland's, hands that might have been made for playing the guitar or piano.

That same afternoon he was waiting for her as she left for her bus. Shyly he asked if she'd go to the cinema with him. She agreed, thinking *Well, why not?* That Saturday they went to see *The Graduate*; he insisted on paying, walked her home afterwards and asked if he might kiss her. He took her nervousness for inexperience, and was so tentative and gentle that she wondered if he'd ever kissed anyone before. It felt like playing the part of a girl with a nice boyfriend, rather in the way she'd played mummies and daddies as a child.

They went to the cinema again the following week, and soon Donny invited her home. His family was an extended one, with aunts and uncles, grandparents and cousins always round at each other's houses for Sunday dinner or tea, games of cards and Monopoly. Gusts of laughter broke out about nothing in particular; there was much teasing and reminiscing and showing of photographs, and everyone was plied at intervals with tea and home-made cake. Sandy looked on in astonishment; never had she met people with such a gift for making celebrations out of the stuff of everyday life. From her first visit, she was accepted as Donny's girlfriend. He was touchingly proud of her, protective, as if the hardships of life might be too much for her to bear alone.

'Have you got brothers and sisters, Sandra?' his mother asked – Donny always called her Sandra, considering Sandy to be a boy's name.

'I had a brother,' she said flatly. 'He died last year.'

Teacups were lowered, faces aghast. 'Oh, no! You poor lass. What a terrible, terrible thing. Awful, unbearable.' Mrs Taverner's eyes filled with tears; one of the aunts got up and enveloped Sandy in an ample, perfumed hug. 'Donny, you be sure to treat her kindly, poor little thing.'

Sandy resisted bringing Donny to her own home. When at last she did invite him, she felt embarrassed for her parents, for their stilted attempts to put him at ease. The Tonbridge house still felt like temporary lodgings; there were too few people in it, too little laughter, too much silence while every remark was weighed and assimilated.

'You've found a nice boy there,' Sandy's mother said, when he had gone home. 'You hang onto him.'

On Thursday evenings, when the Taverner parents went to a ballroom dancing class, Sandy and Donny had the house to themselves. They would watch TV or listen to music, cuddled together on the sofa. Donny's kisses became more searching; his hand groped with her buttons or felt its way up her thigh. He said that he loved her: not as a great declaration, but as if it proceeded naturally from spending time together. He was so uncomplicated, so easy to be with, that she could find no reason not to love him back. He didn't expect sex, just a progression, step by step, of fumbling and exploring; she let him think he was leading her where she hadn't been before.

'We could get engaged, if you want,' he told her, breathing heavily.

Sandy's mother saw this coming. 'You haven't told him, have you, about – you know? You wouldn't be so silly? You've got a good chance here, to settle down with a decent boy. Don't go throwing it away.'

She was in a Thomas Hardy novel. Before, she'd been Fanny Robin, dragging herself to the workhouse. Now, as Tess, she was offered a chance of happiness. In the story, the natural world seemed to throw all its energy into uniting Tess with Angel Clare; it was early summer, there were dewy mornings and long-shadowed evenings, cows in the pasture and fresh milk for breakfast. Tess tormented herself with the secret that she had lived with Alec Stoke d'Urberville and borne his child. The novel was subtitled *A Pure Woman*, a subject on which Sandy had written an essay: Hardy's championing of a fallen woman had been considered outrageous, but even now people talked about *living in sin*.

She thought of telling Donny about what she now thought of as *her past*: but how should she broach the subject? Shouldn't she have told him already? They couldn't plan a life together with such a huge silence bulking between them like an iceberg. The guilt of concealment added to the guilt of the secret itself. She must find a way; he would have to know.

Donny spoke of getting engaged in the summer, but surprised her, one Thursday evening at his parents' house, by presenting her with a small cube-shaped box. 'Open it!' His arm was round her; he smiled at her hesitation.

'Oh, what—?' She knew, of course, that it would be an engagement ring. She'd imagined that some time in the future they'd go and choose one together, after they'd had serious discussions, made plans. In between was a large and comfortable buffer of time during which everything she needed to tell him would naturally emerge. But here it was: a small single diamond, sparkling at her from its nest of satin, promising security, the status of being loved and wanted. Its small circle would enclose her with Donny where no one else could reach them.

'I had to guess the size. I was going to wait, but I saw this and knew you'd love it. Here, let me.' Donny reached for her left hand and slid the ring onto her finger. She extended her hand, turning it this way and that; the ring was so delicate, so pretty. She could be like other girls at college, talking about her fiancé, her wedding plans.

Donny lifted her hand and kissed it. 'You do like it, don't

you? I wish I could afford a better one. But it fits all right, doesn't it?'

'Yes, yes, it's gorgeous.' She twisted the ring off her finger and handed it to him. 'But . . . Donny, I can't get engaged. We can't get married. You'll have to take it back.'

'What are you on about?' He looked at her in bemusement. 'What's all this about?'

'I can't marry you, because—'

'Because what? Come on.'

A tear trickled down her cheek. 'Because I—'

The words wouldn't come; they dried up in her throat. How could she spoil this moment, this little tableau he'd staged? He was so trusting, so good; he wanted nothing more than to please her. If she told him now, if she brought out the black box of her past and thrust it in his face, how would that help? It would mean anguish and tears; it would be punishing him for something he hadn't done. Wasn't it kinder to go along with his wishes, accept the security he offered?

'Because I'm scared.'

Donny let out his breath. 'Is that it? Oh, Sandra, you silly, silly thing – come here.' He took her in his arms, kissed away her tears. 'What is there to be scared of, you and me together? I'll look after you, I promise. I love you. I only want you to be happy.'

They were married soon after Sandy's nineteenth birthday. The week before, Neil Armstrong had stepped onto the surface of the moon, and the world seemed to have entered a new era.

❖ ❖ ❖

# 26

Anna woke to cold dawn light showing through the curtains, and the silence of the back bedroom at Rowan Lodge. She clicked on the radio, the events of the weekend slowly coming back to her.

Rose.

Rose was alive. Rose had a life.

It was the culmination of all Anna had wanted, but she felt no sense of exultation; only flatness, as if she'd lost something, rather than found it. The Rose she'd found in Cornwall, Rosalind Owen, Rosalind Sullivan, wasn't the girl who had been her sister; she would never get Rose Taverner back. The Rose of her memory was bigger and louder; she was cleverer, more beautiful, more ambitious, more talented than the woman Anna had met.

Ruth had driven her here last night, having phoned in response to Anna's text message, offering to meet her at Woodford station. Their last conversation had been huffy, but Ruth had listened, and exclaimed, and asked questions, while Anna told her about Michael, about Rose, about the life they had made for themselves.

'When are you going to tell your parents?'

'Soon. But I've no idea how. I'll have to go home – I can't do it on the phone. It's too complicated.'

Now, stirring, feeling chilly air against her shoulders as she emerged from the cocoon of duvet, Anna noticed the shabbiness and bareness of this room in the early light, and thought without relish of the journey to work, the uneventful day ahead, and her return here alone.

It's a start, she told herself, a new start. That's how to think of it. There's no point looking back. It'll be spring soon, and everything will look different.

Ruth had mentioned that Martin would be at a conference in Norwich from Tuesday to Thursday. He didn't tell *me* that, Anna thought, but saw an opportunity to clear her things out of his flat. She hired a car for Wednesday evening, and did the job briskly, not letting herself linger. Books and CDs, clothes, shoes and toiletries: her belongings didn't amount to much, and it was easy to remove all trace of herself. There were a few kitchen items and some bedding and tableware she and Martin had bought together, but she left all those, not wanting him to think she'd taken anything that wasn't rightfully hers. After a final check round she took her door-key off the ring and placed it on the table.

She considered leaving a note, but couldn't think of anything worth saying.

Cassandra is at the hatch, speaking to a patient about physiotherapy. 'Yes, Mr Goss comes three afternoons a week. Here's his card – you can contact him directly. He's very good, people say.'

'Thanks. I'll give him a call.'

'Lucky thing,' Jilly mutters when the young woman has gone. 'I'd lie down on his couch any day.'

'Sorry to disappoint you, Jill,' says one of the nurses, in the office to collect blood test results, 'but he's gay. He lives in Westerham, plays for the same cricket team as my Geoff.'

'No!' says Jilly, eyes wide. 'Are you sure? He wears a wedding ring.'

'Yes, that's right. His partner's called Adam – he's an anaesthetist. He plays sometimes as well.'

Cassandra stares down at her keyboard, feeling her face hot and burning to the tips of her ears. Pauline has noticed; they'll giggle about her after she's gone, Pauline and Jilly, like a pair of fifteen-year-olds; they'll joke about starchy Sandra, so buttoned up, so conventional that she's horrified by the mere mention of homosexuality. 'What century does she think we're in?' she imagines them saying.

That's all right. Let them gossip. There's not a chance they'll ever guess.

Don meets her from work today, in the car; they've arranged to have lunch at the garden centre and look for a white clematis she had admired in her magazine.

'Anna phoned,' he tells her, as she fastens her seat belt. 'She's coming tomorrow evening. Wants to stay the night – that's OK, isn't it? On her own, she said. I had the impression she's got something to tell us.'

She looks at him in surprise. 'Really? Does it mean she's – you know, after all—'

'No, no. It's not that. She wouldn't say. I don't know – when we spoke the other day I got the impression something was wrong between her and Martin.'

339

'Oh, I shouldn't think so. Martin's so reliable.'

Don sighs. 'I know, love. Is Anna, though? That's the thing.'

'Of course she is! What a thing to say!'

Cassandra falls silent, briefly wondering, before her thoughts turn back to Philip Goss. What if he changes his hours, or arrives early one day? He might call at reception for his messages, come face to face with her, in front of the others. What then? Will he pretend not to know her? Maybe he'll see only a dull, respectable woman well into middle age. She tries to comfort herself with that. He probably won't look closely enough to recognize.

But to live from day to day with the threat of that – no, no, it's more than her nerves can stand. What, then – what can she do about him?

Maybe it isn't the same Philip Goss. She's thought of that, tried to convince herself that it can't be. It's not an uncommon name; there are probably hundreds of men who share it. But now, with the news that he's gay – her mind is full of what that means. Or might have meant, back then.

One leaves, another returns. Zanna came that day, so Rose left. Now Phil is here because Zanna's gone. There's a strange logic to it, if only she could work it out. But Roland – Roland will never come back. She knows that. Because of her, and because of him. Because of Phil.

The damage words can do! A few misplaced words. Zanna, on the phone in tears, saying she'd done something terrible, something she didn't mean. A quick look, she said, that's all I wanted. Just to see the house and garden, a glimpse of your life. I'd have gone away quietly. How could I know she'd—

A phone call to add to her stash of secrets. Don must never know. It's part of the pattern. Something said, something done, small actions or remarks that weigh so heavily and can't be unsaid.

But it's not fair that she should carry all the blame. Always, always, that's how it's been.

She firms her resolve. Tomorrow. She'll watch out for him in the car park; there are plenty of shrubs there for cover. She knows what time he arrives. She has to be sure it's him – or, better by far, confirm that it's *not* him. She feels trapped, clasped by her seat belt, guarded by Don. She is held at bay. They're like phantoms, the people in her life, in a complicated dance, of changing patterns and formations. They grab hold of her and whirl her round and release her so that she loses all balance and spins off giddily. She can't keep hold of herself, can't be sure who she is.

'You're quiet, love.' Don is looking at her with affectionate concern. 'Are you all right?'

'Oh, just thinking.' She smiles back at him, amazed at how easy it is, as if she's looking down at herself from some way above, wondering what she might do; he has no idea. 'About the best place for that clematis. Feet in the shade, head in the sun, that's what they like.'

Wanting moral support before she went home to her parents, Anna arranged to meet Ruth on Thursday evening for a meal. Patrick was at home, left in charge of Liam while Ruth and Anna went to a local Indian restaurant.

'When are you planning to see Rose again?' Ruth asked. 'It must be such an incredible thing, getting your sister back. Has it sunk in yet?'

Anna looked at her in bemusement. She couldn't disguise her sense of anti-climax, and a guilty feeling that she ought to feel joyful, that anyone else would be. If only her feelings were as simple – my sister is alive, therefore I'm happy.

'I thought I'd feel different – ecstatic,' she said. 'But I don't think I'm nice enough.'

'Of course you are! It's a weird situation. You need to get to know each other again.'

'If she lets me. Mainly, I can't get over the fact that I'm one of three sisters now. Like someone in a Chekhov play, or *King Lear*. After being an only child since I was thirteen.'

'Yes! Anna and her sisters. Isn't that a Woody Allen film?'

The waiters brought their food, placing the small sizzling platters on candle-heated trays.

'I saw Martin today,' Ruth said. 'I told him about Rose. Hope that's OK.'

'Oh . . .' Anna was taken aback. 'I thought he was in Norwich, at a conference?'

'Yes, he was. He left early, after his presentation, and called in at Holtby Hall. We went to the pub for lunch.'

On the point of asking, 'Why did he come to see you?' Anna realized that it was none of her business. Previously she'd seen herself as the central figure in the triangle, but now that she'd surrendered any claim on Martin, Ruth was the pivot. She looked down, unsettled by the cosy picture of Ruth and Martin having lunch together.

'How was he?'

'He's – he's gutted.' Ruth gave her a straight look. 'And hurt, Anna – deeply hurt, that you kept all this to yourself. He had no idea. You've never talked much about her, he

342

said – you always gave the impression it was off-limits. I don't think you've been fair to him.'

Anna assimilated this. 'Mm. Maybe. But, Ruth' – she had to come out with it – 'didn't you tell him I was meeting someone? I don't see how you thought that would help. Unless—'

Ruth, with a look of being wrong-footed, said, 'Unless what?'

'I – I thought you and Martin might get back together, if I was out of the way. Especially if you both thought I'd gone off with someone else.'

Ruth gave a startled snort of a laugh, looked sidelong at Anna, then shook her head. 'No. No. Is that really what you thought? No. We're OK now, Martin and me, but there's too much . . . too much *stuff*. Did you really think you could organize things so neatly?'

'Yes. No. I don't know.'

'Well, it's not going to happen. It's not what I want,' Ruth said firmly. 'It's not what he wants. And I don't even believe it's what you want. Look – I shouldn't have told Martin. Especially as I got it all wrong. The truth is – I was annoyed with you, for letting me down about the wallpapering. There, it's as petty as that – not because I was scheming to get Martin back. I'm sorry.'

'And I'm sorry about the wallpaper.'

'Stuff the wallpaper! That's the least of our worries.'

They exchanged hesitant smiles.

'Course, if you'd only *said* . . .' Ruth went on. 'And now? You've found Rose, and there she is, where she's been for years, all settled with a husband and children and a nice home. Meanwhile you've wrecked your own relationship –

343

shoved Martin out of your life, when he could have been your best support. It doesn't make sense.'

'You don't know how bad things have been,' Anna said. 'The things we've said to each other.'

'Anna – I saw how upset Martin was today. And for him to let *me* see that . . . well. If you thought you could hand him back to me, like returning a library book, you don't know how much he loves you. If I can see that, why can't you?'

Anna shifted in her seat. 'It's too late.'

'Is it?'

'Yes, really. Please don't say any more. I can't even think about it, just now. Come on, let's start on this.' Anna passed one of the dishes over for Ruth to serve herself. She thought of Martin arriving back at the flat, finding it stripped of her belongings, not even a note left on the table with her key. She hadn't told Ruth about that. As a gesture it could hardly be more final.

Ruth began spooning chicken and spicy sauce onto her plate. 'What about Rose? When will you see her again? And will you try to meet Rosanna?'

'I don't know. There's such a lot to clear up first. Dad doesn't know, I'm sure he doesn't. And who was Rosanna's father? Perhaps this starts to make sense of the odd things Mum's been saying. Talking about Rosanna, when Dad and I always thought she meant Rose. Blurting out her secret, after so many years.'

'Perhaps it means she wants it to be known,' Ruth said. 'Imagine the strain of keeping such a big thing hidden. But . . . where *is* Rosanna now? Your mum must know.'

Anna gave a helpless shrug. 'Surely they can't still be

meeting, with no one ever finding out? Has Rosanna died, or disappeared?'

'I hope not.' Ruth refilled both their glasses. 'There's been more than enough disappearing. Is it a family trait?'

Now. Today. She could keep putting it off, but the worry is snapping at her with such determination that she may as well surrender. Let it eat her whole.

She tells Don that she'll be late home; she's going to Waitrose after work, ready for Anna's visit. He offers to come, but she insists that she'll be quicker on her own. And since there's an hour between her finishing time and Philip Goss's first appointment, she actually does go and shop, remembering her list and her Bags for Life. She puts her bags into the boot and drives back towards Meadowcroft, leaving the Audi in a side street rather than in the car park; she doesn't want to be seen. She shuts her shoulder bag into the boot as well, taking only her keys. An alleyway runs alongside the car park, separated by a narrow strip of trees and shrubs, leading to a housing estate and a children's play area. She walks along this path until she has a good view through bare trees of the back windows of the health centre, and double doors which are usually kept locked. A row of parking spaces is marked DOCTORS ONLY. Will he use one of those? He's not a doctor, but surely he's entitled to a parking space.

Ten to two. She shivers, standing with hands thrust deep into her coat pockets, collar turned up. A scruffy terrier comes along the path from the estate, snuffling busily, followed by an elderly man who gives her a curious stare. She responds with a curt 'Good afternoon!' but feels exposed, not wanting anyone else to see her. Awkward in court shoes and narrow skirt, she climbs the low railing and picks her way into the undergrowth, through rough damp grass, and brambles that snag her tights. Ducking under a branch, she winces as something prongs into her scalp; she raises a hand to disentangle her hair, but her attention is diverted to a car pulling in, a small and jaunty red car – no, that's not him, it's a young woman at the wheel. But behind it comes a larger black estate – and she doesn't know much about cars, but surely he's more likely to drive something like this. She can see the driver's face only in profile, but surely this is him.

Yes. He pulls into a space in the row of doctors' cars, gets out and opens the rear door, taking out a briefcase. She edges forward. He's tall and lean, dressed in dark trousers and a casual jacket, a long scarf looped about his neck. His hair is short and neat, but the face – yes, it's the face she remembers so well: the bony features, the deep-set eyes, all the indefinable things that make a face recognizable as one person's rather than another's. He is Phil. He is the boy she idolized as a teenager, his youthful beauty coarsened in maturity.

He locks his car and turns, and she must have let out a gasp or trodden on a twig; he gives her a direct look, pauses for a moment, and comes towards her. She backs off, intending to walk away quickly towards the housing estate, but in her haste she has enmeshed herself in brambles.

'Mrs Taverner!' he calls.

How does he know her name? She gives him a quick, frightened glance, trying to prise a thorny stem from her skirt. When she doesn't answer he calls again: 'Sandra? Are you all right?'

346

She says the first thing that comes into her mind. 'I'm looking for a – a cat. One of our patients has lost a cat.'

'Here?'

'Yes, she – had it in her car, and it got out.' This is transparently absurd; there is no anxious patient, no cat, no one else in sight; he must know she's blathering. She tugs again at the brambles and succeeds in disengaging herself, though she hears and feels a thorn ripping through fabric.

'Here, let me.' He extends a hand, pushes hawthorn branches aside with the other, and pulls her through, looking at her in perplexity. Feeling her bottom lip trembling, she bites it hard.

'You've cut yourself!' He's looking closely at the side of her face, where she now feels the warm trickle of blood. 'You'd better get one of the nurses to clean that up.' He pauses, still holding her arm. 'It *is* you, isn't it? Sandra, Sandy? Cassandra Skipton?'

'What do you mean?' she says stupidly.

'I saw you in Reception, the first time I came here. You were busy at your desk, but I heard one of the others call you Sandra and I looked again and recognized you. And you're Sandra Taverner who takes messages for me. I've looked for you a couple of times since, but you've never been here.'

'No. I only work mornings.'

'Come on, let's go inside. You look quite pale. Someone else can look for the cat.' Solicitously, a hand on her elbow, he begins guiding her towards the front of the building, to the main doors.

She thinks of the last time he touched her, the first and last – the cry of gulls, the breaking of waves, their shivering bodies coming together for comfort. So long ago that she scarcely recognizes herself, but she can never forget – how can she, when what happened that day has shaped the rest of her life?

Is he thinking of that, too?

She can't go in. She flings herself away from him.

'It wasn't true, what you told me. I know that, now. You lied to me and – you lied to Roland.' The words jerk out of her and echo around the car park in the silence that follows. He steps back in shock.

They stare at each other, then his mouth clenches and twists, in an expression she remembers, and he says, very quietly, 'Yes. I did. I wasn't as brave as he was.'

'His song,' she accuses.

'Yes. I've still got it.'

She lifts both hands to her face, holding in the sobs that bubble up. 'Excuse me,' she blurts, and she runs towards the road. It feels odd to run, strangely liberating, as if she might acquire spring heels the way she sometimes does in dreams, taking giant strides, never tiring. In reality she's clumsy in her court shoes, almost losing one as her ankle twists.

'Sandy!' Phil's voice rises in warning, and a car turning into the drive jolts to a halt, the driver giving her a self-righteous glare. She slows to a walk, but marches on at a fast walk that's almost a jog, gulping down tears. When she glances back she sees that Phil hasn't run after her, but is standing with head high, watching to see where she goes.

He said it. He *said* it. He lied. And his lie killed Roland.

It's come out wrong, too quickly. But now he knows her, he's known all along, and there's only one thing to do. When she gets back to the car she slings herself into the driver's seat and inserts the key in the ignition, her hand shaking. She catches sight of herself in the mirror: tear-stained face, hair dishevelled, blood trickling down her forehead and coagulating in her eyebrow. She finds a tissue in the glove compartment and dabs at her face with it. Her thoughts race, and the feeling of dread is back in full force, her shadow, always waiting. She must run. Run away as far as she can, before anyone tries to stop her.

Don – what did Don say he was doing? He has to be out. She can't face him. She fumbles with her mobile and dials home, and yes, the recorded message comes on after a few rings. He's out. Thank God. If she hurries, if she's lucky, she can get what she needs and be out again before he knows she's gone.

# 27

Arriving at her parents' house, by taxi this time, Anna found her father in a state of agitation. He opened the door, talking rapidly before she'd got inside.

'I don't know where she is! She's gone off somewhere. I would have phoned earlier, only I was sure she'd turn up. But she hasn't.'

'What's going on, Dad? What's happened?'

With a sense of foreboding, Anna followed as he led her inside, talking all the way.

'No note. Nothing. She left the shopping in bags on the kitchen floor. Frozen stuff and all, ice cream melting. Then the phone call.'

'*What* phone call? Dad, tell me what happened, in order.'

They went into the kitchen, Don telling Anna that he'd spent the afternoon at Kathy and Malcolm's, helping Malcolm to cut down conifers in their back garden. This had taken some while, but Don had kept an eye on his watch, having promised Sandra to be back in time for the meal with Anna. Malcolm drove him back, and he went indoors expecting to find her busy in the kitchen. 'But the car wasn't here. I thought at first she'd taken longer than expected, or forgotten something and gone back to Waitrose. Then I saw the bags of shopping. I couldn't work out what on earth had happened. I went upstairs and saw the mess in our room – you can see – it looked like she'd been opening drawers, pulling things out in a hurry. At first I thought we'd been burgled, but her bag's not here, or her keys. No car, either. So then I thought – God' – he covered his hands with his face – 'someone had broken in and forced her to drive off at knifepoint or something—'

'Dad!'

'– and I was about to call the police, when the phone rang and it was someone from the health centre, a physiotherapist – um, Phil, Phil Goss. He was concerned because he'd met her in the car park and she seemed upset. About two, this was. He'd phoned earlier, left two messages. Wanted to check she'd got home safely. He said something about knowing Roland.'

Anna tried to make sense of this. 'He told her he knew Roland? That's what upset her?'

'I don't know. He said she was already agitated when he first saw her. He tried to stop her but she ran off crying.'

'Ran off *crying*? And you've no idea what . . .?'

Don shook his head, unable to speak.

Anna said, 'Have you phoned the police?'

'Yes – someone's been round to take details, a WPC. But, I mean, it doesn't sound very much, does it? A woman goes out unexpectedly.'

'What can we do? Have you tried all her friends? The Oxfam shop?'

'Yes, love. The shop was closed by that time but I found a number for Angela – she's the manageress – but she hasn't seen Sandra since last Friday. I don't know what to do. There's no point going out searching. She's got the car – she could be anywhere. I should have gone shopping with her. I offered, but she said no.'

'Don't blame yourself, Dad,' Anna told him. 'You can't be with her all the time. Something's obviously been worrying her.' She hesitated, wondering whether this was the time to drop the name Rosanna into the conversation, but only said, 'You've tried her mobile, obviously?'

'Yes,' said Don, 'and got voicemail. I left a message saying *Where are you? Phone as soon as you get this.*'

They stood for a moment, looking at the bags of shopping which Don had only half unpacked. He was staring at them hopelessly, breathing fast; Anna looked at him anxiously, afraid he might cry. It was so horribly like the day Rose left: trying to think of every possible explanation, assuring each other that nothing was amiss.

'Dad,' said Anna, 'you finish this, and I'll have a look round upstairs – see if I can work out what Mum was looking for.'

'OK, love,' said Don, with a little uplift of hope in his voice.

Upstairs Anna remembered Ruth's joking remark that running away was a family trait. Had something tipped her mother into desperation? It's as if she knew what I've found out, Anna thought, and she's running away from it. But where to? Where would she go? Anna could only think of the unlikely explanation – no, impossible, surely – that her mother somehow knew where Rose was, and was heading for Cornwall.

In her parents' bedroom a drawer was half open, a

sweater thrown on the bed; the skirt and jacket her mother had presumably worn for work were behind the door, the jacket skewed on its hanger, one shoulder and sleeve drooping. In the wardrobe, other garments lay crumpled on the floor. Picking up the black court shoes strewn haphazardly on the carpet, Anna saw that they were crusted with dried mud. All this was so unlike her mother's usual tidiness that some stranger might have entered the room to ransack her belongings.

Above the main part of the wardrobe was a cupboard space in which her parents stored their suitcases. Anna was looking now for the fabric holdall her mother had recently bought in the John Lewis sale, but it wasn't there with the cases. In the bathroom only one toothbrush stood in the holder; her father must have missed that. Alarm clutched at Anna's stomach as she registered this evidence that her mother hadn't popped out for a minute, hadn't gone to see a friend, hadn't simply wandered off forgetfully, but had decided to leave. In a hurry.

It *must* be connected with Rose; Anna could think of nothing else. Had Rose decided to get in touch? Phoned, told their mother where she was? That seemed highly improbable, but maybe she'd done it on an impulse, or at Michael's suggestion. What else would make sense?

Anna sat on the bed and picked up the mauve lambswool sweater discarded there. Holding it to her face she breathed in the smell of fine wool and a faint trace of light floral perfume. She tried to imagine herself as Mum, to enter into her thoughts, find out where they led. But how well did she really know her mother? She would have said that she knew her better than anyone; but she rarely thought about it, taking for granted that there would always be Mum and Dad, living in this comfortable house, here whenever she felt like returning. This woman who played the role of Mum had secrets, a past she desperately wanted to keep hidden.

How desperately? Enough to drive her to . . . Anna could hardly frame the thought, but she'd been here before – they all had, speculating about Rose, and the possibility of suicide—

A car was pulling up outside. Anna ran to the front bedroom, hoping to see the Audi with her mother at the wheel, but instead it was a police car. She clutched at the windowsill, her pulse beating in her ears. Two policewomen got out of the car and walked towards the front door. She's dead, Anna thought: they've come to tell us she's been found. She's killed herself or smashed the car into a tree. This is the last moment of not knowing.

She went downstairs on unsteady legs, to open the door before her father did.

'Ms Taverner?' said one of two smart young women who stood there. 'Is Mr Taverner here?'

She was half smiling: surely she wouldn't look like that if—

'Yes. Come in.'

'What is it?' Don was in the kitchen doorway, a hand to his chest, prepared for bad news.

'Mrs Taverner's been found! She's quite all right, only a bit shocked and confused. She's at Heathrow.'

'At—?'

'She was trying to get on a flight to Sydney, to visit her daughter.'

'Her daughter?' Don echoed. 'But this is our daughter,

here. Or – no – she couldn't have meant *Rose*?' He looked at Anna. 'Has something made her think Rose is in Sydney?'

The WPC nodded. 'Yes, that's what she said – Rosanna. Don't worry, she's being looked after, and she can be brought home by police car, unless you'd rather go and pick her up yourselves?'

'We'll go,' Don said at once. 'Oh, but the car's not here.'

'I'll phone for a taxi,' Anna said.

'Or' – Don was hurriedly picking up wallet, keys and jacket – 'Martin could come. He said he would.'

'What? When?'

'I rang him when I couldn't get hold of you, earlier.'

There wasn't time to stop and examine this. 'No,' Anna said, 'it'll take ages for him to get here. Quicker by taxi. We'll stop at a cash machine.'

It took several phone calls before she could find a taxi firm able to do the Heathrow run at short notice, but at last they were on the M25 heading west. It was late enough for rush-hour congestion to be over, and the traffic was flowing well; they should be there within the hour. Don had been quite baffled by what the policeman said, as was Anna – but she had to disabuse him of the idea that Rose had been discovered in Sydney.

'Dad,' she said carefully. 'It's not Rose who's in Australia. I think Mum was talking about someone else.'

And now she's not going anywhere. What was she thinking? Why, for a second, had she imagined she could get on a plane and fly to the other side of the world?

Arriving at Heathrow, finding the car park, making her way to the terminal, she thought she'd done it, escaped.

She's got her passport, her bank card, a few clothes in her holdall – all she needs is a ticket.

But, at airline ticket sales, the girl says, 'No. I'm afraid we have no standby tickets for that flight.'

'The next one, then.'

'I'll check for you. Have you got your visa?'

'Visa? You mean my bank card?' She fumbles at the catch of her bag.

'You need a tourist visa to travel to Australia,' the girl says patiently.

'A visa,' Cassandra repeats. 'No. I didn't know. How do I get one of those?'

Had she thought it was like getting on a bus? There are obstacles in her way, obstacles she must somehow get past.

'You've got to let me go,' she pleads. 'Please! I've got my card, I can pay. Can't I get the visa here?'

Someone is standing behind her, a man, shifting his weight from one foot to another. He'll have to put up with it. She's got to persuade them to let her go.

'I'm sorry, madam,' says the girl, behind the mask of a perfectly made-up face. 'You can't travel to Australia without a visa. You can do it online and it'll be electronically linked to your passport. It's only twenty pounds. It'd be better to book your ticket online as well, then you'll be sure of getting a seat.'

Cassandra's mind blurs. Panic trembles through her, clutches at her chest.

'All right, madam?' The girl gives her a bland smile and a flash of white teeth. Already she is looking, with a bright enquiring expression, at the waiting man, who gives Cassandra a scathing look and then a huff as, instead of moving out of his way, she stands there with tears rolling down her cheeks. The airport is a gateway through which she must pass, and she doesn't know the rules, the password. She gives a loud sob, and covers her face with her hands.

Next moment someone has appeared beside her, taking her arm and moving her to one side, asking what's wrong. It's another of the smart girls, so immaculately made up that she looks like a Barbie doll, but this one has kind blue eyes and a gentle voice. Cassandra is trembling as she tries to explain. 'My daughter's in Sydney,' she keeps repeating. 'Zanna. I've got to get to Sydney,' and this girl listens intently, and nods, and says, 'I see.' Something about her sympathy makes Cassandra's tears flow unchecked. They're moving off somewhere now, and people are staring, but soon they're away from the concourse and in a room with high windows and low chairs and a water-cooler. The girl brings a cup of iced water, which she gulps gratefully; soon someone else comes in, an older woman in a different uniform, and asks her a great many questions.

'So – Cassandra, is it? Are you on your own? Did anyone bring you? How did you get here? You've got a daughter in Sydney and you want to go and see her. Is she expecting you?'

'Yes!' Cassandra snatched gratefully at the mention of her daughter. 'I haven't seen her for ages, but we email each other. I told her I'd get there somehow. She's expecting a baby, you see. I'm sorry to cause such a lot of trouble.' She is shivering now with the sense that she's behaved idiotically, embarrassingly.

The nice blue-eyed girl leaves, and someone else brings tea and biscuits, and the policewoman – is she a policewoman? – talks into her phone. Soon Cassandra feels her eyelids dropping with weariness, and the woman finds her a cushion and a blanket, and helps her to get comfortable.

When she wakes, Don's beside her, saying he's come to take her home.

Oddly, it's begun to seem quite normal: a matter of practicalities, of getting themselves back to Sevenoaks. It's taken some while to find the car, but they're on their way, Don driving, Anna in the back. Cassandra, in the passenger seat, looks at the motorway in darkness, white headlights curving towards them, red lights streaming away: a double necklace of light around a wide bend.

They haven't talked much. 'You have a doze, love,' Don told her as they set off. 'We'll soon have you home.' For a while she did sleep, nodding against the clutch of her seat belt, but she woke with a crick in her neck and now she is wakeful but silent, registering that Don is driving her home, and he doesn't seem angry with her for acting as if she's completely deranged.

'Are you warm enough, love?' he asks, and she nods.

'I've been so stupid, haven't I? I'm so sorry. I don't know what got hold of me.'

'I know about Rosanna. Anna told me.' He inclines his head towards the back seat. 'I'm glad she did. Oh, love, if only you'd told me years ago.'

She sits silent for a few moments, then, before she's decided to speak, words burst out of her. 'I'm fed up with it! I've put up with it for too long, and I've had enough!'

'I know, love. It's been a strain, we know that—'

'Don't patronize me!' The voice doesn't even seem to be hers; a loud, strong voice, vibrating with fury. 'Don't talk in that maddening soothing way! What century are we in, for God's sake? Why should I be made to feel like a fallen woman in a – in a Victorian melodrama? What did I do that was so terrible? I've been paying for it all my life, all my *life*—'

'Mum, Mum—'

She has forgotten Anna's with them in the back, so quiet till now.

Don shoots her an outraged look, flickeringly illuminated by sweeping headlights. 'No one's saying any of that! How could I, when I didn't know? How could I understand, how could I help, when you kept everything to yourself?'

'You know now!' she yells back. 'And you'll have to get used to it, because this is me. *This* is *me*! Whether you like it or not—'

Don swerves over to the hard shoulder and stops. She hears the *click, click* of the warning lights, and sees the flashing red triangle on the dashboard.

'I can't drive with you screaming at me,' he says, in a tone of infuriating calm.

'Mum, it's all right,' says Anna, leaning forward from the back seat. 'Let's get home – then you can rest. There's plenty of time to talk. We love you, you know we do.'

Has Anna ever said that before?

'It's *not* all right!' It's as if someone else is speaking for her, shouting, relishing the freedom of being allowed out. 'Don't treat me like an invalid. I need to get away from it all! I'm going to Australia and no one's going to stop me—'

'But why Australia, Mum? Why Sydney?'

'Because that's where she lives! Zanna!' She snaps it out as if they ought to know.

'When did she go there?'

'Sixteen – sixteen years ago she left. You can blame me for everything else, but you can't blame me for that.' Tears are threatening again, her voice wavering. 'It wasn't fair. It wasn't what—'

'Mum,' says Anna quietly. 'Did you know that Rose left because Zanna came back? Have you known that, all this time?'

'Zanna didn't want that! She didn't! All she wanted was to see the house, a quick look. She was horrified when – when she knew—'

But her thoughts are roiling, one surfacing, then another; she can't grasp them, make sense of them.

'All right, love. All right.' Don is looking down at his lap, not at her, but he's talking again in that oddly quiet, controlled voice. 'You've been keeping so much to yourself. I don't think I know the half of it yet. And neither do you.'

'What d'you mean? Half of what?' Cassandra says sharply. Fear clutches at her stomach. A body found, remains, a note. It's the dread that never leaves her. Everything's her fault, no matter what she's been yelling just now.

'Go on,' says Don, turning to Anna. 'Tell her.'

'Shouldn't we—?'

'Go on.'

She feels Anna's hand on her arm. 'Mum. I know where Rose is. She's all right, she's – she's fine. I've met her, talked to her.'

# 28

On Saturday, in the last afternoon light, Anna was standing in Rose's bedroom.

All seemed calm, her mother asleep, Don tidying the kitchen. The house had changed since her last visit. This wasn't a shrine to Rose any more; it was simply the room Rose had left behind.

Anna remembered sitting on the bed beside Rose, with a big atlas open across their knees. 'Look, Anna,' Rose said, jabbing a finger, and Anna would peer at a tiny blob that meant nothing to her. 'Here's where I'll go. Irkutsk. Murmansk. Odessa. Here, then here.' The names had a kind of magic. But Rose hadn't proved to be much of a traveller after all; she had rooted herself in a place too small to feature in the atlas even as the minutest dot.

I should have known, Anna thought, long ago, that she'd head for the sea.

'It was a different world back then,' Don said, in the kitchen. 'I mean, nowadays girls have babies on their own and no one gives it a second thought. Then, well, it was seen as shocking. Even in the swinging sixties.'

The phrase, to Anna, conjured psychedelia and the Beatles, Woodstock, the pill, an explosion of youthful energy. But she knew from reading and films that it hadn't been all freedom and tolerance; attitudes lag behind fashion, at some distance. Now, learning about her mother's teenage years was like watching one of those faded but exuberant films that provoked such nostalgia for the sixties, even for people who hadn't been there.

'You'll be all right, Dad, won't you?' Anna asked.

Don looked mildly surprised. 'Me? *I'm* not the one we need to worry about.'

'But you've had a shock. A double shock.'

'At least. Triple, even. But there's Rose. Soon as Sandra's up to it, we'll go down and see her.'

'If Mum had told you about Rosanna, when you first met,' Anna asked, 'what would you have done?'

'I don't know, love. I'd like to say it wouldn't have made the slightest difference, but the fact is it'd have made a lot more difference then than it does now. All I know is – well, I'm not going to hold it against her, am I? I'm relieved, to tell you the truth. It starts to explain all this strangeness. When we lost Rose – no wonder it hit her so hard, after losing her brother, then giving up her first baby as well. It's not surprising a few cracks have started to show. But what I'm finding really hard is that she never told me about Rosanna coming to the house that day. She let me think Rose was dead.'

'Oh, Dad. But – she didn't know herself, did she? Didn't know that Rose wasn't?'

'I haven't quite got my head round it yet. I just wish – it would have given me something to hold on to. Something to make sense of.'

'So she'd been meeting Zanna in secret, till Zanna went to Australia? It was amazing she could manage that, without letting on.'

'That's right, love – it was a bit garbled, but I think I've got this straight. Soon after our Rose left, this was. Rosanna married an Ozzie and settled in Sydney. Sandra hasn't seen her since, but they've kept in touch by email. Now Rosanna's expecting a baby, after years of trying, apparently. That's what – you know – that business about the shoes was all about. She must have been looking forward to her first grandchild, but with no idea how she'd ever be able to see him, or her.'

'Did Mum say—' Anna wasn't sure she should ask this, but did: 'Zanna's father. Who was he – *is* he? Did she say?'

'Yes,' said Don, 'I asked. That's another thing that's brought this to the surface. She didn't expect to see him ever again. Now he's turned up at the health centre, and that's what threw her into panic. Chap called Phil, the physio there.'

'The one who phoned? The friend of her brother's?'

'Yes, love. He was Roland's best friend, apparently.'

'And Mum's boyfriend?'

'Looks like it. But after this happened – after she got pregnant – she never saw him again.'

'So does he know – about Zanna, I mean?'

Don shook his head. 'This is where things get completely muddled. She's got it into her head that somehow he does, and that's why he's turned up at Meadowcroft, with the idea of broadcasting it to everyone. But at the same time she thinks he *doesn't* know, and she ought to tell him. From what I could make of it, he had no idea. Quite likely still hasn't.

The pregnancy was hushed up – her parents saw it as a disgrace. They sent her away to some kind of institution, and when she came back they all pretended it had never happened.'

'An institution?'

'Home for unmarried mothers, in Maidstone. The baby was taken away as soon as it was born.'

'It sounds awful. Like a punishment.' Anna took this in. 'And in the *sixties* – I thought it was all flower-power and Jimi Hendrix and peace, man. We're not talking about Victorian times, for God's sake!'

'I know. Seems incredible, now.'

'And this was *Gran*! Granny Skipton, and Grandad, who sent her away . . .' Anna's head swam with the knowledge of another adjustment to be made. 'And Mum told you all this? She didn't rage at you, like yesterday?'

'No. We just talked, and she'd say one thing, then another, but I didn't probe too hard. She'll tell me in her own time, I expect. Isn't it amazing,' Don said, 'that you can live with someone for years, day by day, and not have the faintest idea what's going on in their head?'

'So much covering up. It's not surprising she's started to – to behave a bit oddly.' Anna didn't want to give voice to the words that presented themselves as explanations. 'Do you think she'll get over this?'

'I think it's a kind of breakdown, love. Not what you're thinking. I wanted to call a doctor today, but she wouldn't – I'll make an appointment on Monday. Who knows? Having this out in the open might make a big difference. Shock can be the tipping point, I know that. Shock, stress, bereavement.'

'But this is the opposite of bereavement,' Anna said. 'People coming back, people appearing from nowhere.'

'I know, I know.'

They looked at each other with the air of survivors marvelling at their escape. Don sighed, and went to put the kettle on.

'She can stop pretending now,' he said. 'No more secrecy, after all these years of being sick with worry that I'd find out – she thought I'd turn on her and throw her out of the house. It's – it's awful to realize that the person she's been afraid of is *me*. Why couldn't she trust me? That's what really hurts. There was a time, years ago, when I convinced myself she was having an affair, meeting someone. I had it out with her, asked if there was another man. She said no, there wasn't – and that was true. But I could tell she was frightened of something, and that made me sure she was lying.'

'I had no idea of any of this,' Anna said.

'No, well. Things were pretty cool. It was something we had to sort out between us – I'd have hated you to know. But we never did sort it out.'

The phone rang, and Don answered.

'Martin! Hi. Yes, we're OK, thanks. Yes, Sandra's home, a bit worn out, but none the worse.'

Anna felt herself flushing. She busied her hands with mugs and tea bags.

'Did Anna tell you? No? You're more than welcome to come down this evening – yes, she's here. I'll pass you over.'

Reluctantly, Anna took the receiver. She didn't want to talk to Martin in her father's presence. Didn't want to talk to him at all, in fact.

'Hello,' she said cautiously. 'Where are you?'

'At the flat. It feels a bit empty. Why didn't you tell me what was going on? Why did you shut me out? I only know about this from Ruth and your dad.'

'Oh – lots of reasons.' *You were always too busy*, she would have said, but couldn't, with her father in earshot.

'Anna,' he said, and his voice seemed to reverberate through her. 'Look – d'you want me to come down? I've got something on, but I can cancel.'

'No – thanks, but we're OK.'

She rang off; her father was looking at her in concern. 'Is everything all right, love?'

'Yes! Fine, thanks,' she said brightly. 'Are there any biscuits?'

'Well, *I* think she sounds like a complete cow,' said Bethan, over lunch on Monday. 'She must have *known*. How could she leave you all in the lurch like that – never a word, never even a note? I mean, there's such a thing as being a bit of a drama queen, and then there's being completely self-obsessed.'

'I don't know.' Anna felt compelled to support Rose. 'There's something fragile about her. Or perhaps I mean brittle. Something still lost.'

Bethan thumped down her glass. 'Yes, and that bloke of hers seems to have done nothing but indulge her. He should have made her get in touch with your parents. Why didn't he?'

'He did try. But, see, you're using common sense and logic. There's nothing common-sensical about Rose. Probably never was.'

Anna found it hard to convey what she felt: that when she'd been with Rose, for less than a day, she'd been under Rose's spell again, as she always had been. All her negative thoughts had seemed ungenerous, unsympathetic. She should have been happy; if she wasn't, it was another failure.

'Will you go down there again?'

'Yes, and soon. Honestly, I'll be skint by the end of the month, all this train travel and car hire.'

'And . . .' Bethan made prompting gestures. 'You and Martin?'

Anna shook her head. 'There's no me and Martin any more. But I'm not going to talk about that, Beth. I told you I wouldn't.'

'Meaning?'

'Meaning it's over, and that's that.'

'Anna, you're mad. You know you are.'

'I'm not mad. It's best this way. I'm going to look on this as a new start, not an ending.' Anna was trying to catch the waitress's eye to order coffee. 'Anyway! That's enough about me. How are you? And how's sprog-in-waiting?'

On Friday, finishing work early, Anna made the long journey to Cornwall again. She was drawn to Rose by her feeling that there must be more, that another meeting must make up for the reticence of the last.

As the train left Paddington, she checked her mobile and found a voicemail message from Martin. 'Anna, you left your painting behind. You can't have meant to, so I'll bring it over to Rowan Lodge tomorrow. OK. Bye.'

*Shore!* Anna felt a stab of loss. How could she have

forgotten? She saw the figure blurred in haze; the impress of footprints along the tide's edge. She wanted to look at it again, with her new insights. And she wanted the assurance that she'd been considered promising, once, and might be able to resurrect any talent she'd had, and build on it.

Tomorrow would be one of Martin's days with Liam; he'd be at Ruth's to collect him, and again later, bringing him back. Not trusting herself to speak, she sent a text message back: *Not at RL – on way to Cornwall. Easier to leave at Ruth's? Thanks.*

She replayed the voice message twice more, wondering if she could keep it indefinitely, and whether there would be a time when she could no longer recall the unique blend of sounds and inflexions that made up Martin's voice. A memory came to her of both of them looking at the *Shore* picture, soon after they'd met. He was standing behind her, a hand on her shoulder; she had propped the painting on a bookshelf to show him. 'You're good,' he said, his mouth so close to her ear that she felt his breath like a caress; 'really good. Why did you stop?'

How much she had wanted his approval, then; how much it meant to her, even though he knew little about art. She hadn't told him that the girl was meant to be Rose. Perhaps she should have.

'It shouldn't be shut away in a cupboard,' he said. 'Let's hang it in our bedroom.' But they never had. Maybe he'd only been flattering her.

Michael met Anna at Penzance station and drove her to Trelissick Lodge. As it was so late, she wouldn't see Rose until next morning. Michael was the one Anna felt she could confide in, rather than Rose. As they drove along dark lanes following the swathe of headlights, she asked about a possible visit for her parents, how it could best be arranged. Michael would have to be the one to persuade Rose.

'Perhaps it had better be on neutral ground, the first meeting,' he suggested. 'Lunch at the Morwenna Hotel, perhaps? I could book them a room there. Then, if it goes well, we can invite them home. Will you and Martin come too? Would that make it easier? Or should it be your parents on their own?'

'I might come,' Anna said. 'Actually – I'm not with Martin any more. We've split up. I've moved out.'

'Oh! I'm sorry to hear that. Is it – quite definite?'

'Yes. It is.'

Michael gave her a sidelong look, seemed about to ask another question, but didn't.

'It's no big deal,' Anna said. 'And it's not about Rose.'

Two lies. To say any more would be at the risk of bursting into tears. She lifted her chin and turned away to look out of the side-window at nothing but blackness.

'But I don't see – How could Rose have anything to do with it?' Michael asked, and then, when she didn't answer, 'Will you tell her?'

'I'd rather you did. I don't want to talk to her about it.'

Getting ready for bed in the same room as last time, she took out her mobile. No new messages, and of course – now that she felt desperate to send something, just a few words – there was no signal. Tears sprang to her eyes, and she blinked them away angrily. She should have tried while she had the chance. Several times she had told Martin that he didn't understand her; but how hard had she tried to understand him? Not enough. She should have asked, listened, given him the importance that she had freely granted to Rose.

In the morning the wind was strong, carrying rain, the sky grey and unpromising.

'I thought we might walk over to Penarthen.' Rose was clearing away breakfast things when Anna arrived. 'There are standing stones on the cliff, on the way there. I want to get some photos for a painting I'm going to do.'

'You'll need warm clothes,' said Michael; 'it's cold in that wind. Anna, I'm taking the boys to football – see you at lunch time. We'll come straight to the pub.'

Meeting Finn for the first time, Anna saw his strong resemblance to Rose: the dark hair, the flawless skin. A tall, attractive boy, he was shy of Anna; more so than Euan, who seemed unsurprised by her return. Anna couldn't imagine how Rose had explained the sudden appearance of a sister unheard of till now, but Euan had apparently accepted her as a new member of the family.

Euan waved as Michael reversed the car out and pulled away up the hill.

'Ready?' Rose said to Anna, who nodded. Anna was prepared this time, with walking boots, and a thick sweater under her waterproof. Rose was dressed not entirely practically in a velvet coat, her hair piled into a saggy knitted hat in multi-coloured stripes, a purple scarf flying out behind her as she strode up a bouldery path behind the boathouse. Even now, Anna felt drab in comparison, in her more functional clothes. Rose could still do that thing she'd always been so good at, throwing on a few garments and looking stylish and arty. Twenty years had fallen away and Anna still felt dull and ordinary, trailing in her sister's wake.

It was the first time they'd been alone together for any length of time. Anna felt very conscious of that. There was no need to talk at first; the ascent demanded single-file concentration, and was steep enough to leave little breath for words. When the path levelled and became a broad grassy track, Rose stopped to wait for Anna, and they stood looking down over the cluster of houses at the sweep of cliffs to the west, and the sea shining flat and grey beneath louring cloud. Walking on, Rose pointed out landmarks: a lightship, a favourite cove where seals sometimes rested on the rocks, and the dip between hills, some way along the coast, where the village of Penarthen was hidden from view. She talked about a series of paintings she was about to start, very specific to this part of the coast.

'Standing stones, rocky outcrops, like that one ahead. There's something about them, don't you think?'

Increasingly annoyed by Rose's self-containment, her lack of interest in anything other than her immediate concerns, Anna said, 'We need to find a way to get Mum and Dad down here to meet you, Rose. They want to, and soon.'

Rose might not have heard. 'You sometimes see choughs along here.' She was gazing inland, towards a low summit topped by gorse bushes. 'And, listen, there's a stonechat – can you hear? That chinking sound, like pebbles rubbing together?'

Anna looked, made out the small bright bird before it flew away, then said, 'I found out more about Zanna. Rosanna.'

Rose turned her back on the wind, grabbed at a loose end of scarf and wound it firmly round her face, hiding all but her eyes. 'Come on. I want to show you the cliffs up here, where seabirds nest – kittiwakes and guillemots. They won't be there now, but we can look down on the ledges they use.'

Perplexed, Anna gazed after her as she walked off purposefully. OK, so now wasn't the time; but when *would* be? Later? Never? She followed, returning the cheerful greeting of a couple her parents' age who were walking away from what Anna could now see was an overhang, a cliff dropping precipitously away. A notice warned of danger, of coastal erosion. Rose was ahead, walking far nearer to the edge than she'd allowed Euan to go on their previous walk. It was a promontory a little higher than the track, which dipped behind; rock, dry sandy earth, scattered stones.

'See?' Rose turned to Anna, loose strands of hair whipping free from her hat. 'Down there, that's where they nest. I come in summer to watch them.' She was crouching, taking her camera out of her pocket, aiming down at flat rocks a dizzying distance below, where the waves creamed foam.

Anna felt the clutch of fear in her stomach. She wouldn't have said she was afraid of heights, but here, high in the wind, her body knew otherwise.

'Rose, be careful!'

Rose laughed. 'Don't worry. I'm used to it.'

Far below, the tide washed over granite slabs and sucked back, timeless, mesmerizing. Anna inched as close as the clenching knot of fear would allow. She saw herself, it seemed, from a long way off, a figure reduced to tininess against sky and sea and rock.

'Michael would have a fit if he saw me.' Rose's words were half snatched away. 'But on my own, I love it. I'm not scared. You are, aren't you? You're not used to it.' Rose was angling her camera, clicking. 'It's so hard to get a sense of perspective in a photo. Maybe I can do it in a painting.'

Anna dragged her gaze away from the surge and pull of the tide. She stepped back a few paces, making herself breathe more calmly, and think rational thoughts.

Her own camera was in her holdall at Trelissick Lodge. She'd forgotten to bring it today, but had intended to take photographs of Rose, of Michael and the boys, to show her parents – to prove Rose existed, and show them their grandsons. Rose made no suggestion of photographing Anna. Anna disliked having her picture taken but felt a twinge of hurt amusement, all the same.

'Michael told me you've split up with Martin,' Rose said casually, still looking through the viewfinder.

'Did he?'

'Perhaps you're better off on your own,' Rose said. 'Maybe you didn't care about him much. I thought that, last time.'

Anna was goaded by the careless way she said it, her assumption of knowing.

'And maybe I did,' she retorted. 'Maybe I loved him. Maybe I still do. You're not the only one who matters, Rose. What do you know about caring for anyone?'

Rose lowered the camera; her eyes met Anna's, wide and amazed. 'Of course I do! I'm a mother, I've got the boys, and Michael – how can you say such a hurtful thing?'

'After what you did?' Indignation made it hard to get the

373

words out. 'Why, Rose – why did you do it? Why did you never get in touch? Still, now, you're so – so—'

'So what?'

'So *unfeeling*.'

'I'm not unfeeling!' Rose shouted. 'How can you think that? You don't know. You don't know anything.'

'How *can* I know? I can only guess, and I've spent twenty years doing that. What I can't fathom is why you *never got in touch*, not once. You've ruined their lives – does that never occur to you? Mine, too—'

Slowly Rose stood, cradling her camera. 'Don't be ridiculous, Anna. You can't blame me for everything.'

'But I do,' Anna said quietly.

'Yes, well.' Rose gave her a pitying glance. 'That's your mistake. I can't help that.' She turned away, looking down again over the giddying drop. 'Isn't it amazing how the eggs don't roll off those tiny ledges? The chicks stay there till they're ready to fly.'

'Rose, for God's sake!' Anna's voice trembled; Rose swung round, and the urge gripped Anna to push her, to give one shove that would send her over the edge to crash on the rocks below. In that second she saw fear in Rose's face, and recognition; saw in slow-motion the flailing figure suspended in space, then spread-eagled on the granite before the waves washed over and sucked back, taking Rose with them. She saw the moment that would change her life for ever; saw herself running back, distraught, making up a story about an accident, a slip, and then lying, lying, lying to everyone, lying to herself. She would be trapped for ever in this frozen instant when she could have chosen otherwise.

Rose would still have won. Always, Rose won.

'I wouldn't really blame you.' Rose stood firm, smiling hesitantly. 'I knew you wouldn't, though.'

Anna closed her eyes and took a deep breath. She hadn't done it. It was like waking from a harrowing dream.

'I'm not letting you do any more damage, Rose,' she said. 'You've done enough.'

Turning away, she headed back towards the path. Her eyes took in the magnificence of the coast, the immensity of sky and sea, the gusting wind. She had walked away; she was free. Exhilaration filled her, and a sense of herself, of being more fully herself than she had ever felt; full of vigour. She skittered over boulders to the grass track and broke into a run, jogging at first, then fast and faster, the short turf rolling under her, her feet dodging rocks and ruts, the eyes blurred by the wind. *Free, free*, said the rhythm of her running, the pumping of her heart; every stride took her farther from Rose.

She ran until the gradient and the heaving of her lungs slowed her pace. She was hot now, sweating inside her waterproof; she had too many clothes on for proper running.

People were coming down from the brow ahead, a group of walkers, led by a man being tugged along by a Border collie. The man called out to Anna:

'Is she all right? She's a bit close to the edge.'

Anna looked back in the direction of his gaze to where Rose was sitting cross-legged by the cliff-edge, looking out to sea. Perhaps he thought there was an emergency, an injury or something, and that Anna was running for help.

'Yes, thanks. She's always all right,' Anna said, flippant

but serious.

She didn't look back again. She knew what she needed to do. Walking fast, she carried on to the crest of the hill. When Penarthen came into view, a tiny village clustered around a harbour, she hurried down the rocky path and towards the small pub next to the quay. It was already open; another pair of walkers sat defiantly on a bench outside, wrapped up in Gore-tex and scarves. The interior was dark, hung with netting and glass floats; a smoky fire threw out warmth; a woman stood behind the bar, polishing glasses. Anna had the urge for a large drink, whisky perhaps, but there was something more urgent.

'Is there a payphone?'

The woman nodded towards a vestibule between the two bars. Anna took out her wallet, found change; her hands trembled as she keyed in the number and waited for the ringing tone.

*Please, Martin. Please answer.*

Longing for his voice, she was thrown into confusion when a different one answered. 'Yeah?'

'Oh – who's that?' Anna said, startled. '*Patrick?*'

'Yeah. Anna, right?'

'Yes – is Martin there?'

Of course he wouldn't be, she remembered; it was his day with Liam. Why hadn't she stopped to think?

'No, he's away a couple of nights. Gone to Devon.'

'Devon?'

'Devon, Cornwall, wherever. It was all a bit sudden. He picked up Liam last night and they headed off.'

'So where are they now?'

'Dunno.' Patrick didn't sound much interested; Anna

had the impression his attention was elsewhere. 'You'll have to try his mobile.'

'Right. Are you staying?'

'Yeah, a few days, seeing friends. Catch you later.'

Anna rang off and stood by a rack of leaflets for various tourist attractions. She was warmed through with relief – was Martin on his way? – then fearful of assuming too much. She could see no other reason for him to set off for the West Country at short notice, and surely, surely that must mean that he hadn't given her up, in spite of all she'd said and done, and failed to do.

He was coming to find her.

But . . . maybe it wasn't that at all. He could be taking Liam on a surprise outing. Patrick had sounded vague, but now she remembered Ruth saying it was half-term next week. Disappointment numbed her; she closed her eyes, suddenly finding it hard to breathe. Why should Martin want to give her another chance? Could he really be so loyal, so forgiving, after all she'd said and done? Self-disgust rose in her like nausea.

And – even if he *was* on his way, which seemed less and less likely the more she thought about it – how would he find her? He didn't know where Rose lived, didn't even know the name of the village. She stood in indecision; went out to the car park, then came back inside, counting more coins; she found Martin's number on her mobile and keyed it in to the payphone.

Voicemail.

'Oh, Martin—' she began, then thought better of it and rang off.

Outside, she looked up towards the cliff where she'd

left Rose, and saw that Rose was walking down the path; she'd reach the pub in a few minutes. Anna looked at her in exasperation, then in the other direction at a single-track lane that curved down the hillside. What to do? Should she go on down to the cottage? Wait here for Michael?

Frustration jittered through her; she had to do *something*. She looked again in her wallet. She had enough coins for another call. Another chance. Better not waste it.

'Martin,' she said to his voicemail. 'I'm sorry. I've been awful. I want to be with you. I love you. Please believe me.'

Perhaps he'd delete it. Maybe without even bothering to listen. She would wait and wait, and nothing would happen, and she deserved no better. She had emerged from one kind of limbo to create another for herself.

She stepped outside and filled her lungs with air. It should have been invigorating, but she felt hollow, and suddenly exhausted, ready to flop to the ground and lie there. But she saw Rose hurrying along the final stretch of track, her feet skidding on loose stones.

'Wait!' she called, as if Anna was about to head off somewhere.

'What?'

Rose's pace slowed as she came closer.

'What you were asking. Up there. Why I didn't ever . . . I just couldn't. It was too big, too horrible, what I'd done. I couldn't face it. Couldn't bear to think about it. Couldn't ever go back.' She spoke as if stating a simple fact. 'Don't you see?'

Anna gazed back at her, seeing, for the first time, something like pleading in Rose's expression.

'I don't, Rose,' she said. 'I don't see. But I'll have to try.'

Behind her, in the pub entrance, the payphone started ringing.

Rose started again. 'You see, I—'

'Wait. Let me get that.' Anna darted in and snatched up the receiver; her pulse pounded in her ears. *Please, please . . .*

'Anna?' Martin's voice; she closed her eyes. 'Where are you?'

# 29

## July

The engine noise rises from the low sound of taxiing and the forward surge presses her to the back of her seat. Grass, buildings and vans rush past in a blur of speed. She had forgotten that flying, or at least this part of it, the take-off, always frightens her. And of course it's too late: she can't change her mind and get off.

Everyone takes for granted that you can get into a plane and fly to the other side of the world, but it seems crazy and impossible that this big, heavy piece of machinery will launch itself into the air. As she feels the upward tilt and sees how quickly the ground drops away, she knows this can't work; the aircraft will strain and strain to climb into the sky, only to give up the struggle and flop back to the ground, splat on the runway.

Don clasps her hand and smiles, and she takes deep, regular breaths. He's here; it will be all right. And although she remembers – so vividly – the sense of dread taking her over, choking her, blurring all her senses, she knows how to acknowledge the feeling and observe it and wait for it to pass. Her thoughts are beginning to obey her instead of

380

running wild. She knows where she's going and why, and this is the way to do it. It's a different place, now, inside her head, and she doesn't mind going there. She pictures an apple tree, the tree in the garden she is getting to know. Small green apples are forming on its branches. The garden is full of early morning light, and she sits on the bench and looks at it, attuning her thoughts to the slow life of a tree. It's clear in her mind, and she can go there whenever she needs to.

So much change. But she has come through, as the therapist said she would. It's not insanity. It happens to lots of people. There are words for it, explanations, strategies, and that has turned it into something that can be treated and tamed. She is still herself, not lost after all.

Don made sure she had the window seat, and she has a good view. It's a long while since she's flown anywhere. As she gazes out, she thinks of home, down there somewhere: both of them, the Sevenoaks house, and – farther into Kent – the house she can now think of as home, whose garden she already misses. The pattern of roads and houses gives way to green, so much green, stretching so far: shades and shades of it, clumps of forest and fields of crops already turning dusty yellow, but all that soft green is reassuring – you'd think with global warming there wouldn't be so much left, but it's everywhere she looks. There's a glittering thread of river, and a ribbon of motorway, and then scarves of cloud drift by like veils and for a while it's all mist, and she sees moisture flecking the window. The light has changed, it feels like being underwater, and she thinks she won't see any more, but then there's a sense of sunlight above and they're rising to meet it, and suddenly there's a stillness and calm, and all sense of racing and climbing is gone.

And, after all, it's exhilarating rather than terrifying. They've done it, and the plane will take them to Sydney, to Zanna and the baby, her new granddaughter. She settles back in her seat, releasing the clench of her hands, thinking how small the world seems, and how enormous. In Australia there is Zanna, and in London there's Anna, and in Cornwall, Rose. Her three daughters. She can say that, if anyone asks. 'Yes, I've got family. Three daughters, and three grandchildren.' And no one finds that very startling. No one other than herself, because of Rose: Rose who has jumped somehow from adolescence to adulthood, and is a mother herself now and not the same Rose as the Rose who preserved herself at eighteen. This Rose lets herself be seen only briefly; they've met twice now, at the hotel, and Sandra senses that it won't ever be different. She finds this logical, accepting it as her due: Zanna came back, so Rose went away. Somehow, now, they've all balanced themselves, like figures in a dance: they come together, they whirl apart, held in a changing pattern. But she can see their faces now; she can tell them apart, call them by their separate names and know where each one is likely to be.

Now she has more than she ever dreamed, and her only fear is that it will all be snatched away again. The tiny shoes with the daisy fastenings are in her suitcase, and soon, soon, she will be holding a baby in her arms, marvelling at its newness and completeness, and that in spite of everything this child has come into her life.

The clouds and the weather are underneath the aircraft now, fleecy and dimpled and touched with pink, and she could easily think that if she parachuted out of the plane and landed on that cloud mattress she could lie there, drifting and basking. It seems oddly normal to be up here in the sky – hardly moving, it seems now – with stewardesses coming along the aisle offering drinks.

Don is leaning over to look. 'Beautiful, isn't it?'

She laughs. 'It's amazing to think that up here the sun shines all the time. Does that sound silly?'

'No, love,' says Don. 'Not in the slightest.'

And she thinks that if she died now, this minute, she'd die happy.


'Text message,' says Martin, touching Anna's arm.

'Mmm?' She stirs, looking up at him.

He is sitting up in bed, naked but for his glasses, his laptop open on the duvet. 'Your mobile. Just now. Incoming.'

Anna pushes back the bedclothes and fetches the mobile from her bag. 'Dad! They've arrived. They're in Sydney.'

'Good,' Martin says absently. His eyes are on the screen.

He's on RightMove, his new addiction. Anna leans over, propping her chin on his shoulder.

'Isn't it strange,' she says, 'to think that somewhere there's a house that's going to be ours? It's waiting for us.'

'We'll find it,' he says. 'Even if it takes a while. Maybe this is it. Have a look.' He shows Anna floor-plans, a map, an aerial view.

'Nice!' she approves, leaning forward to look more closely.

'There's even an outbuilding – hang on – here. That could be your studio,' Martin says. 'Shall I ring the agent? Perhaps we could go and see, after the Clavering one.'

'Today?'

'Why not? Worth a try.'

'It does look good.'

'And the garden,' says Martin. 'Just wait till I show you the garden.'

❖ ❖ ❖

## August 1987

A beach day, on holiday. A long afternoon of heat and salt breeze, an afternoon that feels never-ending. Rose and Anna, in shorts and T-shirts, were down on the beach at low tide. Dad was reading his book, Mum had gone off for a walk by herself.

They were making a beach collage. Rose had started it, and now Anna was joining in, under her instruction.

'I want more shells. See? Like this.' She was making a huge bird, a large and predatory-looking bird, with wings outstretched. She had sketched it with a stick, had fashioned a rough nest of ribbon-weed and bladder-wrack, and now the bird's plumage must be given a texture. Anna scurried about the rock-pools, wanting to please, wanting to find something special and unusual. She found crab-claws; she found glossy weed the colour of henna, she found small bleached bones which Rose took from her in delight, spreading them out to examine them.

'Oh, yes! It can have those for feet. White bony feet.'

Encouraged, Anna set off again, returning next time with a handful of glass, sharp shards of green and brown.

'Look.' She held them out for Rose's scrutiny.

'That's good! Put them down there. But don't cut yourself.'

There was a small chinking and grating as Anna laid them on the sand. One of the pieces caught her attention; she picked it out and held it in her palm.

'This one's different – see?' It was an irregular shape of soft blue-green, misted over as if by surf, tumbled and sanded into smoothness. She touched it reverently with her finger. 'Isn't it lovely?' she appealed to Rose. 'Like a piece of the sea.'

She had found a small gem, a piece of treasure.

'It's sea-glass!' Rose said, taking it. 'The rest is just smashed bottles, but this is much older – real sea-glass. It must have been waiting for us to find it.'

'Is it valuable?' Anna asked.

'I don't s'pose so. But I'm going to keep it.' Rose crouched, and put the fragment carefully aside from the rest. 'Make it into a necklace or something. The other bits we'll use for eyes. Now, more shells – razor shells, these long ones. I want them for feathers.'

Slowly their shadows lengthened over the footmarked sand; two shadows, crossing, becoming one, separating again. The lull of waves gave a rhythm to their movements. Anna's bare legs were dusted with fine silvery sand; she felt grittiness between her toes, the give and tilt beneath the arches of her feet as she stepped carefully around the spread-eagled bird. Rose selected and placed and re-arranged, stood back to look, made small adjustments. The bird had acquired a life and spirit of its own. Dad came, looked and admired, and asked if they wanted ice creams at

388

the beach café. Rose shook her head: not yet. Not till the bird was finished. They couldn't leave it.

'But when the tide comes in . . .' said Anna in dismay, only now thinking of that. 'It'll be washed away.'

'I know! That's the point.' Rose was moving quickly, cradling shells in her hand, placing them decisively. Anna sensed a briskness in the waves as the breeze freshened; the sand would soon be covered, their work smoothed to nothing.

'I wish I'd brought my camera,' said their mother, returning from her walk.

Rose was satisfied at last; she took several paces back, looked at her creation and smiled. 'But you haven't. You'll have to look and remember. A photo wouldn't catch it properly.'

They seemed caught in the bird's spell, all four of them, held by the sternness of its gaze. Anna imagined it ruffling its plumage of stones and shells, flexing its wings, and soaring over their heads, a dinosaur bird come to life.

We made it, she thought, but it's not really ours.

She gazed down at the bony claws, the staring glass eyes, the wings poised for flight.

❖ ❖ ❖

# Acknowledgements

Several people have read bits or all of this book in its various drafts (and under various titles). Special thanks go to Jon Appleton, Adèle Geras, Alison Leonard and Celia Rees, for their encouragement; also to David Fickling, Bella Pearson, Simon Mason and Tilda Johnson for editorial input, to Catherine Clarke and Michele Topham at Felicity Bryan Agency, and to everyone at Doubleday. As always I owe a big thank you to Linda Sargent, to whom the book is dedicated, and to Trevor for various kinds of support.